From the award-winning auth
series *The Troubadours Quarte*
fantasy trilogy

**Praise for *The Ring Breaker***

*'Absolutely brilliant. A tour-de-force of storytelling, Viking lore, and the rugged landscape of Orkney.'* Deborah Swift, *Italian Renaissance* series

*'A stirring coming-of-age tale forged in love, inheritance and adventure - in* The Ring Breaker *Jean Gill skilfully brings the poetry and magic of the Viking world to life.'* Emily Brand, *The Fall of the House of Byron*

*'An immersive coming of age tale set in Viking Age Orkney filled with court intrigue, sea voyages, and a society where two belief systems battle. The historic details are accurate but lightly woven into the story which takes real skill.'* Grace Tierney, *Words the Vikings Gave Us*

*'The Odyssey kind of epic, yet softer and kinder on the mind, and quicker-paced, but without losing its glorious intensity and genius.'* Jessica Bell *Can You Make The Title Bigga*

*'A skilfully written, beautifully researched coming-of-age story set in Viking Orkney... A rich and compelling read.'* Lexie Conyngham, *the Orkneyinga Murders series*

*'If you're a fan of the Viking Age, the television shows* Vikings *and* Valhalla, *or the excellent works of authors Kristian Giles and Peter Gibbons, the world of* The Ring Breaker *will feel familiar. (In this novel) all of a reader's senses are stirred by rich details of the medieval experience. But what makes for the best Viking tales? The adventures, of course, found in this novel too.'* Lisa J. Yarde, *Sultana* series

# THE RING BREAKER

### 1139: ORKNEYJAR

## JEAN GILL

THE MIDWINTER DRAGON I

Cover design by Jessica Bell

## Jean Gill's Publications

**Novels**

**Natural Forces - FANTASY**

*Book 3* The World Beyond the Walls *(The 13th Sign)* 2021

*Book 2* Arrows Tipped with Honey *(The 13th Sign)* 2020

*Book 1* Queen of the Warrior Bees *(The 13th Sign)* 2019

**The Troubadours Quartet - HISTORICAL FICTION**

*Book 5* Nici's Christmas Tale: A Troubadours Short Story *(The 13<sup>th</sup> Sign)* 2018

*Book 4* Song Hereafter *(The 13<sup>th</sup> Sign)* 2017

*Book 3* Plaint for Provence *(The 13<sup>th</sup> Sign)* 2015

*Book 2* Bladesong *(The 13<sup>th</sup> Sign)* 2015

*Book 1* Song at Dawn *(The 13<sup>th</sup> Sign)* 2015

**Love Heals - SECOND CHANCE LOVE**

*Book 2* More Than One Kind *(The 13<sup>th</sup> Sign)* 2016

*Book 1* No Bed of Roses *(The 13<sup>th</sup> Sign)* 2016

**Looking for Normal - TEEN FICTION**

*Book 1* Left Out *(The 13<sup>th</sup> Sign)* 2017

*Book 2* Fortune Kookie *(The 13<sup>th</sup> Sign)* 2017

**Non-fiction**
**MEMOIR / TRAVEL**
How White is My Valley *(The 13th Sign 2021)* **\*EXCLUSIVE to Jean Gill's Special Readers Group**
How Blue is my Valley *(The 13th Sign)* 2016
A Small Cheese in Provence *(The 13th Sign)* 2016

**WW2 MILITARY MEMOIR**
Faithful through Hard Times *(The 13th Sign)* 2018
4.5 Years – war memoir by David Taylor *(The 13th Sign)* 2017

**Short Stories and Poetry**
One Sixth of a Gill *(The 13th Sign)* 2014
From Bedtime On *(The 13th Sign)* 2018 (2nd edition)
With Double Blade *(The 13th Sign)* 2018 (2nd edition)

**Translation (from French)**
The Last Love of Edith Piaf – Christie Laume *(Archipel)* 2014
A Pup in Your Life – Michel Hasbrouck 2008
Gentle Dog Training – Michel Hasbrouck *(Souvenir Press)* 2008

# MAIN HISTORICAL CHARACTERS

The Norse naming convention, still used today, usually creates a girl's second name from her mother's first name e.g. Ingeborg Asleifsdottir and a boy's second name comes from his father's first name e.g. Kali Kolsson. One exception is when the mother or father is dead and the child takes the survivor's name e.g. Sweyn's father was murdered and he is famous as Sweyn Asleifsson, Asleif being his mother's name.

- *Bishop William* – Bishop of Orkney, later nicknamed 'the Old'.
- *Botolf* – Icelandic skald living in Orkney
- *Frakork Maddansdottir* – 'the witch', alleged murderer, Sweyn's enemy, grandmother to Thorbjorn and Olvir Rosta (see family tree)
- *Harald Maddadson* – Jarl of Orkney, foster-son to Thorbjorn and Jarl Rognvald (see family tree)
- *Hlif (Hlifolfsdottir)* – one 12th century runic message in Maeshowe is signed 'Hlif (female name), Rognvald's housekeeper'
- *Hlifolf* – the cook who killed Jarl Magnus (later Saint Magnus) on Jarl Hakon's orders
- *Holbodi* – Lord of Tiree, who sheltered Sweyn during one of his periods of exile
- *Ingeborg* – Rognvald's daughter
- *Ingeborg (Inge) Asleifsdottir* – Sweyn's sister, married to Thorbjorn Klerk, mentioned in *the Orkneyinga Saga*
- *Jarl Hakon of Orkney* – predecessor to Jarl Rognvald, co-ruler with Jarl Magnus, whom he had killed

- *Jarl Paul of Orkney* – successor to Jarl Hakon, 'disappeared' by Sweyn and replaced by Rognvald
- *Jarl Rognvald of Orkney* (ex Kali Kolsson) – Norwegian-born ruler of Orkney and famous poet
- *Kol* – Norwegian father of Jarl Rognvald, first builder of St Magnus Cathedral
- *Olvir 'the Brawler' Rosta* – Sweyn's enemy, grandson to Frakork on whose orders he murdered Sweyn's father
- *Rognvald's wife* – one of Rognvald's poems mourns his lady but she is never identified
- *Saint (ex-Jarl of Orkney) Magnus* – Rognvald's maternal uncle, murdered on Jarl Hakon's orders
- *Sweyn Asleifsson* – sea-rover extraordinaire
- *Thorbjorn Klerk* – guardian to the young Jarl Harald, clerk and advisor to Jarl Rognvald

- *The Jerusalem-farers* – The leaders: Magnus, the son of Hávard, Gunni's son; Swein, Hróald's son; Thorgeir Skotakoll, Oddi the little, Thorberg Svarti, Armód the scald, Thorkel Krókauga, Grímkell of Flettuness, and Bjarni his son; Erling, Jón, his brother-in-law, Aslák and Guttorm. And of course, most important of all, Eindridi, the man who'd inspired Rognvald with the idea of sailing for Jerusalem.
- *The Maeshowe rune-carvers* – Hlif, Eyolfr Kolbeinssor, Vemundr, Ottar, Ogmundr, Arnfior, Oframr Sigurdsarsonr, Hermundr 'hard', Arnfithr 'food'.

'The price of a man's murder,' his mother said, as she inspected the cold hearth at the centre of cosy living quarters. Stone walls were caulked with peat and only one weakness in the patchwork roof allowed Orkney's bitter wind to knife through, cutting smoke into choking backdraughts.

When the hearth was aglow and the fish smoking above it, the shades of a man, his wife and his son formed in the grey wisps and vanished into the sky. Or so it seemed.

'Your father would have been happy here,' she said, watching the smoke, her face so lined with poverty that grief left no trace.

She died of an ague within a year of his father's death. Her last words were, 'Always remember how your father was rewarded for his loyalty to the Jarl of Orkneyjar.' Presumably, she meant the longhouse. Skarfr was left rich and alone, too young to be either.

As was the custom, foster-parents were sought and their suitability debated at the Thing, their local council. Usually, an orphan would have many foster-homes, with perhaps a year in each to spread the burden, but in his case volunteers were torn between greed and fear. Skarfr's wealth meant he would need one foster-father until he came of age but the rumours of how he got his name made good Christians cross themselves and many men fingered the hammer amulets beneath their jerkins.

'Unnatural, touched by the gods,' they whispered when they thought he couldn't hear.

As always, the ruling jarl spoke for peace and found a solution that nobody could find fault with. Except Skarfr. And what did an eight-year-old know? A lot, as it turned out.

Botolf Begla, a skald newly arrived from the Old Country, was lodging with a family who needed more space and – so Botolf said – who dried up his inspiration with their ceaseless tattle. A skald as famous as Botolf for his poetry and sagas merited better.

Killing two birds with one stone, the Thing chose Botolf as foster-father so he formally adopted a boy now called Skarfr

Botolffson. In silence, the boy refused the name. He was Skarfr Kristinsson, for the two mothers who'd nurtured him.

Botolf moved into the longhouse that would not be Skarfr's for eight years, if his foster-father judged him ready, or for up to thirteen years, should such a judgement be withheld. Botolf began training him as a skald. And beating him when he forgot to feed the chickens or milk the cow, or when he let the fire go out. Or when he could only think of *eagle-feeder* as a poetic term for warrior and forgot all the others he'd been taught. His master was a peerless skald but a poor teacher. Even so, despite lashings from tongue and whip, Skarfr learned.

When Botolf acquired a male thrall to do the heavy work, and a female one to tend to the house and cook, Skarfr's duties lessened and his training as skald intensified. At first, the thralls made overtures of kindness to him but when he opened his mouth to reply to their soft-spoken questions, he saw Botolf's body freeze, from face through clenched fists to his boots that seemed part of the tamped earth floor. That rigidity was prequel to the whip so Skarfr wiped the smile off his face, turned away, pretended he didn't know their names. The ones Botolf never used. Fergus and Brigid.

The sea taught him to swim, cradling him afloat in cold salt, tempting him to dive for shells on the rare occasions the waves unveiled the seabed. Water called to him, cormorant that he was, and he soon discovered that lochs reflected fluffy clouds but hid depths and eddies more dangerous than those of the sea. Such risks meant nothing to him in the joy of weightless twists and turns, less alone among the otters and bobbing eider ducks than in that longhouse where smoked walls made dreary what was once his home.

Botolf was afraid of the sea, which made Skarfr love it even more. The skald never set foot in their faering, a two-man rowboat, but he sent Fergus out fishing and the boy slunk out with him.

Limiting their words to *net, line* and *kreel,* they let the current flow around them and knew smiles over a silvery catch. The boat was offshore, outside Botolf's law.

In the house, Skarfr behaved as if Fergus and Brigid were invisible, and Botolf relaxed, not realising he'd taught his ward to hold in the precious words a skald needs to say aloud, to play with. So it was that Skarfr learned the craft of poetry but not the art. If he had any, it was buried with his grief for his mother and his bitterness over his father's death. Not even his cormorant could gift him golden speech. Botolf had beaten a fatal flaw into his masterwork and was doomed to as much disappointment as Skarfr's parents would have felt.

He was not to make sagas after all, neither to be the story nor tell it. He believed what men said of him, reported with glee by Botolf. Skarfr was 'unnatural, touched by the gods,' and a disappointment, condemned to live with a cold genius of a man.

Until Skarfr was fourteen, when he met Hlif on a beach and they fled the storm of swords that came from the whale's way.

# CHAPTER TWO

B otolf was out on his rounds, harvesting scandal from his neighbours and gleaning the details which would enrich his verse and make his listeners hungry for more. As was Skarfr's habit on such occasions, he sneaked out to the beach, revelling in solitude. Free to roll sand over his feet, then wriggle his toes, leaving tracks like sea-serpents. Free to inspect shells and marine skeletons caught in the curves of sea wrack patterning the beach. Free to talk to the cormorant.

Today was promising. Shimmering from the receding tide, the sand was rippled in the sea's pattern. Waves everywhere. A confusion of glitter as reflected clouds flitted across the wet sand: Týr, the sky god, was whirling his nebulous cloak and Aegir, the sea god, danced with him until the land became a dazzle of watery heavens.

Skarfr picked up a stick, charcoal black from its time in the sea but not yet too fragile to use for drawing. He drew a zigzag in the wet sand. The sun rune Sól, his name-letter. In defiance of the dancing wave-curves, his straight lines said, 'Skarfr carved these runes.' He was here.

His runes were those Botolf taught him, their Old Country

shapes different from his homeland short twig letters but he could read and write both. Botolf said the best skalds and sagas came from the Old Country, also known as Island or Snaeland, so Skarfr must become a Snaelandman in his ways. He must learn by heart the tales of gods, giants and heroes that would make him welcome at any lord's hearth and earn him good coin. Maybe one day the Jarl would break his ring and give a silver piece to Skarfr for his work. If he was second-rate as a skald, he could always be first-rate as a praise-singer. That was often a more remunerative occupation.

Botolf said Skarfr was crippled as a poet by what his homeland lacked. No mountains, no forests, no rivers, no wolves. How could such an impoverished land create poets?

*From wide skies and water, burns and heath, cormorants and sea-eagles,* Skarfr did not say. He had learned the hard way to rein back his words unless told to speak.

'You must travel to the Old Country when you come of age; leave this primitive outpost of posturing peasants,' was Botolf's constant refrain. The long tuft of grey hair, lonely on his otherwise bald head, would swing as he ranted, his mouth ugly.

*Why don't you go back there if you love it so much?* Skarfr did not ask.

Instead, he communed with the cormorant, which was sometimes one oiled black body and sometimes another. Skarfr was not naive enough to think a mere bird had saved his life. He knew of shapeshifters and spirit guides from the verses Botolf made him learn. There were usually several cormorants fishing together in the bay but Skarfr always knew which cormorant held his spirit guide at any moment by the way one looked at him, wise beyond bird nature. Goddess or Valkyrie, he cared not, as long as she watched over him and listened, while he poured out his lonely heart.

Crouching, lost in contemplation of the trickle of seawater

outlining his name-rune, Skarfr was unaware that he was no longer alone, so he jumped at the sound of a girl's voice.

'What are you doing?'

Skarfr looked up and blinked. Bright-haired against the sunshine, a girl screwed her face up in puzzlement, making her eyes so small he could barely distinguish their colour. Stormy grey. Even against the sun, her skin was curdled milk, speckled as Botolf's roan pony with so many freckles they joined into blotches. He'd never seen a girl so ugly but then he hadn't seen many girls at all. Brigid's face, scored with suffering and fatigue, occasionally bore traces of the raven-haired beauty she must once have been.

'Nothing,' he replied. At which stupid reply, the girl opened her eyes fully, the better to bestow contempt on him.

'You shouldn't talk to me. Or even be seen with me,' she informed him with hauteur. 'I'm going to skim stones.'

While Skarfr still sought appropriate words and found none, she selected pebbles carefully, for flatness and size, and walked into the waves. She was barefoot like himself but her girl's apparel was less convenient for paddling. Although she'd rearranged her wool belt to hitch up both her pinafore overdress and her longer undergown, the hems of both must be getting wet.

She didn't seem to care about anything but her success in beating her own numbers.

'Not a good start,' she muttered, as a marbled grey pebble skipped three times and sank.

When she achieved seven skips, she gave a humph of satisfaction. 'I'll stop there.'

She jiggled her remaining stones.

Then hurled one straight at a diving cormorant.

'No!' shouted Skarfr, suddenly freed from his paralysis. He rushed her from behind, made her stumble and lose the rest of her pebbles. Her clothes dipped full into an oncoming wave, that broke around them in a froth of laughter, mimicking the girl. She pushed past him to get out of the water.

'What's the matter with you?'

'Nothing,' he replied, flushing. He couldn't help glancing out to sea. Spear-straight, his cormorant dived again. In the time it took a stone to skip seven times, she surged up, far from where she'd entered the water, silver wriggling in her mouth before she contorted her long throat and swallowed the fish. She was fine.

The girl was staring at him. He felt like a fish wriggling.

'Do you always spoil the fun?' she demanded, her face as red as her hair, her clothes dripping.

'No,' he said.

He considered his answer then, 'Yes,' he said.

Then, 'That's none of your business.'

He liked that answer best because he could repeat it to any other question she asked.

His second impression of her was that she was rude as well as ugly. Although there had been a moment, when she was skipping stones, that she resembled a sea sprite, fire dancing in the water with her blaze of long curls and her russet dress.

'I'm Hlif,' she said, and waited.

And waited, apparently disappointed at his lack of reaction.

'My father murdered Jarl Magnus, who's a saint now,' she told him and stuck her chin out. 'So I'm cursed. And you touched me so now you're cursed too.'

Skarfr surprised himself by speaking the truth. 'It won't make any difference,' he said. 'Things couldn't be worse. You can call me...' he hesitated, 'Long-throat.'

'Well then, *Long-throat*, as it's too late for you to run away and you owe me compensation for my wet clothes and spoiled game, you can keep me company while I dry out. I shall tell you my story and you shall tell me yours.'

Skarfr should have gone home but the word 'story' held a

fascination for him. He was trained to be a skald after all and if *wanting* to compose great verse were enough, he would be the best. But a man can recognise what's great without achieving it.

What a story Hlif must have. Everyone knew that Orkneyjar must be ruled by two jarls, because *'One jarl is for himself and rules by fear but two must heed their people.'*

She picked her way over the sands like a gull, holding her skirts bunched in each hand as if she would curtsey at any moment. Skarfr stumbled in her wake, his feet sinking further as he reached dry sand, which shod his wet feet in abrasive grains. His body seemed dense, his footsteps a struggle, whereas Hlif was still an airy sprite, despite her sodden hemline.

She didn't look back once as she headed up the beach, away from the ebbing waves towards the tussocks in the dunes. She chose a sandy dip, sheltered from view by golden oat's ears, cushioned by marram grass, and she threw herself to the ground, her flame hair spread around her matted grass pillow and her skirt shaken to its fullest so it could dry out.

Cautiously, Skarfr lay down beside her, enjoying the light breeze and sun playing on his face. He shut his eyes and instantly relaxed.

*This is how stories should be heard*, he thought. *In the dark, so the mind can make its own pictures.*

'So, Long-throat. What have you been told about how Saint Magnus died?' Dissociated from red hair and mocking face, the voice already had a storytelling cadence, slower and more dramatic than speech. Unexpected in a child unless of course the child had trained with Botolf. But this was no moment to dwell on his inadequacy. Skarfr tried to match Hlif's tone, to show the skills beaten into him as he retold the story he'd heard so often from Botolf. When Magnus was jarl, his yokemate as ruler had been Hakon, whose jealousy and greed led him to murder his popular rival. Jarl Magnus died with a martyr's courage, blessing and forgiving his executioner.

Then, so the tale was told, a blinding light appeared above Magnus' burial-place. Incurables were healed and certain doom averted for those who prayed to this new saint.

Such events were mere rumours during the life of Jarl Hakon, from respect – or fear. But Magnus' miracles were acknowledged after his death and his sanctity confirmed by Bishop William.

And now, in nearby Kirkjuvágr, their own jarl, Magnus' nephew and successor, was erecting a cathedral to his saintly uncle. A cathedral that would dazzle men with the splendour of the One God, splendour that would also bathe Bishop William in its radiance – and bring considerable income. Their jarl had promised the cathedral to the Orkneymen to win their support for his accession to the jarldom and they were paying heavily for their saint's resting-place.

This is what everybody knew. But what if Hlif's tale was different?

Skarfr finished the story of Saint Magnus, in grand style.

*'Shriven and in prayer when Hakon caught up with him, Magnus made three offers.*

*To go for a pilgrim and never return.*

*"No," said Hakon.*

*To go to Skotland and be a prisoner there with the two men who still kept him company.*

*"No," said Hakon.*

*To be maimed and blinded, thrown into the deepest dungeon, sparing Hakon the sin of murder.*

*"Yes," said Hakon.*

*"No," said his chiefs. "Enough of this rivalry. One of you must die this day."*

*Then Magnus accepted his doom and knelt to receive his deathblow.*

Hakon ordered his standard-bearer to do the deed but the man refused in great anger.

Then Hakon forced his cook Hlifolf to take an axe to Magnus. Hlifolf shook with sobs and Magnus calmed him.

"Be quick," he said. "There is no dishonour to you but only to him who commands such a task." He took off his rich tunic and gave it to Hlifolf in token of forgiveness.

After prayer and confession, Magnus said, "Stand before me and cut the tree of my head with all your strength, a noble death for one of noble birth. God will forgive you as I will intercede on your behalf."

Then he made the sign of the cross, the axe fell and his soul ascended to heaven. Greensward replaced the moss and stones where his body had lain, the first of many miracles. And Hakon became sole ruler of Orkneyjar.'

In the silence, Skarfr heard only seabirds squabbling and the melody of a skylark distracting strangers from her nest. He was pleased with himself. This was the first time he'd *enjoyed* narrating a story, lost himself in the telling. He almost expected his audience to shout their praise. Then he remembered who his audience was. He sneaked a glance and quickly shut his eyes again. Was she asleep?

'No dishonour,' Hlif said slowly. 'If I believed one word of that then I'd hate *Saint* Magnus for lying.'

Shocked by her blasphemy, Skarfr waited.

'Do you believe it?' she challenged him.

He stuttered, 'Everybody says—'

He tried again. 'Sagas need to lift us, be bigger than life – but that doesn't mean they're not true, in their own way. And this is Magnus' story.'

He followed a difficult train of thought, important but only half-grasped. 'Maybe Hakon's story would be different. Everyone says he ruled well and there was peace with only one jarl, despite

the proverb. And he did go for a pilgrim so maybe he was forgiven.'
He wasn't sure how Christian forgiveness worked.

'Well,' said Hlif, 'it's all lies. My father told me his story,
Hlifolf's story. Not a heroic saga, skald-boy—'

How did she know who he was? Skarfr flushed, wondering
what stories were told about the remarkable skald Botolf and his
charity towards an orphan.

'No, this is the truth, the reason I'm cursed. Hlifolf's daughter
lives a half-life in a jarl's hall because of her father's crime.
Forgiven? No. Never. He's lucky to have left this world and I must
keep paying for what he did.'

None of this made any sense to Skarfr but he half-listened. He
saw no point in stories of ordinary men. No inspiration, no
passion, no heroism.

His attention was jolted back to Hlif when she asked him, 'How
do you think Hlifolf was forced to be a murderer when the standard-
bearer said no and yet lived? And how does a man find time for so
much prayer, confession and forgiveness, even a mass? While his
enemy patiently holds the axe over his head, waiting till he's finished
before smiting the deadly blow? Your arm would drop off from
wielding an axe so long. My father told me what really happened.'

Eyes shut, Skarfr pillowed the back of his head on his hands
and let the disembodied voice carry him on choppy waters to
Egilsey. That day of betrayal and dishonour – but whose? His
eyelids felt shade and light as clouds hid, then uncovered the sun,
nature's way of dramatising the tale.

'Hakon's men shamed Ofeig the standard-bearer, for his
cowardice.' Hlif's tone was low with doom and Skarfr shivered.
'When Jarl Magnus pleaded for his life, the tortures he suggested
in lieu of death might well come to his mind for he saw them
enacted. Who could deny Hakon's right to obedience from his
men? 'Riddle me this, young skald-boy.'

Skarfr frowned at both the insult and the interruption to the story but he was intrigued and listened.

'Two jarls met that day to make peace. Both wanted peace in our land. Which one achieved what they both wanted?'

Skarfr understood her well enough but disliked being led to an answer like a pony to a trough. He refused to drink. For once he could follow his own reasoning without a beating to teach him the required response.

'Both did,' he declared, as much to show off his cleverness and annoy the girl as because it was what he believed. 'One brought peace on earth and one brings us peace in heaven. By Saint Magnus' martyrdom and grace, Hakon ruled well in his earthly domain – and died.'

'So you think Saint Magnus is the story,' she continued, unperturbed. 'Maybe you are right and maybe you are wrong.'

Her voice deepened again, ominous. 'Betrayed by his standard-bearer, Hakon turned to his loyal cook Hlifolf and asked formally whether he was a man of honour.

'My father had served Hakon with oar and axe, never failing him and he welcomed the name offered to him by his lord, to pass on honour to his lineage.

'I wasn't born then and my father still hoped for sons,' she interrupted the story in her natural tone, then carried on, '"Men will call you Gall-Cleaver, Cancre-Cutter, Peace-Carver," said Hakon to Hlifolf.

'Jarl Magnus stopped pleading and cast a bane instead. "My killer shall pale from the murder that haunts his sleep and his touch will spread corruption from him to his children and to their children."

'He was in mid-curse, shouting at Jarl Hakon, when my father rushed him from behind and swung his great axe, carving in Magnus' head the simple rune used for his name, Hlifolf. Magnus dropped to his knees, fell sideways and my father swiped again, unable to hew a clean blow, dragging his axe in a ragged line along the other side of Magnus' head, like the slash of a sword but deeper.

'Then Magnus' ragged breaths ended but his curse still lived and found its aim. My father felt it lodge in his heart and Hakon's words confirmed his fears.

'"There is no honour in dealing such a messy death," said Hakon. "Let us go to our homes and bring the peace to this land that has had such a foul beginning." He would not look at my father nor ever did again.

'Hlifolf gazed long at the blood pooling on earth and pebbles while his comrades headed back to their ships, sombre, bearing Magnus' corpse.

'The two companions who had stayed with Magnus had been left unharmed and would tell their story of sainthood across the isles from that time on. One of them, Holbodi, spoke to my father. "You have murdered a saint and will die a miserable death."'

Matter-of-fact again, Hlif concluded, 'My father endured the years left to him and the comfort he took with his wife was his undoing for it created me, the continuation of Magnus' curse. And in recompense to his sainted uncle for the manner of his death, our Jarl Rognvald brought me to his Bu, his home in Orphir, as his ward and his prisoner. I am to be his housekeeper and never marry. The only child and last of the cursed line of Saint Magnus' murderer.'

Stunned into silence, Skarfr wondered what to make of this girl. *Unnatural and touched by the gods?* He sat up and opened his eyes. As if they were two dolls on one string, she had lain back and shut her eyes, her face a red and cream version of the dappled marram grass and sand. Smoothed out now, unwrinkled, her tale told.

*Cursed girl*, thought Skarfr. But he wasn't worried about her infectious corruption. His life *couldn't* get much worse. And he was curious.

'Why did you tell me?' he asked.

'I tell everybody who'll listen.' Her eyes flashed open, reflected clouds scudding across the grey gaze. 'I know you're the skald-boy so I thought you might. But mostly people don't. Or they laugh. But they stay away from me, which is good.'

Skarfr picked a long spike of grass and chewed on it absently, pondering truth as the splash of cormorants and a whisper of a breeze played a background to his thoughts, which were as blasphemous as Hlif's story.

'Do you believe in Magnus' saintliness?' He held his breath.

'Of course I do,' she retorted. 'But when did he become a saint? When he lived? Or when he died?'

Skarfr shook his head and turned to more practical matters. 'How are you going to get the curse lifted?' he asked. He wondered whether he was now cursed too, so the answer was important.

'I need to get Saint Magnus to pardon me. He's the one who cursed my family in the first place.'

That made sense. Skarfr dropped to his stomach in the long grass, the better to concentrate on *how* they would get Saint Magnus to lift the curse. He was too intrigued to miss out on the next part of the story.

That's when he realised that the sea noises had changed. There was a regular splash and creak, men's voices coming nearer. He peeked through the grass and thought Hlif's story was coming to life: they would be chased to a church, hacked to death. But there weren't eight longships coming towards the beach. There were three and the pennants above the sails were not Hakon's. Eight leather-clad men jumped into the shallows and hauled the first boat till its keel stuck.

# CHAPTER THREE

M ore men put their battle-hardened muscles to work.
Within five surges of waves up the sands, the first ship
was beached and turned sideways to allow three ponies to
disembark from a panel that dropped to become a ramp.

Splashing and shouting, the men moved onto the hard sand,
leaving a clear view of the ramp, where a golden-haired giant
offered his hand to a woman who could have been his twin, Freyja
to his Freyjr. Skarfr realised how wrong he'd been. These were no
mere mortals as Hakon had been. The gods had come visiting.
*Star-dwellers, hurt-quellers, truth-tellers.*

From the exquisite gold braid on his cloak to his poise as he
gave orders to his men, their leader commanded attention. With
the ease of habit, he oversaw the unloading of some packages,
which he secured in saddlebags and strapped onto one of the
ponies.

The brooch pinning his cloak at the shoulder caught fire from
the sun, dazzling Skarfr so that the scene shimmered and glinted,
with blurry doubles of men and beasts. He blinked but couldn't
look away from what must surely be a saga in the making.

When the leader's cloak flared in the breeze, more braid

showed, edging a fine blue tunic. Surely he was dressed for ceremony, not raiding. Why was such a man arriving by stealth on a longship? As he came nearer, Skarfr could see the strong lines of his face, cheekbones straight as the water-rune *lǫgr* and a nose sharp as an axe blade.

While his men stumbled and cursed on the shifting sand, he never broke his stride, careful not to inconvenience the lady whose hand rested on his arm. She held her skirts as Hlif had done but the woman moved in a sensual sway, as if the ship's motion still rocked her gently.

As tall as many of the men, she embodied her own version of her companion's coiled power, drawing attention by her silent presence as he did by the authority in his tone. Grace and might, side by side. And if his face was sculpted as a warrior, hers was softened by the pale bloom of her unlined skin, by a gentleness in her blue eyes and by unbound hair rippling in golden waves.

'I would marry a woman like that and cleave to her all my days,' whispered Skarfr, heedless of listeners.

Too engrossed in their own conversation to have noticed their eavesdropper, the couple were close enough for him to hear their words. He ducked his head down to stay hidden by the dunes and was surprised to see his companion's blotchy red face and stubby nose, with no gentleness at all in eyes now grey as granite. He'd quite forgotten his strange new acquaintance.

He put his finger to his lips to shush her and ignored the indignant 'O!' shape her mouth made. They listened.

'Must it be so?' the woman asked, pleading without hope.

His tone brooked no appeal. 'We've *had* this conversation. You know Thorbjorn Klerk is too strong to be left unattached and he'll make you a good husband. We hold the balance of this land between us and we can topple the jarls – or support them.'

'Or support *one* of them,' murmured the woman. Her voice

brushed Skarfr's skin like a warm breeze, raising the downy hairs on his arms. He shivered, omen-touched.

The man laughed. 'That is why I need you where you can best help me, dear sister. You'll be the only woman who matters in that fake-Norðvegr court and you'll see the boy daily. Make him yours, influence him, drive a wedge between him and his foster-fathers without Thorbjorn or the Jarl even noticing. And at the same time, your lovely body and lively mind will bind Thorbjorn as an ally and I needn't fear an axe in the head from that quarter.'

'And Jarl Rognvald in all this?'

A shrug. '*One jarl rules for himself...*'

'*But two jarls must heed their people,*' she completed the saying known by all Orkneymen.

'So we'll watch and wait. Our father will drink to us in Óðinn's Hall and our mother will sleep easy.'

'You have not finished your revenge,' she observed. 'Good. Thorbjorn won't like it though. And the Jarl won't like you causing trouble.'

*Revenge? And who's the boy?* wondered Skarfr, trying to remember all he'd heard about the Jarl's entourage. *Sounds like the boy's important and Thorbjorn is his guardian. And so's the Jarl.* But it was no good. There had been too many names in Botolf's lectures and he remembered only those with stories attached. The stuff of sagas, not facts about boys.

Another deep laugh came from the giant, less amicable. 'Calmer-Jarl. Grown-old-Rognvald. The man likes everybody to make peace as if he's a nursemaid with a bevy of babies. Your marriage will make him smile till All Hallows. He'll be in his Christian heaven to see two strong men united by a beautiful woman.' He kissed his sister's hand, a gesture that Skarfr had never seen before but liked. Outlandish but courteous.

'And I must live on this island, alone.' She flicked strands of hair out of her eyes as the wind plucked at her tresses.

'We are all travellers.' His voice echoed her wistfulness. 'But we return when we can.'

'You still think this a good idea? To surprise the earl and his gathering, arrive by road rather than at Orphir Harbour?'

Instead of replying, the man suddenly filled Skarfr's view, lunging forward to grab him.

'Leave him be!' shouted Hlif. She rushed at the man, a sparrow against a mountain. He scooped her up and tucked her under one arm, where she dangled, lashing out and trying to bite.

'Quite a wildcat,' he observed, unperturbed. 'It seems we have been spied upon. What shall we do with them, Inge?'

Skarfr turned crimson under the full weight of the sister's blue eyes, now ice chips. He must have imagined the warmth in them.

'Our arrival won't be much of a surprise if these two noise it abroad,' she pointed out.

'I won't, my lady,' promised Skarfr earnestly. 'I must go straight home to my master, the skald, to prepare for this evening's entertainment at the Jarl's Bu. We live nearby and won't reach the Bu for hours yet.' He knew he was gabbling but he wanted her to think well of him and if he just kept talking maybe some of the words would make a skald-shaped impression on her.

If only Hlif could behave with more dignity.

'I can't speak for this girl,' he said. 'I don't know her.'

A look of contempt came his way from the bundle of clothing that struggled under the man's arm, then went still as a dead bird.

'You've hurt her!'

In response to Inge's words, her brother put Hlif down so she was standing but still within his grip.

He turned first to Skarfr, his eyes cobalt fire, dancing like the northern lights that flickered in winter skies. 'Tell your skald that Sweyn Asleifsson is come to Orkneyjar and let him pay attention to what he recites so that it does honour to the greatest sea-rover who ever lived.'

From any lesser man such a statement would have drawn at least a cough to cover hidden laughter at such arrogance. But this was not a lesser man. He believed he had earned the title he flung like a challenge.

Abruptly released, Skarfr rubbed his arms and resisted the urge to run away. Conscious of how he might look to Inge, he tried to sound courtly.

'I will announce your presence to my master, whose skill with words is renowned from the Old Country to this.'

The effect was spoilt by Hlif snorting as if she knew very well he was hoping for reflected glory by exaggerating his master's reputation. However, when she spoke, her tone was unexpectedly meek, although she held her chin high.

'I am Jarl Rognvald's ward and wish only that his guests find their way safely to his Bu and the reception waiting for them. If you wish me to forewarn my guardian that you are here, I will.'

Inge and Sweyn exchanged glances.

'I think not,' he said and glanced at her bare feet. 'But we shall save you a walk and you'll ride with us. Wait here.'

There was no chance of running away from a band of armed men and Hlif must have known that. Although Skarfr had been dismissed, he waited, whether to witness the next part of the story or for Hlif's sake, he wasn't sure.

Sweyn was talking to his men, organising the packhorse and two ponies. Hlif watched Inge walk over to join him, a curious expression in her eyes. Not envy but pity.

'A good husband is not what she'll find in Thorbjorn Klerk nor is he a man who'll be interested in her lively mind,' she retorted, then looked at him. 'She'd even be better off with you.'

He flushed, remembering his spontaneous reaction to Inge. He wanted to hit back at her for mocking a feeling so private, so precious.

'Jealous, you are,' he teased her. 'You want me for yourself, don't you.'

Her face smoothed and her eyes were misty, otherworldly, when she spoke, slowly, every word weighted with importance. 'I will marry you when my curse is lifted.' She paused, put all her hurt pride into the second condition. 'And when you are a skald renowned from the Old Country to this, *Skarfr*.'

He flushed deeper red, as if his inadequacy was a banner in front of his face and she'd read it aloud as easily as she'd decoded his name.

She turned away, allowed Sweyn to pull her up in front of him on the pony; the last sight Skarfr had of Hlif, on the day they met, was of her in the arms of the greatest sea-rover of them all, riding away from him, fiery red hair flying below the man's gold halo. And beside them, straight-backed and determined, rode the golden sister.

Skarfr's heart leapt like a fish. He knew two hundred and forty-three poetic ways to say 'woman' and not one of them fitted.

He almost forgot he was cursed.

# CHAPTER FOUR

'Idle boy!'

Botolf had returned early and sober, no doubt to prepare for his performance that evening.

Ducking a blow, Skarfr blurted out, 'Sweyn Asleifsson is come to Orkneyjar. We – I mean I – saw him beach his boat and he's heading to the Jarl's Bu by pony.'

The reaction was satisfying. Irritation at Skarfr changed to amazement, then a calculating look narrowed the hooded eyes in their wrinkled settings, almost sharpening the habitual watery vagueness. The usual sourness about his mouth in repose tilted upwards as he grilled his apprentice about the news.

Skarfr dutifully described Sweyn and his band, finishing, 'He spoke to me, said you must do honour to him in your songs this night because he's the greatest sea-rover who ever lived.'

Botolf looked thunder at being given such instructions and Skarfr added hastily, 'Those are his words, not mine.'

Then he had a sudden moment of inspiration. 'And you must —,' he amended the offending word quickly, '*should* do honour also to his sister, the Lady Inge, who is to marry Thorbjorn Klerk.'

His mind once more on bigger news than his apprentice's

failings, Botolf mused aloud, 'So it is true. Sweyn and Thorbjorn become blood-brothers while Jarl Rognvald looks on and smiles. What will this mean for us?'

Having been taught to recognise a rhetorical question along with the four hundred allusions that meant 'warrior', Skarfr held his tongue.

Botolf started pacing, his usual way in private to stimulate Óðinn's gift, the verse that filled his mind and spewed from his mouth. He warmed up with well-known kennings, those poetic references that gained nods of recognition from all educated men and even some women.

'*Riding on wave-steeds to Ring-Breaker's Hall, where*
*Bold-Hammer and Jarl-Snatcher will down one glad horn*
*and shout skål for their lady, the peace-goddess-born.'*

Skarfr shook his head, marvelling. Why was the god's gift bestowed on a man whose thoughts were as rancid as his unwashed feet? Understanding such verse was second nature to the boy now but he could no more compose such lines than spin gold.

'Well?' Botolf asked him, the cue for him to show he understood and appreciated every word.

'On boats, Thorbjorn and Sweyn come to the Jarl's Hall and seal their alliance through marriage with a draught from the same drinking-horn. The Jarl is the Ring-Breaker because he gives silver links from his chain to those who merit it. And the name-kennings are well found, Master, because Thórr is the hammer and Bjorn is the bear's strength while all know that Sweyn is Jarl-Snatcher because he kidnapped Jarl Paul, who was never seen again.'

'*Horn* and *born* are neatly rhymed. And the Lady Inge is well portrayed too.'

Skarfr knew better than to criticise but his true opinion was that playing on Inge's name as 'peace-goddess-born' was weak, rather obvious in referring to the goddess of peace and fertility, Ing, for whom she was named, and in emphasising the peace her marriage would bring. There was no evocation of the golden goddess who'd dazzled him. The woman in the verse could have been some dumpy matron.

If he were a skald, he would praise her so well she would ... he would ... he sighed and felt the sting of the girl's curse. He would what? *Be renowned throughout this land and the Old Country?* As Botolf was.

The skald was preening at the praise so Skarfr risked a question.

'Do you think our Jarl might react badly to the reminder that Sweyn put himself above a jarl in the past?'

'Yes,' said Botolf, serious. 'It is a warning he should heed. A reminder to Sweyn too that a skald is beyond his orders and obeys a higher power.'

He struck a pose, his belly straining at his linen tunic, his legs thin as a heron's. As he declaimed kennings on marriage and honour that ventured ever further from the common stock of images, his spittle hit Skarfr. Who merely blinked. Unless the skald was completely lost in composition, concern for his apprentice's manners would always take priority, using the tool nearest to hand. Skarfr had been thrashed with bridle, belt and even a cooking pot, which had smashed into soapstone smithereens.

His own name jolted Skarfr back into the present. 'Skarfr, you halfwit. I don't have time for lessons today but you can practise these three lines until they're perfect. And I'll test you on them any time I choose so make sure they are perfect. Before tonight.

*Golden Rán embarks for the heart's world,*
*proud at the prow which ploughs the raven's field,*
*and plants two hollow hand-fires for her and Strong-Hammer.'*

That was more like Inge. Skarfr could see her in his mind's eye as he repeated the lines, singsong, to show he'd memorised them. He would rehearse them all afternoon just so he could picture her, slim and regal, like the sea-goddess Rán, waves of golden hair gilding her dark cloak as she stood at the prow of her brother's dragon ship. Preparing the battlefield with rings for the crop of a marriage.

Skarfr could see layers upon layers of meaning in the lines that he must work to understand before performing them. Botolf would keep the important verses for himself, especially those lauding the two heroes and their alliance, but Skarfr would speak hers, Inge's. He glowed.

His master paid him no attention, too focused on his own work. 'A rough gem but will polish up well enough tonight,' was Botolf's judgement and there was no chance he was referring to Skarfr.

'Why are you still here, boy? There's animals to feed before you pack for overnight at the Jarl's Bu. Check Fergus has brushed, cooled and readied the pony for our journey. The lazy beast did little enough this morning but I don't want him collapsing on the road. Bad bargain that was. I make too many bad bargains from kindness of heart.'

Botolf's hard stare made it clear who else was a bad bargain. His kindness of heart had been dinned into Skarfr so often by neighbours as well as the skald himself that the boy no longer felt the bitterness that used to rise like bile at such a statement. He had learned to stomach worse and learning was his job.

'You won't need much.'

So deep had he retreated into his protective shell that Skarfr didn't take in his master's words at first. Then his heart pounded. He was going too. He would see this gathering of gods and heroes. Sweyn, Thorbjorn and Jarl Rognvald. *Lady Inge,* suggested his sly thoughts. *And Hlif.*

# CHAPTER FIVE

S karfr's first impressions of the interior of the Jarl's Bu were filtered through elbows as men jostled each other and jabbed him in the head if he didn't duck fast enough. He squeezed onto a bench at the back of the hall, guarding the precious pack which would serve as a pillow that night, on the same hard bench, if he was lucky. His feet rested on Botolf's pack while the skald paid his respects to the Jarl and his guests at the High Table.

Then he drew breath and looked around him. All the lesser guests had found seats at benches against two walls. They could see the central hearth and High Table, if their view wasn't hindered by the four pillars that supported the great thatched roof. Wood was scarce in Orkneyjar and no longhouse squandered even pine in beams and rafters, however important the owner. Peat, pitch and wattle and daub were used whenever possible.

Tapestries hung on the walls, stopping draughts and celebrating hunts and religious stories. Skarfr recognised Óðinn in one and Mary, mother of the White Christ, in another, but had no idea whether such fine work was local or from Norðvegr across the sea, where the Jarl had come to manhood.

Apart from the rich decor and solid stone build, the Jarl's Bu was much like Skarfr's own longhouse, but bigger and better. There were curtains behind the High Table, no doubt concealing sleeping chambers for the Jarl, his wife and other family members or guests of high status.

In the manner of a courteous host, Rognvald played cup-bearer to his guests at the High Table before taking his place on the bench between Thorbjorn and Sweyn. Like three different brews of ale, they dominated the hall from their elevated position on the dais. Blond on the left, amber in the middle and dark on the right.

The Jarl was pleasant-faced, his power lightly worn and dimmed by the young men either side of him, who exuded physical prowess and energy, like mastiffs straining at an invisible leash. Their every gesture and expression issued a challenge, not least when they looked at each other. As if 'Prove yourself or get out of my way!' was emblazoned across their tunics.

If he *was* the master holding those invisible leashes, the Jarl seemed immune to his companions' domination of the hall, apart from one nervous tic. He stroked a golden brooch on his embroidered jerkin in the same way that Skarfr reached for his hammer amulet when anxious.

Apart from these three men, nobody else in the hall mattered, except perhaps the glittering prize, the woman who sat beside her brother.

Botolf's self-important nods and bows suggested he thought differently and he barely glanced down the hall to check where Skarfr was seated with his belongings, before he took the place at the High Table indicated to him by a red-headed girl. Honour to the skald indeed.

In clean clothes, with her hair braided and coiled at the nape of her neck, and her face washed, Hlif was a different girl from the wild spirit he'd met on the beach. Skarfr observed her from the shadows at the back of the hall. With minimal nods, she gave brief replies to questions. Never initiating a conversation, let alone talking too much. Dainty manners with the food, which had been served to the High Table first. Eyes cast down. Quite the young gentlewoman. She and Inge were the only women at table so presumably the Jarl's lady was absent.

His attention moved along her neighbours at table to rest on a little boy sitting to the left of Thorbjorn, his curly brown hair so long in front that his eyes were hidden. His clothes were a miniature version of those of the adults beside him: breeks, leggings and a green wool tunic trimmed with bright red woven braid. The boy looked to Thorbjorn as though for guidance, or even permission, before he spoke to his other neighbour.

*The boy.* Skarfr remembered Sweyn's instructions to his sister, to 'win over the boy', and suddenly he knew who this must be. Harald Maddadson, the second ruler of Orkney. Until he came of age, he was foster-son to both Thorbjorn and Rognvald, growing up in the Jarl's court, far from his birthplace in mainland Ness. Waiting for the years to pass so he could claim his inheritance.

*Like me,* thought Skarfr, with a surge of sympathy.

Knowing that this little boy was Rognvald's rival as much as his fellow-ruler, Skarfr looked for signs of ill-feeling between them. And found none. The adult Jarl bent his knee when serving the little boy, made him smile as he filled his plate. An observer who knew no better would have thought from his avuncular affection that Rognvald was the first foster-father not Thorbjorn. But the boy looked always to Thorbjorn, who nodded or shook his head and the gesture was apparently obeyed each time.

Then thralls brought platters and Skarfr lost all interest in politics the moment he smelled smokies and fresh bannocks. The yellow smoked haddock flaked onto his warm flatbread. If only Brigid could bake bannocks like this, he'd be happy to eat nothing else. But hers were dry as dust, only edible if dunked in porridge or gruel.

He couldn't believe his luck as somebody passed him the

platter of crackling skin and chicken flesh hanging tender off the bone. His mouth full, he mumbled, 'Thank you,' and kept chewing.

His neighbour laughed, creasing a weather-lined face that joined his shoulders with no apparent neck. Built like a bull and cheerfully crunching a chicken bone on one side of his jaw.

'Look at the boy,' he said, showing bits of kale stuck in the few teeth he had. 'Half-starved!'

'Skald's a fool,' replied a man with a scar-gashed cheek. 'Starve a mutt and he'll turn one day.'

The grunts could have been agreement or disinterest. It made no difference to Skarfr either way. He knew not to complain. Word always got back to Botolf and he didn't want this to be his only visit to the Jarl's Bu so he kept his head down and his mouth full.

Nobody made him eat the kale so he didn't. And nobody stopped him taking a cup of barley ale though the first gulp made his eyes water and he waited awhile before taking another. The men ignored him as they talked.

'Full of himself as always, Sweyn is,' commented Bull-neck. 'And cool as you please, sitting at table with the relatives of the witch he's just burned alive.'

Presumably taking this as praise, Scar-face nodded in agreement, chicken grease dripping down his beard as he replied. 'He kept his word. He told the Thing he'd take no *manbot* for his father being burnt alive in their hall. He's been chasing Olvir Rosta ever since, the one who did the torching.'

'Hah! That one's well named. Olvir the Brawler, and he's Thorbjorn's foster brother. He's wily enough. He'll keep running. A fast ship and an ocean between him and Sweyn will cool heads.'

Bull-neck disagreed. 'Sweyn never forgives. But settling his score with Frakork will calm him for now. She's the one ordered the burning and who knows what devilment she used to trap those inside.'

'That witch just got what she gave. Death was too easy for her if you ask me, when you think of all she did.' He crossed himself against the dark arts. 'But she'll pay in the afterlife.'

Then he queried, 'Relatives? I know Thorbjorn's her grandson but he'll have to bite his tongue on the subject if he wants the bride, and her brother for family.'

'Why, Jarl Rognvald himself is related to the witch. Frakork is – was – his wife's sister,' said Bull-neck.

'He's probably glad she's out of the way and none of his doing so his wife can't blame him. He'll just say, "Sweyn is Sweyn" and we all know no man controls Sweyn.'

'Where is she anyway, the Jarl's lady?'

'Over in Ness with her folk. Dropped the bairn alive this time but it's only a girl and the mother's sickly.'

'Ay, Jarl Rognvald has no luck with getting an heir so he does well to keep the boy Harald close.'

Skarfr let the gossip float over his head. For once in his life, he ate his fill and was almost regretting that second bannock when he dropped a chunk under the table for the hounds. He'd already slipped a third into his pack, to take home. Cups were filled with ale once more and men were ready to be entertained.

# CHAPTER SIX

W hen Botolf performed, the hall itself listened. His mastery of the craft masked any weakness in his ageing voice. Judging by the reactions to even the most obscure of his allusions, the audience appreciated his inventive wit and recognised their fellow men in his words. Maybe he spoke the truth when he said his daily visits around the neighbourhood were to harvest grist for his poetry mill. Skarfr remained skeptical, not least because of the ale consumption during such visits, but there was no denying the pertinence of the skald's verses.

His improvisation on the topic of the forthcoming marriage fuelled more shouts for the ceremonial horn to be drunk to the dregs by the happy brothers-to-be, who complied with a brief show of reluctance. Easily persuaded, Sweyn swigged the full horn in one competent tilt of his arm, the fully-developed muscles from shoulder to elbow catching the firelight.

Thorbjorn feigned awe, fear of seeming the lesser man, then shrugged, accepting his fate. He raised the full horn as if it were one of his clerk's quills and threw his head back to catch the stream of ale. An arc of amber liquid flowed to meet the curve of throat, which pulsed in swallowing, a primitive rhythm. As he wiped the last drops from his mouth, he looked long at Inge, his eyes glittering. A different kind of challenge. She flushed, looked away, and her betrothed turned his unsmiling face back towards her brother.

'What men are these!' Rognvald stood, proffering all the smiles required. 'With two such men in my party, allies and now brothers, I count myself blessed!'

And so the tension ebbed and flowed throughout the night, as men drank and women – in asides or publicly – needled them to respond to perceived insults. Some men turned rough words to humour. Others took them inwards like those grass spikelets which stick in the skin and work through to the vital organs.

Questions were dangerous. 'Who is the most generous lord who ever lived' went from disagreement to 'Let's settle this outside' within minutes until surface calm was restored by the Jarl, who gave his judgement on each contender for the title and pronounced them equal but different.

Skarfr was all eyes and ears, wondering how the hall did not burst into flames from the accusations and rebuttals hurled across the trestle tables. Then, with careful timing, a cup-bearer would interrupt and the argument was drowned in ale, which of course fuelled resurgence of the dispute if the wrong word was spoken.

'Mother' was always the wrong word but 'sister' came close in sparking disputes and the golden siblings who were guests of honour were not immune to the tensions.

One joined in, loud and confident as befitted the world's greatest sea-rover. The other bestowed her gaze equally and briefly on the men present, including her betrothed.

Thorbjorn was not so restrained. His dark eyes were hungrier each time he turned to her.

'Jarl Rognvald, will you favour us with a poem?' invited Botolf. He had lectured Skarfr a thousand times on the skald's role as praise-singer and his duty to enhance his lord's reputation. Had

Rognvald been less talented, Botolf would never have offered such an invitation.

Affable as ever, Rognvald sent for the triangular hand-held harp that was his preferred instrument. Skarfr had learned enough from Botolf, who played an old-fashioned lyre harp, to appreciate the loud twang on the strings but he preferred a pipe, more practical for a skald and, to his ear, more emotional. Pipes stirred people to dance, to sing, to make love. The harp was insistent, a sharp interruption that jangled on the nerves.

With his harp nestled against his right cheek, Rognvald plucked some introductory notes to set the scene and the audience hushed. Perhaps there were advantages to the jarring noise, surprisingly loud from such a small instrument. And whereas Botolf's harp had gut strings, Rognvald's were metallic, plucked with the nails instead of the flats of the fingers. The firelight picked out some grizzle in his beard and brown hair.

But it was a young man's poem that Rognvald chose to recite.

'A man should know his own worth,' he began. 'The skills a youth learns are his treasures as a man, and these are mine. Old verse but silver skills, freshly minted by practice.'

Then he recited the poem he'd written as a young man; one everybody knew but that took on new meanings in the presence of his guests. His harp underlined each skill with a buzzing jingle. The theme was his own status as Jarl and however genial his manner, he was reminding them that he merited this hall and their allegiance, by birthright from his Orkneyingar mother, by the powerful allies of his Norðman father, and by his own prowess.

*'The Jarl's Nine Skills*

*Who will match himself against me?*
*Chess-master*
*Rune-reader*

*Book-knower*
*Ski-runner*
*Verse-pourer*
*Harp-strummer*
*Oar-wielder*
*True-shooter*
*Fire-forger.'*

Cups were raised in tribute and none took up the rhetorical challenge offered by their host, who spoke again.

'This is a double celebration as news from Ness tells me I am a father. My lady Gertrud has given birth to a fine girl.' If he was disappointed, he did not show it. There was a restrained ripple of congratulations as men made the delicate judgement regarding how to respond positively but without too much enthusiasm at the failure to produce an heir.

As the noise lulled, a childish voice could be heard asking, 'That's good news, isn't it, my lord?'

Harald's innocent remark had men sputtering in their beer at the irony. It was indeed good news for him.

'Yes, Harald, it's good news,' Rognvald replied, without any inflection that showed he understood the sniggers in the hall. He moved quickly on to the second reason for celebration.

'It is good to see such men as Sweyn Asleifsson and Thorbjorn Klerk at my table and for such an occasion. Tomorrow will witness the marriage of Thorbjorn Klerk to Sweyn's sister, and make these two brothers. No Jarl could wish for stronger men serving him or a happier occasion.'

Skarfr received two elbows in his ribs as the men either side of him raised their cups and swigged some ale. Just his luck to be between a right-hander and a *Týrsday*'s man so he took double jabbing. The bullish man was the left-hander and he closed his ham fist around the boy's, directing Skarfr's cup to his mouth.

The Jarl's golden brooch glinted as he returned to his seat at table and Skarfr could pick out some design on it, like runes in a circle. Something mystical.

Rognvald should have mentioned drinking as a skill young men needed, thought Skarfr, as the sour liquid numbed the back of his throat. He felt a little queasy and thought some fresh air might clear his head, if he could wriggle out of his place.

He glanced up at the table to see whether his master was still at a safe distance and was relieved to see Botolf waving his hands and philosophising. *Everything is bigger and better in the Old Country,* Skarfr mimicked in his imagination.

He scanned the High Table. Had it not been for her hair, the red-headed girl might have been invisible. She was motionless and ignored. Jarl Rognvald responded to Thorbjorn, who was nodding assent. The black-haired guest of honour stood up from the table, went behind Rognvald to approach first Sweyn, who also nodded, then Inge, who shrank back. Her brother spoke to her – a command? – and she gave her hand to Thorbjorn, who helped her extricate herself from her seat. He led her out of the hall.

Perhaps they too needed some air, thought Skarfr as he freed himself and followed them. The ale he'd consumed aroused his curiosity.

Perhaps they would kiss and he could watch, imagine the taste of her mouth, lips parting under his. With a beer-induced lurch, he stumbled out the door and a cool wind buffeted him. He ignored the men growling at each other. He couldn't care less whether words led to blows or not. He followed the couple in their fine embroidered clothes, the tunic and the gown, Thorbjorn's grip proprietorial on his lady.

When they turned the corner of the Jarl's dwelling, into the darkness, the boy hesitated. How would Thorbjorn react if he caught Skarfr watching? Badly, was the only possible answer but

Skarfr couldn't help himself. He had to see. He flattened himself against the wall at the corner and peeked round.

Behind him, the loud talk of men heading for the midden or returning to the hall continued unbroken. The rise and fall of arguments punctuated the more distant hum of conversation inside the hall. All of it faded to background noise when Inge spoke, her voice like spring-water to a thirsty man.

'My lord, it does you credit that you wished to speak to me in person, privately, but I think we should go back into the hall now. I can only repeat how honoured I am at your proposal and that tomorrow we will be man and wife in the eyes of God.'

She turned as if to walk back towards Skarfr and he recoiled instantly so she could not see him. He heard her exclamation of surprise or pain, then Thorbjorn's tones, low and urgent.

'That's tomorrow,' he told her. 'I wouldn't buy a horse without riding her first, far less a wife, so ready yourself, if you're truly a maiden.'

Confused, not sure whether this was preliminary to a kiss, Skarfr peered once more around the corner into the darkness. Inge was backed against a wall by Thorbjorn, pushing at him, saying, 'No!' while he gripped her more tightly.

Was this a game couples played? To make the physical adventure more exciting? Skarfr *was* excited but he felt ashamed too. He knew he shouldn't be watching but how else would he learn? There must be more to a man and a woman mating than he'd seen with dogs, cats and sheep.

'Enough,' said Thorbjorn, his voice rasping. He held a dagger to Inge's throat and she stilled instantly. He fumbled under his tunic with his other hand, then scrabbled up her skirt.

'This does neither of us any honour.'

Her words spoke directly to Skarfr's conscience and he stepped out from the wall, took a pace towards the couple. This was wrong and he had to do something.

'You'll find my betrothal sword goes deep enough to honour us both,' slurred Thorbjorn and Inge gasped in pain.

Skarfr also let out an involuntary noise and moved to help Inge.

'Oh no, you don't.' The whispered words were accompanied with force.

Skarfr suddenly found himself as constrained as Inge and his struggles just as impotent. Strong arms were around his chest like a metal band around a barrel, stopping his breath. His feet barely touched the ground but he could turn his head enough to recognise his assailant, his bull-necked neighbour from the hall. And beside the man, an ashen-faced girl with red hair, holding a torch.

Behind her, unnoticed by either of them, was a little boy, eyes gleaming large in the torchlight. Who watched Thorbjorn and Inge with a curve to his mouth that could only be a smile.

# CHAPTER SEVEN

The scuffle had drawn Thorbjorn's attention and without releasing Inge or changing position, he yelled, 'Give a man some privacy, Jedvard!' His face turned towards Skarfr a long moment, then he looked back at his lady, laughed and made ugly thrusting movements.

Skarfr would never forget the two faces lit in red by Hlif's torch, like the demons of the Christian hell. Thorbjorn, eyes darkened by his deed, acknowledged Skarfr with a nod.

*I'll remember you boy,* that nod said.

And the most beautiful woman in the world was wearing a blank expression that Skarfr knew well, from the inside. An *I will not cry* face. Yet, even with onlookers, she couldn't help gasping as her betrothed pounded her.

'Fool youngster,' muttered Jedvard, forcing Skarfr away from the couple, shoving him towards the open door of the hall. There was no sign of the boy who'd been there a minute earlier but Skarfr knew he'd seen Harald there, watching, and it troubled him. Hlif stalked beside them, her face set.

Skarfr declared, 'I shall tell Sweyn Asleifsson that Thorbjorn Klerk forced his sister.'

Jedvard stopped abruptly, laughed. 'And make two dangerous enemies instead of one? Why not tell Jarl Rognvald while you're about it?'

That had been Skarfr's next plan and he said in a small voice, 'I should. It's not right, what happened.'

Jedvard prodded him in the chest. 'Tomorrow, those two,' he jerked his head, 'will be man and wife. What goes on in a marriage is nobody's business but theirs and you won't find any man who says different.'

'But he hurt her,' persisted Skarfr, flushing at the thought of what he'd seen.

Another of those laughs that said, *You know nothing.*

'She'll get to like it,' said Jedvard. 'And Sweyn would say the same if you were stupid enough to tell him. But he'd punish you quick enough for spying. So get back in there and thank this lass for telling me that you were going to stir up trouble.'

Skarfr could no longer avoid looking at Hlif but what he saw in her eyes flayed him worse than any whip. Pity. He didn't need her pity. He didn't need her understanding of what had happened in the darkness against a wall, or of what he had felt, watching.

*Thorbjorn will not make a good husband,* she'd said. How had she known that?

He grunted something that could have been thanks and rushed into the hall, looking for Botolf. Any errand would be better than being left alone with his thoughts. Sure enough, his master was looking for him. Skarfr grabbed his pack from under the table and wove through the people between him and the skald.

'I've been to the midden,' Skarfr excused himself, then wondered why he needed an excuse.

'Now's the time,' Botolf told him.

Skarfr had no idea what the skald was talking about.

'Now's the time,' Botolf repeated. 'Has the ale made your wits even duller than usual? You're to recite the verse you practised, for the happy couple, and end the evening's celebration.'

Without listening to Skarfr's protests that he wasn't ready, Botolf pulled him up to the High Table, announced that his apprentice would recite a verse and all eyes turned to Skarfr. Including those behind him, daggers in his back, as Thorbjorn Klerk rejoined the High Table.

'My lady has retired for the night,' Thorbjorn told Sweyn as he passed, indicating the curtains behind them.

'Everything was to your satisfaction?' asked Sweyn, beaming.

'Everything,' replied Thorbjorn, sardonic. 'Together, we are invincible.'

'My invincible men,' Jarl Rognvald declared in a jovial tone. 'Sit down, sit down, Thorbjorn, and let the boy have his moment.'

Botolf called for attention and enough of the audience were listening for him to nudge Skarfr and urge, 'Begin!'

'Golden ring,' stammered Skarfr and his voice cracked.

He cleared his throat and began again, sweating.

'Golden ring of...' He blanked. What was the sea-goddess' name?

'Freyja,' he substituted the only one he could remember, realising too late what the goddess of fertility would evoke for the men in the hall.

'Rán, you numbskull,' Botolf muttered.

'I mean Rán,' Skarfr tried to continue but he could barely be heard over the raucous comments on Freyja's attributes. He knew they meant Inge. He'd turned Botolf's kenning to innuendo, to filth. He was no better than Thorbjorn.

*The man's appendage like a narwhal's horn, ripping into soft flesh under the fine, bunched fabric of Inge's gown. Her I will not cry face.*

'Thórr's rune bring together the two warriors,' he whispered. Then he leant forward and vomited, to the delight of every man in the hall, except Botolf.

His master pushed Skarfr off the dais with a clip to the head, hissed, 'Get out of my sight,' and opened his arms wide to win back *his* audience.

As Skarfr careered to the doorway, clutching his pack, he heard Botolf's voice over the mocking laughter, jeers and table-thumping.

'You can see what I have to put with! A drunk like his father! But what can you expect from an ill-bred whelp? I was a fool to think I could fashion a skald from a savage. In the Old Country, I could have had my pick of twenty boys but my kindness six years ago has bitten me again, like a snake in my bosom.'

Then bile rose again and Skarfr rushed out the door before he could disgrace himself a second time. He was doubled over in the darkness when a man grabbed him.

'Thorbjorn says you need more than a poetry lesson.'

It was not the bull-necked neighbour nor were the intentions kind. Skarfr kicked out but the clout in return made it clear what his options were.

Was he about to die? He tried to remember suitable prayers, in case, but they were as much out of mind as his praise verse had been when the moment counted. *Now*, he could remember every gods-cursed word he'd learned by heart but reciting verse would not get him to Valhalla *or* Heaven. This would be no warrior's death, nor a martyr's.

He remembered Hlif's retelling of St Magnus' death and how different the truth was from the story. Maybe he should forgive Thorbjorn and die in a state of grace?

*Never*, he vowed. *He will not make a good husband.*

He did not want to think of Hlif, the pity in her eyes before his public humiliation. Maybe this was her fault. She'd cursed him with her sarcasm, known he'd never be a skald. Women were like that.

*No,* he argued with himself. *Women are not like that. Not all.* Hlif had saved his life.

But the evening's humiliations were not over. He knew by the smell where he'd been dragged. The fish midden.

'Where you belong, rotten and reeking,' commented Thorbjorn's man, throwing Skarfr into the pit where fish-heads and bones were chucked, no doubt including those from the smokies he'd so enjoyed at the meal. He lost his footing in the slime and a rat ran past his face.

Where was his pack, with his precious flute inside? And his talisman bone? Stomach heaving, he felt the shifting piles around him, wincing when a shard spiked his hand. He was rewarded by the smooth feel of canvas and he shouldered the pack, heedless of the debris stuck to it. After all, he was in the same condition as his pack.

Alone in the darkness and stench, he clambered up the crumbling sides of the pit, falling back onto bones, trying again. Failing.

Pig-like grunting and black wings overhead distracted him. Óðinn's ravens no doubt, telling him his time was over. A punishment for fouling the art of poetry.

Not ravens – cormorants. Five of them, making deep, throaty noises as they landed. Perched on the bones around him in the midden, they folded their wings like draped flags while they picked at recent fish-heads.

One cocked its head, looked at him. In the darkness, he could see the tilt of the head, feel the bird's stare. It had something in its beak and with a quick flick, it threw something at him.

'Ow!' He picked up the object, a bone of course, but larger than a fish-bone, then he shielded his face as the other cormorants pelted him.

'Crk, crk,' they crooned as they flapped their wings.

*Fly. Watch us flying.*

Their wings whooshed the air past his face, with a reek of fish and tang of something else, oil and salt, a babyhood memory that must have been from his mother's tale. If only he could fly.

But his mother hadn't flown to reclaim him. She'd climbed. He unclenched his fist around six bones the length of cormorant shanks, like the talisman in his pack. The bones felt delicate and yet were maybe strong enough to help him, long enough to stick into the side of the pit, to give him handholds.

He paced his trust in the cormorants. Slowly, carefully, he dug his nails in and drove a bone into the earth, then another a bit higher. Hand by hand, foot by foot, he hauled himself upwards, pulling out each bone to use again. Then he was out of the pit onto steady ground. He lurched with the effort and sat down.

In the distant light from the open door of the hall, he could see the track by which he and Botolf had arrived at the Bu. He remembered the anticipation he'd felt then with disbelief, as if it belonged to a different person. That Skarfr was dead.

'Crk, crk,' the birds told him, flapping their wings again. And he listened to them, knew what they meant.

*Go home.*

He put the bones into his pack. *Seven*, he thought.

Then he got to his feet and plodded towards the track with increasing determination, encouraged by the cormorants' squabbling over choice remnants. They'd certainly profited from coming to his aid. A cheerful thought on a black night.

Not *so* black either, he thought, as he walked further from the hall and a full moon came out from behind the clouds to light his way. The gods might sport with him but they had not forsaken him completely. Best of all, he'd completely lost his sense of smell.

When Skarfr reached his house, he realised it was latched and locked, and the key must be in Botolf's pack, in the Jarl's Bu. He was so near to a comfortable night's sleep he felt like breaking the door down. Even though the hearth would be cold until the thralls lit the fire for Botolf's return, the empty house would have blankets and be warmer than sleeping outdoors.

He thought about the thralls again. How would they get into the house to prepare the fire and food for Botolf's return? He forced his weary feet to take the extra steps to the byre where Fergus and Brigid slept in the straw, called their names, heard only the soft breathing of the cow and goats.

Where would two thralls go in the middle of the night when their master was away?

Maybe...

Back to the house he trudged and knocked loudly on the door. The nearest neighbours were too far away to be disturbed, whatever noise he made.

'Fergus, Brigid, I know you're there. I won't tell Botolf. I need help. It's Skarfr.' He'd used their names, spoken to them directly, but the new Skarfr was not afraid to do so. He'd used up all his fear.

The door swung open. Fergus had an amber halo in the dim light of the tamped-down hearth fire. He screwed up his face.

'You smell. You can't come in like that. Brigid, get a blanket and the boy's spare tunic and bring it to the trough.'

Fergus led Skarfr to the pony's trough and dunked him, rubbing his hair and skin in the freezing water. The boy let the thrall wash him, caring little what happened to his bruised body. His spirit was numb.

With mother-hen clucks of disapproval, Brigid patted him dry with the blanket, threw his tunic over him and bundled him across the yard, back into the house, where a dry blanket was on the floor by the fire, with a roll for a pillow.

'Lie there, boy, and sleep,' Fergus told him. 'We'll watch over you.'

Skarfr curled up in his wool cocoon, shaking, afraid to sleep and dream. Stripes of different yarns, he noticed, as he pulled the blanket tightly around him. He forced his mind away from a dark wall only to remember sea-grey eyes stinging him with their pity.

When Brigid whispered, 'Poor boy,' he heard Hlif, although she'd never said the words. He could never face her again. He could never face anybody who'd been in that hall.

Finally, the warmth lulled him into sleep and when a gentle touch woke him too soon, he was under the protection of dark wings and soft feathers. He blinked as the warm down metamorphosed into woollen stripes and Fergus spoke to him, urgently.

'Come to the byre now. Best we eat there and leave no trace of our presence here except for our work. Best for you too. He won't be happy. Tell him you slept in the byre.'

'When is he coming back?' asked Skarfr. They both knew who 'he' was.

'He didn't say but it's Friggsday today so it will be the wedding day. He'll stay for that and he won't come back at night so...'

Skarfr nodded, avoided the dark place in his memory. 'Yes, the wedding will be today.' Weddings might take place in the White Christ's church but they were always held on the day of the marriage and motherhood goddess, Frigg.

They could sleep in the house each night until the master returned.

'I won't tell,' he said.

'I know.' There was kindness in Fergus' eyes, which no longer avoided his.

'My pack!' Skarfr suddenly remembered, panicking at the thought of losing his flute.

'Is fit only for the midden. We'll throw it away today, apart from this. Your pipe was protected by the oilcloth you'd wrapped it in.'

Skarfr took the pipe and the familiar feel of its smooth wood, its history of melodies played and waiting for his mouth, brought tears.

'It is not harmed,' said Fergus gently.

'And the bones,' remembered Skarfr. 'They are gifts, talismans.'

'And the bones,' agreed Fergus, asking no questions. 'I will fetch them now.'

Even a thrall pitied him. Skarfr could not bear to be looked at in such a way. It unmanned him. He thought of Inge and the courage of women. Maybe she would kill Thorbjorn one day. Or he would. He lifted his *I will not cry* face to meet Fergus' eyes.

Laying his hand on Fergus' arm in a warrior's gesture, he said, 'When I was a boy, I kept to the path our master permitted and he does not see you. I do. And I will not unsee you and Brigid again. You have your stories to tell and I will listen.'

The man put his work-hardened hand on top of Skarfr's, a vow. 'When he is present, we change nothing, for all our sakes. He is a brutal man but we protect each other.'

'Like hiding the bedroll,' said Skarfr.

Fergus nodded. 'When you find us in the byre or he is away, we will be ourselves. And we will give you our stories.'

# CHAPTER EIGHT

By the dull embers of the hearth-fire, Skarfr listened to Fergus and Brigid tell tales of Írland, a land so well-tempered in weather that cattle fed outdoors all year round. No venomous creature could live there and if any were brought from elsewhere, they died as soon as they touched bare earth or rock. So potent was its effect that Irish soil could be taken to another country and would pen any such poisonous beast if strewn in a circle around the devil's creation. The beast would stay there until dead. Even an Irish stick would have the power to draw such a holy circle, so when Irishmen travelled abroad, they would carry a holy staff for their protection.

In this holiest of countries, according to Fergus, miracles abounded. On the mountain of Blandina were two springs, which changed the hair colour of any man or beast bathing in their waters. One spring would turn white hair to black; the other would change all colours to white. If a man should want white wool from black sheep, nothing was simpler than to dip his oddities in the white spring. And an old woman could be rejuvenated by washing her grey hair in the black spring. Skarfr's cormorant could dive after fish there and surface in swan plumage.

He imagined Hlif plunging into cold Irish spring-water, entering the water as a red-haired maid and emerging as a white-capped crone when she came up for air. He felt strangely tender towards the old woman she would become.

Fergus was already telling new stories of a lake that provided bountiful salmon but only to the righteous, and of an island where no disease or females could exist. Of the willow that bore healing apples in response to St Kevinius' prayer and kept its God-given gift thereafter. Of the Themar king who gave unjust judgement, in favour of his friends, and whose great town was upturned by the Lord's wrath, so that towers pointed downwards deep into the earth and heaps of soil were the new buildings.

Skarfr's favourite was a story of holy Patricius; how one clan howled at him like wolves when he preached his faith. Unable to speak above the clamour, he prayed for God to send them an affliction and show His strength. From that day on, and for seven years afterwards, all members of the clan became wolves each winter. Worse than wolves, as they retained men's guile while devouring men as eagerly as other creatures.

Although an amazing display of God's power, worthy of Thórr, this did not seem much of a punishment in Skarfr's eyes. If the clan were content as wolves and human the rest of the year, there were even adventures to be had from such changing. And uses, such as the wolf and bear-changers who gave Norðmen an advantage in battle.

Skarfr pondered the question as to whether he'd rather be wolf or bear and realised there might be some disadvantages in changing to either. What if he should eat Hlif? That would be a foul return for her intended kindness. And if he died in wolf form, neither Valhalla nor heaven would be his lot. No: shifting shapes was for gods, not mortals.

Sometimes, Skarfr dropped off before the story's end, and, without knowing how he'd got there, found himself on his own straw pallet, drowsily aware of soft night-time noises from Botolf's bed behind the curtain. As unlike what had happened against a dark wall back at the Jarl's Bu as melody from cats calling.

Dream and life merged when he felt the light warmth of a woman's touch, stroking his cheek. Brigid? His mother? And when he was carried in arms or a giant beak to be gently dropped, somewhere safe. Fergus or a cormorant?

Each morning, Skarfr erased any trace of night-time presence and headed for the beach to check on Sweyn's longships. When the rover sailed, he would do so early in the day and there was every likelihood that Botolf would return immediately Sweyn had left Orphir, taking saga stories with him and leaving lesser mortals behind.

How Skarfr wished he could follow those stories, sail with Sweyn. Even though his hopes of becoming a skald had ended, stories called to him the way the nine daughters of Aegir were known to lure sailors. He would rather be dashed upon rocks than doomed to such a little life.

Each morning the longships were still there, waterproof covers untouched, and after a fruitless vigil, Skarfr returned to his chores at home.

Now he had allowed himself to see the thralls as people, he devoured every detail of how they looked and how they spoke, their soft pronunciation of the Norn language marking them outsiders as much as their black hair and blue eyes. The combination was not unknown among Orkneymen but spoke of foreign blood. True-bred Orkney hair was every hue of sunshine from ash-white and barley gold through to bronze and sunset red.

Maybe Skarfr was drawn to the black-haired couple because of his own outsider looks, his jet hair, straight as weighted weaving, like his mother's. He wasn't sure what colour his eyes were but their reflection in water showed them dark, probably brown rather than blue. But Skarfr was more like Thorbjorn physically than like the thralls. Ness and Scots background probably, for both of them. The thought that he might in any way be like Thorbjorn evoked a shudder.

There was something about the Irish couple and how they were with each other, that soothed Skarfr's aches. A kindness. Without words, the couple looked out for each other. Fergus lifted buckets of water that were too heavy for Brigid, while she patched a rent in his jerkin. She raised flames from the embers and cooked some of the ling he'd caught out in the bay, hanging the extra fish above the fire to smoke.

When he found his tunic and breeks laid on his bed, smelling of soap instead of fish heads, Skarfr realised that this care had surrounded him too, for years. He'd always been so focused on Botolf – his anger, his teaching, his rare approval – that he'd dismissed the thralls' daily care for him and his home as irrelevant. Not anymore.

Eight days' freedom had passed since the disaster in the Jarl's hall and the sixth day of the week, Laugarday, was always bath day. Usually, Skarfr trudged beside his master the two miles from his isolated longhouse to the cluster of dwellings on the outskirts of Kirkjuvágr, where the bathhouse was situated. Botolf liked him washed and out of sight as quickly as possible so the bard could gossip while Skarfr shivered outdoors, waiting. This Laugarday, Skarfr went to the bathhouse later in the day than was his right so he could keep Fergus company among the male thralls. People might gossip but in their eyes he was a child, and moreover a child whose guardian was absent, so his odd behaviour would arouse little curiosity.

Once in the bathhouse, Skarfr removed his clothes, put them in a pile and sat down beside Fergus on the step below the water level in the stone basin. The water was no longer hot but when a man added a boiling crock-full from the pot over the fire, it became warm enough to suffice. When his turn came, the boy took the soap and scrubbed at his hardened feet, rubbed it over his body and passed it on to the next man.

Naked in the bathhouse, men relaxed. They spoke when words came but mostly they let silence drift like the cleansing steam from the pot above the fire. The scent of juniper burning slipped into Skarfr's sense of wellbeing. He shut his eyes, listening to the music of foreign tongues, understanding the words only when the talk switched to Norn so as to cross the language barriers between the different nationalities of thralls.

Peat-digging and barley harvest held no interest for Skarfr but his attention was caught by the word 'wedding'.

'My master came back from Orphir today, says Sweyn leaves tomorrow and that's the end of the feasting at the big hall. The wedding took place yesterday so all the little lords are happy as lambkins.'

'Yesterday?' Fergus queried, voicing Skarfr's surprise. 'I thought it was planned for last Friggsday.'

'As the head of Inge's household, Sweyn kept upping the amount he gave as *heimanfylgia*, her inheritance for her husband's use, which made Thorbjorn look small in what he'd offered as *mundr*, the bride-price, and there was no end of outdoing each other, with the Jarl speaking his mind on what was fair and reasonable.

'Rognvald declared that Thorbjorn's intended *morgengifu*, the morning-after gifts, were the most generous he'd ever known. Rumour says he slipped his own coin to Thorbjorn to ensure that was so and Sweyn knew he was beaten. He could not be the more generous because his dowry-offering could always be outdone by Thorbjorn the morning after. What a to-do! The couple finally bound their hands in marriage under the lychgate to the Round Kirk and Inge gave Thorbjorn her father's sword, as was proper. With the priest's blessing.'

'And Frigg's,' observed a heavily-accented voice.

'Rognvald is all Christian piety these days, especially since he took on the cathedral project. St Magnus blesses everything. But the Jarl knows his men well enough and makes no war against the old ways. Thorbjorn married in the kirk but he made sure men witnessed how deep he'd buried the sword, the morning after.'

Skarfr winced. Thorbjorn's sword-thrust had indeed been witnessed, and not just the one to the central pillar in his longhouse.

'It's not just that the Jarl accepts the old ways. He's not one for making war at all.'

'He thinks he has two strong men in his camp, brothers by a fine marriage, and instead he's made a two-headed dragon with a clever woman holding both bridles. If the lady aims their fire at Rognvald, he has no defence.'

'Why should she?'

'Well, there were no purple flowers from husband to wife in *that* marriage nor did she sew him a tunic but all know Thorbjorn could be more than a clerk with Sweyn to back him. And he's foster-father to the next Jarl. Rognvald's getting old.'

Skarfr knew only too well how a guardian could control a boy's life and abuse his fortune and he didn't believe Thorbjorn's motive for watching over Harald was born of pure generosity.

'He's a few grey hairs but twenty years more still won't see a white head on him! For the moment, all is as peaceful as Rognvald could want. Thorbjorn can play with his new wife and do his clerking for the Jarl while Sweyn's off raiding again.'

There was silence. Skarfr wondered what 'raiding' meant to these men, knew that each of them had once been an enemy to Orkneymen and perhaps to each other. Killing was not personal and peace was not cowardice. The Thing often pronounced sentence on murder, with blood-price and an end to hostility. Or so the law said. Conversations in the Jarl's hall had suggested otherwise.

He looked straight ahead at the water, while quietly posing the question he'd been longing to ask. 'How did you and Brigid come to Orkneyjar?'

The reply was a whisper across the shimmering surface. 'We lived in the same village. I was on a message from my father to hers, when the raiders came. He worked leather, her father.'

In the pauses, Skarfr imagined the rest. The longships arriving on the beach, the warriors reddening the eagle's claw, taking what they wanted, taking *who* they wanted.

'We were in her house and they wanted girls, so they bound her.'

Skarfr watched his legs wriggle, shortening and lengthening, distorted like a reflection in a metal cup as the water moved. He thought of Thorbjorn.

'I was young. She was older, quick-witted. She lied, said I was a noble's son, worth a ransom, so they took me just in case, brought me to Orkneyjar. Botolf bought her and, the gods be thanked, his needs were not those she feared, though he is not an easy master.'

Skarfr trailed his right hand across the water. Five ripples.

'He said he'd keep me till the ransom came. The bargain was even better than he thought. He paid nothing for me, the ransom never came and he has my service.'

'What about the man ransom was owed to?' asked Skarfr. 'Who took you from the village? Don't you belong to him?'

'Died.' Before Skarfr could ask any more questions, Fergus stood up. 'The water's getting cold,' he said, although another scalding scoop had just been added.

Skarfr took the hint. It was none of his business how Fergus had avoided the noose of false identity tightening around his neck.

*His* business was to go with Sweyn and *become* a warrior instead of reciting hundreds of kennings for one. Poets and storytellers didn't have lives. They just leeched off other people's. He should fulfil the cormorant's prophecy to his mother and be the stuff of sagas. Botolf had unmanned him with all that verse.

With a pang, he decided that tonight must be his last night of home fare and Irish tales. Tomorrow, he would wait for Sweyn on the beach and sail with him, become a wave-rider and bring back so much booty from his raids that he could free Fergus and Brigid, who would come back to work for him when he came of age and inherited his mother's longhouse. He would leave Botolf and curses behind him and there would be no women to confuse him.

'Skarfr?'

Fergus' puzzled look made him realise he'd been wool-gathering and he came back reluctantly to the present.

At first light, Skarfr grabbed two of yesterday's bannocks and wolfed one down with a drink of milk. The other went into his pack, where his spare tunic, a comb, the talisman bone, a knife, a leather bottle and his pipe had already been stashed, along with two silver bits he'd stolen from Botolf's 'secret' box.

He stammered, 'Thank you,' to Brigid and Fergus, who looked pointedly at the pack and observed, 'The master will likely be back this afternoon. He's not one for an early start if he's comfortable.'

Skarfr took this to mean that their idyll was over and that he should expect punishment for failing Botolf at the Jarl's Bu. Even more punishment if he was shirking his duties rather than meekly waiting at home for Botolf to return.

He shrugged. He had no intention of coming back at all. Not until he could claim the house and his life as his own. Until then he'd go a-roving, among real men.

He hoisted his pack onto his shoulders and trotted off on the familiar path towards the beach, undaunted by the drizzle. Rain was no deterrent to an adventurous spirit. Although he wished he had a cloak and was soon wet through, he didn't remember one mention of dampened enthusiasm in the sagas. Storms, whirlpools and raging seas, yes. But not the light pitter-patter of *dagg*. Nor the myriad other forms of Orkneyjar rain from *eesk* showers to bitter-cold *aitran*.

Nevertheless, he sought shelter on the beach. The shrub-tufted dunes offered none, nor did the grey sands stretching out to the steely sea. The only option was to sneak under the tent cloth protecting Sweyn's longship and seek permission after the event.

He loosed one of the ties enough to clamber over the side of the beached ship and onto a rower's bench. It was no harder than those offered to guests in Rognvald's Bu and he had the luxury of its length to himself so he stashed his pack under his head for a pillow and made himself comfortable.

He shut his eyes and practised his request.

'My lord, I want nothing more than to sail with you and become a man.'

Truthful but too blunt. Should he start with praise for Sweyn? Along the lines of, 'All have heard of your exploits, how you captured Jarl Paul...' No, that story had a doubtful ending and might be taken as criticism.

'How you defeated a hundred men one-handed in battle and challenged the wolves that chase the sun to race your dragon ship redder than the sunset.' That was more like it. Heroes merited a proper telling of their sagas. Poetic truth, not boy's bluntness.

Maybe the allusion was a little obscure for rovers. How well-versed was Sweyn? He hadn't seemed impressed by the Jarl's nine skills but perhaps that was because of the manner in which Rognvald had asserted his authority rather than the quality of the lines.

Skarfr racked his brains but among all the stories of Sweyn's prowess, none came to mind where his retorts were clever lines rather than axe-blows or night-raid.

Skarfr's thoughts shied away from the other poems recited in Rognvald's Bu and hoped a week's drinking had made all present forget the first evening.

No, maybe Skarfr would be better to take a man-to-man bluff approach, say how keen he was to learn from a master, show he could pull an oar and live as lean as need be. With such cheerful thoughts and the rhythm of raindrops for a lullaby, he drifted into a shallow sleep.

# CHAPTER NINE

'We've a thief!' The rough voice was followed by even rougher hands, hauling Skarfr up from the bench, dangling him over the side of the ship and dropping him on the wet sand in front of Sweyn.

Ice-chip eyes looked him over. The hero was cloaked against the rain, his hair peeping out from his hood like gold coin from a dark purse.

'What have you taken?' Sweyn asked, placing one booted foot on Skarfr's back, pinning him to the sand with enough pressure to hurt.

'Nothing,' gasped Skarfr, arching his neck to hold up his head and avoid taking in sand as he spoke. The boot gave no leeway and he crunched back down on the wet grit.

The same hands that had grabbed Skarfr held up his pack. 'This was with him,' growled the man.

'Search it.'

Sand rasping his cheek, Skarfr watched his possessions tossed over the side of the ship after being enumerated in a guessing game.

'One. Item: dirty linen,' yelled Growly Voice.

It wasn't. Brigid had washed it only two days ago. Skarfr bit his lip, listened to the mew of hungry gulls and put on his *I will not cry* face.

'Tunic,' the men shouted back and they cheered when the item of clothing flew over the side of the ship and proved them right. One of Sweyn's men wiped his sweaty face on it before dropping it on the sand and calling, 'Next?'

'A fine blade!'

'Sure to be a sword,' came the reply.

'No, an axe!' joked another.

'Wrong! Guess again!'

Skarfr's knife was joined on the sand by his leather water-bottle, emptied of what the men insisted was ale, dangerous for a growing lad.

'Seven saints.'

'That'll be beads on a string.'

'No.'

'Magic stones,' guessed another.

'No,' crowed Growly Voice, triumphant. 'It's the real thing!' He intoned like a priest, 'One, Saint Peter's thigh-bone,' and over the side of the ship he threw one of Skarfr's bones. The catalogue continued until the seventh bone was allocated to a vulgar part of saintly anatomy and dumped in the sand.

To much laughter

Then, as the jesting grew stale, came the moment he was dreading.

'What's this?' Growly Voice couldn't hide his surprise and Skarfr imagined him pulling open the pouch strings, peering inside, pulling out—

'Well, well, well.'

'Stop teasing the men and tell us what you've found, before I jump in that ship and see for myself. It's time we caught the tide.'

Sweyn's tone held an edge but the man in the ship seemed oblivious to the change in mood on the sand.

'Eight. Item. Wooden mouth-game.'

Skarfr's heart sank. After a few guesses and more clues, his precious flute was thrown like rubbish onto the sand. Nobody moved to pick it up but nobody suggested it proved he was a thief, unlike—

'Nine. Item. Pieces of friendship.'

'Would they be silver?' queried the quickest of the men guessing.

As Growly Voice yelled, 'Silver bits!' Sweyn was already hauling Skarfr to his feet by the scruff of his tunic neck.

Skarfr scrambled to stand quickly enough to prevent his best tunic being ripped. If it was only a seam, Brigid could mend it. But he wasn't going to see Brigid. He was going to sea.

*Be a man,* he told himself. *Now's your chance to talk.* Especially as he *had* stolen the silver, or so most people would judge. It was too complicated to explain to Sweyn that stealing from Botolf wasn't really stealing because the longhouse and everything in it belonged to him, Skarfr.

'Master Botolf, the skald, sent me to you with the coin, Lord Sweyn. It's to thank you for taking me roving with you and teaching me the seamanship a man should learn.'

Sweyn's expressions were not as easy to read as the moods of sky and sea but a small narrowing of his eyes suggested calculation. Skarfr was used to judging his daily fate by such slight changes in a man's face and he thought the odds on a whipping had lessened.

'Throw me the pouch, Grith,' yelled Sweyn, 'with the strings tight. And if you keep so much as one bit, you'll wear stripes on your back for a fortnight and have salt rubbed in them.'

Instantly the pouch arced in Sweyn's direction and he caught it one-handed, with an elegance that Skarfr would have admired in different circumstances. Sweyn loosened the strings enough to check the bag's contents, then tied it to his belt and grinned at Skarfr, who allowed himself to hope.

'I learn fast, work hard and I can row. And I don't eat much,' he added.

An unexpected ally spoke up.

'We were all boys once,' pointed out Growly Voice, 'and hardened into men on a ship. Maybe he'd bring us luck?' Then he tempered his support with a practical alternative. 'And we can always toss him overboard if he's too much trouble.'

Skarfr swallowed, hoping this was another joke.

'Luck?' Sweyn's gaze swept his men. 'Don't you recognise the boy? He's the skald's apprentice who forgot his fine words and wet his breeks in Rognvald's Bu the night before the wedding.'

He sniffed Skarfr and jumped back dramatically. 'Still stinks of fish.'

Hearty laughter made it clear that all the men there understood the joke, knew where Skarfr had been dumped in Orphir. Skarfr felt the heat crimson his face and wished he were dead but he forced himself to look up and meet Sweyn's eyes when addressed directly.

'Do you think you're lucky, boy?'

'No,' whispered Skarfr. 'I think I'm cursed.'

This time the laughter was uneasy. Some men crossed themselves and others fingered the hammer amulets round their neck – or did both.

Sweyn threw back his hood, let his hair fly over his forehead.

*Like a lion's mane*, thought Skarfr. Like one of the splendid beasts from the Old Country Botolf had told him about.

'No, I don't think you're lucky, either. Nor do I think you can row to our rhythm, watch someone's back or carry enough treasure to be worth your weight on my ship.' He made a little bow. 'But I'll keep the skald's thank-you and you can tell your master I taught you a lesson and took payment for it.'

With a casual thwack across Skarfr's backside that was almost friendly, the boy was dismissed. After staggering to a safe distance, he watched the men move about their accustomed duties as Sweyn focused on launching the ship. Skarfr's dream of joining them was dashed but he could not leave, not while his belongings lay scattered on the beach. Cursed indeed.

A coarse cackle came overhead and three cormorants flew over Skarfr, one so low she could speak to him. He knew her for a liar. He would never make sagas and he refused to listen as she squawked her pagan message. Let her fly and dive with the wave-riders, who were busy stowing the tent cover in a tidy roll.

As if she'd heard him, the cormorant dived as low over Sweyn as she had over Skarfr but with a different message. The hero shouted an order just as the bird was over his head. Then he ducked too late and swore volubly as filthy droppings, grey and white, hit his blond head and trickled down. His orders were even more curt as he wiped at his face with his cloak, no doubt smearing the guano further.

'Luck, my lord,' Growly Voice attempted to cheer up his leader as men hid sniggers behind their hands and coughed instead.

'Luck,' agreed Skarfr with a sarcastic edge, suddenly feeling more cheerful. Even a god looked less heroic with bird shit on his head.

Belongings and boots were thrown over the side onto the rowers' benches, and finally the roller blocking the prow was removed and shipped.

'Run!' Sweyn instructed and the men on either side of the ship hefted it as if it were an axe, gliding it over the wet sand to the sea where they jumped through the waves into the ship, hauling in the slowest of the band. Oars flashed into rowlocks and after the first bumps, the twenty oarsmen worked to the same rhythm. Wave-riders seeking adventure. *Foam-harrowers, Sea-tillers, Storm-bravers.*

Skarfr watched the ship until it was a dot on the horizon, then realised it was no longer raining. A pity, as he needed fresh water to wash himself and his belongings. He gathered up his possessions slowly, inspecting each one, trying to turn them back into *his* things, to brush off the taint of mockery. He turned his spare tunic into a makeshift pouch and packed comb and knife. They were soon joined by six bones but he had to search some time before he found the seventh, chipped. He knew each nick and bump of all seven and this was not his birth talisman, which was intact. His gods were still with him, in their ambiguous fashion.

The pipe was gritty with wet sand and he had no idea how much damage the salt water had done but he dried it as best he could on the tunic he was wearing and added it to the pack, along with what had been protective cloth, now screwed into a ball.

He would have to go back to the longhouse and face Botolf.

'Skarfr!'

How long had she been there, the cursed girl, Hlif? He flushed. She was picking her way through the grass tussocks towards him, skirts bunched in her hands, in the fruitless attempt to keep the hem clean, just like the first time they'd met.

*Hah!* He was in no state to poke fun at sandy clothes. What must he look like? When she was close enough, he stared her in the eye, daring her to show the pity that still made him flinch from remembering their last encounter.

She stared back, turned it into a cats' duel of who blinked first.

He lost, blushing again and looking away, but not before he'd studied every yellow fleck in the cloudy grey irises, more in the right than the left, fish in a troubled pool, the shine and movement hiding what lay beneath.

'Now you know how it is,' she said, matter of fact. 'Sweyn and

Thorbjorn are two sides of the same coin. Being cursed has its uses.'

Still none the wiser as to whether she'd seen all his humiliation, Skarfr had no idea whether she meant herself or him. He had yet to see the benefits of being cursed.

'The Jarl will give you work if I ask him,' she said simply.

His automatic rejection of charity died on his lips, held back by knowledge of the alternative. Not fear. Worse than fear. Resignation. There must be something better.

Before he found an answer, she hammered him with words so fast he wondered how she could breathe and talk. Out they spilled, *bang, bang, bang.*

'You can wash, meet my guardian, get work as a table-boy or apprentice bootlicker, I don't care what! He won't say no because he owes me but he won't let me live a normal life because he owns me and I'm tired of it all, tired, tired, tired!'

She paced the sand and even if Skarfr had found the words he wanted, she was too deep in her own outburst to have listened.

When he'd woken that morning, he'd seen his future as a warrior in a dragon ship. Instead, he might be considered as pot-boy. He could always go back to his own longhouse, to Brigid and Fergus. And Botolf.

'All right,' he interrupted Hlif's rant. 'I'll work for the Jarl, if he'll have me.'

# CHAPTER TEN

They found Jarl Rognvald watching two of his men compete with staff slings, aiming three shots each at the tin eyes of a straw doll. The main advantage of the long wooden staff over a hand-held sling was that its steadiness and consistency made for greater accuracy in firing a stone – once a man had mastered the technique. With one hand on the slingshot in its cord loop at the end of the staff, the man swung the stick over his shoulder like a fishing-rod and let go of the sling, which flung the stone. The clang of a hit was greeted with cheers by the onlookers and in the pause, a lad ran out to move the target further away.

Hlif told Skarfr to wait while she broached his situation with her guardian. He was surprised at how confident the girl was in approaching the Jarl and at how readily Rognvald left his men to consider what she had to say. He strained to hear but Hlif had carefully stopped him short, out of Skarfr's earshot. He felt like a lame pony at market, trafficked to look like a good buy.

Then Rognvald was striding towards him across the yard, with Hlif trying to keep up, five steps to his one.

'You want to be a table-boy! Given up on your skaldic ambitions, have you?'

Now that it was directed at him, the Jarl's humour did not seem so affable. He flinched, his skin so thin that one more mocking smile would surely flay him alive. He'd been wrong and Botolf was a better alternative after all. At least *there* he had Brigid and Fergus, and could sneer at Botolf behind his back. What witchcraft did the cursed girl possess that he'd followed her here? To be laughed at. But he wasn't drunk and he wasn't running out of this court a second time.

With all the dignity he could muster, he drew himself up straight and said, 'My skills were overestimated.' *By me*, he thought bitterly. 'I have not drunk the true mead of Óðinn and will not be among those regurgitating the dregs without knowing any better. So yes, I have given up on my skaldic ambitions.' He clamped his lips shut before their trembling betrayed him. They were all the same: Rognvald, Sweyn, Thorbjorn. All men hardened by raiding and fighting who made themselves look big by cruel jokes targeting those who couldn't fight back. He must become like them.

Rognvald raised one eyebrow, a twinkle in his eyes that boded ill for Skarfr's composure. 'So, you think I'm one of those who drank what Óðinn dropped in the mud outside Asgard walls and I have but eight skills.'

Now Skarfr knew he was being teased. The Jarl was at much at ease in his toned mind as in his muscled body. Not young but well-exercised and as happy to respond to a verse challenge as to a wrestling match. He could spin verse on the spot, about anything from a swim in a sea cave to a woman's strange head-dress. Even Botolf had recited Rognvald's verses with admiration for his ninth skill.

The Jarl's fine garments showed off his broad shoulders and Skarfr remembered how easily the jibes had been shrugged off during the celebratory feast. If only he had shoulders as broad. Close up, he could see that the design on the golden brooch was circular, a wheel of arrows, rune-like but not runes – or not ones he knew. A sigil of some kind.

'Not runes, although they look like them,' Rognvald confirmed, observing where his attention had wandered. 'I call it *Vegvísir*, the pathfinder. When I was given this brooch, I was told, "Wherever you go, you will never be lost. When you seek direction, the pathfinder will answer you. Óðinn and Thórr will recognise you from now on." I keep it for sentimental reasons.' He made the sign of the cross. 'I have found the true way now and will not stray from it.'

*That doesn't stop him fingering the brooch,* thought Skarfr cynically. But weren't Orkneymen all alike, praying in the kirk on the Sun's Day and yet wearing amulets?

A strong hand raised his chin, forced eye contact; there was an unexpected kindness in Rognvald's eyes.

'Do you know what they called me, boy? Before Orkney accepted me as Jarl?'

Politely, Skarfr shook his head but he knew the story. The king of Norðvegr, overlord of Orkneyjar, declared Rognvald jarl by right of his mother's line. All Rognvald had to do was to sail from Norðvegr, smile on his people and move into his Bu. Or so he thought, when he still called himself by his birth-name, Kali Kolsson.

As if Orkneymen would accept a jarl just because the king of Norðvegr said his claim over them was true! There was more than a wide sea dividing Orkneymen from Norðmen. Botolf called them bumpkins but Skarfr took pride in his countrymen's fierce rejection of the king's authority. He might be king over Orkneyjar but he was away over the sea and Jarl Paul was one of their own, not some Norðman. They'd backed Jarl Paul as sole jarl and sent the naive pretender back to Norðvegr, without his ships. Without his claimed birthright and without honour. Whatever names were used about Rognvald would not have been kind.

'Kali Brown-breeks,' the Jarl told Skarfr. And he laughed.

It took a moment for Skarfr to understand and then he was the one who flushed at the insult.

'Don't mistake me, lad,' the Jarl told him. 'It hurt, all of it. My mother taught me to be proud of Orkneyjar and I thought her people would be my people, would welcome me as rightful heir. Instead, they dirtied the name I was born with.'

Skarfr smelled rotting fishbones and heard the clatter as he slipped in slime and bones. He pictured cormorant droppings, oozing over a hero's head.

'My lord,' he began slowly but plucked up courage. 'Those who call names might not have the last laugh.'

Rognvald laughed openly then and tousled Skarfr's hair. 'Indeed, my young skald.' Skarfr winced but could hardly object. He'd been reminded that there were worse terms.

'Indeed. The last laugh is mine for I won these islands and their stubborn men. But I made sure to change my name.'

He didn't need to explain his choice. The previous Rognvald had been the greatest Orkneyjar jarl in the history of the isles. The present incumbent had given himself a name to live up to, an assertion of his leadership, just like his poem about his nine skills. Laying claim to Orkney by more than his mother's blood.

Rognvald returned to the matter in hand. 'Hlif wants to hire you and she is to be my housekeeper so she must learn the measure of a man and take responsibility for her choices.'

It was time for Skarfr to look down at his feet again, observe the line of dried mud around each one, like a cargo limit in a trading ship. One leg twitched as he resisted the urge to rub his feet clean against his calves, each in turn.

'You have many lessons to learn in my household,' Rognvald began, deep and serious in tone.

Did that mean Skarfr was to stay? He sneaked a look sideways at Hlif but she was a different girl from the one he knew. Pale and silent, still as a stone saint, neither storm nor sky in her eyes but deep well-water instead, empty of expression.

'Laugh first at yourself and last at others,' Rognvald told him. 'Make a jibe at you into *your* joke and tell it better than they do. A skald can use words as a weapon. No, don't shake your head, Apprentice Skald, just because you failed once. Use what you've learned and work to be the kind of man *you* respect. Then others will.'

He made it sound so easy and it was all very well Rognvald talking about past failure from his position now. Skarfr's failure was very much in the present.

'Don't let them beat you, Fish-eater! Do you understand?'

Skarfr was stung as much by the change in tone as by the cruel play on his name. He breathed heavily, counted to ten in silence. Then wondered *why* 'Fish-eater' should be an insult. As a kenning, it wasn't bad and the gods often took bird form. As he well knew.

He bowed, sweeping his arms wide in the style of a skald about to perform. '*Fish-eater, wave-spear, storm-rider* and *wind-arrow*, at your service,' he replied, thinking up ever more extravagant kennings for a cormorant until his name felt like a title of honour. He grinned.

Rognvald nodded, then attacked again, holding his nose. 'I smell dead fish. Does anybody else find the company in here rank?'

This time Skarfr understood the game and wasted no time feeling hurt, managing a hearty laugh as he said, 'That joke's starting to smell worse than dead fish!'

Rognvald nodded again and grunted. Then he said, 'Recite a verse for me, Apprentice Skald.'

Skarfr's bravado shrivelled to a lump in his throat and he shook his head.

Rognvald waited.

Eventually, Skarfr cleared his throat and stammered, 'At least some of us know when we spout Óðinn's dregs not true mead.' His earlier words sounded pathetic and childish now.

The Jarl's smile was kind again but there was a rebuke in his words. 'All skalds speak of Óðinn but in my court we never forget that two gods were hanged on a tree. Óðinn brought us poetry but the living Christ brought us redemption and the old gods must give way in our lives to the new, whatever the stories we tell by the fire.'

Skarfr said something respectful but his heart ignored his lips. The new gods had not been there when he was born and he'd seen nothing of them since.

'You have time to rehearse your reply, lad. In language more suited to my court.'

Skarfr flushed again.

'And remember that if your response is sharp and hits home, you make an enemy. Weigh your words. It is no sin to be humble and say you have much to learn and will not presume to know more than you do. Your time as skald will come.'

'Never,' whispered Skarfr.

'Your father was loyal to the death and I will make good your price to your guardian without any need to take the matter to the Thing. As they agreed, Botolf remains your foster-father but you work for me, with his consent. What is your assessment of your worth to him, failed Apprentice Skald?'

Skarfr didn't have to think. 'Ten silver coins.' Then he owed Botolf nothing. 'And tell him you will pay for my food and shelter until I come of age.' *And get what belongs to me, like Kali Brown-breeks did.*

One eyebrow raised, Rognvald asked, 'Will you be worth so much and for so many years?'

Then Skarfr had the chance to make his speech, the one he'd prepared for Sweyn Asleifsson, only putting 'table service' before 'ship' and 'rowing'. After all, Rognvald put to sea often enough and why should Skarfr not learn from him instead of from Sweyn?

'You drive a hard bargain, lad, but for your father's sake and for Hlif's so be it.'

Rognvald looked gravely at Hlif. 'You have hired your first worker and now he must learn his duties. Take him to Arn and say Skarfr is to be my table-boy. He'll do all that needs to be done.'

She bobbed her head. 'Thank you, Sire. And sheep-shearing is now complete so I've taken an inventory. We have enough surplus to make one sail this winter so I've put that to one side.'

'Good. I want to have one spare sail without paying Norðman prices. You've asked Bodil to explain the process to you?'

'Yes, sire. She sorted the required quantities into two and treated the wool for the undercoat with fish oil. The spinsters will need to make two different yarns, loose and well fulled for the insulation, coarse and tight for the overcoat. Then the work goes to the weavers. It will take the whole winter but you shall have your sail, waterproofed and with eyelets for the rope, by springtime.' She smiled. 'In blue and white stripes.'

Rognvald nodded in approval but the whole conversation could have been in Latin as far as Skarfr was concerned.

'Tell Jorgen to load his wagon with cheeses and flour and distribute them among all the sailmakers,' Rognvald told her.

She nodded.

'Good work, Hlif.' A softness came over Rognvald's expression that lingered even when he turned back to Skarfr and dismissed them both.

Arn was a fussy man with a belly and florid complexion that suggested he sampled the kitchen provisions with diligence. He continued organising produce and people while bombarding

Skarfr with instructions, advice and random observations. He was much taken at the coincidence of their names, Arn meaning 'eagle'.

'I suppose the Jarl thinks it's funny putting a Cormorant to work for an Arn but the joke will grow stale before the milk in that pail curdles.'

Arn suddenly pointed across the kitchen at the offending pail and yelled at the boy standing beside it. 'Move that bucket, boy! And get me twenty ling from the smokehouse. Now, where was I? The Jarl was educated in the king's court in Norðvegr so he expects manners that are not habitual to the peasants of this island.'

Arn paused, a drinking horn in one hand and a cup in the other, to look down his nose at the offending peasant.

*Am I a peasant?* Skarfr wondered, as he moved to allow one of the scurrying boys access to the large cooking-pot hanging over a fire-pit. Was this a new version of Botolf's old theme, with Norðvegr the home of civilised behaviour instead of Snaeland?

'Jarl Rognvald wants to elevate those around him to be more refined, show restraint in their drinking and fighting and what-have-you, but he's trying to milk bulls if you ask me. Still, he does as he says is right and we're to do our best so, no foul language if you please. And if you don't understand someone's words to you, don't say "Eh?" or "Hvat?" like a simpleton, say "Herra?", "Sire?" or better still, "I'm sorry Sire, I didn't quite catch that," and always use formal speech, whatever you hear from others.

'It's not polite for people to overeat or drink themselves silly but of course the Jarl isn't going to tell his guests that and neither are you, so when plate or cup is empty, you should be there to fill it but without pushing, to allow anybody who is self-restrained to be so without looking like he's turning down what's offered. Not that turning down food or drink is likely, except, as I say, by the Jarl himself.

'And if it looks like a fight's brewing, which is likely when the drink flows and the pissing contests start, then it's only common sense to move anything breakable somewhere safer. You get to be a magician at slipping objects out of the way.

'If the Jarl takes the cup from you to honour a guest by serving him, you should follow and stay behind him, ready to fetch more wine but in no way interfering in his gesture or getting close enough to eavesdrop. Predict what is wanted and be invisible!'

Skarfr jumped when Arn raised his voice again to fire instructions round the kitchen at whoever responded to the name 'you'.

'You, fetch water and you, prod that fire or supper won't be cooked till cockcrow. And speaking of poultry, I've seen more life in a headless chicken – get on with it!'

Skarfr noticed that Arn did not use the polite form of 'you' to his staff or indeed polite anything. But their reactions suggested the workers were accustomed to his manner and took no offence.

'What you have to understand is that our Jarl doesn't keep godliness for church days and fast days.'

With a start, Skarfr realised that this last was aimed at him and he hoped his attentive expression hadn't slipped while his imagination chased a headless chicken.

'Service is important to him,' continued Arn. 'That's why he serves at table sometimes, to show humility and follow in our Lord's footsteps.

'God's body, watch where you're walking!'

As Arn swore at a lad who'd tripped over a basket of wild roots and bulbs, and nearly dropped the basket of eggs he was carrying, Skarfr was able to disguise his involuntary snort of amusement as a cough.

'Watch the best and copy them.' Arn glowered after the unfortunate lad disappearing out the door. 'And you'll know quick enough when you displease your betters because I'll tell you.'

He looked around and shouted, 'Harald? Somebody fetch me Harald, this instant.' Then he spoke to Skarfr again. 'You follow

Harald today and he'll show you what he does. He's a good little boy.'

*Harald?*

Skarfr's heart sank. He'd hoped for anonymity and tasks worthy of him. Not to be partnered with the young Jarl of Orkney, Harald Maddadson, who was presumably following in the footsteps of their two lords, Jesus Christ and Jarl Rognvald. Or worse still, in the footsteps of his guardian, Thorbjorn Klerk.

# CHAPTER ELEVEN

R ed-faced and breathless, Harald brushed his curly brown hair out of his eyes and reported for duty, employing the formal 'you' and polite language. His courtesy was diminished by a childish lisp and his face marred by a stubby chin and wayward eyes, wild as two shots rolling in a sling, so you couldn't be sure where he was looking. No wonder he kept his hair hanging over them.

Skarfr flushed almost as red as the boy but not from running. He knew his cruel thoughts were born of resentment. It was not Harald's fault that he was so young, hardly a suitable mentor for Skarfr. Nor was it Harald's fault that he was so much higher in rank that there was no way Skarfr could object to the embarrassment. And it was certainly not the lad's fault if he was ill-favoured.

Harald was as keen as a pup. To judge by his response to Arn's instruction, Skarfr was just another stick for him to fetch while he wagged his tail and waited for the pat on the head that must surely come. At his age, Skarfr had become an orphan and Botolf's ward.

'And show him all the workshops and where we sleep and be back here before service. And if I must run errands, Skarfr comes with me,' Harald dutifully repeated Arn's instructions, then his entire face screwed up in thought. 'I have to go back to the training ground now, quickly. Let's go.'

'Go,' Arn dismissed them both.

And Harald was charging off again, at full pelt once they were outside. Skarfr kept up with him easily, jogging a little behind to show respect. Whatever his feelings, he was an Orkneyman and Harald was his jarl. Or rather, one of them.

*The boy,* Sweyn had called Harald, the boy Inge was to woo and win, while also wooing in a more intimate way his foster-father, her husband. Skarfr's heart skipped a beat, remembering the golden goddess, Sweyn's sister, as he'd first seen her on the beach.

Then his insides twisted at what he couldn't forget, what the boy had also seen. Whatever the child had made of his foster-father's behaviour, he would not see Inge as a goddess.

*Don't think of her. Think of politics, like Botolf would.*

Harald was growing up in Rognvald's court but who was more of an influence on the child? Rognvald or Thorbjorn? And what exactly was Thorbjorn fostering in his charge? Did it include perfect amity between the old Jarl and the young?

For the first time Skarfr wondered what evil fate had established two jarls to rule Orkney. Although the saying was *One jarl rules for himself: two jarls must heed their people,* history told only of rivalry and betrayal, maiming and murder. Rognvald had called Skarfr's father 'loyal' but there had been only one jarl for that brief, peaceful interval. Between murders.

How could a good Orkneyman be loyal to two jarls if they fought each other? Skarfr glanced at the dogged little figure running ahead of him, pumping clenched fists to go faster. What if Harald grew up to want more than Rognvald allowed? What if Harald was encouraged to want more?

'There,' Harald flung the words over his shoulder in breathless gasps. 'Wait here and watch what I do. You can take a turn if you like but I can do it all by myself.'

Skarfr was back at the place where Hlif had brought him, watching Rognvald's men at target practice with staff slings, two at a time. The target dolls were two upended bales of straw with tin eyes that clanged when a warrior hit his mark.

Each man had his own weapon, the stick rising to chest height when placed upright on the ground, with a hook at the top and two cords attached to the leather sling. When a man's turn came, he took a practice shot at his target, then adjusted the cords. It seemed to Skarfr that the shorter they were, the further the stone flew. Each man had four stones, carried in a pouch, marked with his rune or sign. One for practice and three for the competition.

And Harald was the lad who ran out to collect the shot and move the targets as demanded, tasks he was taking up once more, with different men. Then the new competitors stepped up. One ruffled Harald's hair, smiled, then glanced towards the new table-boy. His smile died.

*Thorbjorn.*

Thinking of a dozen responses to the insults he anticipated, Skarfr was taken unawares by perfume and laughter behind him, then passing him before he realised that ladies had come to watch the men, Inge among them. Thorbjorn's expression set hard as his eyes followed his wife's approach. Perhaps his gaze had never rested on Skarfr in the first place.

Harald was waving frantically, beckoning his fellow-servant over to a better position for fetching and carrying, receiving orders, running errands. To receive orders, Skarfr had to be close enough to listen, and if he couldn't help hearing what was spoken between Thorbjorn Klerk and his lady, that wasn't really eavesdropping. He was merely obeying Harald and doing his duty.

Keeping his head down, Skarfr trotted after the ladies and past them to join Harald.

'I don't need help,' whispered Harald, puffing the lie to his words, 'but Arn said you should learn our duties so you can move the targets when my lord says so. Some of them like the challenge of greater distance.

'That's Thorbjorn Klerk,' he said with pride. 'My foster-father.'

'He looks a fine man,' Skarfr forced himself to say. And yet it was the truth. Swarthy in complexion and strong-jawed, peat-brown eyes lit with exceptional intelligence and a young man's body, honed with physical work and a warrior's training. A dark mirror to Sweyn's sunshine.

Thorbjorn raised the stick to its diagonal position, placed the stone in the sling, eyed the target and was about to loose the cords when Inge's voice rang sweet and piercing across the yard.

'You always shoot to the left, husband. Remember to adjust.'

Thorbjorn's shot went so wide it hit a pitcher of water, with a resounding ping.

Inge and her ladies tittered. She walked up to her husband and lowered her voice, although her words still carried clearly across the yard. 'Too much of an adjustment, I think. Maybe if you drop this shoulder a little.' She caressed his left shoulder as she applied a little downward pressure, then stepped away quickly.

'Much better stance,' she approved, almost purring. Skarfr longed to be the recipient of such a tone, such a touch. No wonder Thorbjorn had reacted as if burned by the open longing in her touch. How had such affection come between them after such a start?

'God's breath!' swore Thorbjorn as his shot went wide again, the other side of the straw target.

His opponent muttered, 'Bad luck,' then took his shot without the benefit of suggestions from the audience and scored a competent hit with a resounding clang.

Grim-faced, Thorbjorn adjusted the length of his cords.

'Never mind, dearest. The fates will be with you next time,' Inge soothed, unfortunately just as Thorbjorn was taking his third shot. Which hit the ground short of the target.

Thorbjorn pre-empted the other's shot with a shake of his head and ordered, 'Boy! Fetch the shot but leave the target where it is. I must go. I have work to do.'

Harald nudged Skarfr, who rushed to obey. So his name was 'Boy', just as it had been with Botolf, and he wasn't important enough to recognise, let alone mock. And Inge loved Thorbjorn. She was clinging to his arm when Skarfr ran to them to give back the stone shot.

'I hope I didn't put you off,' she was saying. 'I so want to help you perform better.' She emphasised the word 'perform'. A man guffawed and Inge turned on him.

'I don't know what's so funny,' she berated him. 'A wife should help her husband perform his best and all men have their off-days, when nothing works the way they'd like.' There was a wistful note in her voice and she seemed innocent of the impact of her words.

Men hid their sniggers. Thorbjorn glowered at them.

'Do you want Harald with you, dearest? He always cheers you up and he's just the man to challenge at whatever sport you choose!' She chucked the beaming boy under the chin as she flattered him. 'You can show him how things should be done.'

'No.' Thorbjorn was curt. 'Harald can stay as runner for the men. I have bookwork to do and can stay no longer, sadly. My lady.' He nodded in leave-taking and she shook her head playfully.

'Books are best left to monks, dear husband, for they don't mind the ill effects of so much study.'

'I'm not made for a monastery, my lady,' retorted Thorbjorn, bantering, 'although it's true there are no wives there.'

She laughed, lightly, taking every word in fun and watching him stride off to his books.

'Do you still want to marry her?' teased a voice Skarfr knew well. Hlif. She must have been among the ladies with Inge and she'd materialised beside him. Her clothes and demeanour made her seem older but her tone held the same childish provocation as when they'd first met on the beach. Far too honest to be an adult and yet too knowing to be a child. As well-trained in stewardship as he was in skaldcraft. But she would be a housekeeper and he would be – what?

He didn't deign to reply but his heart thumped at the question. Did he still want to marry Inge? Or even some woman like her? This was his third vision of the golden goddess and he was confused by her infatuation with the man she'd married.

'She needles him at every opportunity. Worse when they're alone,' observed Hlif.

His understanding took a heartbeat to catch up with his ears, his interpretation of Inge's behaviour thrown completely into doubt. Not wifely affection?

'What?' he asked, breaking the first of Arn's edicts. And then, 'How do you know what they do when they're alone?' He flushed as he said the words aloud, fearing the answer.

Grey eyes danced as if she'd read his thoughts. 'Because he tells the women he beds and they tell me.' Then her eyes clouded. 'She uses women's weapons, unmans him and he daren't hit her or she'd tell Sweyn. So he hits other women instead.'

'That's not her fault,' Skarfr reacted instinctively, wondering what women's weapons were and definitely not wanting to ask Hlif. 'He treated her badly.' He didn't have a word that was big enough for what Thorbjorn had done to Inge. It seemed that forcing his woman against a wall was a man's right but hitting her was wrong. The sagas made clear that no good came of domestic blows but they said nothing of the other thing. It made no sense and Skarfr was glad he was not a woman.

'He is a cruel man.' Hlif's oblique reply seemed to be agreement with Skarfr's defence of Inge. 'I told you I didn't envy her and that it couldn't be a happy marriage. But now she's turned him into a devil. And she's the only one who won't feel the damage she's caused.'

Before Skarfr could think of anything to say, Hlif was back with the other women, demure and silent.

# CHAPTER TWELVE

The novelty of Rognvald's court soon wore off as Skarfr scurried about on the same menial tasks he'd carried out for Botolf, but with heavier buckets, more people giving orders and no lessons in skaldcraft. Sometimes he almost missed his brutal master but then he'd remember the physical chastisement that followed tongue-lashings on the slightest excuse, or with none at all. He also remembered the shame of the wedding feast and any urge to recite skaldic verse fled.

Like the legendary Greek hero toiling in the stables, he would serve his time in the lowliest work and redeem his name with some glorious act of courage. He liked how that sounded and was willing to leave the detail of the glorious act for the gods to reveal to him later. Especially when he realised that Thorbjorn had recognised him.

Ordered to accompany young Harald, Skarfr had found it impossible to avoid Thorbjorn. Looking at the ground while the child held his foster-father's attention worked as a strategy until Harald drew Thorbjorn's attention to his new friend.

'I forget the manners you've taught me, Lord Thorbjorn,' the innocent havoc-bringer began. 'This is a new boy called Skarfr and

I'm training him for kitchen work. He wanted to be a skald but he wasn't any good at it so Jarl Rognvald is buying him from Skald Botolf.'

Thorbjorn gave his foster-son a fatherly pat. 'I'm sure you'll teach him well.' The smile died on his lips as he turned stony eyes to Skarfr. 'He is lucky to be pot-boy and stir a fish soup.'

Skarfr flushed. Now was not the moment to spar with words as Rognvald had suggested.

'Yes,' agreed Harald. 'And I am lucky to be Jarl. Everybody should know his place.' A thought struck him. 'It's not fish soup today. It's mutton.'

'Then fish soup will be for another day,' promised Thorbjorn, his gaze relentless. 'In tiny, chopped morsels.' He flexed his arm muscles, flaunting his trained strength.

Skarfr stared back, willing his expression blank, but his insides liquified to soup and mush, nothing as courageous as chopped morsels. His own arm muscles were well-developed from menial tasks but merely slingshot in a string compared with those of the warrior looming over him.

'Now young man,' Thorbjorn turned his attention back to Harald. 'I have a gift for you. Guess what it is and you shall have it.' He pointed to a wooden box on the ground. It was about three handspans by two.

*What a waste of precious wood as mere wrapping for a gift to a spoiled child,* thought Skarfr but he was intrigued as to its contents, despite himself. And envious.

The guessing-game was an uncomfortable reminder of how his possessions had been treated by Sweyn's men but he was sure the box did not contain bones or a spare tunic. Maybe a musical instrument like his pipes or a weapon, a dirk or slingshot. Too big a box for adornment like an armband.

'A puppy!' guessed Harald.

And received a smiling headshake.

The second guess was equally unrelated to the type and size of container. 'Bow and arrows!'

Another headshake but this time Thorbjorn gave a clue. 'What flies on water but is beached on land? Its head breathes fire and its tail is forked.'

*A dragon ship.*

Harald gave the answer after long reflection that wrinkled his brow. At Thorbjorn's nod, he whooped, prised open the box and lifted out a carved longship that was too beautiful to be abused as a child's toy.

Skarfr looked at the young Jarl's shining eyes. This child would have his own full-size dragon ship before the pot-boy found a way out of kitchen duties.

'Carry the box for Jarl Harald,' Thorbjorn told Skarfr. 'And see the toy safely stored in my lady's chamber when he gives you the order.'

'Yes, my lord.' *Everyone should know his place.*

'I want to show Lady Inge,' Harald told Skarfr, a new peremptory note in his tone. 'Bring the box.'

Thorbjorn ruffled the boy's hair while his eyes rested on Skarfr, checking they understood one another. The reprieve was temporary.

'Look!' Harald's face was radiant as he held out the carved wooden longship for Inge's appreciation. 'My foster-father made this for me. Here's the thwarts – they're the benches where the oarsmen sit – and the oars go in those holes but they'll fall out so they've been stowed on the floor in the boat until I can sit down and play properly.'

Inge took the toy and held it as carefully as if it were made of glass. She inspected the detail: dragon prow and serpent tail, its square sail woven in red and white stripes, a work of love. The planes of her beautiful face were knife-sharp in the northern sunlight and her eyes chips of blue quartz. The pale rose of her mouth did not soften its hard lines. Skarfr held his breath, fearing for the exquisite craft.

With a smile, the lady sailed the ship back to the boy's open hands, teasing him with dip and rise as if great waves tested the vessel until it dropped suddenly, far below his waiting hands, then soared up into them, cresting the last roller sent by the sea-god.

Harald crowed, triumphant as his ship beached safely in his hands. His eyes shining, he told Inge, 'You should have lowered the sail in stormy seas like that. You can untie the rope. I'll show you.'

'I'd like that,' she said, her voice honeyed. 'Your foster-father has made a dragon ship as beautiful as that of Sweyn Asleifsson and you shall be a man just like my brother, whose name is known throughout the civilised world. The best sea-rover and the best warrior, beloved of the gods, whose deeds are both matchless and honourable, who has the *best* adventures.'

Harald looked down at the ship, puzzlement wrinkling his open face. 'This is Sweyn's ship?'

'Yes indeed,' confirmed Inge. 'And its name is the *Death-bringer*. See the red sail? Red is the colour of blood, to strike fear into all who see my brother's ship come to their shores.' Inge happily ignored the white stripes.

*Which is why 'reddening the eagle's claw' means 'killing' in the language of skalds,* Skarfr thought, but did not say. His skaldcraft must remain in his head from now on.

Harald was still puzzling over Thorbjorn's gift of what he now believed to be Sweyn's dragon ship. Smoothly, Inge wove glitter into her tissue of lies to make it pretty. 'Your foster-father is the best of carvers and in making words. He is called Thorbjorn Klerk because he is so skilled in carving runes and in making marks of all kinds, reading and writing. Nobody is better than

Thorbjorn at recording how many skins of wine have been drunk.'

Harald's face cleared. 'So he is the best. I thought so.'

'At reading and writing. And Sweyn is the best for adventures. Men are made for different fates. When I look at you, I can see what kind of man you will be.' Such tenderness as she turned on Harald would have melted Skarfr when he first saw her on the beach. But now his insides liquified for a different reason. Although he bore no liking for Thorbjorn, he felt sick at Inge's manipulation of a child's feelings in her subtle war against him. Poison could be injected in more subtle ways than the embroidery of a lethal tunic.

And then Inge glanced briefly at him, as if she'd known all along that he was there, watching. Their eyes met, as had happened once before. But this time *I will not cry* had been replaced by *See how I have my revenge.* Knowing what Thorbjorn had done, how could he blame her?

'What do you think I will be?' asked Harald.

'I think you know,' she teased the boy, her attention fully on him now. 'Would you like to be a Klerk, the best at reading and writing? Or another Sweyn, the bravest of raiders and warriors, but even more famous, because you'll be a jarl?'

The boy did justice to his foster-father. 'I think reading and writing is very important,' he judged, 'but a man has to follow his own fate and mine is more adventurous than that. Do you think Sweyn will teach me?'

'I think he will, Harald. I think he will see in you what I see in you. My bravest of warriors, my guardian. Will you swear to protect me always and never let anyone hurt me?'

Once more Harald's open face showed confusion. Was he remembering what he'd seen by a dark wall? Remembering who had hurt Inge?

'No matter who it is who wants to hurt me?' emphasised Inge.

'You'll stand in for Sweyn while my brother is away and you'll protect me?'

Mention of taking Sweyn's role wiped Harald's expression clear of any conflict of loyalties.

He put his hand on his heart. 'I swear.'

'That shall be our secret,' she whispered to him, mouthing the words clearly to make sure Skarfr could see what she said. She looked again at Skarfr. Was she asking for his protection too? As well as his silence.

'You may go back to your work,' she told him. 'Harald is staying with me.'

'Yes, my lady,' Skarfr stammered.

Inge had already turned back to the young jarl. She sat down on the grass, her skirts spread around her as she spread out a blue scarf as sea between the land masses of Orkneyjar and foreign territories.

'Let's sail Sweyn's longship to Írland to do battle with the savages and bring home treasure.'

*Savages.* Brigid and Fergus, with their kindness and stories of their homeland. Something else Skarfr must keep in his own head and not talk about.

It was too late to protect Inge and never let anyone hurt her. Maybe Hlif was right and Inge's revenge would lead to more women being assaulted in some never-ending contagion. As if the gods had marked Thorbjorn's heroism with some flaw that would cause his downfall, as in sagas. And a man like that would not go down alone. As he watched her lay claim to Orkneyjar's heir, he almost pitied the man who had hurt her so deeply.

'Where have you been? Food doesn't cook itself and fires need fed even more often than people do.' Arn grumbled at the high-handed ways of ladies and Harald's dereliction of duty, before setting Skarfr to chores which needed no explanation. The Bu's need for water entailed an endless trek to the well and back but as he fell into the rhythm of filling, carrying and emptying buckets, Skarfr's mind was free to consider all he'd seen and heard.

Inge had recognised him and, worse still, so had Thorbjorn. And it wouldn't be a carved wooden ship coming Skarfr's way from either lord or lady, so he should stay alert, but there wasn't much he could do to stave off trouble. There was nowhere he could go. He would have shrugged his shoulders if they hadn't been balancing buckets hanging from a pole.

He envied the little boy with the golden future. What would he, Skarfr, be? Like Harald, he'd been sure of his future, from Botolf's apprentice to skald, composing the history of all his Sweyn-like adventures in immortal verse. Making sagas and fulfilling the cormorant's prophecy.

Then came his public humiliation. Not Óðinn's mead but Orkney ale had revealed the truth. He only had to think of reciting a poem and his stomach heaved. He'd overestimated himself to Rognvald. He was worse than second-rate, a braggart and simpleton.

Yet, he could not rid his head of the words he could not speak without murdering them. He could hear the music of verse like the rise and fall of Harald's wooden longship on a pretend sea. He could feel in his blood the connection between kennings and the core of all things, on the loom of history where brave deeds glittered in gold thread.

He liked the phrase, memorised it in silence. *So be it,* he told himself. He would practise all he'd learned and enjoy his words, in silence. Never embarrass himself or others again. Rognvald was wrong, believing all men to be like himself, seeing failure only as a stepping stone to success.

Skarfr could learn from Rognvald but he could not be like him.

*You know who you want to be.* The words echoed and Skarfr suddenly realised that Inge had not once mentioned Rognvald. Of course a little boy would be drawn naturally towards youth and adventure, whether Sweyn's sunshine or Thorbjorn's dark fire. Rognvald was grizzled, past his raiding days, and of his nine skills, only his poetry could be sure of claiming a winner's prize. But he was Orkney's Jarl and Harald's guardian, the obvious model of virtue for a small boy. Virtue was as attractive as clerking to a boy with a dragon ship called the *Death-bringer.* It took no great powers of deduction to guess why Inge had not mentioned Rognvald. Just a memory of a conversation overheard on a beach.

# CHAPTER THIRTEEN

Arn grumbled but acquiesced, as he did every time Hlif said she needed Skarfr as protection on one of her outings. Nobody pointed out that her need for protection varied with her mood and she saw no problem gadding about alone when it suited her. Her position as Rognvald's ward and housekeeper gave her a unique status and her strange manners compensated for her youth. Whether Arn thought her cursed or not, he seemed unwilling to test the limits of Hlif's authority. Skarfr just did as he was told and hoped that something interesting would happen.

On this occasion, he was required to carry soapstone ware, which he was more than happy to do for a change of scenery. And, as Hlif pointed out to Arn, the pots were for the kitchen so he should be pleased too.

She was explaining their errand to Skarfr as they started off westwards, following the coastline. Beyond the grazing sheep and scrubby grassland, the sea glittered on their left, fringed by dunes and dark curves of sea-wrack.

There had been a new delivery of soapstone from Hjaltland and Hlif wanted first pick of the utensils for the Jarl's Bu. 'I give Trygve Trader a pot of honey each month to make sure he tells me first when his brother has brought him new stock. Word gets around fast as soon as the boat's beached so I have to get there quickly but he won't sell anything till I've had my pick. I want three cooking-pots but they'll be far too heavy for you to carry so I'll have them put aside until Rognvald's carter can pick them up. And I need two oil lamps – you can carry one back – and thirty loom-weights – they can wait for the carter.'

'So you don't really need me at all,' observed Skarfr. 'The carter could have picked up all that you select.'

Hlif screwed up her mouth, as was her habit when anybody challenged her or disagreed with her decisions. 'Protection,' she said firmly. 'I'm a woman now and must behave as such.'

Once, Skarfr would have laughed but now he held back. He'd listened to Hlif's conversations with Rognvald about more than sailmaking. He'd seen her management of the supplies needed to keep the Jarl's household fed, clothed and lodged. She knew the Jarl's people and the work they did: who would provide raw material; who would make a finished product; and how to connect the various workers. She would never sneer at Thorbjorn's clerking because every day she checked his ledgers and worked out what would be needed.

If she said she was a woman, he would respect her delusion, although he was still sceptical as to her inconsistent desire for protection. Maybe she liked his company. As he liked hers. The realisation caught him unawares but it was true. He no longer thought her the ugliest girl he'd ever seen. Although there was nothing comely about her skinny frame or speckled face, her expressions could be endearing. She was clever and funny. She was Hlif and there was nobody like her.

He walked beside her, easily adapting his pace to hers, noting her bare feet taking two steps to his one. He'd grown too since they first met a year ago. At fifteen, the gawky lines of his body had filled out and he'd outgrown both his clothes and his footwear. He had considered wearing boots on this outing but his feet were tough enough until winter tested them and besides, he couldn't squeeze his feet into the ones he owned. Perhaps he could swap them at the cobbler's for a pair someone else had grown out of or for a dead man's boots. He'd hardly worn his own but they'd been ill-used by their previous owner so he'd be lucky to strike a bargain as Botolf had done. No doubt the neighbours' mockery of Botolf's meanness had goaded him into making basic provision for his foster-son.

He was engrossed in his boot dilemma and feelings of being hard done by when Hlif broke the silence.

'Sweyn's on Gareksey and he's coming here to meet up with Holbodi.'

*Who? Why? How did Hlif always know what was happening?*

'I listen to the women talk,' she answered his unspoken thoughts. And sighed at his obvious ignorance. 'You don't know who Holbodi is. Or why Sweyn's coming. You probably don't even know that Sweyn's lord of Gareksey.'

'I do so!' retorted Skarfr, stung into forgetting about boots. 'And he was given it for winning Orkney for our Jarl with his trick with bonfires and sails. Only that's not the way Rognvald tells it.'

'Well he wouldn't, would he. Men like to be heroes of their own stories.'

'So do women.'

Hlif's smile was condescending. 'What would you know of women, cormorant friend?'

'I know you. And you are always the centre of your own story.' He wondered whether she'd meant he was her cormorant friend or that he was a friend to cormorants.

She conceded the point. 'I suppose that's true. But that's just natural, wanting to get un-cursed, to make something of my life. I'm not trying to be a saga hero.'

'You'd have to be evil to be worth putting in a saga,' Skarfr told

her, trying to regain his lost superiority. 'Like Frakork the witch.
Only evil women are important.'

He sensed the change in her, a stillness even though she kept
walking and congratulated himself on scoring a point.

'I see her,' Hlif said quietly. 'Frakork.'

The hairs rose on the back of Skarfr's neck. 'But she's dead,' he
said. 'Sweyn burned her with her longhouse.'

'It's a sending. I don't know what it means but I see her as clear
as I see you now.' She stopped and fixed him with cloudy grey eyes.
Her gaze slipped over his shoulder, widened; he shivered, not
daring to turn around.

Her eyes returned to his, dulled with fear. 'I don't know that I
should speak of it.'

'Then don't,' he said quickly.

'But I trust you.'

Skarfr wasn't sure he wanted to be trusted but he could hardly
say so and part of him wanted her to go on.

'I see her in the Bu and I see the jarl who was murdered there,'
whispered Hlif. 'His mouth is open in a scream and he tears at
himself as if his tunic's on fire, burning him alive. He's screaming
the name of his killers.'

Her voice was so quiet Skarfr had to strain to hear her but he
knew the story of the poisoned jarl and so must Hlif.

'His own sisters.'

Skarfr named them and declaimed the whole story as Botolf
had when rehearsing it for Skarfr's edification. Jarl Paul's own
sisters, those witches, Frakork and Helga, who made a beautiful
tunic of finest linen with glittering gold thread for their brother,
steeped in poison. But Harald, the brother they loved insisted on
wearing the tunic, too jealous to trust them when they pleaded
with him not to, and so the wrong brother died.

He left a dramatic pause, then in his normal voice told her,
'This is just a story, Hlif, and has been told well enough to show

you its deeds in dark and candlelight.' He suddenly realised he'd already broken his vow of skaldic silence but as it was only to Hlif it didn't count. It was more like speaking to himself than speaking in public.

'No,' she insisted. 'He is there. Frenzied, clawing at his breast and neck, screaming in silence, pointing at *them*.' Her tone dropped lower.

'I can see *them* too. The witches. One is shadowy, in the background as if it wasn't her idea or as if she's taking shelter. The other is fierce and strong. She grows as the murdered jarl rushes at her, accusing her. She points her wand at him, mutters spells, but he keeps coming towards her until he touches her and *boom!* she catches fire. Not poison fire like him but flames as a high as a funeral pyre. A judgement bonfire.

'It's all screams. I can feel them even though it's silent. And then through the flames I can see the wand turning to a walking stick, lengthening, touching the ground so the witch can support herself. And she's not a witch anymore, just an old, sad lady turning to ashes, crying for her grandson until she disappears.

'And then I see Sweyn and Thorbjorn and another man. At first I thought they were real, then I recognised the third man and knew they couldn't see me. It's Harald grown to manhood and they have swords drawn. Sometimes they jump on each other as if to fight, sometimes they are shoulder to shoulder, seeking, searching – and I know what they want is bad.'

Awed despite himself, Skarfr waited, unsure whether Hlif had paused or finished. Apparently, there was no more.

'That is a sending,' was his judgement. 'But it doesn't tell us more than we know already. They are powerful men, who could be allies or could be rivals.'

'I know,' she said. 'So I haven't told my guardian. I wait for more to be revealed.' She hesitated. 'Once, this Sweyn-sending came so close to me I felt the chill of Valhalla, and I saw what was on the chain around his neck. The head of a man, in small. Not Rognvald and yet something in my mind whispered 'Jarl'. I don't know whether the head speaks of the past or of the future.'

Skarfr shook his head. 'Rumours and stories,' he said again, recalling Botolf's glee in reporting the news. 'Jarl Paul was never seen again after Sweyn kidnapped him and cleared the way for Rognvald. But you must know all this, without any ghosts, and your imagination is making play of shadows.'

'A little,' she said. 'But the women do not talk of such matters and I can't ask Rognvald whether he profited knowingly from a man's murder.'

*Or even arranged it*, thought Skarfr, remembering Rognvald's pride in taking Orkney. Though it had been through Sweyn's stratagem, in truth. Maybe he'd also used Sweyn's help to remove Jarl Paul, permanently. Maybe he'd been gifted the isle of Gareksey for more than his cunning play with beacons and sails.

Some rumours said the kidnapped jarl was blinded and in a Scottish monastery, on his Ness daughter's orders. He had not been loved by the women in his family. Where his sisters failed, maybe his daughter succeeded, thanks to Sweyn, who'd been banished by Jarl Paul and had his own reasons to wish him ill and support Rognvald.

Jarl Paul's daughter: Harald's mother. After installing Rognvald as ruler, Sweyn had backed Harald as second jarl, the choice of Ness and Skotland too. Rognvald had agreed and so Sweyn had put both jarls in power and secured his own future interests. How did Thorbjorn fit in? Ness born, the foster-father, the clerk, always present when Sweyn was roving.

*Sweyn. On his way from Gareksey.*

Skarfr shook off the dark talk, crossed himself and touched his hammer amulet. Never mind ghosts and sendings. How was the real Thorbjorn going to react when the real Sweyn arrived? And who in Thórr's name was Holbodi?

'Why is Sweyn coming and who is Holbodi?' he asked.

Her eyes glittered in triumph, her moods changeable as a winter sea. 'Holbodi is lord of the Suðreyjar and he's taking dragon ships to Bretland.'

Hlif was clearly holding back the most important information to tease him. 'What's that got to do with Sweyn?' asked Skarfr, impatient.

'Holbodi is hoping Sweyn will add his ships to the venture.' She paused, enjoying his attention. 'And he's going after Olvir, Frakork's grandson. He'll offer Sweyn revenge for his father's murder.'

Everyone knew of Sweyn's outbursts in the Thing, refusing to accept the *manbot* payment from Frakork and Olvir, after they torched his father's holding in Ness, burning alive all in the longhouse over some land dispute. That was the day Sweyn Olafsson took his mother's name instead of his father's. Perhaps, when his father was murdered in the family home, the gods had touched Sweyn with the same darkness they'd laid on Thorbjorn. Skarfr remembered the golden giant, laughing at his ambitions and wished them both a fall. Preferably into a fish midden.

'Maybe you can go to Bretland with the dragon ships, with Holbodi,' said Hlif.

'Maybe not!' Skarfr would not seek humiliation a second time and Hlif should know that.

'I just wondered but I'm glad. They might be away for years. You should serve in the hall when Holbodi pleads his case, so you know what's happening. There might be opportunities.'

The water closed in on both sides as the path took them to a small settlement between the sea and the loch of Steinnesvatn. Boats were beached on the lakeside as well as by the open sea, some upturned for a longer stay ashore.

Before Skarfr could respond to Hlif's suggestion, she spoke again, her tone lightened. 'Here we are.'

They had reached a longhouse which was easily recognised as belonging to Trygve, the soapstone trader. In the open portion of the house, where others might keep dogs or a goat, there were shelves stacked with soapstone ware. Pots, jars, lamps, plus two boxes that attracted Hlif's attention straight away. One contained loom-weights but the other made her eyes sparkle. She fingered the blush-pink beads.

Trygve himself came from the interior shadows where he'd been watching his goods.

'Those would suit you, Hlif,' he greeted her with the informality of long acquaintance. 'And the colour is rare for soapstone. It's from Hlidi's Bay.'

He pointed at the grey pots and lamps, tinged with orangey-brown. 'The usual stone-quarry is turning colour with the peat in the water so we're getting more of that rust in the grey. And they've started excavating from another quarry which gives grey-green.'

She sighed and put the beads back. 'Pink beads and red hair – not a good combination. And dull grey is for cooking-pots. What I'd really love is that grey-green.'

He nodded. 'I'll pass on the word. You never know your luck. What are you after today? These are the finest goods my brother has finished.'

Hlif reeled off her shopping list, picked up a cooking-pot and inspected its base and the two holes for suspending it over the fire. 'Yes, nicely finished, smooth and strong. Tell Skarfr how they're made.'

Trygve was only too keen to launch into an explanation of his brother's trade, from cutting slabs out of the rock face with chisels, to hardening the finished utensils with heat.

'It's as near alchemy as I've ever seen,' he said. 'It's so soft you can scratch it with your fingernail when it's fresh quarried. You can even chisel out bowls direct from the quarry but the soapstone goes hard when it's in the air and harder still once it's heated. There's nothing else like it and it's rare. My brother calls it *kleber*. If you clean it gently with hot water it will last for years.'

*And don't throw it at your apprentice,* thought Skarfr.

'I'll take these.' Hlif showed her choice to the trader and, with the confidence of previous transactions, they haggled over a price until they were both happy, although Trygve pretended otherwise, like any trader worth his salt.

'You'll be wearing gold beads while I'm so poor I'll be eating soapstone.' He grimaced in mock-pain. 'I'll put your pots inside till your carter comes,' he confirmed as they sealed the bargain with coin from Hlif's purse.

She picked up one of the oil lamps she'd bought and gave it to Skarfr. 'We'll take this one with us, to show the quality of your ware.' She looked around the stacked shelves. 'You won't have anything left in a week's time.'

He beamed. 'Thank you for your custom. You can tell the Jarl he always gets first pick.'

'I shall,' she replied, 'and you shall have your honey from the carter when he comes.'

As Skarfr and Hlif left, two women arrived and went straight to the box of beads, trickling them through greedy fingers, discussing strings and fasteners, complementary gowns and brooches. They had reluctantly moved on to the utensils as Rognvald's representatives moved out of earshot.

'Blonde hair. They'll buy beads,' stated Hlif sadly. She waited.

Skarfr had no idea what she wanted him to say.

'You could at least say that red hair is pretty. Even if you don't mean it.' She tossed her head, wisps of the offending locks escaping her clean, womanly coif. A matron while she was still a maid, because of Rognvald's decree.

Should he say it now he'd been told to? He certainly wouldn't mean it. Red hair was not pretty. But it was ... striking. While he considered the matter and the choice of word, the silence lengthened and he was almost relieved when somebody overtook them from behind on the open track between village and Bu. A distraction and a change in conversation.

But when the man turned to face them and blocked the way, Skarfr's guts lurched.

'Run away home, Hlif,' said Thorbjorn Klerk. He wore casual fighting gear: padded leather jerkin and breeks, boots and a sword. 'I've a mind to continue the boy's fishing lessons and a maid would get in the way.'

She hesitated.

'Go,' said Skarfr, his voice unsteady. 'You'll make it worse.'

Hlif ran, without looking back.

# CHAPTER FOURTEEN

As Hlif's figure vanished in the distance, Skarfr faced his doom. He could run across the heath but unless he could shrink to mouse-size and hide behind a tussock of grass, he would be caught easily. If he reached the sea to his right, he could always wade in and swim ever further from the shore until Aegir took him and pounded him to death against the rocks. The drama appealed but the death didn't.

Thorbjorn just stood there, solid as a ship's mast, eyes narrowed. The pause before the punishment reminded Skarfr of Botolf's violence. The subtleties in inflicting pain. How much waiting, knowing what was coming, added to the hurt. But Skarfr had found that easier to endure than the shock of unexpected punishment, lightning changes of mood, from almost-praise for skaldcraft to whiplashes. Neither mind nor body could control the instinctive flinch that branded them 'cowards', a reaction that became habit. Skarfr had become sensitive to the slightest change in Botolf's expression, lived with his own permanent sense of guilt at needing such punishment. Even though he knew Botolf was a cruel man, daily repetition of their lessons had left its mark, made him feel he was to blame.

Was this what Thorbjorn saw in him? Why he still wanted to torment Skarfr? Did he see a victim?

'I don't like the way you look at me,' growled the warrior. 'You need to learn respect.'

*Run! Hide!* The little boy in Skarfr's mind yelled at him but he did not move. He had overcome such fear too often to give in to it now. He held a soapstone lamp clutched to his chest, a reminder that he was the Jarl's man. Thorbjorn would not kill him as he was not worth *manbot* or exile. He was an annoying pot-boy, good to kick when a man was angry. And Thorbjorn was always angry. What Thorbjorn didn't know was that Skarfr had been kicked – and worse – so often, a thrashing held no new terror for him. He would live through this.

He put the lamp down, carefully, and moved far enough away from it that he would not break it by falling when he was hit. He made a bargain with the gods. If he endured Thorbjorn's attack in silence, then they would preserve the lamp, unbroken, and he would survive.

Then he stood, waiting. And sure enough a fist came, caught him in the stomach. He doubled up, winded. As he straightened, breathed more easily, he felt a surge of impotent fury. He should hit back, go down fighting. And go down he would, he knew. He'd felt the controlled impact of the first punch, the muscle behind the restraint, the leashed storm that would make his own anger seem like a raindrop in a tempest if Thorbjorn went berserk. So he too controlled himself, judged what would defend him and what merely provoke more violence.

Rognvald had said to use words but the Jarl was capable of wrestling a man like Thorbjorn, his physical equal, to the ground, so it was easy for him to give such advice. Skarfr readied himself for more blows, heard the shriek of metal and saw the sword being drawn from the scabbard. Hoping it would be the flat he received, he wondered what words would reach a man so focused on assault. He'd seen Thorbjorn's expression like this before, jaw slack, eyes burning and vacant, losing all awareness other than the damage he could cause another's body, the relief he gained.

Inge had suffered, endured, done nothing. What could she have done? What could any woman do? What would Hlif do?

Then he knew, suddenly.

'I see you with the burning witch,' he said, imitating Hlif's otherworldly manner when she spoke of ghosts, his voice sing-song and his eyes fixed on some space beyond Thorbjorn. 'I see the dead who walk the Bu, the witch on fire, screaming and the jarl she poisoned. And I see you with them. The witch is pointing at you, telling you something...'

Thorbjorn flinched, his nostrils flaring and eyes wide, like a spooked pony.

Having captured his audience, Skarfr dropped his voice to a whisper. 'I see things yet to pass.'

Thorbjorn's body stilled. He sheathed his sword. A shadow passed over his face. Fear? The animal bloodlust in his eyes was softening, becoming human again.

'You, fully armed and splendid as the warrior-god Týr,' embroidered Skarfr, 'with Jarl Harald, a man, your sword at his command and his trust at yours.'

Skarfr knew the dizziest heights of success when Thorbjorn's hand moved to his neck, seeking his amulet.

In his seer's voice, Skarfr added, 'And Sweyn...' Then he stopped, frightened by the vehemence of Thorbjorn's curse and gesture. But this time it wasn't aimed at him.

'Sweyn!' spat Thorbjorn. 'Always Sweyn!' He calmed, sat down on the grass and motioned Skarfr to sit down beside him. He started to speak, then stopped, as if mustering his thoughts.

Was Skarfr supposed to continue with his strange voice and visions? Mimicking Hlif would be no help to him now as he'd used up her store of visions.

'Tell me more,' ordered Thorbjorn.

Whatever he did now would be dangerous and Skarfr did not trust his invention of further visions to produce the required effect, so he hesitated. 'I'm sorry, my lord, but my gift is unreliable.' Well, that was true enough, though it wasn't prophecy he had in mind.

Thorbjorn's black hair flopped straight as a mare's tail over his eyes so his stare winked in and out of view. A predator glimpsed through trees.

'Sweyn,' he prompted. 'Was he alive? *With* me?'

Skarfr wasn't feigning the difficulty of recall. 'I felt he was alive,' he concluded. He knew what Thorbjorn was asking and the future seemed a dangerous place to pretend foreknowledge about. He remembered the gossip at table and adapted Hlif's vision to suit his audience, as good storytellers are wont to do.

'I don't think Sweyn is *with* anyone but Sweyn, except in the moments it suits him. In my vision he stands apart, alone, and the witch Frakork curses him with her burning hand raised. He shrinks back.'

Thorbjorn humphed a noise of apparent satisfaction and Skarfr's heartbeat calmed enough to appreciate how unlikely it was that he should be sitting here on the grass as if he were best friends with the volatile courtier.

'Where was the Jarl in all this?'

'Nowhere. I mean, I haven't seen him.'

Another satisfied reaction. Skarfr was glad Thorbjorn could read meaning into his desperate inventions as he had no idea where his answers were leading. *As long as he and the lamp stayed in one piece.*

With a shuddering sigh, Thorbjorn spoke. 'Rognvald wasn't there because he is *never* there where he should be, to face Sweyn and his mockery of all laws, the Jarl and the Thing, *all* authority – he does what he likes. He murders my grandmother, sister to the

Jarl's wife and yet Rognvald does nothing.' Thorbjorn slammed his hand down on the grass.

Skarfr forbore from commenting on the somewhat twisted familial relationships between Frakork and her siblings.

'That's what my grandmother is saying in your visions when she points at me. "Do something, Thorbjorn!" But what? My marriage is like a blood eagle, spreading me open, bleeding me slowly, painfully, killing my manhood. The threat of Sweyn's enmity is held over me with every word I speak to her, Sweyn's sister.'

Skarfr winced. The blood eagle was the rarest, worst of punishments, never used in living memory. And yet, he had not forgotten Thorbjorn's assault on Inge. Or forgiven.

'The gods put you in my path for a reason,' mused Thorbjorn. 'And not the one I thought.' He turned his hawk's gaze full on Skarfr. 'Learn to hide your judgements, boy, or your face will have you killed. You do not know enough to judge men. To judge me.' He swallowed, chose his words. 'You should not have witnessed what you did. You thought me harsh and perhaps I was. But I was drunk. You should know what that does to a man, failed skald!'

For once, Skarfr felt no shame at the words. From Thorbjorn, it was a truth shared.

'So lucky to marry Sweyn's sister. Every man, woman and child at that gods-cursed banquet told me so until I could take no more. As full of bile as beer, I needed to show her she was marrying a man with a name of his own. So I forced her.' He shrugged. 'I would have courted her afterwards. She's fair and clever.'

His expression hardened again. 'But she'll always be Sweyn's sister, never Thorbjorn's wife. To the Jarl, to his followers, to the gossips – and to me. Trapped in this alliance like a crab in a pot.'

He stood up suddenly, loomed over Skarfr, a dark mountain of a man, showing no hint of the weakness he claimed. 'Know this, fish-boy. My blood lays claim to thanes and *mormaers*, Skots rulers equal to the Jarl. Sweyn's name is his own, nothing behind him and nothing to follow. No wife, no children.'

His face darkened from the storm of emotion shaking him. 'I shall have heirs, bearing *my* name.

'One day, you'll understand, fish-boy. You remind me of myself at your age.' He studied Skarfr, tousled his black hair. Skarfr felt the instinct to jerk away but also a conflicting enjoyment of the attention.

Thorbjorn continued, 'They say my colouring came from an Irish great-grandmother. Perhaps yours too. And your second sight.'

'I don't know,' stammered Skarfr, repelled by the comparison and not sure he liked the idea of Irish ancestry. Brigid and Fergus were kind people but they were not true Orcadians. Thorbjorn seemed almost proud of such a background. Perhaps Skots saw matters pragmatically. Rovers did sometimes take a fancy to the women they took and even married them. Was that so different from what Thorbjorn had done to Inge? If she were gentler, not so proud, would she have forgiven her husband? Should she have?

Skarfr's head ached and he stumbled to his feet, dizzy as if drunk.

'My lord, I'm just trying to do my work. I know nothing of high-born matters.'

'No,' agreed Thorbjorn. 'But the gods do and they speak to me through you.' He reached some kind of decision. 'It shall be as you have told me. Whatever the consequences.' His eyes shimmered with sunlight and fierce resolve.

Skarfr pitied whoever was to be the target of that resolve. He opened his mouth to say he hadn't meant Thorbjorn to act on his words. Then he shut it again. He couldn't say he'd made it all up and draw the warrior's fire down on him again. He shivered. Let the fates decide.

Before he could change his mind, a horse and wagon rolled

into sight, creaking and rumbling. Dust flew up around the horse's hooves and the cart's wheels but he recognised the two figures on the drover's seat.

'Skarfr,' called Hlif as the cart drew to a halt beside him and Thorbjorn. Her eyes flicked between them; presumably she noted that Skarfr was still in one piece. 'We're going to Trygve's house to collect the pots. You could come with us.'

Skarfr should have been touched by her clumsy attempt to rescue him from Thorbjorn but he wasn't. He didn't need a girl to rescue him. He could look after himself and Hlif had to learn that.

'You don't need me,' he told her airily, meaning that *he* didn't need *her*. 'I shall accompany my lord back to the Bu.' He picked up the lamp and passed it up to her. 'It can go in the back with the other goods, to save me carrying it.'

She took the lamp without meeting his eyes. 'I see how it is,' she said quietly.

'It is in one piece.' Skarfr pointed to the lamp, triumphant, deliberately misunderstanding her.

Thorbjorn was right. Women should know their place just as he'd been told to know his. And he would never tell Hlif that he'd escaped a beating by acting like her, stealing her visions.

'If you're going to accompany "my lord", you'd better start walking,' observed Thorbjorn drily. Then his whole face lit up in a way Skarfr had only seen once before. 'I should thank you with a lesson of a different sort. What say you to wrestling? I can teach you some holds that will serve you well in the future.'

'I would like that very much,' said Skarfr, his stomach leaping like a salmon at the thought of training with such a warrior. He felt like he'd been given a hand-carved wooden dragon ship by a foster-father.

# CHAPTER FIFTEEN

Thorbjorn's attention was a fiery beacon lighting up Skarfr's monotonous life in Orphir. When he stripped to his breeks in the training yard, he expected mockery but the warrior merely assessed his body as if he were a horse. Then his mercurial opponent faced him, in the unnerving stillness of the calm before the storm, before moving in to grapple. The dance was brief, arms around each other's shoulders and circling sun-wise. Jittery with nerves, Skarfr hooked his leg around Thorbjorn's, was pushed further off-balance and found himself on his back.

He had no more success when he waited for Thorbjorn to make the first move. The warrior employed what seemed to be exactly the same hook, his foot behind Skarfr's calf, but might as well have been a stone cairn for all the response to Skarfr's shove. Instead, Skarfr toppled once more.

Thorbjorn judged his moves with precision, wasting no energy, mastering without violence. His breathing gave the slightest hitch with the effort of a throw but was barely audible over Skarfr's ragged gasps and snorts. Lightning-fast grappling and footwork landed Skarfr on his back on the grass. And then on his stomach, with no chance of wriggling out from the weight of his opponent, from the arms pinning him to the ground.

When Skarfr did grab an arm or calf, oiled muscles slipped through his fingers like fish. His own body glistened with sweat, acting as lubrication, the smell salty as seaweed, but his adversary's hands caught him every time, sure as cormorants' beaks.

Winded, panting, Skarfr stood doubled over, unable to speak, the happiest he'd been in his entire life. This was what it meant to be a man. As soon as he could, he raised his head, showed he was ready to begin again.

Thorbjorn grinned, shook his head. 'Now you practise,' he told Skarfr and he demonstrated one hold at a time, slowly.

'When you hooked my leg, so.' He imitated Skarfr's first hold. 'You were leaning backwards, so you were easy to push. Look how I was standing.' He tilted his upper body towards Skarfr, maintaining a strong centre of balance while he whipped his foot around to destabilise his student.

He taught Skarfr how to roll out from under a man pinning him down, made Skarfr think up a defence and try it, learn from failures. Always with restraint.

'We are just training but in a battle this could gain you enough time to save your life. Remember that the ground is your enemy. Your opponent's friend is waiting to stamp on your head or swing an axe down. You must get up from the ground and fight again.'

*Fight again.* Skarfr thought of Botolf, who'd beaten him senseless but never won. He could do this. He didn't want to stop though he ached to the bone from stretching, bending and falling. He'd never been so aware of his own body, a young mirror of his wrestling partner's.

'Enough for one session,' decreed the warrior, stepping back, breaking the physical contact.

Skarfr stumbled, dizzy.

'Enough for one session. When I come back, I expect to see you at the training-ground. I'll leave word. And remember to keep moving.' He rubbed a cloth over his face, then chest and back, dark hair curling over the muscles Skarfr could still feel as dents in his own skin.

Thorbjorn carelessly threw on his tunic and leather jerkin, fastened his belt. His thoughts were obviously elsewhere already, volatile as his moods.

'Keep your visions to yourself,' he warned. 'They are meant for me. They tell me what I must do.'

Skarfr's glow of well-being faded as he made his way back to the kitchen, wondering what fires his fabrications had sparked. Thorbjorn's words echoed in his head while he served at table, clumsy enough to earn a clip across his head from Arn.

*When I come back. Your visions tell me what I must do.*

Thorbjorn was not in the hall but Hlif was. She studiously ignored him and he knew she had every right to feel peeved. He also knew she'd come around when she needed to talk to someone. But that wouldn't put things right and the sense of foreboding grew.

For hours, tossing and turning on his thin pallet, he let himself dream of wrestling and weaponscraft, a warrior's training, even sea-roving. Everything that Sweyn had thrown back in his face with laughter, Thorbjorn would give him. As long as he recounted his false visions.

But he could not let Thorbjorn leave on some gods-given mission. He could not enjoy his new status, the patronage of a lord, based on a lie. He could not steal Hlif's gift. Something bad would come of all this.

'Skarfr, wake up!'

Harald was shaking him and the sun showed way past dawn. Cursing, Skarfr threw on his clothes, brushed Harald aside and ran as much of the way to the beach as he could manage, trotting when he was out of breath.

He was in time.

Thorbjorn and forty of his men had removed the rollers from his dragon ship but had not yet run it down to the water.

'Wait!' yelled Skarfr, waving his arms as he ran. A capricious wind warped the words into whistles and squeaks. The men put their shoulders to the ship, strained, set it in slow motion down the sands towards the breakers.

There was still time. Skarfr would swim to the boat if he had to, serve ten years as an oarsman as his punishment, offer his loyalty to Thorbjorn as himself, not as a seer.

The ship began to glide across the sands as the men started to get some momentum going.

Skarfr yelled again and some of the men must have seen or heard him. Their faces turned towards him.

Then winged creatures rose black from the sea, blocked the sun as they flew over the ship towards Skarfr, cawing and clacking in dismay. All but one of the cormorants settled on the sand, waving their wings in the wide gesture they used for drying them or warning off attackers.

'Crk, crk, crrrrruck!' screeched Skarfr's spirit cormorant. She flew straight at him as if she would peck out his eyes like crows did corpses'. He instinctively put his arm over his face and tripped in the sand, dropping to his knees as the whoosh of air from the cormorant's flight brushed the top of his head.

She circled and returned to dive at him again but Skarfr had understood the message. He stayed on his knees in the sand, watching the ship reach water, the men jump in and the sail rise on the mast.

Tall and proud as a dragon figurehead, Thorbjorn waved at him from the deck. Pointed at the cormorants and to the chain on his neck, and waved again.

A good sign.

His cormorant had landed in front of Skarfr, was watching him from sea-green eyes with her head cocked to one side.

'What have you done?' Skarfr asked.

She cackled a reply, flapped her wings and stretched out her long neck, clacking her beak in accusation.

*What have* you *done?* she returned.

# CHAPTER SIXTEEN

'Where have you been?' Arn asked Skarfr, when he arrived back at the Bu. Not waiting for an answer, he continued, 'The Jarl wants you and Harald in the hall. The boy's gone already. So hop to it!'

Obedience and service were easier than brooding over what might come of his imposture so Skarfr hopped to it, slowing only when he reached the Jarl's dais and realised that Rognvald was sitting on the platform in deep discussion with Harald, who was sitting beside him.

Rognvald acknowledged his presence with a nod but gave no instructions so, unwilling to antagonise yet another powerful lord, Skarfr stood and waited. He made every bone in his body show respect. What had Thorbjorn said? His eyes were the problem. Dumb insolence. How was it just to punish a man for a crime he hadn't committed? For his restraint? Skarfr almost shook his head then reminded himself, *Respect.*

Harald was studying the chequered board between them, on which carved game pieces were placed. These were nothing like the plain counters which Botolf had used for games of *Hnefatafl* when he was too bored or too drunk to shun Skarfr's company.

Rognvald held up a crowned character with a sword on his lap, made of gleaming ivory. 'This is the king and you win the game when you capture your opponent's king,' he told Harald. A glance made it clear that he was speaking to Skarfr too, who relaxed. This would be easy. It would be much the same as *hnefatafl*.

As Rognvald introduced each of the pieces. Skarfr realised the differences. Although the king could be cornered by strategy and numbers, as in *Hnefatafl*, instead of there being only two types of piece, the king and his house karls, here there were six and they all moved on the board in different ways and held different values.

'A jarl is like a king,' Rognvald told the young heir to Orkney. 'He has many enemies and must bind men close to him so they will protect him. You can put the white jarl back in his place.'

Skarfr could see the dragon eating its tail in the knotwork carved on the back of the king's throne.

'This is the new game of *tafl*, that they play in Norðvegr, and there are two kings, like there are two jarls of Orkney. This is the red jarl and he is the enemy of the white jarl. Only one of them can win the game.'

Harald reached out to take the red piece, which was identical to the white one, even down to the dragon in the throne's knotwork. He raised mud-brown eyes to meet Rognvald's.

'Will we be enemies, when I grow up?'

The small hairs on the back of Skarfr's neck rose as if Hlif's visions blew cold on the naked skin. Two jarls at a game board. *Pawn-pushers. Knight-crushers. War-wielders.*

Rognvald showed no such concern. 'Men will try to make it so but you will always have a choice. As do I. And by my choice you are kin and hearth-guest, as boy and man. I shall teach you all I know of leadership so we can rule these unruly isles together.'

'But we can kill each other in sport?'

Perhaps Rognvald perceived the unholy light in the boy's face.

'Capture,' corrected Rognvald softly. 'On the games board, all is permitted within its Rule of Law. As in life, where the Thing calls us to account, by different laws. How will you *capture* the other jarl on the games board?'

Harald could have modelled for a gargoyle on the new cathedral, so screwed up was his face as he pondered such weighty matters. 'You said the king moves but one square?'

Rognvald nodded.

'He's not much good at attacking then.'

'No,' Rognvald agreed. 'He's not. He represents too many people to put himself at risk. He is responsible for his realm.'

'Then,' decided Harald, his face clearing. 'He must instruct his men to kill the king. I mean capture him.' He beamed. 'And then they could kill him.'

Invisible ants marched up and down Skarfr's arms as he realised how dangerous this conversation was, not just for the boy jarl but for him as a witness. What if Harald 'disappeared' like Jarl Paul had done? By the same hand and for the same reason?

Not a hint of scheming crossed Rognvald's open countenance but he did not redirect the exchange. Quite the reverse. He built his own construction on Harald's answers. As impressive as his father Kol's cathedral-building but in a different plane.

'When a jarl kills a jarl, what do his people learn?'

'That he is strong?' Harald's voice rose, uncertain.

Skarfr couldn't help himself. He answered, 'That any jarl can kill another or be killed. That jarls do not respect the Thing and the Rule of Law. That jarls cannot be trusted.'

'The apprentice skald has been well taught,' Rognvald told a scowling Harald, to Skarfr's dismay. Surely the Jarl *knew* that nobody liked a know-all. If only he could keep quiet and not just refrain from spouting verse but from making all unsolicited contributions. And solicited ones too, he thought ruefully. But the little flame of hope that still burned deep inside flared a little higher in Rognvald's approval. Maybe Harald's dislike was a small price to pay. He'd known worse.

'What do the ordinary men, the karls, learn from a jarl who breaks the law? What do their goodwives learn?'

Skarfr left the easy question for Harald to answer. Which he did, with a sideways *See, I beat you* look at Skarfr. The little flame did not falter.

'They learn to despise the Thing and the law.'

Harald was rewarded with the same even-handed praise Rognvald meted out to all who showed what he called godly virtues. Other men used different terms.

Although he beamed at his success, Harald must also have been thinking of other men as he burst out, 'Sweyn doesn't do what the Thing tells him.' Admiration glowed in his eyes, with no attempt at concealment.

'Which is why he was exiled,' replied Rognvald smoothly, unruffled. 'And he is not jarl so he is...' He picked up one of the pieces, a helmeted knight bearing a shield, quartered with his device. His horse wore a fringed carapace, all carved in ivory. 'This is Sweyn,' Rognvald stated. 'He is a warrior valued by his king – or jarl.'

Harald's eyes glowed. 'So he's the best fighter because he's free to do the things the king can't. He can move fast can't he?'

'Fast but not far,' qualified Rognvald and he showed the knight's move.

Harald's disappointment vanished when he realised there was a second knight. 'And this is my foster-father Thorbjorn,' he declared. 'They're the two best fighters.'

'Yes, they are. Like all loyal subjects, they will lay down their lives for their lord and it often happens in a game that you must sacrifice a knight to win.'

Skarfr thought of his father, of the price of loyalty. Laying down one's life for one's lord did not sound like Sweyn or

Thorbjorn but Skarfr could see the points Rognvald was hoping to make. But he was not the only influence on the young jarl.

'This looks like a woman. What's she doing here?' asked Harald with what would have been a sneer from a man but came out as a sulky objection from one so young. He was holding the throned companion to the king, her throne less ornamented, her hair neatly hidden in a wimple beneath her crown and her head resting on her hand. No sword for the queen.

Rognvald's face showed his forty years, lined and weary. 'Without her the king is lonely,' he said. 'She can move far and fast, do what he cannot. She can win the game for him and when he loses her, no other piece can compensate. See how she has her head on her hands, weeping for those who die. She brings compassion.' He whispered, 'Like Gertrud.'

'Like Inge,' said the boy firmly. 'I understand now. And these?' He held up in turn the bishop, with his crozier, the tip turned sideways; the warder, solid as an Orkney stone tower; and a berserker chewing on his shield in battle frenzy.

'Next time we shall play a game and you can count how many go to Valhalla from our match. You can go about your duties now. I wish to speak to Skarfr.'

Another resentful look came Skarfr's way, at being excluded from whatever conversation was to follow. Skarfr would have been only too happy to go about his duties, especially when the question he dreaded came.

'Where is Thorbjorn?'

# CHAPTER SEVENTEEN

R ognvald's expression was as affable as usual and yet Skarfr had difficulty in meeting the frank hazel eyes.

'Thorbjorn is nowhere to be found and I would like to see him and Sweyn, together. Do you know where he is?'

*To make sure they don't kill each other over Frakork's murder.* 'No, my lord.' Which was true, as far as it went.

'Hlif said she thought you might know. Why would she think that?'

*Because her feelings were hurt and she'd spoken to get back at him.* 'Because she saw me with Lord Thorbjorn yesterday afternoon.' Now Skarfr did feel he could lift honest eyes to the Jarl's. 'He said it was time I trained with the men, as a warrior.' If his resentment showed, so be it.

A shadow passed over the weary face. 'And I have kept you a pot-boy. Used fine steel to stir my pottage. Is that what Thorbjorn told you, to win you as his man?'

'No, sire, he did not!' But he did not deny being Thorbjorn's man although he knew he should. The words stuck in his throat, would lead to him declaring whose man he *was,* an oath he no longer wished to make. How strange to think he would have sworn allegiance to Sweyn, and gladly, such a short time ago.

Rognvald spoke as if to himself. 'One moment you are at odds, the next you are back-to-back against the world, against the rule of law. And I must protect you from each other, then protect myself from you. So it is with knights. And who shall watch my back? Oh my dear one, who shall rest her head in her hands and grieve over the waste of life in men's squabbles when you are gone?'

Although the Jarl's words made no sense, Skarfr could see his fatigue, his shoulders stooped from the burden he carried. How weak Rognvald was compared with Thorbjorn – or Sweyn.

As if summoned, the sea-rover strode into the hall and up to the dais, ignoring Skarfr as if he were invisible. He would rather Sweyn did *not* remember him so he kept his eyes lowered, barely breathing as he realised he might hear a private audience between the Jarl and the unpredictable pirate.

'This cannot wait, Rognvald. Every day I delay here, waiting for your decision, Holbodi is nearer Bretland without the support he needs.'

Rognvald's cheeks furrowed deeper. '*You* are in Holbodi's debt, Sweyn, not I, and just because you need ships, that does not automatically mean I can do without them. They are *my* ships. I told you I would give my decision when I have made one.'

'So conscientious about being Jarl.' Sweyn blazed impatience. 'You're right, a man must honour those who helped him gain his rightful place, *Sire*, and respond to their need. What about your debt of honour to the man who placed you here?' His gesture included the hall and implied the wider realm as he leaned over Rognvald. 'Do you want to be known as the lord who let the Bretlandmen burn our neighbours' villages and gave only encouragement?'

Rognvald remained sitting, solid and unruffled, his gaze

remaining on the game board as if the petitioner's anger was merely a blustery breeze.

'You shall have your answer tomorrow, Sweyn.'

'When you've found Thorbjorn to ask his permission!' The sea-rover stooped over Rognvald and swiped the pieces off the board into a tumbled heap.

'This is what your dithering shall bring – your friends fallen and a double-tongued advisor at your side. What legacy do you leave your heirs with this cowardly peace-dance?'

Sweyn's eyes blazed as his temper fired words that could not be unsaid. 'But you have no heirs, do you. Your seed is as weak as your rule. One sickly daughter from all your years swiving. Or maybe your White Christ only allowed you to swive once in twenty years to avoid holy days!'

Rognvald jumped to his feet, a full head shorter than his subject but as worthy an opponent as ice against wildfire. 'Enough, Sweyn. You forget yourself and you may leave to cool your head.'

Sweyn was far beyond reason. 'I need no man's permission to stay or leave. If my sister tells me of one insult to her or to me from that whoreson she married or any other man,' he glared at the Jarl, 'this misbegotten alliance is over.'

Sweyn stormed out, with a clatter of boots and squeak of leather, axe-belt against jerkin, leaving Skarfr uncertain as to whether he was threatening to break off from Rognvald or from Thorbjorn, or from both.

Rognvald sat down again, heavily. He disentangled the queen from the pile of pieces and set her throne carefully, almost lovingly on the board. Then he picked up one of the berserker pawns, inspected the crazed expression, teeth champing down so hard on the shield Skarfr could almost imagine the mouth frothing in divine frenzy.

'And will she take your place in my Bu?' Rognvald asked the

queen and shook his head. 'She is not fit to do so.'

Embarrassed by the Jarl's moonstruck behaviour, Skarfr didn't like to attract his attention, so he stood still, wooden as the central pillar in the hall, mulling over the likelihood of Rognvald giving Sweyn ships and ignoring the insistence of his unsettled guts that Thorbjorn's absence boded ill.

'Thorbjorn had the right of it,' said Rognvald eventually, startling Skarfr with the direct focus of his gaze, once more returned to the world. 'You should train with my men.' There was a slight emphasis on *my* and the Jarl's knuckles were white with the intensity of his grip on the berserker game piece but Rognvald's tone showed nothing but his habitual calm.

'I shall send word for them to expect you in the yard tomorrow morning after breaking fast. And let me know when Lord Thorbjorn returns.'

Skarfr's stuttered thanks were ignored as the Jarl was distracted by yet another visitor. No armour clanking this time and to judge by the softening expression in Rognvald's eyes, even an attempt at a weary smile, the person approaching was held in affection.

'Sire, should we set table for Lord Sweyn and his company this evening or are they leaving?' Hlif's practical question sucked the tensions from the air and Skarfr breathed freely again.

'He stays tonight and leaves tomorrow. I have been remiss in letting you know, my young housekeeper.'

She studied her guardian, without denying his fault. 'I understand,' she said.

Rognvald pulled himself to his feet with the awkwardness of a much older man, stretched and loosened cramped limbs. Taller than Hlif by an arm-span, he patted her shoulder as he passed.

'Go with Hlif to the kitchens and make yourself useful for whatever extra work is needed for our guests,' the Jarl told Skarfr, who relaxed and watched his liege leave the hall.

The instruction had been clear enough but Rognvald still seemed abstracted, his gait unsteady at first. Then he rallied, strode to the door. To any onlooker he seemed a leader with a purpose.

Alone with Hlif for the first time since he'd appropriated her visions and rejected her helping hand, Skarfr felt the accusation in her stormy eyes and her silence. He would not apologise for behaving as a man and he could not tell her of his real crime, not as he'd left things with Thorbjorn, but he fumbled for a conciliatory topic.

He knew Hlif hated constraints, hated the limits placed on her by her guardian, resented him.

'The Jarl is not himself,' he observed, then whispered the treason that would surely renew their former rapport. 'I fear he is growing too old to rule.'

Hlif looked at him as if he were a beetle, hardly worth stamping underfoot. Dressed for domestic duty, her wiry red curls netted under a clean linen coif, she showed no trace of the wild spirit he'd first met on the beach.

'And how would you behave,' she asked him, 'if your wife was dying, a sea-voyage away from you? With your newborn baby struggling to survive? I can well believe that *you*,' she delivered the coup de grâce with hauteur, 'would feel nothing.'

She gave him no chance to reply but swished her skirts round to march ahead of him towards the kitchen.

His face burned at the injustice. How was he supposed to have known? And how dare she insult him? He didn't try to catch her up, merely followed the stiff-backed swinging gown in silence. With some satisfaction, he noticed that her feet were still bare and as dusty as his own. She might pretend to be above him but she was no more a lady than he was a lord.

Thorbjorn was right. Women were impossible. And where *was* Thorbjorn?

# CHAPTER EIGHTEEN

Although nobody lacked food, thanks to frenzied activity in the kitchen, the evening meal was a sombre affair. The Jarl was listless and even Sweyn's brilliance was dimmed. He too showed little interest in his laden trencher but fretted like a bridled stallion, snapping at Inge and ignoring Rognvald.

Some well-meaning scion shouted a poetry challenge at the Jarl, who had never turned one down. He nodded, drew himself slowly to his feet, stood looking at the backs of his own hands, spread on the table in front of him, as if they might offer him answers or at least verse. The silence lasted long enough for the audience to begin whispering Skarfr's thoughts aloud.

*He is too old. His rule is over.*

Then Rognvald raised red-rimmed eyes and spoke, his voice reaching the back of the hall with the ease of a practised skald.

'Forgive me if my thoughts turn towards Ness and my skaldcraft follows them. The lady of Orkney, *your* lady,' his voice broke a little then steadied, '*my* lady, is worthy of our acknowledgement.'

Then he came out from behind the table, clapped his hands

and gestured to a boy to bring his harp. The waiting no longer weighed heavily now that entertainment promised.

The moment Rognvald held his instrument, he straightened into his performer's stance and his hands moved to their accustomed places on the strings, expressing his feelings once more. The jangling notes laced drama with pain, touching the melancholy humour in all listeners. As the reverberation faded, he spoke, plucking a desolate commentary when the words paused.

> 'Border-weaves, beads and ivory combs
> I take her, not as gifts
> but grave-goods.
> While she lies fevered
> I wish back hot-headed youth
> chasing hawk, hound
> and each other
> through marsh and mere.
> Now my words wear jesses –
> a vain attempt to tether grief.'

Skarfr felt his heart would burst and spill out of his eyes in sorrow for his father, his mother, his childhood, even for Hlif and all that could not be because of death and fate. Nobody spoke.

Rognvald nodded sadly, passed his harp to the waiting boy, and left the hall.

Conversation started up again when he'd gone but the solemn mood hung over the evening, black as a Christian funeral pall, smothering laughter.

Skarfr was relieved when his duties were over and he could help himself to leftovers among the dirty pots, and relax in the warmth of the kitchen, away from the tensions in the hall. The following day would surely see Rognvald grant Sweyn his ships and both men leave Orkneyjar; the Jarl for Ness and his wife's bedside, and Sweyn to join Holbodi. The following day would also see Skarfr training with Rognvald's men, sanctioned by the Jarl himself. And by Thorbjorn, wherever he might be.

Any envy of the men who would leave with the ships, to Ness and to Bretland, was easily suppressed in anticipation of his first step towards joining the warriors.

*Brand-bearers. Heart-hewers. Wolf-brethren.*

Next time ships sailed, he might be on board.

Speculation and hope left his chest with his breath as he exhausted the small store of wrestling moves Thorbjorn had taught him. But pride remained as he endured the bear-grip of his opponent and was rewarded not just by encouragement from the circle of men watching the bout but also some practical suggestions. Motivated by the support, Skarfr kept moving, twisting, grabbing. Even though he suspected his adversary was holding back, he felt the rush of success-blood to his face. He belonged.

'Take his hands so you can break free!'

'Come on Skarfr!'

'Grab his legs!'

'From the inside, from the inside. That's it!'

All too soon, their turn was over and another pair took the centre so all could learn from mistakes and tricks.

Bear-grip threw a heavy arm around Skarfr's shoulders, laughed when the boy winced. 'You shall have your revenge,' he promised, with what was probably a smile. His mouthful of black-painted and missing teeth offered little confirmation of good humour but he kept his word. 'Now,' he told the others, when a changeover was due. 'I need proper training.'

He lay down on his belly and began push-ups, his rhythm as

relentless as a drum, while the watchers roared the beat and Skarfr lost count.

'Kick him,' the red-beard who led the instruction and criticism told Skarfr. 'From the side. He has to tense his chest muscles, make them strong.'

Tentatively, Skarfr aimed a kick at the man who'd defeated him. He'd never kicked anyone before. Or anything.

'Harder!' the men yelled. 'Make him strong.'

Skarfr lashed out. Not even a grunt in response and no change to the rhythm of the push-ups.

'Catch him out,' ordered Red-beard. 'You're kicking to a rhythm, tricked by your body into copying his. Make your kicks unpredictable.'

This was surprisingly hard and Skarfr had to recite kennings in his head to kick out first to a different rhythm, then without pattern. Who knew that the body had instinctive poetry in its movements, sought the beat? He stored the knowledge for another time.

Both Skarfr and Bear-grip were lathered in sweat when Red-beard called, 'Enough!'

Skarfr held out his hand to the man on the ground, to help him to his feet. With a black grin, Bear-grip took the arm offered, from respect not from need, his muscles rounded and hard as roof-beams.

'You have potential,' Red-beard told him gruffly before ordering the next pair to clinch and begin their bout.

Someone threw them linen cloths and as Skarfr dried his body he became aware of the ripples underneath his own chest, muscles there less developed than in his arms but no longer a boy's. He would work on his body as Botolf had once worked on his mind, make it a weapon. He didn't rush to don his tunic, considering his assets and faults in comparison with the men around him. He was tall for his age, long-limbed and strong but he was slim and clumsy, inexperienced in how to keep his balance. He would practise alone on the log across the beck, he determined.

Awareness that he was being watched broke into his thoughts and he slung the cloth around his shoulders. He glanced around the circle of men, found a gap where a woman stood, her lips a tight line of disapproval. He shrugged, aware even as he did so of the muscle movements rippling his naked chest.

Hlif looked away and Skarfr slipped his tunic over his head.

'Skarfr,' she called. 'The Jarl wants you.'

She anticipated his question as they walked towards the hall. 'I don't know why.' She stopped, added, 'He hasn't asked for me.'

She turned to go her own way but hesitated, bit her lip and then the words came out in a rush. 'I saw you kicking that man.'

'He asked for it,' explained Skarfr.

Her face whitened. 'You are indeed Thorbjorn's man.'

By the time Skarfr realised the misunderstanding, she was gone. That was the trouble with women. They were too ready to believe ill of a man and too ignorant to know what men did.

Composing his expression into one more suitable for his liege, Skarfr entered the darkness of the hall and found Rognvald seated at the table in formal attire, his pathfinder brooch pinned to his cloak and catching the torchlight. No sign of the game board.

He wasted no time on niceties, his face set.

'I've invited Lord Sweyn to join me and I want a witness in case I should take a dispute to the Thing.'

Skarfr swallowed hard. If Sweyn showed no remorse for his disrespect of the previous day and Rognvald went to the Thing for grievance, the result would be exile for the sea-rover. With who knew what consequences. And Sweyn had never shown remorse. Exile was not new to him, though not previously at Rognvald's hand.

'You have no dog in this fight and can speak clearly of what transpires, should that be needed.'

The clatter of a warrior's approach preceded Sweyn into the hall and he strode up to the table with no pretence of humility. And he had not politely deposited his weapons on entry.

Rognvald pre-empted any arrogant speech. 'You have asked me to offer you ships and I promised my response today.'

The reminder seemed to calm Sweyn, who showed enough restraint to hold his tongue.

'Your comportment yesterday did not help your case,' began the Jarl.

Sweyn's jaw tightened but what either of them would have said next was prevented by a rumpus at the back of the hall and a group of men rushing in, all shouting at once.

Rognvald and Sweyn had automatically reached for their weapons and remained alert, although it was now apparent that the intruders were bursting with news, not violent intent.

'Two men, without warning or mercy,' gasped a man in a weatherproof jerkin, who'd reached the table first but addressed himself to Sweyn rather than Rognvald, perhaps because he was the nearer and his weapon therefore more of a threat.

Then another commotion brought Inge rushing through the hall to her brother's side, livid spots flaring in her pale cheeks, her words cutting through the confusion.

'Thorbjorn has raided Gareksey, murdered two of Sweyn's men in coward's manner, taking them unawares. He cannot get away with this ... this lawlessness! Sweyn must leave now and deal with this criminal.'

She looped her arm through her brother's, heedless of the fact that she was thereby preventing him from rushing out of the hall.

Irritated at being pre-empted, the messenger added, 'The men were among those who fired Frakork's longhouse.'

'Nobody moves,' roared Rognvald, looking grim, his impassivity shaken. 'It is but weeks since Thorbjorn – your husband, madam – came to me with the same accusation, regarding Sweyn's obsessive pursuit and burning of Frakork, despite accepting *manbot* and hearing the Thing's judgement.'

'I said I would not accept *manbot* for my father's death!' Sweyn shouted and the angry echoes fired back from the stone walls.

In calmer tones, Rognvald said, 'Forced or no, you took the payment, then killed Thorbjorn's grandmother. In his eyes, he has grievance. And his deed is lesser than yours. If it had been you he killed, the Thing would have a harder judgement to make but you stand before me.' Almost as an afterthought, he said, with emphasis, 'Seeking ships.'

'Leave,' he ordered, 'all of you but Sweyn and Inge.'

Skarfr moved to leave with the others but Rognvald snapped at him, 'Not you, boy.'

He spoke to Sweyn first, curt and to the point. 'You spoke much of honour. Do you want to pay your debt to Holbodi? Do you want ships to support his revenge? Or do you want to waste your time on the next spat of tit for tat against Thorbjorn in a game of *who's-the-hardest*? Two men are worth what to you? More than your honour? More than five ships?'

'My honour is touched by these murders,' growled Sweyn.

Rognvald shook his head. 'Not if compensation is paid. And I shall see to it that Thorbjorn knows my displeasure.'

Sweyn's lips curled in contempt but it was Inge who spoke. 'He won't care a rat's pizzle about your displeasure.'

Eyes narrowed, the Jarl regarded Thorbjorn's wife. 'Apparently he's not the only one,' he observed. 'Those with manners address me as Sire.'

Inge flushed crimson and bit her lip.

Rognvald was unmoved. 'Let's mince no more words, madam. Do you seek a divorce?'

Inge's eyes filled and she hesitated.

Sweyn snapped, 'Of course she doesn't.'

Inge's hand slipped from her brother's arm and she looked down.

'Then go to your husband's house, await his return and – what were your words?' Rognvald asked Sweyn, sarcastic. 'Ah yes, play peacemaker.'

As Inge swayed on a lonely route through the hall to go back to her husband's house, the Jarl asked Sweyn, 'Well?'

Between gritted teeth, Sweyn said, 'I'll take the ships.'

Rognvald nodded. 'Take them and set sail today. I trust your voyage will be both successful and of long duration. When you return to Gareksey after some years, you will be grateful you left.'

It was an order.

# CHAPTER NINETEEN

Thorbjorn came home with a victor's swagger to find that he'd missed Sweyn's visit by a few days and that, as Harald's guardian, he was to take Rognvald's place while the Jarl went to Ness to be with his wife. If disapproval *was* expressed, it made no more impact on Thorbjorn's jubilation than it had on Sweyn.

Skarfr couldn't resist discussing the dramatic scenes he'd witnessed with the only person who would never tell. He went further in trying to win back Hlif's friendship and said he was willing to accompany her to Kirkjuvágr while Rognvald was away from Orkney, to petition St Magnus on lifting the curse.

Although he'd made the offer, he'd hoped the crazy plan to visit St Magnus' shrine would be forgotten but no such luck. And he *had* given his word he'd go with her. When Hlif appeared in the kitchen and told Arn that the table-boy was to accompany her on a trip the following day to check supplies from Kirkjuvágr, Skarfr had hidden a groan and tried to seem enthusiastic.

Sharing the back of a wagon with sacks of wool, they talked as if Skarfr had never chosen Thorbjorn over Hlif and his guilt eased. But his misgivings about the trip returned.

'We shouldn't be doing this,' Skarfr told Hlif as they bumped along the track in the back of a trader's cart, with sacks of wool for company. 'If the Jarl finds out, he'll be furious.'

Pale pink lips pursed in irritation. 'He can hardly object to me making my devotion.' Then she grinned, her cheeks flushed and freckled. 'Especially if he doesn't know about it until afterwards, if at all. Everybody is used to me carrying out my duties as housekeeper.'

'Apprentice housekeeper,' corrected Skarfr, who had listened well while about his boring errands.

'Not for much longer,' retorted Hlif. 'I'm of an age now to run the Jarl's household and he owes me that status.'

'Then why do you want the curse lifted? If you want to be the housekeeper and you're going to *be* the housekeeper, you would only lose all that if you were to marry, so why does it matter that you can't?' He kept to himself the thought that with her looks she should be grateful to have such an appropriate role, given that nobody would want to be her husband without some large incentive. Perhaps a farm, some livestock. As she had no father or brother, Rognvald would be the one to agree *mundr* for Hlif. And pigs would fly before he did so!

A thought struck Skarfr.

'You don't have some man in mind for husband?'

Hlif's face went a blotchy beetroot. 'No,' she said. Then, after a long pause, 'I would just like the choice.'

'And,' pursued Skarfr, enjoying his own logic and heedless of its impact, 'you said being cursed was protection against—' *Being backed against a wall and forced.* 'unwanted attentions. So you're better off as you are.'

She said nothing and he felt smug, having won. It wasn't like her not to have the last word though.

'The ghosts are getting more violent,' she said, in that quiet voice which made Skarfr shiver. 'I don't mind how people look at me or not getting married and not having children. And I do want to be a housekeeper. But if the curse was lifted, I wouldn't have to see *them*. And I don't know what they want from me.'

He asked. 'Who do you see? What do they do? Tell me everything.'

She paused. For a terrible moment he thought she knew why he was so curious.

'It helps me to have someone to talk to,' she confessed.

Skarfr felt even worse. But he needed Hlif's visions so he could feed them to Thorbjorn and stay safe.

'I don't just *see* Frakork,' she said, her eyes distant. 'I *feel* her death. Smoke slipping into my nostrils, then my throat, choking and burning from inside while the charred scent of my own flesh mixes with flame and pain. *She* carries that death with her even as she walks, whole in my visions, brandishing her wand, her magic intact.

The timbre of Hlif's voice came from some dark underworld, as if from Helheim itself. 'I see you too.'

Skarfr shuddered but he couldn't help asking, 'Older, like Harald? What am I doing?'

She opened her mouth to answer, hesitated, then shook her head. 'I won't say. Maybe saying will hang the loom-weight, fix the cloth and the pattern. Maybe I'm not seeing it true.'

Not knowing what she saw was an itch to his curiosity that he couldn't scratch but he knew she wouldn't tell him. Not now but maybe in the future – before the vision *became* the future and was no use at all.

She shuddered, whispered, 'Do you think of your own death, Skarfr?'

The cartwheel caught in a pothole, jolted sacks and people against each other as it bumped out and the cart straightened again.

'Up, up, Loki,' Viggo, the trader, encouraged his horse. Any beast less suited to bear the name of the mercurial sex-changing god of trickery, Skarfr could not imagine. To his ears, the alternation of praise and reproach guiding the horse was in some foreign language, with as many clicks of the tongue as syllables. And Loki plodded on, with no noticeable change in rhythm or enthusiasm.

'Of course,' he answered, already thinking how he would use Hlif's words to make Thorbjorn feel good about avenging Frakork. He shied away from the thought that two men had already died because of Skarfr's fake visions. He wasn't a target anymore, and neither was Hlif, which was all that mattered.

'I shall die with an axe in my hand and carouse in Valhalla until the last battle. No hearth-waning for me.' *Carouse is a good word,* he thought, *and hearth-waning too.*

To show Hlif that he was not thinking only of himself, he added sympathetically, 'It is a terrible fate to be a woman, inferior in this world and barred from Valhalla. I admire the courage of women bearing such a burden.'

However, Hlif had clearly not quite forgiven him for choosing Thorbjorn. 'The main burden for most women is men's stupidity. As a skald, surely you know of Freyja's Hall.'

'An inferior afterlife, for failed men and for women,' Skarfr dismissed it airily.

'Well perhaps a failed skald might consider the company there to be quite suitable.'

How could any man keep patience with somebody so determined to provoke him? 'I'm no longer a skald. I'm training as a warrior. With Thorbjorn. And with Rognvald's blessing.' *There, take that.*

But she'd followed her own thoughts. 'You don't know the names of Freyja's cats.'

He sighed. 'Nobody knows the names of Freyja's cats.'

'And you've never thought that strange? I hate to be the first to tell you but *women* do know the names of Freyja's cats and a lot more besides. It's for women to know and pass on to other women. And I'd rather go to Freyja's Hall when I die and call her cats by name than endure more banquets and drinking competitions among bragging warriors.'

He shrugged, 'Then I hope you get your wish.'

Considering the matter further, she said, 'Rognvald wants us to go to Christian heaven. We could be together there.'

Skarfr doubted any such heaven would accept as sinful a man as himself but he didn't want to explain this to Hlif so he let her have the last word on the subject. He would be happy in Valhalla. With Thorbjorn. *And Sweyn*, suggested his impish imagination. No doubt Óðinn was more skilled than Rognvald in dealing with belligerent guests. Otherwise, Hlif might have a point.

'Why doesn't Inge ask for a divorce?' he asked Hlif, changing the subject. She was always happiest explaining women or politics to him. 'She hates Thorbjorn and it's even worse since he killed Sweyn's men.'

'Pride. Divorce is a public admission of failure. If she could accuse him of something, that would sweeten it but he has done nothing a husband shouldn't do and much that shows her respect.'

'But—' objected Skarfr.

Hlif rounded on him. 'You want her to talk of intimate matters? Make herself a laughing-stock? Worse – get a divorce by making herself into a woman no man will marry? It's not as if she's produced an heir. No, she won't give up on the power she has as Thorbjorn's wife, guardian to the young Jarl. And she won't give up on needling him. It's the only way she can cope.'

'One day, she will go too far and he will hit her,' Skarfr said.

'What happens in the sagas when a man hits his wife?'

'Trouble always comes of it.'

'Then trouble will come of it. But for now, trouble comes of it for other women instead. And you don't care.' There it was again, the burr fretting at their friendship, his enjoyment of Thorbjorn's patronage.

'A man can appreciate another's talents without condoning his behaviour with women,' Skarfr defended himself.

'No,' declared Hlif, 'he can't. Some defects are too important to overlook.'

He glanced sideways at her and looked quickly back at the dust blowing up from the track they'd travelled over. Her eyes were screwed up, her fists clenched and he did not think how ugly she looked. And she *had* confided in him so he owed her something of himself in return. He had an overwhelming urge to hug her as Brigid had hugged him.

But he didn't.

'I brought my bones,' he said and immediately regretted opening up so much.

'What bones? Why?' she asked, as he'd known she would.

He hesitated but he couldn't with any courtesy tell her it was personal and to mind her own business.

'Just things I collected on the beach, birds' bones.' He shrugged. 'I don't have precious things and you're supposed to offer something to the gods when you pray so I suppose it's the same for a saint.'

'And you brought them for me so St Magnus would hear my prayer.' She spoke softly. 'Nobody has ever done anything like that for me before. Thank you.'

It was his turn to flush crimson. He could hardly tell her that the bones were *his* offering for *his* prayer. Now what could he give? His mind shied away from the other object in his pack. He had lied. He did have precious things.

The cart shuddered to a halt and Skarfr realised the people around them were not walking to market. They were *in* the market and Viggo had drawn up his wagon in the space between a leather goods trader and a cheese stall.

'This is where you get down,' confirmed the carter, dropping the back of the cart so his human cargo could descend and his wares be displayed.

# CHAPTER TWENTY

H lif ignored Viggo's extended hand and jumped down onto the well-trampled earth, followed by Skarfr. They brushed the dust and specks of fluff off their clothes and looked around to get their bearings. It would be easy enough to find their way back, as the foundations for the new cathedral were in front of them, within a stone's throw, with all the noise of masons and their apprentices at work. Not that these stones could easily be thrown. Huge red blocks were being unloaded and added to the stacks all around the site, presumably in some organised plan to which the masons held the key.

Their carter raised his voice above the hullabaloo of builders, traders and customers. 'Be back here when the bells ring for nones.' He exchanged nods with his neighbours and was already showing samples of wool to the first customer curious about the content of the sacks.

'Wait!' Skarfr chased after Hlif, who was marching towards the only part of the cathedral-to-be which had recognisable walls and a makeshift covering for its roof. The construction filled the north-east corner of the building site, already startling in its height and red sandstone exterior.

They negotiated blocks of stone and boys carrying buckets of water. Skarfr's shoulders ached in sympathy just watching them but his attention soon shifted to a man splitting a block with a hammer and chisel. He would have liked to linger and watch the stone cutter at work but duty hastened his feet in pursuit of Hlif.

She stopped at the entrance to the covered section and peered in. When Skarfr joined her, he was tall enough to see over her head and gawp at the impossible way the red stone curved. How had those blocks turned into such grace? The Jarl's Bu was a pigsty in comparison to this building, even at such an early stage. But Hlif was in no mood to appreciate architecture.

'There's nothing here.' All the vivacity and anticipation of the journey had evaporated. 'They call it St Magnus Cathedral but the rock stacks on the headland are higher than this! Three years' work and there's no cross, no shrine. The saint's bones aren't here and there's nowhere to pray even if they were. We might as well go home.'

'They must be somewhere,' reasoned Skarfr, as much to gain time among the stoneworkers as to comfort Hlif. 'People can't be waiting for the cathedral to be built before they have somewhere they can pray.'

He approached one of the masons, a burly man with a pate as bald as his well-worn leather apron. Waiting patiently for a pause in the tap-tap-tap of hammer on chisel on stone, Skarfr watched the cut lines appear, shallow and even, like a rune marking but no character that he knew.

The man looked up, gruff. 'What?'

'I don't know that rune. Is it your name? Why are you putting it into the stone?' asked Skarfr, distracted from his mission.

'You wouldn't know, would you,' replied the man smugly, 'because you're not a mason. Years in the trade I've had, from boy to man, and we,' he waved his hammer around to include his fellow-workers, 'came here when we finished Dunholm Cathedral.'

Years with Botolf had accustomed Skarfr to the tone which required awe in response but he opted for information instead. 'I don't know where Dunholm is,' he confessed. 'Or anything about its cathedral.'

The mason sighed. 'We were told how backwards you were on these islands but I still can't believe how little you know. Dunholm is St Cuthbert's holy place and the cathedral we built there, well, let's just say it shows that we're the best. And we earned the place in heaven that we were promised. Not but what it wouldn't hurt to have better pay here on earth, rather than wait till we're dead for our reward. How we'll make it through winter again, laid off in this godforsaken hole till work starts up again in spring, I don't know.'

He looked around quickly. 'But that's dangerous talk. And this, young master long-nose,' he waved the chisel at the marks he'd made on the stone, 'is to make sure I get paid what's due. I'm on piecework, see, and this is no rune. It's my mark to show which stones I've cut. That's not all we use the marks for but you'd have to become a mason to find out more trade secrets.'

He looked Skarfr up and down, from his rough-chopped black hair to his bare feet. 'And you don't look the type to me.'

'Excuse me, stonemason,' a haughty voice interrupted. 'I need some information.'

Unimpressed by Hlif's manner, the man weighed her up in the same way he had Skarfr, from her unruly red hair escaping from a clean coif, to her dusty feet, also bare.

'Information is what I'm giving,' he replied stolidly, 'and the Lord knows why I'm bothering, when you don't know the first thing about—' He struggled for a big enough word 'about anything. I'm not a master mason though I could be one day. That's our master mason, over there, talking to Lord Kol.'

The two men indicated formed an island in the stream of activity. The boys with buckets and the men carrying blocks walked around their superiors without breaking stride. The master mason could easily be distinguished by the ubiquitous leather apron and a less tangible air of authority, equal to Lord Kol's. The man holding the purse-strings to the project built imaginary walls with his hands, only to have the man responsible for the structure's safety reduce the size of those walls with even firmer gestures.

Skarfr's stoneworker shook his head in disgust. 'Always want things done quicker, these lords, and they think we're all slacking if it's not finished by Christmas. He'll be more than lucky if he lives to see it finished.' He sucked his moustache philosophically. 'The glory of God takes more than a man's span of years, and stone takes the time it takes.'

After a quick glance towards the two men in charge of operations, Hlif moved so that her back was towards them.

Answering his puzzled expression, she muttered, 'Rognvald's father,' which did not explain her odd behaviour.

The mason nodded. 'Aye, the Norðman is father to your Jarl, right enough.'

Hlif drummed her fingers against her skirt. 'We wouldn't want you to be accused of slacking because of us,' she said with an insincere smile. 'So if you could just tell us where the saint's bones are, we'll be on our way.'

The man shook his head again. 'Where else would they be? In the church of course.'

'And where's the church?' asked Hlif, between gritted teeth.

'St Olaf's Church it is, north-east from here, a short walk. It's Norðman-built in the old-fashioned way but solid enough for its time. Your St Magnus will be one-up on St Olaf when he moves in here.' He laughed until he choked and told them, wheezing, 'Dust in my pipes.'

'You should take a honey and thyme posset,' Hlif told him, which was as close to kindness as she could manage, her impatience to get going manifest. 'Thank you.'

Skarfr watched the chisel and hammer return to their work, marking a different block with the same open triangle crossed by a line.

'Skarfr!' Hlif called to him. He sighed, then jogged to catch up with her.

'Why didn't you want Lord Kol to see you?'

Hlif stopped dead, right beside a pie stall, which Skarfr eyed sideways with a grumbling stomach. As usual, the soggy pastry was wet from leaked filling but it kept the meaty contents as fresh as their baker claimed, judging by the smell. Only the starving poor ate the whole pie but Skarfr was so hungry he was tempted. Of its own volition, his hand fished a coin out of the pouch on his belt and made the exchange with the pie-keeper.

'Why do you think, stupid?'

'Because he'd recognise you? And then tell Rognvald you were here?' mumbled Skarfr through a mouthful of stewed meat.

'Oh he'd recognise me all right. I'm the daughter of the man who killed his wife's brother!' she hissed. Even though they kept their voices down, they were attracting attention, especially from the stallholder whose customers they were blocking. Skarfr took her elbow and moved her on down the row of traders.

'That's not your fault.'

'You don't understand, do you.' She lapsed into gloomy silence for the rest of their walk. Both of them kept their eyes on the ground: the hazards of rotten vegetables and animal droppings threatened their bare feet as cows, sheep and horses were driven between pens and purchase.

# CHAPTER TWENTY-ONE

S t Olaf's church was easy to recognise, humbly offering its
stone comfort among ramshackle village cots that were little
more than sheds. The new cathedral might have land around it but
the field was churned into mud by the stoneworkers and the small
church had the virtue of being walled and roofed. Orkney's new
saint was better protected from the frequent drizzle here in the
company of his Norðman co-martyr than in the imagined
grandeur of his future sanctuary.

Hlif pushed open the great wooden door, adjusted her coif for
modesty and entered the cool darkness. She crossed herself and
Skarfr followed suit, although the gesture was not habitual for
him. As one of Rognvald's household, he was expected to attend
church but he still had to copy others' behaviour to conform to the
rituals, as he forgot them frequently. Botolf had treated all
Christian practices with impatience, seeing them as an
interruption to Skarfr's chores and his own pleasures, so church
attendance had been rare and prayer was a literary conceit rather
than a daily duty.

But if St Magnus could help him, Skarfr was willing to pay
more than lip service to the Christian saint and his God. He might

have given up on his future as a skald but he had no intention of remaining a kitchen boy. His conscience pricked him. And of course he hoped St Magnus could lift the curse from Hlif.

As his eyes adjusted to the gloom, he realised that a robed figure stood at the altar, his back towards them as the priest lit one candle from another, then glided to a stone side-alcove and placed the light in a niche. His mouth worked in the candlelight, no doubt in prayer or blessing and he touched a long wooden box illuminated by the new flame. He bent down and picked up objects from around the box, put them into a basket and half-turned, at which point he became aware of the intruders.

'Those are offerings. St Magnus' relics must be in the box. You're a man. You ask him,' whispered Hlif, hanging back in Skarfr's shadow.

Her words made him feel taller and he addressed the priest, quietly as befitted the solemn atmosphere. His words came from stories and seemed the right ones for the occasion, although his voice shook as he spoke.

'Father, we are penitents come to beg forgiveness on the bones of our dear Saint Magnus.'

The priest's voice quavered even more than Skarfr's and as the penitents drew nearer, they saw wisps of white hair around his shiny bald pate and his lined face showed his age. His long brown robe created the illusion of a gliding walk but the stick on which he leaned could now be seen.

'Of course, children. Kneel and open your hearts. The saint will hear your prayers.' The priest turned back to the wooden box and opened it so they could see inside. Skarfr could hear Hlif's sharp intake of breath as she looked at the remains of her father's victim.

Bones were set out at random, with no attempt to show relationships between them. But what drew attention was the skull. In those sockets, a man's eyes had swivelled, opened and blinked. The teeth were all there and gleamed like walrus ivory although such assets were of little use to Jarl Magnus now. Would the cuts from the axe show in the bone? He peered at the skull, wished he could turn it to see the back.

'Skarfr,' hissed Hlif, pulling him down to his knees beside her as the priest began to frown at his inappropriate curiosity. She shut her eyes, screwed up her face and he did likewise. Was he supposed to pray aloud? Hlif wasn't doing so and he almost smiled at the thought of how the priest would react to her plea.

*Please*, he began, then the entrance door creaked open, light footsteps tapped on the stone and a boy's voice disturbed the silence.

'Father, Bishop William is coming to talk to you about the holy relics. I ran ahead to give you warning but he's on his way now.'

'You did well, my child. Walk with me and we will welcome him to our church in a proper fashion.'

With no thought to his two penitents, or the open box of bones, the priest walked slowly to the back of the church with his young acolyte and stood in the doorway. Skarfr watched from half-closed lids, then when he was satisfied that the priest's attention was elsewhere, he concentrated fully. Now was his chance.

*Our Saint Magnus in heaven, please send me on a longship to have adventures and become a true Orkneyman. They said I should bring an offering and these are my special things I'm giving to you. Amen.*

He stood up, checked that the priest was still otherwise occupied and opened his pack, turned it upside down over the box of holy relics and fished out his precious bones, distributing the birds' skeletal remains among the saint's relics.

There. It was done and the bargain was sealed.

Hlif's eyes were round, her pupils dilated and suspiciously wet in the dim candlelight.

'Nobody's ever done something as nice as that for me, ever,' she whispered, a catch in her voice.

Skarfr couldn't tell her the truth so he pacified his conscience with a postscriptum of a prayer. Without kneeling – surely that wouldn't matter? He shut his eyes and prayed.

*One more thing, Saint Magnus. Please lift the curse from Hlif and make her be a normal girl. Amen.*

An offering. He needed an offering. And he had nothing left. What could he give? Thoughts racing wildly, he remembered his earlier vow, to speak no poetry. He could make it official, a proper vow. And nothing would show so Hlif wouldn't know the bones hadn't been for her.

*I give you my vow of poetic silence.* He remembered his dramatic recital of the poisoned-tunic story and he added hastily, *Except to Hlif because she doesn't count. And in my head of course, because that's silent.*

He opened his eyes, pleased with himself. He felt so magnanimous that he held out his hand in a courtly gesture, to help Hlif to her feet. She even accepted it and smiled at him. And then a voice rang out like thunder from the doorway, a rebuke from Thórr.

'What is that cursed child doing in God's house? Get out, demon!' The bishop's arm was lifted, his finger pointing at Hlif, exorcising her from the church.

She dropped Skarfr's hand, grabbed her skirts and scuttled to the doorway so fast that she had ducked under the accusatory arm before the bishop realised her intention and made a move.

'You,' he roared at Skarfr. 'Move away from the holy relics.' Skarfr wished he'd made a run for it with Hlif but felt he should put up some kind of defence so he took a few steps backwards then stopped.

Bishop William, younger and more vigorous than the priest, strode to the saint's alcove, inspected the wooden box and harrumphed.

'There doesn't look to be anything missing,' he declared with apparent disappointment. By this time, the old priest had joined him. He too peered in the box and was satisfied.

'No, my Lord Bishop, I don't see that anything's been touched at all. They wanted to pray for forgiveness and they were so sincere...'

Hiding his amusement at the two prelates' ignorance of the bird bones among the holy relics, Skarfr responded to the implied doubt.

'We *were* sincere,' he blurted out, 'and we have the right to pray to our saint. We took nothing.'

The bishop looked at him as if he were a dog turd. 'The sins of the fathers are visited on the children. And on those who keep them company. Leave now and don't come back or you'll see the inside of a prison cage. And you may be sure I'll have words with the Jarl about his household.'

Mention of the Jarl stopped Skarfr saying more and he hurried out the door, wondering whether he could catch up with Hlif. If he succeeded, what could he say to her? Was this Saint Magnus' reply to their prayers?

He looked around without much hope or enthusiasm and quickly accepted that Hlif had gone. No doubt she'd show up back at the cart when the nones bells rang and she'd had time to lick her wounds. He had no idea where she'd gone so perhaps it was better if he looked around the market, maybe went back to watch the stoneworkers, made the most of the outing for himself as he couldn't fix the disaster for Hlif.

'Do you want a woman?' a voice breathed in his ear.

He jumped, looked at the speaker, saw a lot more of her than was usual when glancing at a woman's bodice.

'Yes,' he said.

'Follow me.'

Skarfr obeyed, his heart pounding, trying to ignore the jeers and innuendos sent his way by the traders and their customers.

The woman had no such reticence and she seemed to know everybody by name.

'If you want to give a girl a hard time, you know where to find me later,' she yelled cheerfully to those disappointed she was no longer available..

Skarfr blinked at her crudeness but then what had he expected? Before he could change his mind, he was inside one of the ramshackle cots, the earthen floor little cleaner than the street outside, muddied by recent leaks in the roof. A straw pallet was so close to the door he could have fallen onto it and he had difficulty edging around to the far side. He saw a stool and two pails, one full of clean water and one empty, smelly enough for its purpose to be clear.

'That'll be a farthing, proper silver mind, and I like payment first,' she said as she closed the door and only an outline of light remained around the ill-fitting rectangle.

How stupid he was! He'd known she was a whore but never thought about how he'd pay. He wasn't sure whether he was more disappointed or relieved that he could escape without causing offence.

'I don't have any money,' he stuttered. 'I don't have anything. This was a mistake and I'm really sorry but I can go and no harm done.'

Hand on hip, she looked him up and down, presumably seeing better than he could. This was the second time today he'd faced such a calculating look but with a very different set of criteria. And outcome.

She shrugged, letting her loose top slip down off her shoulders and a breast swing free, pendulous as a loom-weight and ten times the size. 'I like the look of you so this will be a taster.'

She gave him a sly look. 'And then you might come back to Freyja another market-day.'

She stepped out of the garment that passed as a gown and the outline of her naked body was more pleasing than any door-rectangle.

Skarfr swallowed. 'I've never done this before,' he owned up.

She stepped forward onto the pallet, closed in on him and rubbed her body against his.

'I don't think you'll have a problem,' she observed.

He remembered Inge against a wall, Brigid's soft noises, such different acts of the night. He controlled himself just long enough to say, 'I want to know how to be kind, give pleasure, if that's possible.'

She laughed and pulled him down onto the pallet, where he found out that it was indeed possible.

When the door opened again for Skarfr to leave, he was shocked to see the woman who called herself Freyja, in full daylight, without the glamour of lust. There were grimy lines around her mouth and shrewd eyes, missing teeth and slackness in her arms and stomach. She must be at least thirty. Freyja, goddess of love and desire.

'Be good to her,' she told him. 'The woman you marry. And meanwhile, you come back when you want.'

Then she gave a grin more honest than her profession. 'And then it'll be a silver bit, however much you play Óðinn to my Freyja.'

Skarfr's hand went to the hammer around his neck, warding off evil at such a mocking reference to the gods. But although he told himself it was nothing, just a rut with a whore, he walked taller, felt different, had much to think about and only crude words for what had happened. Were there better words?

He remembered the words the woman had used and blushed.

Was he as attractive to women as the woman had said? Or was that her trade speaking?

The afternoon light was softening already as Skarfr arrived back at the market stalls in front of the cathedral building site. Traders with further to go than the carter were packing up what wares they had not sold but the hammering of the stonemasons continued its rhythm.

From this direction Skarfr had a fine view of the harbour just beyond the limits of the cathedral's land. The broad hulls of knarrs, the trading ships, dominated all the fishing boats that were tied or beached. *Like a full-breasted woman and her children.* Skarfr added the image to his secret store of poetry.

More prosaically, he thought one was probably Kol's ship, maybe the very one that would take him overseas, to the Old Country, sailing through storms and around whirlpools, evading kraken and the net used to capture men by Rán, the sea-goddess. There would be women, welcoming the heroes wherever they landed. Freyja's invitation had surely been a sign that St Magnus had heard his prayer and now he was a man, adventures abroad would follow.

He could see his transport home was empty. The carter was chatting, relaxed, so his day must have gone well. Skarfr glanced at the sky. There was just time to take a closer look at the knarrs in the harbour, ships built specifically for cargoes, their hulls shorter, deeper and wider than those of the drakkar dragon ships. He strode off through the builders and their boys, recognised the stonemason who'd talked to him earlier that day. He couldn't resist stopping to watch once more.

'You again,' observed the man, tapping away, hammer on chisel. He looked up at Skarfr. 'Do you want to try?' He held out the tools.

'Yes,' said Skarfr and took them. It was a day for saying yes.

He squatted on the ground, imitating the mason. The man

sniffed him and wrinkled his nose, smiled wryly but spoke only of stone cutting and dressing. He pointed at a pile of red stone blocks.

'Those are for a pillar. But you can make your mark on this.'

A disappointingly grey block was to be Skarfr's test piece.

The mason picked up a stick and drew the sign Skarfr had seen earlier, in the earth. He gave the hammer and chisel to Skarfr, showed the lines he'd drawn in charcoal on the stone.

'Use the chisel edge to chip down the line, then make it broader with little taps of the hammer on the chisel. My mark's a guarantee of quality, made by me or an apprentice under my supervision. And it secures my pay.'

'Pay?'

'Aye, as I told you afore, those show what work I've done, for when we're paid by the piece.'

Skarfr liked the feel of the chisel and scoring stone was satisfying. His hammer-taps became less tentative as he began to gauge the impact of the tools. *Mason: stone-scorer, granite-cutter, rock-cleaver.*

'Not as easy as you thought, is it?' The mason sounded smug. 'But you've made your mark and that's a start.'

Skarfr looked at his carving with pride. 'People will see the mark I've made, for hundreds of years.'

The stonemason laughed. 'Oh, it will be there all right, but under a good layer of lime and whitewash. Nobody will know our names are there.'

Skarfr felt foolish. Then he said, 'But we'll know.'

The man smiled. 'Aye, that we will.' He took the hammer and chisel back, added, 'If you're back this way, come and see me. I'll let you know if there's a place for a lad willing to work.'

'Thanks,' said Skarfr, with no intention of taking up the offer, any more than he intended to return to Freyja's cot.

He continued on his way towards the harbour but his elation diminished when he recognised a forlorn figure in a dun dress, trudging towards him. Poor Hlif. But why should she spoil his day? He would say something comforting and leave her. Something comforting like—

His mind was still a complete blank when Hlif reached him.

'Where have you been?' he asked, buying time to find warm, helpful words. 'I've looked everywhere for you.'

Her expression lightened a little. 'I went to the sea,' she said.

He'd often gone to the sea when he missed his parents, when he was hiding from Botolf, when he needed peace and cormorants.

He was going to say so when she sniffed him. Her face took on a pinched look, the freckles bunching and uglier than usual.

'I can smell her on you,' she spat and stalked past him. 'Worse than a fish midden. Stay away from me!'

He flushed, realising that the stonemason had guessed too.

Trailing behind Hlif like a beaten cur, Skarfr plodded back to the wagon, where Viggo was folding the empty table and talking earnestly to a herdsman, easy to identify from his crook and his knife, leather pouch, awl and scissors, hanging from a rope belt. And from the smell of sheep.

Without looking up, Viggo said, 'Skarfr, you can walk back with the drover and the sheep we've gained from today's trade.'

His accent so thick the words took time to make any sense to Skarfr, the shepherd said, 'Rest and sup with me in the barn tonight. We'll set off at daybreak.'

Skarfr grunted assent. That suited him fine. He could avoid company and conversation. He didn't so much as glance at Hlif as he followed the shepherd but he knew from the coldness on the back of his neck that she was ignoring him. Until now, when it was broken, he hadn't realised there was a connection between them, a pact against the cruel world, defiance of the fates themselves.

Still, he told himself. It was worth it. He scratched himself between the legs absent-mindedly.

The shepherd looked at him, sniffed and smiled.

*Surely not over the stink of sheep?*

'Ewe's grease rubbed on your cock and armpits,' advised the man, without breaking his stride. 'Or you'll be scratching till you bleed in three weeks' time.'

Mortified, Skarfr said nothing. When they reached the outskirts of the town where the flock was penned in a large stone fold beside a bothy, he was relieved to see a water trough. Feigning nonchalance, he stripped and doused his body, scrubbing with his nails. Was it his fate to freeze in water troughs after evil-smelling encounters? This time he could blame nobody but himself and there was no Brigid here to comfort him.

The shepherd entered the bothy, came out with a blanket, which he passed to Skarfr, who wrapped it around his goose-pimpled damp nakedness.

His breeks and tunic laid out on the low peat roof to air, Skarfr went into the shelter and sat huddled in his blanket on the straw, as near one curved wall as he could manage. Meant for one person, there was barely room in the bothy for the two of them and the smell of sheep from the shepherd was overpowering as he passed cheese and a stale bannock to Skarfr.

He hunkered down onto the straw, beside the one blanket for his own night covering.

Skarfr suddenly realised what the gift of food, shelter and warmth meant to the shepherd.

'Thank you,' he said, accepting a swig of ale from the leather bottle offered. He wondered what he could give as guest-offering to his host. It seemed to be a day of offerings and he mentally reviewed what remained in his pack.

He pulled his flute out of the pack.

'Shall I play for you?'

'Aye.' The shepherd nodded and closed his eyes, his back propped against the stone wall.

Skarfr tested the notes. Thanks to his weathering of the pipe, playing a tune daily, it had taken no harm from its manhandling on the beach and had regained its plaintive tone.

He played a merry scale. The start to the day, anticipation and friendship.

Then he let the music take him somewhere darker, flight from rejection, Hlif and he separate, each one alone.

Slow and sensual, the pipe recalled a woman's touch, a body soft and curved, opening to his own.

Wonder and then loss, as the last note lingered, a long kiss goodbye to a boy's innocence.

Skarfr wiped the pipe clean of his spit with a rag-wrapped rod. *So it is,* he thought. *There is saliva in the making of music. The body makes magic in the way of this world, with mess.*

The shepherd could have been asleep, his face immobile and his eyes still closed, but tears glistened on his cheeks as they grimed tracks down to the folded hands.

Skarfr's sense of shame lifted and he lay down to sleep, lulled by the music that played on in his mind.

# CHAPTER TWENTY-TWO

When the sheep were safely penned near Orphir, Rognvald's shepherd came to count and check the new flock. He released them five at a time to the care of some ragged children and he tallied each group with a notch on a stick, in the manner of his profession. When he was satisfied that the trade deal had been fulfilled, the two shepherds broke bread, drank together and shared some advice on treating murrain and other ovine maladies. Skarfr waited, witness once again to a bargain but this time the outcome left only goodwill.

'Here, take this.' With a wink, the Kirkjuvágr shepherd gave Skarfr a rancid rag that stank of sheep. 'Sheep grease,' confirmed the shepherd.

*Thank the gods the man hadn't said what it was for.*

Rognvald's shepherd was more interested in somebody approaching from behind Skarfr. 'All's as it should be, Hlif. You can tell the Jarl I thank him and the carter did well. You can be sure we'll have a full wagonload of bales for market next year.' He waved a hand at his new flock. 'I'll take these up to top pasture now.

'Yes, do.' Hlif had that air of distance she assumed in her role of steward – or when she was too annoyed with Skarfr to speak to him. He soon wished that were the case.

'The Jarl gave me coin for beads and ribbons, a while back,' she said, without meeting his eyes. 'But I bought this instead. For you.' The words were fired at him like sling from a shot and he flinched.

Whether he took the double-sided bone comb or not, he could not redeem himself, so he erred on the side of courtesy, without risking more words than, 'Thank you.'

'You'll find the fine-toothed edge particularly useful,' she told him, her lip curling.

Skarfr felt the heat rising to his face, knowing full well why she thought he'd need a nit comb.

'If I do, you can show me how it works,' he challenged her, swaggering a bit as he'd seen men do when they were chasing a woman. The words had sounded wittier in his head than spoken but flirting was a new game he was determined to master now he knew where it could lead, if he was lucky. Not with Hlif, obviously.

'I'm sure you'll find someone more suitable,' she spat back but her face betrayed her embarrassment, bright blotchy red and she almost ran away from him, back towards the Bu.

*Still a little girl,* thought Skarfr airily, as he put the comb in his pack. Just in case. And the workmanship was good so he would use the wide-toothed edge to tame his black tangles.

He barely had time to stow his possessions in the shared chest, when one of the pot-boys told him that Thorbjorn was looking for him. His elation over his adventures fizzed into acid in his throat. Which Thorbjorn would he meet? His enemy, his mentor, or the man afraid of the gods' message?

'There you are!' Thorbjorn's eyes were clear Madonna blue, innocent of sin as the Virgin herself. 'I want six men to go with me to the Big Island of the Papar. You can row?'

What had Skarfr expected from a seasoned warrior? Bloodied

hands, a racked conscience, some trace of two men's murders in their killer's face? Instead there was peace and purpose.

Although he'd never rowed to others' rhythm, Skarfr nodded. It was music and he'd pick up the beat.

'You're not afraid of men in dresses?' The light tone would have alerted Skarfr to the jest even if he'd not been tutored by Botolf and forced to learn all the Jarl's poems.

'Not if they're half-men of the White Christ,' replied Skarfr, as he remembered the lines inspired by Rognvald's first visit to Papey Meiri, the isle of the Pope's men.

*The strangest sixteen girls I ever saw,*
*a tuft of hair on each smooth brow.*
*No tresses*
*nor decoration on their dresses*
*but on this isolated island*
*reached by stormy seas,*
*each man-maid prays and then confesses.*

For all his piety, even Rognvald had been startled by a community of monks, whose appearance was against nature, both in their strange hairstyles and in their women's garb. Had they not been Christian holy men, the Thing would have pronounced a sentence of exile on men who dressed as women. But, distasteful as their ways might be to any who respected the old gods, the monks were scribes and guardians of precious books, so Thorbjorn's purpose in visiting them was not difficult to guess. It was Thorbjorn as Klerk who was setting sail for Papey. But first they were all warriors and seamen.

Two hours march to Kirkjuvágr, where one of Rognvald's ships waited, then four hours by sea, sheltered by islands on both sides. Time enough for a lord to tell his seer, 'Your telling was true and

Frakork can rest. Grith and Jedvard died slowly, watching their own guts spill. With no weapons in their hands.'

Skarfr's stomach rolled like the sea and with his inexperience as excuse, he turned away from the bloodthirsty glitter in Thorbjorn's eyes to spill his last meal over the side of the ship.

*Grith.* Growly Voice, who'd humiliated Skarfr and thrown his possessions onto the sand in mock auction.

*Jedvard.* The bull-necked neighbour from the feast night, who'd saved Skarfr from his own best instincts. Who'd been kind to a drunk dimwit of a boy.

Though Skarfr could not find it in himself to care about Grith's death, he had served Jedvard a foul turn. He had not known the man was Sweyn's. *Would it have made any difference?* his conscience asked. *You would have peddled the same false visions, knowing that the gods would not take your sacrilege lightly.*

Nor would Hlif.

But it was done and could not be changed. A man lived with his actions and their consequences.

Skarfr straightened, wiped his mouth on his sleeve and took his turn at the oar, which stilled his churning mind and settled his stomach. *Oar: wave-dipper, foam-sweeper, bark-whipper.*

Luckily, Thorbjorn too seemed focused on the rise and swell of the sea, the dip and turn of oars and showed no sign that he found Skarfr's reactions odd. His frown was for Skarfr's rowing technique.

He shook his head. 'Sit tall, put your back into it and use your stomach muscles. Stop working your arms so much. Watch me.'

Thorbjorn took over the oar and demonstrated a fluid movement that didn't strain the back or arms. He shipped the oar and stood up from the bench, cat-like in his agility despite the rolling boat. He punched Skarfr lightly in the shoulder.

'Your muscles are solid but a man who uses this—' he punched Skarfr a little harder, in the belly this time, which tensed automatically from *glima* training, 'a man who uses these muscles will row faster and better.'

The route was easy in calm seas, sheltered between the islands of Hrolfsay, Eday and Vestrey, and with a simple entry to the beach at Papey Merei where men in tonsures and brown sacking dresses greeted them in the name of God and Jarl Rognvald.

'Jarl Harald,' corrected Thorbjorn. 'With Rognvald away from the islands, Jarl Harald is sole lord and, as his guardian, I speak for him. Show me the books. My men would appreciate ale and victuals while I work. Come, Skarfr.'

Startled, Skarfr followed the abbot and Thorbjorn, with a wistful backward look at the men heading towards the tables laden with food. He need not have worried. Two brothers brought them jugs of ale, with bread and creamy curd cheese, which they ate in the abbot's private chamber, a small area curtained off, furnished with four stools, a bed and a small table. The abbot said grace with rather more piety than was customary in the Jarl's Bu, then they set to. A wooden crucifix hung on the wall but the suffering of Christ did not interfere with the priority of sating hunger.

In between mouthfuls, Thorbjorn grilled the abbot on lambing, beekeeping, the weather and cheese-making. Skarfr could tell from the sharpness of the questions and from the abbot's replies, that Thorbjorn was tallying numbers in his head and following up any discrepancies. His skill at calculation made the shepherd's notches on a stick seem as primitive as using fingers.

When he was presumably satisfied he'd covered all the information needed to audit the written accounts, Thorbjorn was ready to see the books. The abbot led the way to what he called the scriptorium, which was as sophisticated as the sleeping quarters were rustic.

The stone walls were clad with woven fabric, as well caulked against draught and damp as a ship's timbers, and not a speck of dust dared approach the two shelves which housed the books. One shelf carried the ledgers, which were similar to those Hlif consulted for her stewardship. Nothing there to interest Skarfr although he knew that Thorbjorn would inspect them in all their boring detail and conclude the *tiund,* the percentage of income due, and the rents owed by the church to the Jarl. Thorbjorn would keep some of the monies, Rognvald would take his share and the second set of accounts would declare the adjusted sum owed to *his* overlord, the king of Norðvegr.

Skarfr was only too aware that the sums discussed could set him up as a lord, buy a horse, weapons, even a dragon ship, but such dreams were painful. The only way he could survive the never-ending years until he came into his inheritance was by not thinking of his future freedom.

But one book on the other shelf was so far beyond even his future means that his hand reached out of its own accord to touch the leather binding, trace the gilt letters with a fingertip.

'Don't touch, boy!' warned a brother, who'd stopped his work to guard his precious library from the rustic visitors.

Skarfr jerked back as if scalded but Thorbjorn and the abbot seemed undisturbed.

'Show the boy your work, Brother Kristian. Shine a light on his ignorance and he will teach others the true value of the holy word.'

Brother Kristian's sour face showed little enthusiasm for his task, which no doubt meant he was all the more holy for carrying it out. He moved slightly to let Skarfr join him at a lectern, just like the one the priest used in Orphir's round kirk as a stand for the bible, from which he read in Latin.

On this lectern were two books, both lying open. Skarfr gasped at their beauty. The black lettering looked the same in both books but in the margins, white-tailed hawks flew in sage-green forests. Branches twined like snake-knots and leaves shimmered. Demure ladies leaned graciously over their kneeling knights, silk dresses blooming in primrose, ochre and a turquoise that would gladden Hlif's heart. If he were ever rich, he would give her a robe like this, elegant drapes of silk in her favourite colour. The comb she'd given him was carefully wrapped in linen among his other treasures.

'They're exquisite, aren't they?' Thorbjorn's voice startled him, so lost had he been in contemplating this mythical world.

'How can this be a bible?' asked Skarfr. 'There is no hunting or... ' he sought a polite word, 'courting in the priest's words in the kirk.' *Except to say they're sins*, he thought but was conscious of the monks listening to his foolish outburst.

The abbot replied, 'Brother Kristian brought his skills as a scribe from Dunholm, along with his tools, inks and books to be copied.'

'That's where the cathedral-builders came from, the ones working in Kirkjuvágr,' Skarfr realised.

One eyebrow raised, the abbot observed, 'You are knowledgeable for one so young. Yes, Brother Kristian came with them as advisor to the artists glorifying our St Magnus but he suffered from the clamour of the town and found peace again here with us as soon as his work was done. He copies and illustrates God's Word in this beautiful manner so that men open their hearts in wonder at the sight of it. Just as they will do when the apse of St Magnus Cathedral arches over them to the heavens. A reminder of the ineffable glory of the one God.'

Brother Kristian added, 'Common sinners see God more easily in a tree than in a litany of repentance so we scribes draw on our earthly knowledge to add colour to the sacred word, to make a rainbow that leads men to the Lord.'

With reverence, he turned the pages so Skarfr could see the finished work.

Glorious colour indeed, although Skarfr remained as sceptical about whether pictures of big spotted cats encouraged devout contemplation as he was about there being only one god. No doubt all these creatures represented some vice or virtue but all he could see was the way they leaped off the page, so lifelike.

He couldn't imagine the priest telling his congregation a funny story about an upside down world where two hares formed a hunting party, slinging a man's body on a pole between them after a successful day. You couldn't look at such misrule without smiling, as on Twelfth Night when the world was turned topsy-turvy for entertainment, when a boy could be bishop.

How could such a morose cleric produce these jewelled cameos? Surely a man's interior no more matched his exterior than the ermine lining of a shabby cloak.

Brother Kristian pointed to the row of shells and pots on the second lectern.

'Glue and tempera to bind the inks to the page. And the colours pooling in the shells are inks. Black from gallnuts for the text and outlining: red cochineal, blue azurite, green verdigris and yellow saffron. Gum arabica to keep the ink on the nib but not bind to the page, good for black, so you can remove it if need be.' He indicated a leather wineskin. 'A little ale for thinning.'

He turned back to the page he was working on and now Skarfr could see the ruled lines to keep the writing straight and all the different inks. They looked so much brighter on the page than they did in the shells, as if the ink was wet. But if that were the case, the pages would have stuck together when Brother Kristian showed them his previous work.

'How do you make the pictures light up that way?' he asked.

The monk picked up a glimmering silvery sheet from the lectern holding his tools.

'Precious silver or gold foil illuminates the manuscript,' he said. 'I paste this onto the parchment as a base before I outline and colour with inks.'

This one page was probably worth more than the longhouse Skarfr would inherit.

*Scribes: quill-gilders, virtue-touchers, angel-sketchers.*

'In a different world, I would have done such work as this and been happy,' Thorbjorn mused. 'No carping women and no quarrelling knaves. May I add one small creature here?' he asked, pointing at a small blank space at the bottom of the left-hand margin.

Brother Kristian frowned and shook his head but the abbot spoke first.

'Lord Thorbjorn's hand is fine and steady. You may entrust him with God's work.'

'Young man.' Skarfr jumped as the abbot addressed him. 'Brother Kristian carries the burden of an extraordinary talent. You ask yourself why this is a burden?' The abbot paused to allow reflection, in the manner of one accustomed to instructing acolytes in theology. Botolf had talked in the same pedagogical style, so Skarfr knew not to speak.

'It is a burden because with talent comes the sin of pride. Brother Kristian has laboured as many years on his spiritual illumination as on that of manuscripts and his humility is hard won.'

He smiled ironically. 'Indeed, I should not praise him as that makes it even harder for him. Lord Thorbjorn, your offering is accepted.'

Skarfr looked at the priceless parchment, imagined a quill's nib scratching a hole through the paper, a blob of crimson bloodying the damsel's fair oval face; his stomach lurched on Thorbjorn's behalf. But, instead of looking daunted by the pressure, Thorbjorn Klerk's face was sunshine-clear, as joyful as when he wrestled.

He smiled again. From his mischievous expression, Skarfr expected the creation of some humorous little beast, a mouse in a lady's bodice or some such misplaced feature, to amuse the reader. He bit his lower lip in concentration, lightly etched a silhouette in thin black. A bird.

*Probably a hawk.*

Thorbjorn made jagged rocks with swift black lines, then browned the gallnut ink with saffron-yellow for fill, and a little verdigris green for seaweed. Azurite blue ripples of sea. Then the detail of the bird, its black feathers, shape proud as any eagle as it hung its wings wide to dry and stretched its sinuous throat upwards.

*Cormorant*, Skarfr recognised with a jolt.

And there it was, the expected touch of humour but surprisingly gentle, respectful of the book. Thorbjorn used the penknife to reveal a wriggle of foil, and at once a silver eel slithered around the cormorant's beak, trying to escape the long stretch of throat. The beak pointed upwards to swallow its prey and the eel's upper body writhing towards the scene above, so that it seemed to be a serpent seeking a tree.

Thorbjorn's style was bolder, with fewer lines and a simpler representation than Brother Kristian's work but the execution drew the eye back up towards the scenes above, in completion and homage. And it *was* a cormorant.

'There, fish-eater.' Thorbjorn stepped back to check his work, glanced at Skarfr, who flushed. 'You can make one point for the eye as the head is turned. And then I'll silver the beak. Use the point of the penknife to scrape off a tiny circle of black ink. Make your mark.'

Brother Kristian exclaimed in horror and the abbot looked disapproving but nobody stopped Thorbjorn passing the penknife to Skarfr, who remembered watching the stone sculptor.

*A steady hand and a confident mark.* Heart thumping, Skarfr took the knife. Praying the hardest he'd done in his life, he made the tip pirouette on the place where he knew the eye should be, then he gave the penknife back to Thorbjorn. Two sure strokes and the beak was limned in silver.

Brother Kristian grunted. 'It's good work,' he acknowledged.

The abbot peered at the open page and read a line in Latin, then smiled and translated for Skarfr. 'The Lord Christ sayeth, 'I will make you fishers of men.' Most apt,' he told Thorbjorn. 'Very amusing illustration but well executed too.'

Radiant, Thorbjorn said, '*This* will last forever, young Skarfr. *This* is why you should learn to read and to write. And why the sagas will be forgotten when the last forgetful old man is unable to pass on the misremembered words he was told in his youth. *This* is the Christians' master-stroke.'

'The Christ Jesus is the Christians' master-stroke,' rebuked the abbot, but without anger. Thorbjorn politely tilted his head and smiled in acknowledgement, without professing a change of opinion.

Instead, he spoke to Skarfr, as if just the two of them were in the alcove. He nodded towards the pages open on the lectern, glowing in vermilion and gilt.

'The men, including Sweyn the hero, say this is women's work, boring, but they are no more civilised than swine. What's boring is hacking off heads in endless feuds but,' he shrugged and gave a dazzling smile, 'I'm good at that too.' He looked almost boyish in his exuberance and the evidence of his penmanship turned arrogance to statement of fact.

The abbot shook his head but the corners of his mouth twitched and there was no mention of the danger of pride.

'Learn to read and to write, Skarfr. I will teach you and Harald together.'

He *could* read and write, Skarfr wanted to say, and his head was full of verse, but he knew his runes fell as far short of this miraculous book as swine did in courtly ways.

# CHAPTER TWENTY-THREE

They'd been sparring on the training-ground but Skarfr no longer felt the same enthusiasm. Not for months, not since Harald had proved inept at literacy and Thorbjorn had dropped the lessons. Skarfr's quickness merely added salt to the wound and before he realised he should hide his ability, both Harald and Thorbjorn had turned cold to him. His insistence that Frakork was satisfied and no more visions had come to him dropped his value further in the Klerk's eyes and Skarfr was unremarkable among the men training, Rognvald's men – or at least at first. What would once have been a dream come true tasted sour now he'd known a lord's confidences, attention that lit up both of them with a thirst to learn, to achieve, beyond 'hacking off heads' as Thorbjorn had said.

But he worked, until he too could now say he was a skilled fighter, at least in practice sessions. He earned respect from the others for his co-ordination and strength, his perfect timing and, above all, his keen observation which had beaten many an opponent, whose weakness was always spotted and used against him. Not only that but Skarfr was doggedly working with a variety of weapons in both hands, as determined to master them all as he'd once been to recite kennings.

From the corner of his eye, he noticed Inge and her women coming to watch, as they often did. His heart sank at the prospect of the vinegar in that marriage souring even the simple pleasures of physical work. But Thorbjorn's attention was elsewhere.

*As always.*

A bonny fair-haired lass had flirted her hem just enough to show her fine ankle and her willingness. Sure enough, with little pretence at decorum, she had detached herself from the group and was hanging on Thorbjorn's arm before the couple vanished out of sight.

*Looking for a wall, no doubt.*

Skarfr tried to focus on his archery but he was at the end of his session and the day was spoiled. He handed the bow and quiver to the next man, wishing for the thousandth time that he had his own weapons and didn't have to adjust his every shot and strike to whatever misshapen lump of wood or metal was his penance for the occasion.

'See the girl in green with the brooches above her station?' The acidic voice interrupted his petulance. Skarfr instinctively followed Inge's suggestion and there *was* one woman in green, her face like soured milk.

'She was the one before this brazen whore.' Inge sought his eyes, challenging. 'And her expression looks like yours. He gets bored quickly, you know. I'm almost glad I saw the real Thorbjorn before he tried the charm you all see. I had the antidote before the love potion and now it will never work. But I pity you. My husband does wreak havoc wherever he goes.' She might have been talking about a market-trader who sold short measure, for all the emotion in her voice.

Neither his experience nor the verses he'd learned gave Skarfr a suitable response but courtesy demanded he say something.

'I'm sorry,' he stuttered. 'It must be difficult for you.' He looked in the direction in which Thorbjorn and his bawd had gone.

He had not expected Inge to be amused by his words.

'You don't think I'm jealous, do you? Or feel slighted?' She looked closely at him. 'You do, don't you!' She laughed 'It's been a long time since my lord risked his manhood wilting in my bed, I can assure you, and I shall keep it that way.'

So Hlif was right. *Women's weapons.*

His mouth engaged before he could stop himself. 'But how will you get children?'

She seemed even more amused. 'Are you offering your services, my fine young man?'

Luckily, she didn't wait for a reply and ignored Skarfr's scarlet face. She chucked him under the chin, trailing a white finger down to the opening of his jerkin. 'If I thought Harald would grow into a man of your attractions, I might consider him as a future prospect but,' she shrugged her slim shoulders, jiggling the brooches on her pinafore straps, 'he will become even uglier.'

Shocked and seeing no escape, Skarfr thought he'd lose nothing by being bold. 'Why don't you ask for a divorce?'

Her face hardened. 'You heard my brother. Sweyn's sister has a job to do.'

Now he had successfully diverted her thoughts and her playful fingers, Skarfr was almost disappointed to lose her attention.

'I know what he sees in you,' she told him. 'But he will destroy you. Or Hlif. Or both of you.'

She walked off in the opposite direction from that taken by her husband, leaving Skarfr with the lingering scent of roses and thoughts like tangled wool. Inge talked of Hlif as if she were attached to him in some way. Was he treating her badly? Even if he hadn't been spending so much time with Thorbjorn or training with the other men, he could hardly have gone on errands with her when she turned her back on him at every opportunity.

*Like you do when Thorbjorn comes to training. To see whether he notices you. And he doesn't.*

With a sigh, Skarfr sought out Hlif. When he tracked her down, she was poring over account ledgers in a quiet corner of the Bu. Her pose reminded him so much of Brother Kristian, leaning over an open book placed on one chest, while she used another as a stool. But this page was devoid of colour, as were its contents.

She pretended she hadn't noticed him until he addressed her by name.

'Hlif, have I offended you?' he asked.

'No,' she replied. 'And if you had, why would I care?' She looked back down to her ledger but he thought her finger was underlining a row above that she'd been reading when he reached her.

He considered her reply. It made no sense.

'What are you reading?'

'Two sacks of bere barley; five sheep; seven beehives...' She glanced at him from under her lashes and he knew she was mocking him. Maybe he deserved it.

He remembered his disastrous lessons with Thorbjorn. 'Well you know I can't read those fancy curls, only runes. So you could tell me that it's a recipe for stuffing pike or a witch's brew and I wouldn't know the difference.'

She flushed, was quiet, then looked at him as she had on the beach when they first met. As if she was a wild creature worried he was a predator. Then she'd decided to trust him, her eyes gleaming silver, like the dot he'd opened up on an illustration of a cormorant.

'I could teach you to read,' she said softly.

His pride wanted to say no but the abbot had warned him against the sin of those who were talented.

'I would like that,' he said carefully, not wanting this little bird to fly away again. 'Thank you.'

With a spark of the old friendly sparring, she challenged him. 'You said accounts are boring.'

He didn't rise to the bait. 'If I can read those words,' he pointed at the ledger, 'I'll be able to read anything.'

'Like recipes for stuffing pike or witches' brews.'

'Quite so.'

She made room for him at the lectern and he was aware of her warmth against his side, her scent – dried fruit and spices, not roses. He looked at the squiggles all over the page like an anthill. He picked out one ant, the smallest, and asked, 'What does that say?'

And so it began. First he learned to recognise whole words, then he learned the Norn letters. Hlif didn't know Latin but the letters were the same she said, so one day he might work on that too. Nobody would stop him learning.

When Rognvald returned from Ness, Skarfr and Hlif carried on with their lessons and he did nothing to stop them.

He came back widowed, dull-eyed and curt with anyone who encroached on private matters. He quashed any suggestion that he need not resume his duties as Jarl straight away and, after interrogating Thorbjorn about the past months, he tasked that lord with visiting the furthest islands to audit and report back. Smarting from the obvious demotion and the temporary exile, Thorbjorn had no option but to relinquish the power he'd enjoyed in Harald's name. Rognvald's incessant praise for the role played by Thorbjorn in his absence rubbed salt into the wound, because it was true and because giving such praise was an act of authority. When the Jarl broke a bracelet and gave Thorbjorn three silver rings in gratitude, the message was clear. Rognvald was the Ring-Breaker and he was back. His substitute could now return to his own duties.

Although there were dark circles under the Jarl's eyes, his grasp of politics was sharp and he'd brought news from Ness that almost made Thorbjorn's sullen mouth twitch into a smile. Sweyn had of course succeeded in his support for Holbodi and driven the Bretlandmen from Tiree. They fled from there to the Isle of Man, where they killed the local chieftain before continuing westwards.

When Sweyn reached the Isle of Man he found a rich angry widow and no foes. So he offered her marriage and revenge, a combination that allowed him a warm bed when he felt like it and raids up and down the coast of Bretland when he didn't, which was most of the time.

Rognvald heaved a sigh of relief at Sweyn being fully occupied so far away and at Thorbjorn's apparent compliance with the Jarl's demands.

In such comparative calm, three years passed. Skarfr learned to read the tides and the black squiggles of Norn and its mother tongue Norrøna. He filled out with muscle; competing with him had become the measure of a man's strength and skill in training. He earned respect through his manner.

Sweyn stayed away. If Thorbjorn was stung by Sweyn fathering two sons while no woman bore him any, his face conveyed nothing but his usual mercurial moods, passionate for a project – or a person – one day and bored the next. The Jarl read his moods and kept him travelling around the islands.

One Yuletide, when Skarfr was eighteen and mistletoe from Ness decked the Bu, a symbol of the new year's birth, Hlif kissed him. One moment she was pink-cheeked, saying she'd heard about his recent successes in the training yard and the next she'd stood on tiptoes, pulled his head down towards hers and their mouths had met. Lips touched and parted so quickly Skarfr wondered if it had really happened.

But she'd drunk too much ale and he wasn't the only man she

kissed. It meant nothing. Rognvald spoke sternly to her about wanton behaviour and she complained to Skarfr that a woman couldn't be expected to live like a nun all her life. But the curse and constraints were still on her and Skarfr pretended nothing had happened between them beyond friendship and reading lessons.

Despite his pretence, his mouth remembered the taste of hers and his mind made a verse.

*Mistletoe*

*No harm to Baldr*
*swore the boulders, bears and*
*all of nature's blades.*
*All but mistletoe made vows*
*to Frigg his mother*
*not to harm a hair on Baldr's head.*
*No harm in mistletoe, thought Frigg.*
*So young and green-white innocent,*
*so Frigg his mother thought*
*before her fears shaped tears.*
*Could Baldr's bane be Skarfr's too,*
*Loki's meddling mischief thrown by blind Höðr,*
*who would heedless stop the bolder heart?*

Thorbjorn asked Skarfr at regular intervals whether he'd seen any visions. When told no, he shrugged and forgot his prophet, following whatever skirt or scheme attracted his attention. That suited Skarfr.

Then Sweyn returned.

# CHAPTER TWENTY-FOUR

The day began badly. Skarfr heard that Hlif had been looking for him but there was no sign of her. He finally tracked down the vague information that she'd headed off towards the ring of standing stones at Steinnesvatn. He'd told her often enough that she was too old now to gad about alone, but she still argued that the curse protected her and, anyway, Rognvald was her guardian. If she didn't listen to him, why should she listen to someone barely older than her?

The man who'd seen Hlif head out of the village added, 'Lord Thorbjorn went the same way, not long after, in a foul mood.'

Skarfr's heart stopped.

'Jarl Harald was with him.'

*No need to worry then.* And yet Skarfr's stomach still churned with apprehension. *They probably won't even meet up. And they pass each other daily in the Bu without Thorbjorn ever having noticed Hlif in that way. And Harald is there.*

Harald had grown into a youth every bit as unprepossessing as Inge had predicted, as stolid and competent in all practical matters as he was dismissive of reading, writing and statecraft. If Rognvald's lessons on ruling wisely had taken root, there were no signs of the resulting fruit. Thorbjorn had changed tack when the reading lessons failed. He'd taken Harald with him on voyages around the islands and flattered the boy's self-esteem with fights he'd fixed in advance. Sweyn's absence had weakened the sea-rover's hold in the young Jarl's imagination and Inge was just a woman so Harald now followed his foster-father like an orphaned yellow chick follows the goose it mistook for its mother. They would never be of the same kind however much the chick copied the goose but Skarfr understood the compulsion.

He had tried to remain aloof from Thorbjorn and found this easy when the lord ignored him. But the moment he was singled out again, he was drawn into something that was neither friendship nor respect. He felt special, dazzled by Thorbjorn's unpredictable combination of action and intelligence, so that life became more colourful, cochineal on silver foil instead of charcoal numbers in a drab ledger.

Thorbjorn's renewed interest would always begin with a question about Skarfr's visions but despite the temptation to gain status with further lies, the answer was always, 'None.' Even when Hlif's latest visions filled his mind, could so easily have been adapted to pique Thorbjorn's interest, Skarfr said, 'None.' One small act of atonement for the lie that had murdered two men.

Thorbjorn's humour still blew in Skarfr's direction sometimes, vacillating but irresistible.

'I'm going to Papey Meiri. I want you with me,' made Skarfr's assent a certainty. Although the magical moment of the cormorant's creation was past and never mentioned, Skarfr would be allowed to leaf through the bible and travel by illuminations. Creatures and landscapes he only knew from verse and saga, he saw for the first time. Foxes and tigers, snow-capped mountains and deer-filled forests. Skarfr's head filled to bursting with the poems he would not permit himself to speak aloud. Another penance and a promise to a saint, for which he was rewarded with a warrior's life. Far different from a pot-boy's; his horizons were growing with every book he studied.

One time, when Thorbjorn was busy elsewhere and Skarfr was alone in the scriptorium with Brother Kristian, he had asked casually for the words that meant 'Go and be fishers of men', that he might see them written in the sacred book.

The monk had thrown him a sharp look, not taken in by this display of piety, but said only 'Gospel of St Mark or Gospel of St Matthew. Let me see...' and had turned first to the one that was not the cormorant's page.

After enjoying Skarfr's pretence of enthusiasm for a moment, Brother Kristian relented and said, 'You should see the same story in Matthew too' and turned the pages with reverence until he reached what Skarfr would always call 'the cormorant page'.

The bird stretched to swallow its prey, eye and beak-silver bright, just the way Skarfr remembered. His heart clenched like a fist. It *meant* something when a man offered you a glimpse of his soul in this way, a gift beyond price that could never be taken back. Skarfr stored his knowledge of the real Thorbjorn beside his poetry, deep and secret. The connection when they'd wrestled had begun Skarfr's joy in his own body. The conversations about stars and tides, fate and gods had shaken his mind free of Botolf, free to soar into dangerous thoughts. More poetry.

Inge was wrong. Hlif was wrong. Women could never understand a man like Thorbjorn. They could never keep up with his brilliance of mind or restless body. He, Skarfr, could forgive Thorbjorn's treatment of others because a hero should not be judged by common standards. One woman could never be enough for him and his wife spurned him so what was he to do?

*But not with Hlif.*

Skarfr broke into a run.

He almost ran past the standing stones because their grey domination of the flat grassland showed no hint of human colours.

Then something moved behind one of the big uprights at the back of the circle.

He sprinted straight through the middle, past the long flat slab laid like a table-top. He didn't even touch his amulet for protection against the ancient spirits that haunted this place, so intent was he on reaching the people behind the stones. A change of angle revealed the whole scene.

Harald was lounging against one massive standing stone while Thorbjorn had a woman pinned against its neighbour. *Hlif.*

This time Skarfr would not back away like a good boy. He would not witness another woman's *I'm not afraid of you* face.

'Go on,' urged Harald. 'Same as you did with Inge.'

Blood rushed to Skarfr's head and he charged at Thorbjorn, shouldering him sideways with the impetus of his move.

Taken unawares and when his hands were otherwise occupied, Thorbjorn was panting, confused, his eyes blank.

Skarfr didn't wait for him to recover but knocked him to the ground and pinned him there, watching the lord's face as he realised he was immobilized in a hold that had no way out.

Gradually the light of intelligence returned to Thorbjorn's eyes and his body stopped struggling. He smiled, tried to speak, coughed.

Skarfr loosened his grip but didn't move to stand up.

Thorbjorn managed a pale copy of his usual ironic drawl. 'You should have said she was your whore. You've kept that secret, haven't you! I should have known when she tried the "I have visions" trick on me to get me to stop.'

Startled, Skarfr released Thorbjorn completely, got to his feet and looked at Hlif for the first time.

Her red hair was loose and wild around her bare shoulders. One side of her pinafore top was ripped and hanging, the other side wrenched down her arm. As she adjusted her clothes, tried to pin the bodice back up with her strap brooches, Skarfr could see the silken white skin from her throat to her fingertips, as freckled as her face.

*Like fine lace.*

'Are you all right?' he asked. Thorbjorn was standing now, breathing deeply. Harald merely watched as if the scene had taken a different but equally interesting turn, for an observer.

Hlif's eyes blazed. 'My virginity is intact, if that's what you mean.'

Thorbjorn grinned at her. 'So you say.' He winked at Skarfr, who maintained his self-control with difficulty. 'But you shouldn't have lied about having visions.' He shook a finger at her as if she was a naughty child. 'Your lover here told me about his second sight years ago and the gods won't look kindly on your pretence.'

Hlif looked at Skarfr in anguished silence.

He only hesitated for a second then said, 'They were her visions, not mine.'

Thorbjorn laughed. 'You don't think I'm going to believe that! Very noble to lie for your lady but it won't work with me. I have a nose for the truth and have known you a long time.'

He cast a look of regret towards Hlif. 'Which is why you can fuck her instead.' He gave a mock bow, as if to a king. 'Come on Harald, let's find other sport.'

Skarfr clenched his jaw and fists, told himself Thorbjorn was one Jarl's foster-father and the other's trusted advisor, that a fight would achieve nothing. He needed to swing an axe, cut off Thorbjorn's head –and he needed to stay calm. His body shook with the clash of instinct and reason.

Hlif started walking back towards the village, still in a state of disarray. He knew from her straight back how angry she was. Not just with Thorbjorn.

'Wait! Hlif!' He caught her up but she wouldn't look at him or speak.

He took off his cloak and gave it to her.

She took it, pulled the hood over her spill of bronze curls and marched steadily back to the Bu.

'I'm making sure you get back safely whether you like it or not,' he told her.

Still no word.

Just before they reached the first building, Skarfr came to a decision. 'I'm make a formal complaint against Thorbjorn to the Jarl. For what he tried to do to you.'

Hlif looked at him with contempt and still said nothing. She stalked through the entrance to the Bu, followed by Skarfr, but when she slipped behind the curtain veiling the women's quarters, he could go no further. He turned back and sought the Jarl, full of righteous indignation, increased by his pangs of conscience. If only he could explain to Hlif why he'd stolen her story. The fear, the heat of the moment. He'd done the same as she had for the same reason.

*But they weren't your visions. And you could have confessed then. It's too late now.*

It couldn't be too late. He'd get justice from Rognvald for Thorbjorn's assault on Hlif and all would be well.

# CHAPTER TWENTY-FIVE

S karfr could not believe how difficult it was to make a formal complaint. After finding Rognvald, he had to ask for a private word and the furrows of the Jarl's brow suggested this was not a good time.

Nevertheless, Skarfr owed it to Hlif to persevere and so he insisted.

'Well?' snapped Rognvald, when nobody was in earshot.

Which is when Skarfr realised he had no idea what words to use for the thing that had happened. He knew it was wrong and he knew it shouldn't be allowed to happen but he was speaking on Hlif's behalf and that tied his tongue.

He had to say something, if only to stop the Jarl glaring at him. 'Sire, I witnessed Lord Thorbjorn...' What *had* he seen? He couldn't describe the state of Hlif's clothes without seeming vulgar. *Skin like fine lace. Clouds of red freckles on white marble.*

He swallowed and tried again. 'Sire, I witnessed Lord Thorbjorn being unmannerly towards Hlif.' Rognvald looked at him sharply and Skarfr corrected himself. 'Towards Lady Hlif, your ward. Physically unmannerly,' he stressed, hoping Rognvald would get the message. 'I'm bearing witness, making a formal complaint.'

'Are you indeed.' The Jarl looked down his nose at the source of such an unpleasant statement. 'Has my ward been injured?'

Did he mean wounded or did he mean raped? Or both? The answer was the same in either case.

'No,' said Skarfr 'but if I hadn't been there...' He tailed off, thinking of who else *had* been there.

'*If* is a horse nobody rides,' responded Rognvald curtly. 'My ward was no doubt behaving in an unseemly fashion yet again, attracted Lord Thorbjorn's attention and you misunderstood the situation.'

'No!' blurted out Skarfr. 'I did not misunderstand the situation.'

'Was Lady Hlif alone, far from the village?'

'Yes but...' Rognvald had entirely the wrong impression. What could Skarfr say to put him right? 'She meant for me to accompany her but she hadn't found me.'

Now the Jarl's eyes narrowed. 'There were no other suitable protectors available?'

'No. I mean yes.' Skarfr flushed, knowing full well Hlif's friendship with him would not please the Jarl.

Rognvald's tone was icy. 'You're right. I should speak to my ward about her reputation. So forget this nonsense about Lord Thorbjorn and forget my ward. You're not a boy anymore and although her looks are against her, she has other qualities. But she's not for you or any man.'

Skarfr couldn't believe his ears. Rognvald thought *he* was a threat to Hlif. He stuttered a protest but Rognvald cut him short.

'No doubt you think I'm cruel, withholding consent to her marriage. You imagine the joys of the marriage-bed, children...' He held Skarfr's gaze and repeated heavily, 'Children. Whose grandfather murdered a saint, whose mother has passed this cursed blood on to them. The lure of her youthful body would quickly pass and no marriage would survive the curse of Hlif's lineage.

'It is because I care about her that I forbid marriage! She will never watch a husband's eyes accuse her of destroying his life. She will never see her children doomed to end their line or pass on such a curse.

'As my housekeeper, Hlif has a worthy occupation, respect and security. No man who cares for her would take that from her! Do you understand yet?'

'No,' said Skarfr stubbornly.

'Then stay away from her until you do. And then stay away from her *because* you do. That's an order. She is not your concern. Nor is Lord Thorbjorn.'

Banned from seeing Hlif. Not until the sentence had been passed on him did Skarfr realise how much their time together meant. He had seen her as a friend, not... *Fine lace freckles on porcelain skin.* It was unjust. Thorbjorn should be the one rebuked by the Jarl, ordered to stay distant from Hlif.

'My reading lessons...' he queried tentatively, hoping.

'Are ended.' Rognvald exploded. 'God's blood! Don't take me for a fool. If you haven't learned to read in however many years you've been taking *lessons* from my ward, you never will.'

Skarfr turned to leave, knowing his resentment was expressed in every stiff line of his body.

'I haven't dismissed you,' growled the Jarl. 'And there are more important matters brewing. You can put your restless mind to work as witness to Sweyn's petition and my judgement.'

*Witness again. But only when it suited Rognvald.*

'Lord Sweyn has returned?' Skarfr asked, curious despite himself.

'He has settled his wife and sons on Gareksey and sent word that he comes here today. You may expect him to be foul-tempered and, unlike Lord Thorbjorn—' the Jarl fixed Skarfr in an accusatory stare 'Sweyn has no loyalty to Orkneyjar or its rulers.'

Foul-tempered was an understatement. Sweyn paid the barest of respects to Rognvald before launching into a tirade against his erstwhile bosom friend Holbodi, which finished with, 'bastard runt of a spineless litter shall not cruise the Western Isles with his new friends the Bretlandmen thumbing his nose at Orkney.'

Skarfr gathered that Holbodi had left Sweyn in the lurch to form a more profitable alliance with his former enemies, the very raiders he'd enlisted Sweyn's help to pursue. The falling-out was due to a miscalculation on Holbodi's part. Seeing Sweyn's dragon ships outnumbered, he had withdrawn his own from the battle, expecting Sweyn's death and a negotiation with the victors in calmer times. Instead, Sweyn's superior skill had triumphed over his opponents and he'd survived the encounter despite Holbodi's cowardice. But he'd lost one ship and a younger brother. He was not in a forgiving mood. He wanted ships. And vengeance.

'Again,' said Rognvald. 'Why should I risk men and ships again, this time for your quarrel with Holbodi, the very man you begged me to help last time you petitioned me?'

Sweyn threw his head back and laughed, enjoying the confrontation. He was made for battle, his body as honed as his axe. If rumours were true, his Irish princess wife held little sway over him and his sons would only claim his attention when their blades were steel not wood.

'For plunder, Sire,' Sweyn told him. 'Lend me four of your ships, with your best captains, and we will bring back riches beyond your dreams.'

'That too I have heard before,' said Rognvald but his tone had changed. Cathedrals were expensive to construct.

Sweyn knew he had the attention of the men listening. 'Thorbjorn,' he called. 'Sister's husband. Would you sail with me and be a wealthy man?'

Skarfr had avoided looking at the man he'd named to Rognvald as a criminal but his eyes were drawn to the tall, dark lord in well-oiled leathers with his gold brooches, torque and arm-rings. That he displayed wealth was evident but whether a man in his position could afford such tastes was debatable.

Thorbjorn spoke to Rognvald not to Sweyn and the balance of power shifted again.

'The Bretlandmen are an irritant too near our islands. I could spare the time to make an example of them. Relieving them of their ill-gotten gains seems our Christian duty, don't you think, Sire?'

Rognvald nodded heavily. 'I'll listen to my advisor.'

Thorbjorn smiled. The message had been sent but Sweyn was too busy detailing ships and personnel to show any reaction to how he had got his way.

Giving his own instructions, the Jarl did not forget Skarfr. 'You go on Thorbjorn's ship,' he told him. 'You'll need seaworthy clothes and a pack. Get them from the armoury. And when you return, you will have forgotten the grudge you bear.'

Skarfr's stomach clenched. 'Yes, Sire,' he said and rushed off to find Hlif.

# CHAPTER TWENTY-SIX

'Did you think Rognvald would thank you for witnessing my dishonour? Do you think *I* thank you for stealing my visions, my only weapon against men like Thorbjorn? You left me helpless and then you expect gratitude for rescuing me?

'You didn't ask whether I wanted you to shame me with your tattle-tales against Thorbjorn and I suppose you're upset that you can't have your reading lessons any more. Well, you stupid, lying oaf, you've cost me more than the *pleasure* of *your* company. I won't be able to talk to *anybody* without some carefully chosen ugly dullard glued to my side.

'Go stick your oar in where it belongs, with the rest of the blood-crazed crew Thorbjorn attracts.

'You betrayed me and you mocked the gods with your lies. I hope you have nightmares from here to Tiree and if you survive, don't bother me ever again. Go and enjoy your boat trip, your dream come true!'

Every scathing word was regurgitated by Skarfr's masochistic memory as the horizon heaved and the dragon ship surged from the shelter of Skalpaflói out to the open sea. With a splash and a wooden thunk, Skarfr's oar dipped and rose, turned in its port and slid down again. Splash, creak. Splash, creak.

His muscles remembered what Thorbjorn had taught him on the trips to Papey Meiri. A man who rows with his back and stomach will always be faster and more efficient than one who relies on his big shoulders. Skarfr had both the technique and the arm strength, and he settled easily into the rhythm.

Hlif would be sorry when he died heroically in the coming battle. She would wail at his funeral and regret the last words she'd spoken to somebody who had rescued her, who was her friend. Her only friend. And no wonder, with a temper like that. And the curse didn't even bother him except on her account. So unfair.

'Shake out the sail!' yelled Thorbjorn and the rowers paused. Ahead of their ship, Sweyn's was already sporting its red square, a guide to wind strength and direction for the other four captains.

In front of Skarfr, a dozen men hauled on the ropes, checked that the gigantic sail was unrolling without any hitches. They smoothed out some folds caught in the lines. Hlif could have told him how many women and how many fleeces had gone into making the weave but all a man cared about was the beautiful moment the sail filled with a bellyful of wind.

On Skarfr's right, furthest aft in the ship, Thorbjorn adjusted the wooden steerboard and judged the angle to catch the breeze without the sail flagging or turning directly into the wind, where the ship would stall. The sailors in the mid-section made fast the running rigging and they were under sail.

Soon there were five longships under sail and they were flying, more like dragonflies than ships as their shallow keels skimmed the waves. *Your dream come true.* Hlif was right. Skarfr was riding the white froth on the *Surf-rider*, sailing in the company led by the world's greatest sea-rover, salt spray spritzing his face and verses writing themselves in his head.

Not ships but creatures of the sea kings; *wave-elks on the highway of the sea-prince, Glammi.* Not ships but *wooden serpents; the skis of the swan-plain* and *the steeds of the wind.* Storm-skippers and feather-blown planks. Skarfr's chest swelled and sank like the water all around him. Not sea but gull's land, the earth's girdle. He was surrounded by all the poetry he'd learned by heart and now he was inspired to make more. No wonder that skalds' verses teemed with images of sea-roving.

He shipped his oar and swivelled the wooden cover back over the hole in the side to prevent water coming through. At that moment the sea was calm but who knew what wild winds and currents were in store for them?

'Moderate and a nor'easterly, thank the gods,' observed the weathered seaman who stood by Thorbjorn.

'Why is that good?' Skarfr spoke aloud and the oarsman behind him leaned forward to answer loudly in his ear.

'Usually sou'westerlies here and a westward current, which means we fight both wind and water to go west to the Cape. If the nor'easterly blows strong enough, it can even change the current and lift us around that gods-forsaken headland.'

'Can't we go a different way?' asked Skarfr, watching his home coast disappear out of sight. This was nothing like the predictable voyage to Papey Meiri where the boat steered a comfortable course between Egilsey and Eithee.

Even when fishing, he'd always kept land in sight and nothing had prepared him for this ever-moving expanse of steel grey. No landmarks. The only distinctions marking one patch of water from another were the seabirds and occasional seals, all in perpetual motion.

The gulls followed them hopefully for a while then drifted back towards an unseen shore.

'How do the captains know which way to go when there's no

landmarks?' Released from rowing duty, Skarfr turned to face the oarsman who'd answered his first question.

'First time on a longship? I'm Torsten Holdfast. Everyone calls me Holdfast.' The man was ten years or more older than Skarfr and his face testified to seafaring and raiding: it was leathery and scarred, his eyes glittering ultramarine against the grimy skin.

'Sun and experience, lad. Stars at night in the darker months. Too light in summer,' said Holdfast. 'There's always men on a ship who've done this journey a hundred times, know the tricks and turns of wind and water.'

'What if there's no sun or stars?'

'Then there's just experience and guesswork.'

'If the wind changes or drops?

The sailor sat bolt upright and intoned a prayer, clutching the claw hanging around his neck to ward off spirits. 'Keep your evil words in your head, lad, and don't bring bad luck on us. I've never been blown back by a contrary wind yet and I don't want to be. Rowing out a calm is no fun either.'

As if conjured by his words, a gust of wind took Skarfr by surprise, blowing his hair back off his forehead and chilling the bare skin. With a thump, a black bird blown off course landed on his bench. Equally startled, the cormorant dropped its catch, cocked its head, looked at him out of one knowing sea-green eye, stuttered, 'Crk, crk, crrrruk,' and flew off.

'May Aegir preserve and keep us!' Holdfast looked with horror at the silver mackerel slapping its tail and thrashing about. He crossed himself. The sea-god's name provoked uneasy shuffling among the seamen as they stared at the omen. Better to avoid drawing the gods' attention. And all men knew that a cormorant could carry the spirit of a man dead at sea, back to his own hearth to rest there in peace. Was one of them to know such a fate?

Thorbjorn tagged his second to take over the steerboard,

picked up his axe and ended the wriggling fish with one blow from the handle.

'A gift from Aegir to our newest crew member,' he declared loudly, smiling. 'Skarfr brings us good luck. To fame and fortune we go!'

His shout invited a response from his men and those nearest him roared, 'Fame and fortune!'

The cry was taken up midship, then in the bow as each section caught the mood and yelled a welcome to Skarfr the cormorant, their new mascot.

So easily did interpretation turn bad luck to good: a lesson for Skarfr. How could he hate a leader so skilled and talented, who knew each sailor's work and how to best carry it out? Yet how could he not hate a man who'd tried to force Hlif?

Turning his easy smile on Skarfr, Thorbjorn said, 'Scale and gut it, get Cook to add it to the salt bin with the others. We'll have a grand fire and feast when we reach Skio.' Then he returned to his work as Steersman, watching the two wind-tell ties either side of the sail and watching the other four ships, one hand always on the wooden paddle that steered the ship.

'When will that be?' Skarfr asked Holdfast.

'Three days. Now get some sleep. It's not your watch.'

The ship was divided into six sections of eight men, with duties that matched their placement. Aft with the steersman, Skarfr and his fellows were responsible for the braces and sheets, the ropes attached to the wooden yard spar and the corners at the bottom of the sail. By pulling on these lines or loosening them, they could change the angle of the sail. Like all the crew, they would also row, if required. The day was also divided into six sections: watch and sleep, three times a day, whether sun or stars were in the sky.

Skarfr rolled himself into his sheepskin cover, thankful for the greasy topcoat and heedless of the prickly under-hair. He might be cramped between thwarts, lying on planks that already released the smell of fish and forty men's sweat but at least he was warm.

He knew he should grab sleep while he could but he didn't want to miss any of the journey.

'Will it all be like this?' he asked.

Without taking his eyes off the yard and the sail's angle, Holdfast replied, 'If I'm lucky, we'll cross the Pentlandsfjord like this. But then there's the Swelchie and the Cape. And they'll be on your watch.'

His stomach fluttering, Skarfr shut his eyes and feigned sleep.

# CHAPTER TWENTY-SEVEN

Huddled between the thwarts, Skarfr lay with his eyes shut but that only augmented the intimate stink of men in close quarters. The overlapping planks beneath and beside him had soaked up all the smells, not just the salt water, and the concoction they returned to the air was not conducive to sleep. If he opened his eyes, he saw damp wood, each strake nailed to its neighbour, flexing invisibly as the *Surf-rider* ploughed a white furrow through the waves. Rows of iron clinker nails kept the hull from falling apart. Each nail had been carefully placed, the tail broken off and the head hammered a hundred times, hardened and water-tight. From the nails to the great sail, every part of the ship was seaworthy and each man must keep it so. Seaworthy and clean.

The bucket privy was rough-sluiced, if at all. Each man was supposed to empty it overboard and rinse it after use with seawater from the companion bucket, but some were more fastidious than others. Identifying excrement and culprit could easily escalate from crude jokes to divisive resentment on a long voyage but on a short trip like this one, the captain let the men sort themselves out without rancour.

'Hey, Bent-nose, this looks like your sister,' observed a hoarse voice, followed by laughter and a splash as the offending turd hit the water below.

'More like your wife,' was the cheerful reply.

Tuning out the banter was easier than ignoring all the wooden groans and wave-bumps, so different from Skarfr's usual sleeping environment. The bench in the Bu was hard wood but it was dry and – gods be thanked – didn't buck around like a bee-stung pony. He longed to stretch out full-length and be peaceful in the dark. Never had he appreciated the comfort of that bench in the Bu until now, tossed on a dragon ship. He'd rather be on watch, with something to do, even looking out for the Swelchie, a whirlpool 'the size of a whole village, that would take us down to Hel,' according to Holdfast. The stuff of legend.

Skarfr's heart beat faster, remembering the old poet's words.

*When the world was not full-made, King Frodi of Denmark came by an enchanted quern called Grotti, which would grind out whatsoever he wished, be it peace or riches. On a ship, in secret, he ordered his thralls, Fenja and Menja, to grind out gold and so they sang the Grotti song, heaping gold upon gold, covering the deck.*

*'More!' cried the king.*

*'Are you sure you want more from us and Grotti?' asked the exhausted women.*

*'More!' cried the king, his greed inexhaustible.*

*The sisters shared a long look and began singing again, an ominous note darkening the Grotti song.*

*As the gold petered out, the quern ground out the form of Mysingr, the Sea King, who murdered Frodi and claimed Grotti.*

*'Grind salt!' he ordered the sisters and they did as bid until the ship sank and a* svelgr *whirled in its place, where the sea swirls frothy white into Grotti's eye, the* quern-auga. *And so the sea became salt, thanks to the work of Fenja and Menja, who grind away beneath the sea and take ships as payment.*

Skarfr did not want to die but he longed to add Grotti's song to the verses in his head. If he possessed a magic quern, what would he grind?

*Forgiveness.*

Foolish Christian answer to a foolish question. He had done nothing that wasn't justified. He hadn't been the one who'd killed two men. And the last thing he wanted was forgiveness for others. For Thorbjorn. For Holbodi. They should pay for their crimes. He imagined Sweyn forgiving Holbodi and laughed aloud. What was the point of *manbot* if so much forgiveness was required by the White Christ? It was a man's right to decide whether to forgive and the Thing's work to set a fair price on atonement.

A punch to his shoulder. 'Your watch, lad, before you drive us all mad with your muttering. We're in the aft section and that's where we stay. Check the braces and sheets and don't get in others' way. Pass messages on from Lord Thorbjorn or the other helmsman as men in the foreship don't always hear orders from the stern. The sail itself is not our job, but watch and learn. And if you see the Swelchie I'm already a dead man, so let me sleep.'

With that, Holdfast assumed a foetal position between the thwarts, pulled a cover right over his head and took his turn in sleep – or in writing poetry in his head for four hours. Who could tell what a man did in the privacy of forced rest. Two others in their section were already under their weatherproofs and the two on watch with Skarfr grunted at each other in friendly acknowledgement.

For Skarfr, 'watch' literally meant 'watch'. He watched ropes while his fellow sailors adjusted them, sometimes from instinct, sometimes at Thorbjorn's orders. He saw how the braces turned the yard. The sheets controlled the bottom edge of the sail. Everything affected the sail so Skarfr watched that too.

When the wind picked up and was too fierce, Thorbjorn yelled, 'One reef' and the men midship rolled up the sail to reduce its size. When the wind dropped enough, they unfurled the reef.

Tireless, vigilant, watching over the whole ship from his position by the steerboard, Thorbjorn had taken no rest and his confidence was the wind in his men's sails. Although Sweyn in the *Death-bringer* had taken the lead from the harbour, the five ships were now neck and neck, edging ahead and falling back according to the skittish currents of the Pentlandsfjord and their captains' adjustments. The *Death-bringer* and the *Surf-rider* were the only two with sculpted dragons at the prow and serpent tails, easy to distinguish. The other three longships had sleek curves, curling at the tips of prow and stern, functional and anonymous.

Thorbjorn watched Sweyn's ship as closely as his own, hurling instructions, finding the course to maximise the wind power until he yelled, 'Let's take him!' and with one final adjustment to the sail, the *Surf-rider* stormed ahead of the other four, raising shouts of triumph from the crew.

From that moment on, Sweyn and Thorbjorn competed to find the edge: a gift from wind or tide, an adjustment to sail or steerboard. The two ships played leapfrog, their crews roaring each time their ship took the lead. The other three ships' captains took a staid, less tiring course and let the two dragon ships compete.

Whenever Sweyn pulled ahead, Thorbjorn swore loudly and a rapid volley of instructions spread tension from the serpent's tail screwed to the stern of the ship to its dragon-head prow.

'Land!' yelled the watchman in the foreship and the call was passed back to Thorbjorn, to make sure he'd seen the long run of cliffs, five times the height of Orkney's. He felt the changing currents where the seas clashed with the headland.

'Cape Hvarf!' yelled Thorbjorn.

Skarfr's heart raced like the tide, knowing that the Cape of Turning was the furthest point west before they turned into the shelter of the Suðreyjar and headed south to Tiree. But the Cape also meant a lethal conjunction of conflicting currents, sending cold death out miles from the shore. In a strong wind there was no passage at all but today's prevailing blow was moderate, although it was the unhelpful westerly that usually prevailed here.

Expert captain that he was, Sweyn had already adjusted his course to give the Cape as wide a berth as possible and three longships followed his. But not the *Surf-rider*. Not while the *Death-bringer* was in front.

Black hair flying wild in the wind, Thorbjorn shouted, 'Hold fast!' The seas swirled in angry turbulence, crashing in white stallions, foam at their mouths.

Sleepy-eyed, Skarfr's fellow sailor emerged from his blanket, looked over the port side to the swoops of terns and guillemots clearly visible on the knife-edge cliffs and his eyes quickly returned from dreams to a waking nightmare. He swore long and low but quietly. The captain was still the captain.

'Now! All hands to starboard! Tack north!' The men in the second section, behind the foreship, went into frenzied activity, controlling the front of the sail as it swung.

At Thorbjorn's command, the men all moved starboard, human ballast to take the ship away from its dangerous course too near the Cape.

Lurching at the sudden change of direction, the ship shipped some of the bigger waves and the sail faltered.

A rocky outcrop rose above the crashing waves to starboard and it was the wayfinder who shouted in jubilation, 'Duslic Rock,' as the ship was steered south of the twin crests showing above the water. Skarfr glimpsed two cormorants glistening black as the rocks where they perched, watching over him. Or saying goodbye. He clutched his hammer amulet, praying to any gods who'd listen.

The midshipmen bailed water, men readied themselves to reef and row, and the gods declared for Thorbjorn.

Aegir the sea-god gave them a westward current. The sail stopped fidgeting like a nervous horse, filled and accepted the new direction. The ship sped away from the land and, with careful adjustments, zigzagged on its tack around the cape, far ahead of the other four ships which fought the eastward currents further north. Slower but safer.

'Back to your positions.'

Shaking, Skarfr saw that the men who'd jumped from rest to action were taking over and that his watch was ended. And that they were all still alive.

'What about the Swelchie?' he asked Holdfast, controlling the tremor in his voice.

The seaman looked at him and laughed. 'Thorbjorn's not daft enough to go anywhere near Stroma. We passed the whirlpool by miles during first watch, following Sweyn's lead. He knows this route like the back of his hand, does the sea-rover.' He glanced backwards and added hastily, 'As does Lord Thorbjorn.'

Relief flooded the crew as they rounded the dangerous Cape. Thorbjorn handed the steerboard to the second helmsman now they were heading south and in calm waters, sheltered between the Suðreyjar islands and the Skottish mainland.

'He knows well enough,' he repeated in a whisper, 'but the mad bastard will kill us all to be one up on Sweyn. No good will come of this.'

For all ears, he continued loudly, 'We're on the best ship with the best captain. Look at them, following us like wee doggies.'

The men around him laughed and passed the joke up front to the dragon's head. And they *were* proud of outsailing the greatest sea-rover in the world. But Skarfr too felt no good would come of it. He also wondered where the lash would have landed if Thorbjorn had lost his race. He would not want to be the shroud-pin that broke.

# CHAPTER TWENTY-EIGHT

A night's sleep on Skio, the misty isle, restored the men's good humour. Stomachs full, they'd stretched out for sleep by a cookfire on the beach. A handful of stalwarts had kept watch on each ship and Skarfr thanked the gods he wasn't one of them. As he stretched to wake up, he could feel his legs and arms lengthening, his spine straightening, as his body recovered from the cramped position of 'rest' on board.

Sweyn and Thorbjorn had camped with their men, not needing to speak to each other so not overtly avoiding contact. But the sullen resentment of the former and the glittering triumph of the latter were reflected in the moods of their respective crews. The other three captains and crews shared cookfires and sailors' tales before rolling up in their blankets and leaving this world for the sea of dreams. Whether they had smooth sailing or rode rough mares, all woke up with one thought. *Tiree.* This day, they would show Holbodi what Orkneymen did to allies turned traitors.

Running the *Surf-rider* into the water, Skarfr's blood was pumping more in anticipation than in the heat of a training bout. His first battle. All his work with dagger, shield and axe would be tested in the field, where courage and cowardice could both lead to death. What mattered was not death but honour. Skarfr swore that Hlif would hear only great things of his deeds this day. He *would* be saga-worthy, as his cormorant spirit had foretold.

Early mists lifted and the five ships rode the waves proudly, in a wedge like migrating geese, behind Sweyn, the leader. Thorbjorn's orders were relaxed, with no attempt to draw level. If anything, he let the *Surf-rider* lag behind as if he were saying, 'I can take you any time I like and you know it.' Even when displaying subservience, he conveyed a mocking superiority.

The island of Tiree did not offer the easiest entry, protected by reefs and drying rocks that showed in low seas but ripped apart unwary ships during high tides. But the weather gods stayed with the Orkneymen and Sweyn knew the way to his former friend's stronghold as well as he knew the course home to Gareksey.

Swift as sharks, the ships entered the bay, skimmed the surface with their shallow keels until the first drag of sand underneath slowed them and the men jumped out to complete the beaching. They grabbed shields, axes, daggers and donned whatever protective outerwear they'd brought. Most wore leather jerkins like Skarfr's but he noted with envy that some were padded. The captains all boasted chain-mail byrnies, better protection than leather but stiff from salt spray and in need of oiling. Only Thorbjorn and Sweyn wore helms, which made them easy to spot as they tore up the white sands and headed across the marram grass dunes towards the nearby village.

The bay looked perfect for landing, waves breaking on a long beach. But a misjudgement in poor visibility could easily take a ship too far east where the run into the beach was between two rocky spurs. A sounding with stone and line would deceive, showing depth even while the stone vice crushed the hull. Tiree was not an island to approach without a waymaster who knew the hidden dangers. That made the islanders complacent and they did not expect outsiders.

Even if a lookout had spied the square sails and recognised the threat, the Orkneymen were upon the villagers in Balevullin before they had time to run. Then, run they did, like rabbits.

Taken unawares, flight was the only sensible option but some of the younger men made a stand with whatever tools came to hand: ploughshare, pitchfork or even an iron kettle.

Skarfr had not expected such pathetic opponents, nor the confusion, mess and uproar: buildings and bodies battered and set on fire, smoke masking friend and foe alike. Had they really practised shield-walls in training? The disciplined overlap of shields, shoulder to shoulder, as they marched against equals, was as impossible in this brawl as any form of honour.

Reluctant to kill farm boys, Skarfr fended off any feeble attacks with his shield as he advanced with the others into the village, towards Holbodi's Bu. Only when some unseen foe came at him yelling, then feinted and nearly stuck a dagger in his thigh, did Skarfr instinctively respond. There could be no pause to muse on killing a man for the first time and all he could do was continue, obeying his orders.

The two helms of Sweyn and Thorbjorn were clearly visible in the lead, as the two avenging angels left death and flames in their wake.

Shouts of 'We're coming for you Holbodi!' scattered what was left of resistance and any villagers not dead or held prisoner fled for their lives, pursued inland by the Orkneyman to Holbodi's stronghold.

Leaving a trail of devastation, Sweyn and Thorbjorn arrived at the biggest longhouse in Tiree. Whatever was yelled through the Bu entrance resulted in a speedy exit by pot-boys, thralls and menials but no warriors came out.

'They're all gone, Lord Holbodi and his men. They heard you were coming for them and sailed yesterday,' insisted one of the servants, a towheaded youth who smelled of the smokehouse, too young to know he should hold his peace.

Sweyn didn't believe any of them. He cursed and swung his axe, ensuring that the young man would never speak out of turn again. His head rolled in blood and dust, a last moment of shock in eyes that dimmed already.

The deed had no connection with those casual words, 'hacking off heads'. Skarfr could only stay upright by shutting off compassion as he had once shut off the pain Botolf inflicted. There is a place in every man's spirit that can stay separate from blood and gore, while enduring, watching or carrying out acts of violence.

His guts lurched but Skarfr remained standing. He thought of Hlif's father, commanded to carry out this act against Jarl Magnus. He did not ask himself what he would have done. He watched Thorbjorn and Sweyn, bloody-handed, raging at the stubborn residents of the Bu.

Even after watching their fellow dispatched so brutally, the remainder stuck by their story.

'Go and check the hall,' ordered Sweyn.

'Why don't you just fire the Bu?' jeered Thorbjorn. 'That's what you usually do. Or is that only what you do with old women?'

Like two fighting cocks strutting and pecking at each other before being untied.

Scarlet-faced and brittle, Sweyn said curtly, 'I want that dung beetle to see what's coming to him, not just die.'

But it was true. The Bu was empty of people and probably of valuables too, judging by empty kitchen and caches. The bird had flown the nest and they'd missed him by only a day. If they hadn't rested on Skio, if some messenger hadn't spotted their ships and arrived here first...

Unable to resist another jibe, Thorbjorn pointed out, 'That's two of your sworn enemies playing catch-me-if-you can from ships faster than yours.'

No man loves the one who spells out his failures. First Frakork's grandson Olvir Rosta had eluded Sweyn's revenge and now Holbodi. Maybe it was the reference to his father's murderer that broke through Sweyn's limited self-restraint but Skarfr could have sworn he heard the sea-rover mutter, 'Three,' beneath his breath and his expression set like stone.

'Plunder!' roared Sweyn. 'Take all you can carry and pile it on the beach. Let's go home covered in gold, silver and glory.'

Holbodi had taken all the personal wealth he and his men could carry but he'd omitted to warn the villagers or his priest of the coming raid so there were lucrative pickings in the obvious prime location, the chapel. Then servants and prisoners were pressed into action, revealing hidey-holes and chests in buildings all the way from the inland settlement back to Balevullin beach.

As soon as he'd witnessed the pillaging of the chapel and sent the treasures to the beach, Sweyn rushed back to Balevullin with his men, sweeping together through the buildings like a plague of locusts on a wheatfield. Canny as Loki, the trickiest god, Sweyn had reverted to his piratical habits. With less distance to carry the goods, he'd collect more, and also be in place to receive all the loot sent by the other captains.

Only with hindsight did Skarfr – and the gulled captains – realise how the trickster had pulled off his revenge on the one tormentor who was within reach. While Thorbjorn methodically sacked Tiree and sent all he found to Balevullin, Sweyn coolly assessed the heaps of metal, weapons and even some jewellery. He chose the best pieces and his men carried them aboard. And he kept choosing until half of the haul was on his ship.

The two captains witnessed their spoils disappear. They didn't dare intervene but they later gave Thorbjorn and the fifth captain an impassioned account when these two arrived on the beach to see Sweyn's sail diminishing in the distance.

'He said he'd taken the leader's share, as was his right,' finished a captain, breathless at the injustice.

As white with rage as Sweyn had been red, Thorbjorn shielded his eyes as he watched the last trace of the sea-rover vanish over the horizon.

'We'll take this matter to the Jarl.' His every word came out like a knife jab in the ribs. 'Let each man take his fourth of what is left.' There were no arguments between them as they picked through Sweyn's leavings and saw them loaded onto their ships, but the atmosphere was thunderous.

As Skarfr took his allotted burden of pewter cups and gewgaws, he thought he heard Thorbjorn say something between gritted teeth. Only the expression on Thorbjorn's face helped Skarfr jump at the meaning of those half-heard words. He'd seen that same expression outside the Jarl's Bu, against a wall, on the night of the wedding dinner.

'Sweyn's sister shall pay,' Thorbjorn had vowed to himself.

The voyage back to Orphir was easier sailing than the route out, with favourable tide and wind, but heavier in heart. An invisible cloud hung over the ships and jokes were few. Thorbjorn stared at the pile of loot as if a magic quern would grind it bigger but there it stayed, disappointing, Sweyn's leavings.

In his rest time, Skarfr relived every anticlimax of the voyage, wondering how sagas could be made from stuff like this. Men had blackened their grooved teeth for nothing. He enumerated his experiences as if they'd turn heroic. *His dream come true.* He'd sailed in the finest of dragon ships with an exceptional captain. He'd fought and killed at the side of the two most revered warriors in the world. He was sailing home on a ship full of treasure.

The words didn't change what he felt.

He opened his eyes, saw the row of nails hammered along each wooden strafe to attach the plank to its overlapping fellow. That's how he felt. The poem shaped itself in his head and he knew what he had to do the moment he set foot on Orkneyjar soil again.

*One hundred hammer-strokes clinked his heart iron-hard, manly,*
*fit for stormy passage and rough seas, for reddening the raven's claw,*
*an overlap of brothers' wooden shields sealing out*
*the heady drink of women's wiles and words*
*that capsized unwary warriors.*

# CHAPTER TWENTY-NINE

With such a head start, the *Death-bringer* was no doubt home on Gareksey when the *Surf-rider* beached near Orphir. Thorbjorn barked orders and stamped off towards the Jarl's Bu, the other captains hot on his trail.

Excusing himself, Skarfr headed in the same direction with the same urgency. But he turned left before the Bu, towards the finest longhouse in the village. Thorbjorn's.

Brushing past a woman servant, he found Inge sitting on a stool in her weaving alcove, staring bleakly at the loom as if her fate was written there and she could lay no hand to it. She acknowledged Skarfr with a slight nod and puzzlement in her eyes.

He had no time for courtesies. 'Lady, you must leave now. Go as far as you can. Sweyn has robbed Thorbjorn.'

Understanding dawned in those blue eyes, in the face that mirrored her golden brother's.

'He will kill you this time. There is nothing will stop him, whatever he might pay afterwards.' Skarfr's words were like shot from a sling and Inge took them on the chin.

She stood up, pale but self-controlled. 'I will not run from him. I promised my brother I would be a wife to this man, shape him and the young Jarl, and I am no coward.' Her lip trembled a little but her voice was resolute. 'Death is better than dishonour. I will not run back to my brother like a beaten cur, to throw myself on his charity.'

Skarfr had not considered the possibility that a woman would take such a stand. He was stymied, torn between respect and frustration. 'But you must,' he stammered, 'you're a woman...'

'And you're a very stupid man,' said a familiar voice. Hlif. 'But well-meaning,' she conceded.

She ran to Inge, knelt in front of her, held her hands. She jerked her head at Skarfr. 'He has no idea what you've been through. What you've achieved. But I have. So do all the women here. Give them a story that inspires.'

Inge did not withdraw her hands but she shook her head and her voice was ice. '*He* cannot be changed. The world would be better without him. But Harald... I've failed with him too. If I leave now, my name will carry only shame.'

Hlif shrugged. 'Harald is young and—' she glanced at Skarfr, 'all young men are stupid. His time with you is seeded deep and will bear fruit one day. Rognvald tends him too. Thorbjorn's charm wears thin as boys grow up.' Another fiery glance in Skarfr's direction.

She pressed the argument further. 'You won't know what the future holds if you're dead. Living, you can wield a woman's power, the weaver who sees all the threads and drops the loom-weights into place.'

'I don't know.' Inge was wavering. 'Even if you're right, how can I get away? He will follow.'

Desperate, Hlif pleaded. 'You must leave now. I agree with Skarfr. I heard Thorbjorn shouting at Rognvald, what he's threatening to do to Sweyn. He will do it to you instead and death will be a kindness. This is not cowardice but courage. Take your life back. You have the right to be free and everybody will respect you for your choice.'

A tabby cat meowed, brushing against Inge's leg. She bent down, let her fingers trail though its fur, watched it perform a somersault after an imaginary mouse then freeze, staring at a ghost. Skarfr shivered. They were running out of time.

'A sign from Freyja,' declared Hlif, pointing at the cat. 'You have earned your place in her hall when your time comes, among the cats whose names you know. She wants you to go, to live.'

Inge picked up a loom-weight, jiggled it in her hand, her mouth pursed.

Seeing his opportunity, Skarfr said, 'I can get two ponies from the Jarl's stables. It's natural for a man to ride out with a girl after a week a-viking and I'll make the sort of jokes they understand. Hlif can be that girl.'

He felt her bristling.

'You can keep your hood up,' he said hastily, 'but it'll be obvious you're not Inge, even if men discover she's missing and ask questions.'

'True,' muttered Hlif, chewing her lip. Even cloaked, her figure was nothing like the tall, slim blonde.

'Inge can meet us at the edge of the village, on the road to my longhouse. We'll all three ride there.' How strange to call it *his* for the first time in such circumstances.

'Hlif can bring the ponies back, riding one and leading one. Easy enough to get a boy to take them back to the stables. And,' he looked at Inge, swallowed, 'we'll take the faering. I'll row you to Gareksey in it.'

'You have thought it out,' acknowledged Hlif with growing respect. 'It would work,' she urged Inge, whose face was expressionless.

Death or flight?

Finally she said, 'Not Gareksey. I won't put my mother and

Sweyn in danger, nor his family. Rognvald might make peace between them while they are so far apart. I will go to our home in Ness.'

Skarfr gulped. Rowing to Gareksey was hard work but rowing across the Pentlandsfjord he'd just conquered on a longship with a crew of forty men? But he could see from the set of her face that she was adamant. He would not leave her to die. They could argue about destination later.

'We need to go *now*,' stressed Skarfr. 'Tell your woman-servant nobody was here and she knows nothing. Get your cloak.'

'There's something I must do first.' Inge went behind a curtain, to a cubicle which reminded Skarfr of the scriptorium. Books on a wooden shelf, a quill by a stone inkpot, a lectern.

Inge took down the book on the right-hand end of the shelf, opened it to the latest writing. A ledger. Numbers and items in neat script.

She put the inkpot on the lectern, dipped in the quill and scrawled in huge letters across the meticulous accounts.

*I dimand a divors*

*Inge Asleifsdottir*

Leaning over the book, she added her rune signature to prevent any legal challenge at the Thing, then she stood up, as straight as the '*I*' she'd scored so hard on the paper that the nib cut through to the other side. She left the ledger open, not just for the ink to dry.

'I like to think of him seeing this,' she said. Her face lightened a touch.

'Hurry,' begged Skarfr.

Inge nodded and went behind one more curtain, returning with her cloak and a small chest.

'My *mundr*, my bride-price,' she said. 'It belongs to me.'

'Hurry,' Skarfr repeated. How on earth he would get the chest onto a pony? Inge would never accept hiding it somewhere in the village and anyway, there wasn't time. *Put the contents in saddlebags. Ditch the box somewhere.*

His mind racing, he left for the stables with Hlif, praying that Inge's servants would cover for her, that she would stay anonymous and careful, and reach their assignation point before Thorbjorn discovered her escape. If the gods were with them, Rognvald would spend hours calling witnesses, establishing facts, then promising amends, and penalties for Sweyn's wrongdoing. If the gods were not with them, Thorbjorn was heading back to his longhouse, where the spoiled ledger awaited him. Inge and anyone who helped her were doomed.

A tall, hooded figure in the all-night twilight of summer, Inge was already waiting for them when Skarfr and Hlif rode past the last buildings in the village. To Skarfr's relief there was no sign of a chest and she had brought only one bag with her, the strap crossing her chest and one shoulder, practical.

'One of Sweyn's men serves me and I trust him. He's taken a rowboat and the chest, gone to Gareksey to warn my brother. Thorbjorn will think I've gone with him and we'll have enough time to be well clear before he finds out otherwise.' She raised her bag. 'I've brought enough with me to serve.'

Her voice was bitter. 'Thorbjorn was only generous with my bride-price to compete with my brother. I am also entitled to all the wedding gifts and the *heimanfylgia*, the dowry Sweyn gave but,' she shrugged, 'it's payment in exchange for my life. My brother will have to steal it back if he wants any of it! His pride will make him put a good face on my return, with or without my coin.'

Skarfr jumped down and helped Inge onto his pony.

Then he mounted behind Hlif, and took the reins from her. In the circle of his arms, she murmured, 'You missed your chance there,' and for all the anger they faced, he felt laughter bubble that she was teasing him again.

'You weigh less,' he replied. 'I'm only thinking of the ponies.'

He clicked his tongue to stir the beast into action and Inge followed suit.

Illuminated like one of Brother Kristian's manuscripts, the heavens glowed. Purples, mauves, reds daubed in wide bands on gold foil as if time had stopped in an endless gloaming. The wolf Hati could race across the sky but he would no more catch the moon on a magical night like this than Thorbjorn would catch Inge. Skarfr felt Hlif's warmth against his chest and the sure-footed pace of the sturdy grey, and he knew peace. If the gods made this ride endless, he would not rail against his fate.

A memory ambushed him. So many years ago. Sweyn riding this very road but in the opposite direction, Hlif up front and Inge beside him, just like Skarfr this night. Had Sweyn felt this consuming tenderness, this need to protect, this sense of purpose? Would the sea-rover defend these two women to the death? Skarfr would. The certainty lodged in his heart, a tiny dart piercing the shield he'd erected against Botolf.

Too soon they were at his longhouse, where Botolf still claimed possession, and all the memories Skarfr didn't want flooded back. After selling Skarfr to Rognvald, Botolf's appearances at the Bu had been few and unwelcome until he'd stopped going there. His diminishing talent as a skald combined with the humiliation of his apprentice's performance had finished his reputation. Skarfr had not seen the skald for years.

He beat the door with his fist and called once for Botolf. His former master did not appear at the door to welcome him back. Did not appear at all.

'Come with me,' Skarfr told the women and led the ponies towards the cow byre.

'Fergus, Brigid,' he called softly and sure enough, the two thralls left their straw beds and came to his bidding.

Skarfr outlined the problem and the need, then, despite Fergus' protests, they went back to the house and forced an entry.

Quivering by the hearth, Botolf had diminished to a gaunt, wide-eyed sack of bones, too afraid to speak. What did he think Skarfr had come here to do? Take revenge? Gut him?

The hearth-worm flinched and shut his eyes when Skarfr spoke.

'In three years, your *fostering* is over, old man, however you dispute my rights, and I will keep to the law. But I have need of Fergus.'

Botolf opened his eyes and apparently gained confidence from the fact his head was still on his shoulders. 'Who?' His voice trembled.

Of course. He never had known the names of his thralls. 'Your manservant. We're taking the faering and will return it in a few days. This lady,' he gestured to Hlif and the skald's eyes widened in recognition, 'will rest here in my house tonight and return to Orphir tomorrow with the two ponies in your stable. When Brigid – your maidservant – has seen to the ponies, she will sleep here beside the lady and see to all her needs.'

Botolf's eyes glittered. 'There's another lady,' he observed. 'Something unlawful going on, I can smell it.'

Inge came out of the shadows, her dagger drawn. 'I should kill him, Skarfr,' she said. 'He'll talk and make trouble for you. If he gets you killed, he can have your house.'

'No. It shall not be said I didn't appreciate what this man did for me.' Skarfr's voice was iron. 'And he should know what will happen to him if he breathes a word of this. Firstly, if I die, I have declared before witnesses that my heir is the Lady Hlif.' He ignored her gasp. He would make good his lie when he found the time.

'Who will *not* give you hearth room so you must seek it elsewhere should anything happen to me.

'Secondly, Thorbjorn will torch my house and kill you in it if word gets out as to who called here this night.

'Thirdly, Sweyn will torch this house and kill you in it if word gets out you caused harm to his sister.'

'But I haven't caused harm to his sister!' protested Botolf, his eyes flicking from Hlif to Inge as he took in who they were.

'You'll find it hard to convince him of that if anybody knows of us calling here,' Skarfr continued, 'but I do know what I owe you.'

Botolf flinched again and Skarfr enjoyed a moment toying with his old tormentor.

'I won't throw you out, not now, nor in the future. But whether you eat will depend on your treatment of Brigid and Fergus. From now on, they live inside this house and are your watchers. If you do not show gratitude, live as the old supplicant you are, you will be cast out and I doubt anyone else will have you.'

Inge sheathed her dagger.

His mouth trembling with outrage, Botolf said, 'You will regret this.'

Skarfr ignored the empty threat and addressed the real problem.

'We can't go to Ness,' he told Inge. 'It's too far. We must go to Gareksey.'

She shook her head, stubborn as he'd known she would be.

'Ness,' she said. 'I will not go to my brother.'

'I dare not, my lady,' Skarfr told her. 'Even if I could row that far, I don't know the way and death by wreck and drowning is no better than death at Thorbjorn's hands.'

Defiant and pale, Inge faced him. 'You forget,' she said, 'I have made the trip a thousand times between Ness and Orkneyjar. I'm a sailor's daughter, a sailor's sister and I can navigate for you better than any man you know apart from Sweyn. You *can* row that far! Please, Skarfr.'

'Can it wait till morning?' asked Hlif. 'You could stay here with me, get some sleep.'

A warm hearth, rest, the clear head a new day brings. So tempting. Skarfr made a quick calculation. The *Surf-rider* had beached on the incoming tide this morning and they were now at the hour any sensible man would go to bed. But no man could argue with the sea.

'No, we must go with the tide and that means now. The next outgoing tide will be twelve hours from now and Thorbjorn will not be idle,' Skarfr said. If only Inge hadn't left her defiance scrawled in the ledger, they might have feigned a legitimate absence for Inge, gained time. But she'd feigned too much for too long and her bid for freedom had unloosed all her shackles.

Fergus exchanged a look with Brigid, who nodded. 'Get the poor girl safe away from here,' she said. 'Whatever it takes.'

So it was that Skarfr found himself rowing across the Pentlandsfjord at night with a thrall, a runaway wife and a pack of bannocks with smoked herrings that Brigid had pressed on him.

# CHAPTER THIRTY

G *odspeed.*

Hlif's last word and the manner of it was sweeter to remember than the last time Skarfr had parted from her. But his activity was the same. Lean forward, dip, splash, pull on the oars as you lean backwards, lift the oars, lean forward, dip... All that Thorbjorn had taught him. The stronger your mid-section, the faster the boat. Fergus lacked technique but he was strong and pulled evenly so the boat set off at a fine pace, aided by the current and lack of wind.

As on the dragon ship, the oars were firmly attached to the boat by rope bands but instead of the modern oar-holes, there were traditional wooden *kjeips*. Nailed to the gunwales, each block had a small tree fork, from which a shield could be hung and to which the oars were tied for security. The *kjeips* also offered a brace against which to row. They felt and sounded different, less of a *clunk-clunk* knocking noise, than the oar-holes had.

Skarfr adapted quickly to the rowboat and as he found the oars' rhythm, the shore moved ever further away. Sitting on the bow thwart, he rowed backwards into the future, relying for direction on the coast of Orkney visible on his right and on the woman who faced him, sitting upright and proud on the middle bench. Like Skarfr, she was watching the coast with which they ran parallel but she also looked behind him, out to sea.

Sometimes her eyes flicked to his, then away again. Or was he the one who looked away first, leaning into his stroke and straightening again? Arn had never instructed him in the niceties of such a situation and the magical blue half-light added to the strange intimacy. If Inge had stretched out her legs, she'd have bumped into Skarfr's.

Behind Inge, using the second pair of *kjeips*, was Fergus, his arms moving in great sun-wise wheels. Like Skarfr, he was rowing backwards, facing the receding shore, his two companions invisible to him. His back moved to and fro with his oars and Skarfr adjusted his own stroke to work efficiently with the other man. Dip, splash, pull...

Work warmed the men but Inge shivered and pulled her cloak close against the chill of the sea. Three blankets had been stuffed hastily beneath her bench, alongside the pack of food and bottle of ale provided by Brigid. They would need them all at landfall. If they succeeded in making landfall.

When words came, they were like night-birds flying wild and free, then roosting in silence.

'Never again,' stated Inge. A vow or a realisation?

Ripple, splash. A tease of wind blew long strands of gold hair across her mouth and she tucked them back in place. One hand clutched her bag of worldly possessions. Skarfr thought of his own, stowed in Rognvald's Bu, his pipe, the bone and the comb Hlif had given him. He hoped Inge's were worth rather more in coin than his, for her sake.

'I owe you my life,' she said. 'What *manbot* would have been paid for my killing? You should have that amount.'

The insult stung. Not all men sought coin like her pirate brother. Skarfr held his tongue, counted ten oar-strokes before replying. That a woman held to the same code of honour as a man, in debt and repayment, had never crossed his mind before.

He realised that if he *had* hoped for reward, he couldn't answer her question. He knew of no *manbot* for any crime against a woman. Maybe such crimes were rarer than feuds between men. Had *manbot* been offered for Frakork? No, because Thorbjorn had not reached the Thing with his charge but had been pacified by Rognvald. The *manbot* price depended on a man's rank so his best guess for Inge would be the same as the price of a karl of good lineage.

Although he knew the system of *manbot* had ended many feuds over hundreds of years, Skarfr suddenly found it distasteful, looking at this lady worthy of sagas and wondering what coin would replace her.

Fergus' broad back showed no awareness of the conversation behind him as he swung into his stroke. What about Fergus? What was he worth? The night hid Skarfr's flush of shame as he remembered that a thrall was property. If Thorbjorn killed Fergus, a small payment to his master would be due. To Skarfr. His thoughts circled back to Inge again.

How could he release this lady from feeling beholden?

'A man sometimes behaves badly,' he began. 'And cannot put right his errors. But when he sees a chance to help another, he can hope that a good deed will weigh against the bad at Ragnarök.'

'Might you be such a man?' asked Inge, her voice like a murmur heard in a seashell.

Skarfr nodded. 'You owe me nothing.' He hesitated. 'But should you wish to thank the gods by an act of charity, there is a man deserves reward though he asks none.' Skarfr flicked his head towards Fergus.

A small smile and the bargain was concluded. 'It shall be done,' she said but she didn't let him off the hook. 'And *manbot* for my murder would be...?'

'Two thousand pennies,' invented Skarfr.

Even in the dim light, he saw the shadow flit across her face. 'So little,' she said.

He hoped she would never find out what price would truly be set.

Even in such a light wind, white-caps played around them in the swirls of oil-dark sea. The last sight of the Orkneyjar coast left a void in the horizon and Skarfr's stomach. Their lives depended on their navigator's skills.

'We keep a straight course.' Inge's voice was steady, confident. 'Feel the current and keep it with us. By the time the tide turns, we'll be out of the Pentlandsfjord and around the headland. The only landmark we care about is Muckle Skerry. Keep it in sight to port and you'll stay clear of Stroma, where the Swelchie is, to starboard.'

Skarfr's insides threatened to return his last meal. 'The faering won't survive the Swelchie.'

'No.' Her tone had not changed. 'And neither would a dragon ship. Which is why we keep close enough to the skerry not to be drawn anywhere near the Swelchie. I'll tell you when we reach it and how close to pass it by. There's no mist so we should be fine.'

*Should be* would have to do.

'That's Muckle Skerry,' she told him. 'Hold steady.'

The rocks loomed white in the distance. Not mist but masses of white that shifted, made short flights and settled again. Terns night-roosting. Skarfr envied their downy warmth, their freedom in flight, and kept pulling the oar. A slower route to freedom. He pulled again and again, through the deep blues of sea and sky, until finally Inge gave them the news, a note of triumph in her voice.

'We've reached Skotland! South-east now and follow the coast. We go with the current and will make landing at Vik well within half a day.'

Relief lent extra vigour to the two men's strokes and the reassurance of the sombre coastline on their left settled Skarfr's nerves. In emergency, they could land in one of the coves that indented the cliffs. But Inge had brought them this far, safely, and he trusted her. Not long to go now.

'Now!' Inge's face glowed. 'Pull in here.'

'Fergus, use your right oar only. We'll turn her!'

Skarfr used his left oar and the faering spun in a circle, till the land had disappeared and Inge said, 'Stop! Forward now.'

And then they were moving towards the land they couldn't see, with Inge describing how far to go, then slowing them, then – gods be thanked – the drag of sand on the keel. The men jumped out into the shallows and ran the boat up the beach with Inge still in it, as if they were showing St Magnus' holy bones in his saint's-day procession.

Amid laughter and tears, Skarfr helped Inge out of the boat. She still clung to her bag and stumbled as she adjusted to the movement the land was making in her imagination.

'Bannocks, smoked herrings and ale, or Brigid will flay me when I go back,' said Fergus, his face bright.

'Fire first,' said Skarfr. 'We'll sleep here. I can't go one step further.'

Foraging offered enough driftwood to make a fire and Inge once more proved her practical worth and her Ness origins. She emptied slivers of glowing touchwood from a waxed pouch onto the laid sticks, then she blew sparks until the wood caught. The touchwood fungus didn't grow on Orkneyjar but Skarfr knew that slivers were imported from Ness, treated in urine on the island and carried smouldering, by men skilled in their use. And by a woman, it seemed.

She smiled at him. 'My father taught me and my brothers.' The smile faded and Skarfr remembered their fates. Her father burned in their house by Frakork over a land dispute. Her eldest brother drowned with his men mere days later, on his way to Jarl Paul's Yuletide celebration. No wonder Inge and Sweyn wore their tough exteriors like armour.

Never had sea-salty stale bannocks with herrings tasted so good. Washed down with ale, they made the perfect end to their journey. Although the sky was now pale with the coming dawn, they rolled up in their blankets and dropped into sweet oblivion.

Skarfr was roused by a movement from sleep so deep he wasn't sure if he was still dreaming.

'Steady now, it's only me. I was cold,' a woman's voice told him, as he gripped the potential assailant who'd joined him under the blanket.

*Inge.*

He dropped his hands, ashamed, but unable to move politely away from her in the roll of the blanket.

'It's all right,' she whispered, taking his hands and putting them back where they'd been. 'I want to wipe his face out of my memory, to be with someone kind, just once.'

She made clear what she meant and if Skarfr's sleepy conscience warned him that no good would come of this, his body was already telling him the opposite. He shut his eyes and as gently as he knew how, he obeyed Inge's wishes.

She flinched once and when he looked at her, he saw sky-blue eyes luminous with tears. Confused, he asked, 'Am I hurting you? Should I marry you to make things right?' Something prickly in his heart rebelled at the prospect but he would do it. He remembered his boyhood wish when he'd first seen her and wondered whether this was his fate, to have what he knew was not right for him and never had been.

'No,' she declared. 'I will not wear the yoke again. And no, it's not you that hurts me still. Nobody could be less like him than you.' She stared at him boldly, nothing modest about her look or touch. And so, in the arms of Thorbjorn's wife, Skarfr learned that the lord had been wrong about that as in everything else when he'd seen his younger self in his protégé.

Skarfr was his own man and whatever took place on that Skottish beach laid some of his ghosts as well as Inge's. It was thank you and pleasure and farewell all rolled up in a blanket, while Fergus' back was as discreet as it had been on the faering.

When second sleep was over and Skarfr woke fully, the other two were toasting the last bannocks and mocking him as a lazybones. As if nothing had happened.

The men escorted Inge to the nearby village, where she was recognised as Thorbjorn's wife and she didn't disabuse the folk who greeted her warmly. With a promise of a wagon and company to her family home later that day, Inge was safe and the flight was over.

Skarfr signed to Fergus and tried to slip away but Inge caught him.

'We owe each other nothing,' she said, 'but know that you have a powerful friend in Ness, if ever you should need one.'

Where once he would have laughed at the very idea, Skarfr had learned much about women and felt honoured. He wished there was some way he could show this, some gallantry, but neither Botolf nor Rognvald had taught him any gesture of courtesy that fitted. His mind shied away from those other men who'd influenced him.

Instead, he hoped his eyes conveyed what his words didn't.

'Ness gains the treasure Orkney lost.'

'Take care on the way home. It will be harder work against the current in the Pentlandsfjord but if you go now, you'll catch the tide home to Orphir. And remember—'

'Keep close to the Muckle Skerry and if you can't see it, you're too close to Stroma,' Skarfr grinned.

Her mouth smiled back but her eyes didn't. They told of a new life ahead, divorced, disgraced.

# CHAPTER THIRTY-ONE

L ight drizzle numbed Skarfr's hands but not his spirits and
the faering crossed the Pentlandsfjord like a doughty pony.
No fancy prancing but reliable. Skarfr was warmed by his good
deeds and by the pouch of coins Inge had given Fergus. Whatever
plans this fortune allowed him, Fergus did not share, and Skarfr
preferred the sounds of the sea to conversation as he cautiously
prodded his own feelings, tested the changes.

He pictured Inge, stroked again the silk of her body and hair,
accepted the gift she offered him. No simple union, with the dark
charm and darker cruelty of Thorbjorn present for both of them.
An act of defiance and a flood of quiet tears released, his and hers
both as they were freed, even from each other. His final act with
her had been a kindness and now he could name what he felt for
this woman, goddess springing from the sea, shrew who'd
shrivelled Thorbjorn's manhood, foster-mother who'd tried to
form the young Jarl, brave soul who'd faced death open-eyed,
skilled navigator and unforgettable bedmate. Inge was all of these
and her poetry shaped itself in his thoughts. But what he felt for
her was pity.

The moment he'd asked Inge's hand in marriage, he'd known

what was missing. He wanted a woman who took away the loneliness he'd felt all his childhood; a woman to share secrets with; a woman to watch his back as he watched hers; a woman who walked partly in this world and partly with the gods, who accepted his cormorant as he did her fey visions; a woman who knew that furs came down a wide river from the frozen Slav wasteland and that salt came from Venice, and who could organise supplies of both to the Jarl's Bu; a woman whose mouth had touched his only once in Yuletide laughter, the trace of which still rang in his ears and tingled on his lips.

How had he ever thought her ugly? He remembered their first meeting long ago on the beach, but now Sweyn and Inge no longer had the starring roles, however tall and fair they were. He only saw a water sprite with fiery hair, who'd confided in him and listened to all he said as if his words mattered. *Hlif.*

The melody that was Hlif played the pipes in his head to accompany her verses. The words danced like a sprite on a beach and Skarfr knew this poem would be a lifetime in the making, never ending.

She could never be his but that hadn't prevented their friendship until his naive accusation of Thorbjorn. They would take up where they'd left off, with the shared secret of Inge's escape to bond them even more closely. Maybe, one day, Rognvald would relent, maybe pronounce Hlif free of the curse. There must be a way. Until then, he would be patient, see whether she might feel the same. One day.

Such noble intentions carried Skarfr through the journey home, also noting the Muckle Skerry on his left, then the coast of Orkneyjar and eventually, he and Fergus negotiated the entry to Skalpaflói and beached the faering. He spent the night in his longhouse to reinforce the new regime but Botolf was a spent force, who sought only food and a warm seat. He hadn't recited in public for years and would never do so again. Skarfr satisfied himself that Fergus and Brigid could continue running the smallholding, as they'd done for years, but now with every right to do so and with the wherewithal to purchase stock and supplies as needed. They seemed to care little that they were property but Skarfr meant to go about freeing them as soon as he could find legal advice.

All his good intentions hit reality and shattered when he returned to Orphir and the Jarl's Bu. And Hlif.

It was as if he saw her for the first time. So much he hadn't noticed before. She was wearing a dark blue plaid overdress in fine wool, trimmed with teal braid that matched the three rows of turquoise soapstone beads So, she had commissioned her beads. He should have bought them for her. His eyes followed the slim lines of her gown down to a pair of teal slippers. No longer a barefoot girl.

Her belt had more pouches than a shepherd's, filled with the tools of her stewarding work. Scissors, weights, keys and a sewing kit.

She'd been right. Turquoise suited her red hair, which peeped in wiry curls from under a demure cap. The cream linen of her undershift enhanced the cream skin of her neck and her fine-boned face overlaid with that unique tracery of freckles he'd seen continue down to her bare shoulders. Peerless.

Her eyes studied his, anxious, storm-grey whirlpools in which he could lose himself.

But they could not talk here, in the Bu, with people all around them and work to do.

'Meet me in the kirk,' she told him and rushed off to organise payment for a delivery of fish destined for the smokehouse.

Luckily, the kirk was empty and Skarfr hadn't been on his knees long before Hlif joined him. Nobody could accuse them of inappropriate behaviour in such public view and pious pose but Skarfr was reminded of their embarrassing visit to St Olaf's. Even if St Magnus had heard *his* prayers, Skarfr was angry at the saint's treatment of Hlif and felt disloyal in feigning worship of the White Christ. The walls loomed, disapproving, enclosing him in their circle.

'I'm so glad to see you. I've been so worried.'

If Skarfr could have bottled the warmth in Hlif's words, he'd take a sip every day and live contented.

Her tone changed to the singsong of vision. 'The sighting, the one I didn't want to tell you. I see it more and more. You're burning, consumed by flames. Yet you never blacken or shrivel, not like Frakork did. I daren't touch you for fear of you setting me on fire too. And I'm afraid, so afraid.' She shivered.

With a heartiness he did not feel, Skarfr told her, 'These are fears, not true visions, or they are puzzles that mean something different from what's on the surface. Now I'm here and you've told me, you can stop worrying. Thorbjorn hasn't been near my longhouse and there's been no burning. Unless something has happened here?'

In a breathless stream, Hlif gave him the news.

'When I came back, Thorbjorn was off hunting otters on Hrolfsay, for which everyone was truly grateful, as he was in a towering rage.

'Rognvald judged Sweyn to be in the wrong and has gone to Gareksey to negotiate with him. He'll have as much chance of making Sweyn pay up as getting a whale to cough up a seal he's swallowed.

'To pacify Thorbjorn, our Jarl has made good the deficit to all four captains from his own coffers until he can recover the plunder and make all good between Sweyn and Thorbjorn again. If the gods are kind, Sweyn will go a-viking again.'

Hlif sighed and crossed herself, showing no awkwardness in

courtesy towards any deities present. 'Rognvald sees the best in people and can sometimes bring out that goodness in them. But his Christianity blinds him. All that peace and forgiveness when we're talking about *Sweyn* and *Thorbjorn*.'

She shook her head and her tone was grave as prophecy. 'Thorbjorn will never forgive Sweyn for this insult. Nor his sister. But only we know the truth about Inge. He's saved face by bragging that he's put up with Sweyn's barren shrew of a sister long enough and has sent her back to her brother as used goods that he's welcome to peddle elsewhere. He's asking for a divorce.'

Skarfr winced. 'So unfair to Inge,' he said, earning a sharp look.

'Seeing himself as a hero, with Sweyn his enemy, and divorcing Inge as a way of evening the score, might spare some other woman the fate we've saved her from,' said Hlif tartly. 'He has a way of making someone weaker pay when he's humiliated. Your turn now. The crossing went fine? You saw her safe home?'

Skarfr smiled as Hlif pre-empted his responses. 'Ay, the crossing was fine. She told true about navigating and she found the way without hesitation.'

Hlif made a little noise which Skarfr took to mean respect for Inge's skills and pleasure that he was acknowledging a woman could have them. He congratulated himself on his new-found understanding of the fair sex.

'We were exhausted, all the same.' No harm in building up how hard he and Fergus had worked. A little nudge towards them being seen as heroes. Not like Thorbjorn but just for Hlif to know.

'We were near to dropping with fatigue when we made land,' he continued, 'so we slept together on the beach.'

'Slept together,' she repeated slowly. Heedless of the kirk setting or what an observer might think, she took his face in her hands so she could study it, read his eyes. 'Did you?' she asked. 'You and Inge.' She read the answer in his eyes and her hands dropped. Her eyes were flint.

'I suppose you'll marry her now,' she said, toneless. 'Make all your dreams come true.'

'No.' Words tumbled around his head as Skarfr struggled to find the ones which would put Hlif right, explain the revelation he'd had, without betraying the raw moments he and Inge had shared. He could not feel remorse.

'She said no,' he told Hlif and all colour drained from her creamy skin, leaving her freckles a feverish red.

'I'm no man's second best,' she said. She jumped to her feet, shook out her tunic and strode out of the kirk.

Words lined up in his head, all the words that should have been said. Too late.

# CHAPTER THIRTY-TWO

Rognvald returned from Gareksey grim-faced and sharp-tongued. Skarfr inferred that the attempt to make Sweyn face up to his guilt had gone as expected. The Jarl's sole achievement had been to send Sweyn off raiding again so there was less chance of any confrontation between him and Thorbjorn. Given the sea-rover's restless spirit, he would probably have taken to sea again anyway, without being prompted. Gareksey never claimed his attention for long, perhaps even less so now that his wife was in residence, not just his mother. Nobody suggested that Sweyn was a family man, except when it came to avenging murdered kin. And vengeance was as much to his taste as sea-roving, so the combination of duty and pleasure was little hardship, more of a purpose in life.

But Sweyn was Sweyn. Orkneyjar was calmer without him, if only for a brief respite.

His dark counterpart, Thorbjorn, made much of putting aside his wife, accompanied by allegations against her entire family that would have sparked one-to-one combat had any male representative been present. Which was of course the aim. All in

Rognvald's Bu breathed a sigh of relief that those insulted were well out of earshot.

As if in a dance measure where each man changed partners, Skarfr hid his avoidance of Thorbjorn in the pattern of daily movement and Hlif disguised her avoidance of Skarfr in the same manner, all of them polite as traders abroad.

When Skarfr observed a steel-capped wooden stick attached to Hlif's belt, he wondered what it was. When he saw her open a leather pouch, draw out wooden runes and cast them in front of some goggle-eyed maidens, he knew what she was up to and he didn't like it. He watched, heedless of her irritation. When she'd finished her singsong prophecies and the girls had gone, he caught her elbow before she could escape.

'Really, Hlif – a wand and rune readings! Playing the witch is dangerous!'

She shook off his hand as if it were a beetle and her eyes blazed. 'Not "playing", Skarfr. Just choosing my weapons, ones you can't steal! As you pointed out, when you said I wasn't worth a saga, Witch Frakork was more respected than mere wives and mothers – or housekeepers.'

She stalked off and he hurled the words at her retreating back. 'Yes and she was burned for it!'

The next time he saw her, she was glacial politeness once more. Trudging through this pretence, racking his brains for how to undo the damage of his words on Hlif without making matters worse, Skarfr's only solace was work. He was the first to volunteer, whether cutting peat, rebuilding houses after storm damage or cleaning out the bilges in the ships. He made an occasional sullen trip to market in Kirkjuvágr, where he spent what coin he had on ale and willing girls. More particular in his choices than on his first visit, he still wanted to learn what pleased them.

'You know your way around a woman's body,' one told him, swinging her black hair. *Not red,* he thought. *Never red.* 'And you know how your own parts work.' She ran a teasing hand down the curled hairs on his groin. He quivered, a hound scenting game.

'But once a man learns how all women are alike, he should learn how we are all different. What *this* woman wants from you.' And then she showed him.

Afterwards, he felt a void. There was only one woman worth learning.

He took a deeper pleasure in checking on the slow progress of the cathedral. Stone by stone it grew and its makers still seemed untroubled that they would not live to see it finished.

The stonemason of Skarfr's first visit let him carve another apprentice symbol in the stone and there was a strange thrill in making such a mark, knowing it would be seen by generations yet to come. Skarfr could almost understand the builders' patience, work as an act of worship. But he was young and restless, disappointed in love and life, raging against the cruel fates. His mood was not fertile ground for spiritual contemplation.

When Rognvald summoned him, he hoped it was for a task that was bloody, lengthy and elsewhere.

'It's Sweyn,' said Rognvald, tight-lipped.

*It's always Sweyn.*

'Margad, the steward of Sweyn's lands in Ness, is robbing his own people in Sweyn's absence and they've petitioned me directly as Jarl. Maybe they don't trust Sweyn to take their part against the steward. I must show that an overlord cannot act in such a manner with impunity so we set sail today. Thorbjorn will captain one of the ships but I want you on mine.'

'Of course, Sire.' *But why not on Thorbjorn's? Rognvald knew they'd sailed together before.* Skarfr shifted uneasily under the Jarl's penetrating gaze.

'Thorbjorn speaks well of you and I am pleased that you keep a respectful distance from my ward.'

Skarfr swallowed and responded to the news from Ness, which suddenly seemed a safer topic. 'Surely Sweyn will deal with this man Margad and spare you the journey?'

Rognvald's smile was wry. 'Sweyn has indeed heard of the charges and has sailed to Ness, where he's joined Margad in punishing any man who has spoken out and in plundering rebellious villages to make a point about loyalty to their lord.'

Was Inge caught up in this abuse of power? Would she be faced with Thorbjorn when Rognvald's men caught up with Margad? Over Skarfr's dead body!

'So,' Rognvald continued, 'I must make the same point. By punishing Margad. And thereby reminding Sweyn he is not above the law.'

Skarfr couldn't decide whether Rognvald was deceiving himself or merely trying to shape the story he wanted told.

'Jarl Harald will sail with Lord Thorbjorn. And I want you with me,' repeated Rognvald, as if the two statements were connected. 'You have the qualities I value in a man: strength, skill and skaldcraft.'

Skarfr shook his head in denial but Rognvald had not finished.

'My verse and my saga should not die with me. You have a skald's training and you are young. You will live by my side so you experience what I do, so that you don't just memorise my poetry – you understand how it was born as well as the allusions. And you will pass on all my words, a monument as towering, as immortal, as St Magnus Cathedral.'

'Sire,' stammered Skarfr. 'You know I can't speak in public.'

'Yet.' Rognvald's tone brooked no contradiction. 'And while you are mute, you have more space in your head for my work.'

Skarfr could hardly say that his head was full of his own compositions. And besides, he already knew Rognvald's work off by heart and would enjoy learning from such a master. He would have an excuse to listen to all the word-duels Rognvald started for the sheer fun of spontaneous versifying. He would have access to the highest level of repartee and skaldcraft without the pressure to perform. Rognvald and his skalds would always perform their own work so he would never be called upon. And he would have a reason to be there, a role. He could say he was a witness, remembering for posterity.

'A witness,' he said, marvelling at how well this would suit him.

'Yes,' agreed Rognvald. 'So my words live on.'

Skarfr was being told he must build that monument one day but anything could happen between now and Rognvald's death, which was years away. He might die himself before that happened, a hero's death in battle. Meanwhile, he could enjoy the advantages of his new role. And he wouldn't be on Thorbjorn's ship.

'It would be an honour, Sire,' he said. And he meant it.

On this voyage, Skarfr was now a full member of the crew. He took a turn with the steerboard, under Rognvald's supervision. The Jarl was an experienced, reliable captain and his even temper kept his crew and ship sailing smoothly. No risks and no races. Even Thorbjorn maintained a respectful course, no doubt salivating at the prospect of settling scores with Sweyn.

Their mutual quest for vengeance was another dance of narrow misses and distance. Holbodi and Olvir Rosta had thumbed their noses up at Sweyn, sailing on with their lives, as he had done to Thorbjorn.

While he kept watch with the Jarl, Skarfr studied him. Yes, he was older than Sweyn or Thorbjorn, his peat-brown hair and pleasant face lacking their dynamism, like a carthorse beside colts. Yes, he preferred making peace to making war. But he'd earned the scars on his muscular frame and, now he knew Rognvald better, Skarfr would not bet coin against him in any contest, from swimming to wrestling. His vaunted nine skills were no braggart's claim. Unlike Sweyn and Thorbjorn, the Jarl considered the cost of winning before he competed. A verse tournament left no dead bodies or wounded pride.

Without taking his eyes off the sail and his crew, Rognvald dropped random thoughts like tasty morsels for his newly appointed saga-maker to chew on.

'It is hard seeing my daughter only when I go hunting in Ness but she is better off with her family there than with me. We must do what is best for others and for Orkneyjar. She cannot be Jarl and I must think about the future, about an heir.

'Thorbjorn is effervescent; sparkling company but mere froth. He has neither poetry nor statecraft. Harald will not learn from his godfather how to care for his people and juggle with his warriors' conflicting natures.

'I sometimes wonder whether the Orkneyjar tradition of two jarls is not a recipe for constant strife, splitting loyalties and making succession a hundred-handed-giant of rival claims. And driving a wedge into any division, making mischief, is King David of Skotland, the most irritating of neighbours, always pushing his latest favourite as jarl, via the murder of the present incumbent.'

He spoke of his own murder – or Harald's – in the same tone he used for 'Move the steerboard a little sun-wise, smoothly as you go.'

'Erlend Haraldsson might become a problem. He is braying his rights to anyone who'll listen, egged on by his woman and her Skottish clan.'

*Erlend, son of the jarl murdered by Frakork. Direct heir to a jarl versus Rognvald, son of a jarl's sister and choice of the king of Norðvegr.* There were Orkneymen who thought the king of Skotland should have more say over their jarl's appointment than their own king, who never left Norðvegr.

Erlend's claim was stronger but Rognvald was in situ. There were always two jarls. *Two must heed their people.* Was it *Harald* who was vulnerable?

'His woman?' queried Skarfr.

'Harald's mother, Margaret Hakonsdottir, an embarrassment to all who know her, but it's obvious what Erlend sees in her. Lustful as a cat and hasn't lost her sleek looks. After Harald's father died, she lived in sin with Sweyn's brother Gunni before Erlend claimed her. They spread word that Erlend took her "by force" to Hjaltland but I doubt there was much force involved as she's with him still. Don't mention her to Harald unless you want a tirade against sluts.'

*What stronger claim to the jarldom than a jarl's son married to a jarl's daughter? Harald's claim came from his mother and from Skottish support so Erlend matched him on both counts and outbid him with his lineage.*

'But I fear no challenge while I have Thorbjorn,' stated Rognvald, as if marshalling his pieces on an invisible board.

He sighed. 'And Sweyn.' Who was in his tower of Lambaburg, with his steward Margad and sixty armed men, preparing for siege. *Men only, may the gods be praised.*

Skarfr had expected a saga story. Not a shield-wall, which he now realised was as rare an event as a swallow in winter. But at least a traitor within, unlocking a secret door or a hero, perhaps himself, scaling the wall at night and opening the barred gate. Or even the longer process of starvation, stopping water supplies, building a battering ram. But no.

It wasn't Rognvald's fault. He held firm in parleys, would brook no concession and demanded that Sweyn give up Margad.

Unfortunately, not only was Sweyn predictably stubborn, saying that he would give up nobody, but he also executed a plan so outrageous that the Orkneymen were left surveilling an empty coop. The two chickens had fled, leaving the men in the tower fearful of reprisals but grinning at the manner of the death-defying escape.

Sweyn had gathered and knotted together all the rope in the building, lowered Margad down to the sea, then shinned down himself. They swam to the nearest landing-point then fled to shelter in King David's court, where they were plied with a heady brew of sympathy and admiration. The Skottish king knew how to woo powerful men.

Another letdown for Skarfr to add to his store. Raiding, battle, siege – as exciting as rope-burn. Which he hoped Margad and Sweyn had to a painful degree, in their privates. No saga story, just days camped on soggy earth, hearing two men trade disagreements like bairns over a bannock, ended by the news of Sweyn's escape. Trickery again but executed with such panache that men hid their smirks.

Thorbjorn's expression would have withered barley and improved little when Rognvald stayed his hand, refusing to make an example of the men in the tower. Instead he ordered his mercurial captain to chase Sweyn, taking the *Surf-rider* and forty men.

The air lightened with Thorbjorn's departure but Skarfr still expected a sombre voyage back to Orkney, licking wounds and pretending they had not been royally fooled.

Not wanting to be kicked for their lord's appeasement, the crew of the *Fjord-hound* worked with careful precision and Skarfr also tried to avoid drawing Rognvald's attention. But he could not ignore the Jarl's direct address and he steeled himself against the storm, as if he were once more facing Botolf's lashings.

'He scaled down from the cliffs from a tower window, using a mish-mash of badly-knotted ropes,' said Rognvald, his voice deep with a hint of growl.

'Scaled down the cliffs from a tower window,' he repeated. 'Rocks below and perils at sea.' First, he shook his head. Then his whole body began to shake. He was trying to wipe the tears streaming from his eyes but he kept doubling up, clutching his stomach. Skarfr had never seen such all-consuming rage. Then he realised.

The Jarl was laughing.

When he could speak, breathless with convulsions, he said, 'Only Sweyn.'

And then again, '*That's* your saga story, Skarfr. *Sweyn.*'

He was right. A story was not always where you looked for it.

Open smiles spread from the steerboard to the dragon's head and the mood lightened. Men even chuckled, began to tell each other the story of how Sweyn escaped in the night. And they'd been there, as they would tell their children. That they had lost no longer seemed important against such an adversary.

Skarfr's heart lifted with the wind. He loved sailing and he was suddenly glad that Rognvald was his captain, not Thorbjorn.

The *Fjord-hound* did not go straight home. While the men camped and relaxed with dice and bawdy stories, Rognvald went alone overland on a visit that Skarfr suspected had much to do with a little girl and nothing to do with politics.

# CHAPTER THIRTY-THREE

Everyone thought they knew Hlif and Skarfr had to pretend polite interest when her name cropped up. Hlif had made a rota for maintenance and cleaning, of everything from armour and weapons to furnishings and blankets. Hlif had organised stocks of peat, ale, dried meat and grain stores. Hlif this and Hlif that. Hlif, a brand burnt into his skin and soul.

She was aloof and polite to him, as if they'd never exchanged more than the time of day. She was Rognvald's housekeeper and ward, and the closer to him the Jarl kept Skarfr, the more he saw of Hlif and the less chance there was of speaking to her alone. Especially when she kept propriety between them like a wall.

Maybe she'd accepted her guardian's decree and her single fate. No man went near her in any familiar way, for which Skarfr thanked the curse upon her. Remembering Thorbjorn's assault boiled his blood and he wouldn't hesitate to kill if such a situation recurred. Hlif might welcome some other man's advances: killing seemed appropriate then too. Maybe he had been changed by his sorties on dragon ships after all.

The Jarl made his regular hunting trip to Ness and brought back mistletoe but Yuletide brought no sweet kisses for Skarfr. His only consolation was that Hlif stayed aloof from all men, not just from him.

He reached twenty-one, the age of unquestioned inheritance and took official possession of his longhouse, after so many years waiting for liberation from Botolf and trying not to think about the prospect. Another anticlimax. He'd already settled matters when he'd confronted the hearth-worm and placed Fergus in charge, with Brigid at his side. All that remained was to buy their bonds from Botolf, then purchase their freedom. Which he told them again that he would do, as soon as he knew what was required.

They both duly expressed gratitude but Skarfr could tell the change in status would mean nothing to them. He'd already given them all they wanted. Yet one more inadequate development in a flaccid saga. His story was barely worth living, let alone telling. There was no rush to entangle himself in the legalities of making bondsmen of thralls but he would keep his word. Some time.

He threw himself into his work, storing in his memory the verses composed by Rognvald and his skalds, who responded to the Jarl's inventive challenges with gusto. Rognvald's verse was always best but, in his head, Skarfr added his own compositions to those he heard and his collection grew in quality as well as quantity. The saga of Sweyn was quiet and elsewhere while the skalds took to the platform in the Bu, attracting all eyes and ears as they declaimed their words.

Days, months and years passed, blending into one as Skarfr turned twenty-two and then twenty-three.

The daily bread of island life was leavened with occasional surprises.

A whale washed up dead on the beach and for weeks the men stank of blubber and blood, the women of meat and smoke. The frenzied work against time to butcher, prepare, salt and dry the strips of fresh black meat was helped by the wintry weather. One day in salt, one day hung in the bitter north-east wind, dripping blood and body fluids, and one day smoked, with Norðvegr juniper branches added for the last two hours. Not even the poor would starve that year and there would be oil for every lamp.

Harvesting the bere barley at summer's end was another task where strong men were welcome and Skarfr lost himself in the rhythm of the sickle. Lost himself so far from the golden field of ripe grain that scything the last stalk came as a shock, followed by men's cheers and shouts of, 'Skarfr wins the *bikko*.' One of the women gleaners was already plaiting strands from the last sheaf to make two pricked ears, a long body and snout, four sturdy legs – the straw dog, the *bikko*.

As the man who'd finished the harvest, Skarfr was ceremoniously presented with the *bikko* as a traditional token of the spirit that could be seen on windy days running through the barley field. Norðvegr-born Rognvald said it was Óðinn's wolf. Whether dog or wolf, the spirit in the *bikko* would protect Skarfr's home from trolls until the spring, when the straw figure would be burned in the field, to run free again through the new crop.

With due respect, Skarfr placed the *bikko* on a ledge in the Jarl's Bu, which was more of a home than the longhouse he never visited. He did not fear trolls nor seek the tongue-in-cheek status bestowed on him during his brief reign. But he had no desire to insult others' beliefs so he accepted the teasing 'Sire' when his fellows spoke to him and he played up to the role he'd been given. That's what all of his life felt like, merely playing a role, confiding in nobody, composing poetry in secret.

He would walk to the old stone circle at Steinnesvatn or further away to the ring of stones at Brogar, giant watchers brooding over the loch until Ragnarok. He would play mournful tunes on his pipe, hail the cormorant when she flew over or perched on a rock, watching over him. She gave him neither encouragement nor warning but she was there.

Tormented by daily public contact with Hlif, which was almost worse than none at all, Skarfr welcomed Rognvald's latest project.

'It is time to go back to Norðvegr, speak to the king, commission new ships and all the goods my housekeeper says we lack. I want you and Harald to sail with me. Thorbjorn can take my place in Orkneyjar while we are away. We should go in early spring, after the winter ice and as soon as the westerly winds blow.'

*Norðvegr. Rognvald's homeland and their sovereign's court.*

First, they had to cross the sea they called North but was still the West Sea to those Norðvegr-born like Rognvald. They would head east for at least four nights across trackless water. Four nights turned into six due to the variable wind but Rognvald knew these waters of old and when the lookout called, 'Land!' he negotiated with ease the sheltered channel north to Biörgvin. The coast of Norðvegr extended trolls' rocky fingers to grasp at the ship from both sides and Skarfr saw fjords for the first time. Narrow passages of deep water between forbidding granite cliffs that rose higher than eagles flew in Orkneyjar. Dizzying vistas of forests and stone above, cold blue all around them. So cold that chunks of ice drifted towards the ship. Skarfr saw death in every feature of this fantasy landscape but Rognvald declared the ice as harmless as the rocky islets that gave the illusion that they were speeding past the ship, rather than the reverse.

Only now did Skarfr appreciate Rognvald's poem of Doll's Cave, celebrating his swim into Hel, so deep and dangerous was the half-submerged sea-cave that only one other man risked the attempt, with a rope between them as they swam.

*I raise here a stone cairn,*
*commemoration of courage,*
*where we fought the water,*
*sought the goblins' treasure*

*in dismal Dollshellir, too*
*dangerous for ships to glide*
*like snowshoes near such*
*treacherous turbulence.*

The three ships were crammed full of men so that there would be enough to crew the new ships home as well as the old ones. By the time Skarfr reached the rocky fjord entry to Biörgvin, he was more interested in lying down full-length to sleep than in meeting King Ingi.

Over the summer, Skarfr became accustomed to the Norse accent that twisted his homeland's Norn words into something other. As Rognvald slipped into the speech of his childhood, and gossiped with friends and family, he too seemed something other than Orkney. He kept Harald close to him but he sent Skarfr to discover the city and to train with the king's men.

While wooden planks were cut and shaved, overlapped and curved into two ships' keels for Orkneyjar, Skarfr discovered merchants and mercenaries, along with their goods and services.

He trained with the king's elite fighting force, the Hird, and found their duties and manners surprisingly familiar. Arn would have approved of the warriors' distinction between the familiar 'thou' and the formal 'you.' But Skarfr was more interested in learning new skills, such as combat from horseback.

After his humiliating first attempt with a crossbow while mounted, he persuaded his hosts to teach him the basics. They started with his inadequate clothing, so that he finally gained a mail hauberk, a padded gambeson and a steel helm with visor. They showed him the high-bowed saddle and other protection worn by the horse, similar to his own in padding and mail harness. They demonstrated use of their weapons: the two swords they all bore, one hanging from the saddle's pommel and one on the warrior's belt; spear and dirk; and a shield attached to a shoulder belt.

Skarfr couldn't see any of Rognvald's mounts carrying so much weight but he applied himself to the new skills with an enthusiasm that only increased when the Hird offered to teach him how to fight on board ship.

All manner of weapons he'd never considered before could be useful. Long-handled scythes and broadaxes, darts, crossbows and longbows, along with his own familiar staff shot – these were not surprising choices. But he would never have thought of coal and sulphur, to fire the enemy ship.

Nor had he imagined how useful two spears could be, not just for throwing but when boarding. One should be long, to cross the gap between ships and one shorter, a stabbing weapon.

He learned how planks could form a boarding walkway or a defensive breastwork. But the best protection was always the soft linen gambeson, well padded and thoroughly blackened as befitted a warrior's garb, plus a good steel helm.

Whatever the Hird taught him came with the same principles which ruled them in the King's court.

*Be resolute in combat but not hot-headed and least of all boastful. Fight on sea as on land with an even temper and with proper strokes only. Never waste your weapons by hurling them to no purpose.*

The notion of a code of conduct in battle was new to Skarfr and did not fit with his experience. In sacking Tiree, there had been neither restraint nor calm heads. If Thorbjorn and Sweyn had any code, then it was the opposite of everything the Hird taught, in detail if not in essence.

*A man's name is all. To kill by whatever method is to earn renown and show your manhood. Praise your own deeds so all hear of them. In this manner, you shall earn Valhalla.*

Skarfr only knew one man who tried to live by the code of the Hird and to bring Norðvegr courtesy to Orkneyjar. In his verse,

Rognvald showed no false modesty, nor did he sell himself short when telling Skarfr his life story. But there was no self-aggrandisement either and in his dealings with people, the Jarl often sought to emulate the White Christ. He thought humility a virtue. After training with the Hird, Skarfr was closer to understanding why, although he could hear Sweyn's laughter in his ears at such a thought. And Thorbjorn's mockery. Were they right? Was he being naive?

How strange that the stronger and more skilled a warrior he became, the less he admired those he'd once thought to be heroes.

With such unsettling thoughts troubling him, Skarfr was further perturbed by Rognvald's enthusiasm for a new venture, an ambitious expedition. He'd been spending more and more time with Eindridi the Young, recently returned from Jórsalaheim, whose portrayal of the Holy City fired Rognvald's imagination.

'Eindridi will return to Jórsalaheim with me if I lead a party,' the Jarl told an astounded Harald and Skarfr, 'and I have sufficient men willing to join me in this adventure which can only bring us glory. King Ingi has given his blessing along with two ships. They are small but specially built for rowing at speed, the fastest I've ever known.'

Harald scowled. 'What shall I do in Jórsalaheim?'

Rognvald ignored the ill humour and told him, 'I'm hoping you will rule Orkneyjar while I am on pilgrimage. With Thorbjorn to support you.'

A change came over Harald's face, his contorted lips and brow increasing his likeness to a gargoyle. His expression shifted from resentment to understandable excitement but there was a flicker of something less virtuous in the young Jarl's eyes, something quickly suppressed.

*One jarl is for himself and rules by fear but two must heed their people.*

'I shall spend two more winters in Orkney, preparing, and

those from Norðvegr who are coming with me will join me there when they can.'

Disappointment at the delay clouded Harald's eyes briefly but they brightened again at Rognvald's next words.

'You shall have your first ship, Harald. The *Arrow* is yours and I shall keep the *Saviour*. I want you to captain the *Arrow* home. Skarfr will be my second.'

King Ingi called together all those who wished to sail with Rognvald and plans were laid. As leader, Rognvald was to have the only ornamented ship but other new ships were commissioned and would be ready by the Jarl's return to Norðvegr in the following spring. The King bestowed as many gifts and goods on his subjects from over the seas as their ships could carry. Hlif would be able to tick off all the items on her trading list. The mood was buoyant and the two ships were heavily laden when the *Saviour* and the *Arrow* set sail.

Whether the Orkneymen were dreaming of Jórsalaheim and full of holy fervour or whether they were driven by the more immediate desire to get home after months away, there was a dangerous confidence on the return voyage. Knowing the way and waters so well, Rognvald made light of the mists they travelled through. Even when the storm broke, they didn't realise how far north of their course they'd been driven, along with their sister ship, the *Arrow*.

Only when they escaped the oily swell into what they thought would be safe harbour, did the experienced hands realise with horror that they'd not reached Orkneyjar at all but were probably on the coast of Hjaltland in the worst weather possible. Crashing waves and turbulent swirls of current made them regret leaving the open sea. But it was too late to turn back.

# CHAPTER THIRTY-FOUR

The steerboard bucked like an unbroken stallion amid a confusion of breakers and wild gusts of wind. Skarfr had to use all his strength to steady the ship's course while Rognvald hurled orders that were barely audible above the howling gale. Torrential rain, salted and stinging, blinded the men, reddened eyes already sore from lack of sleep.

'May Aegir preserve us!'

The men prayed to their gods as they fought with ropes and bailed water that surged onto the deck as fast as they emptied buckets. The sail had been taken down long since and half the crew manned the oars but the sea-god mocked the ship's vaunted speed, rendered oars useless in a stomach-churning swell of tide against wind. Without its sail, in heavy seas, the ship rocked like a child's cradle possessed by demons.

Through the mists that ghosted across the water like the dead haunting their barrows, the men glimpsed the craggy entrance to a narrow bay and thought they were saved. First the *Saviour*, then the *Arrow* made it into the cove. There the swell of the open sea changed to a frenzy of breakers, waves whipped to white froth, crashing against the cliffs and surging in all directions as they rebounded.

Land was within reach but they would not make it.

Skarfr held tight, closed his eyes and blinked to clear them, opened them to men screaming like boys as knife-edged rocks emerged from the whirling water, just missing the steerboard side of the ship. They were close enough to see the black bird perching in a deep fissure, still as a Madonna in a chapel niche until it flapped its wings after a deluge. Then it hunched up again.

His cormorant. A last farewell.

*'I'm sorry.'* Skarfr would never be the man of the cormorant's prophecy. Even his death would be an anticlimax, fitting end to a life not fully lived.

The cormorant stared intently at him, bashed its wings against its rocky shelter, then disappeared beneath another gigantic wave that crashed over the outcrop.

Smashed against rocks. Skarfr faced his fate and did his job, holding onto the steerboard as if he could fly the ship with it.

Then he understood the cormorant's message. Smash them against the rocks. The ships.

He abandoned his precious steerboard and lunged for Rognvald, grabbed his arm to get attention, shouted over the Jarl's angry instructions, made him understand.

'It's our only chance of saving the men and some of the cargo. Head for shore, hole the keels on the rocks then get as near the beach as we can so we get ashore. The ships will sink but the cargo will come ashore and some can be saved. If we're carried out to sea, we die and lose everything. We need to sacrifice our queens.'

Rognvald's face was grim beneath the rainwater rivulets coursing down grimy tracks, white-edged with salt. He nodded. 'Desperate times.'

He glanced over at the *Arrow*, cresting a wave three times the height of the ship and plummeting in a keel-breaking descent.

Months in the building, the best of Norse ship-building skill and materials. Rising again on the next wave, a bold little mare tossing her white mane, defying the combined rage of sea and sky. Doomed.

Rognvald jumped onto a thwart and Skarfr instinctively grabbed his leg as tight as he'd held the steerboard, wondering for a heartbeat whether the Jarl intended to throw himself overboard. But no. He waved his arms like a windmill, pointed and gesticulated, a madman in a storm hoping to communicate something to Harald, across the savage waves. He stumbled and Skarfr pulled him down to the deck as the *Saviour* dipped and shook. It felt worse after watching the *Arrow*, knowing how small the ships were and how vast the sea.

'It's up to Harald now. Whether he realises what we're doing is deliberate and follows suit. Do what you can with the steerboard.'

Skarfr braced himself for the shock as he grabbed the paddle again, stopped it veering wildly and made it work against the forces of nature. He watched Rognvald giving instructions to the men nearest him. The words flew the length of the ship like crows on a battlefield, ill omens.

Jagged rocks loomed port-side, the beach was close enough for them to see the shingle, and every oarsman on the steerboard side rowed for dear life while those men port-side shipped oars. Skarfr pulled the steerboard sun-wise and the ship turned so that the next wave rebounding from the rocks rammed the port side against unyielding stone.

Water poured in as all the oarsmen rowed, away from the rocks, towards the shingle. Every yard counted, brought them nearer safety, and the men were waist deep in the sinking ship, struggling to pull an oar or even move at all, when Rognvald yelled, 'Now!'

Into the thrashing waves, struggling against the undertow, the men threw themselves overboard and waded towards the beach.

Skarfr held onto the steerboard, waited until last man left, to give the crew as steady a platform as he could, then he let go and jumped.

Suddenly released, the paddle veered wildly, caught Skarfr a clout on his back that unbalanced him. The undertow did the rest, dragging him against the stony seabed like a plough over a field.

Pelted with pebbles and debris as he curled up and righted himself, Skarfr kicked his legs, pushed down with his arms and aimed for the surface with a swimmer's instinct. Thought had long since left him.

But the tide was too strong and the sea-god wanted a trophy. Skarfr broke water and breathed, long choking airfuls, but he was weakening and he could feel the pull of the wild sea.

'Skarfr!'

Only one other man was a swimmer strong enough to make the attempt. The man who'd reached Doll's Cave and who counted swimming among his nine skills.

Rognvald wrenched Skarfr's shoulder when he reached him, turned him and won him back from Hel's gate. The distance between life and death was barely a yard or two, just enough for Skarfr to be hauled on his back, then raised to his feet on the pebble shelf that sloped upwards to what was theoretically dry land. Where he collapsed to the ground and surveyed the disaster he'd survived.

The *Arrow* did follow the *Saviour's* example and soon the drenched company was gathered on the shingle, men shaking with relief and shock, freezing and exhausted.

Their arrival had not gone unnoticed and a file of local residents descended to identify those shipwrecked, then shepherd them to warmth. The *Arrow* and the *Saviour* had indeed reached Hjaltland – and would never leave there.

# CHAPTER THIRTY-FIVE

When Einar the farmer was finally convinced that the Jarl of Orkney in person sought shelter after a shipwreck, he made the men welcome at his hearth. Food, warmth and a night's sleep revived most of the men and Rognvald was galvanised by events into composing funny poems to lift their spirits.

Still shivering despite dry clothes and blankets, his skin pitted with small wounds from the pebbles that had struck him, Skarfr listened to the recitation, unable to appreciate it fully but smiling despite the pain.

In spontaneous rhymes and neat kennings, the Jarl joked about the sea nymphs who'd dragged the ships down and were currently examining their prizes with puzzlement. As he named his men and the objects they'd lost to the sea nymphs, every man laughed at the picture he painted of these mythical creatures wearing Hawknose's oiled hat or pinning hair up with Cerid's sling used as a hair decoration.

He turned the disaster into a saga story, where all were heroes who'd lived to tell the tale.

When the lady of the house presented him with a fur, he declaimed,

'Here I shake a shrunken fur coat;
surely 'tis not ornamental.
All our clothes are in the ship-field
and it is too wide to seek them.
Lately all the sea-horses
left we dressed in splendid garments,
as we drove the steeds of mast-heads
to the crags across the surges.

'This bear skin is most welcome for
a bare skin's all I have that's dry.
Our clothes are seeded in the ship's field
of wide waves and will be seen again
only on the white sea-horses
we left such splendid gifts,
as we pounded our wooden steeds
against the sea-god's craggy spears.'

Skarfr was reciting the lines, consigning them to memory as he slipped into a restless sleep, aching and shivering.

The next day he was worse and as he dipped in and out of consciousness he was aware of being carried, on a journey by cart, being carried again, so cold.

And then he began to burn and sweat. He threw off bedclothes, thrashing around in delirium. His whole body was on fire and his head pounded.

Somebody, a woman, forced a vile potion down his throat and he lost consciousness again, only to surface in freezing sweats, no blanket warm enough. Then the flames of the White Christ hell consumed him. He see-sawed between ice and fire.

Then more foul-tasting liquid.

Skarfr wanted to keep flying and resisted the attempt to pinion his wings to his sides.

'No,' he protested, flapping in panic.

But they could never imprison a wild bird like himself. He pretended to submit, his wings straight as fins. Then he dived, streamlined as an arrow, so deep they could not follow.

He chased silver shoals that turned and twisted as one creature but they were not fast enough to evade his sleek burst of speed, his own twists and turns. If he was hungry, he'd open his beak and slip a fish down his long throat in one swallow. If he wasn't hungry, he'd play.

When he needed air, he surfaced far from where he'd entered. By the time they spotted him, called, 'Skarfr!' in their soft voices that teased his memory, he'd already dived again.

Deep in a shimmering world where sunlight became fishes, tiny wriggles of gold that disappeared when he ate them.

'Come back, Skarfr,' the voice urged, so kind, so gentle, he was tempted.

But he knew such voices were an illusion and the sea called him back, dancing in white lace, opening to him in warm currents that tickled and caressed.

The voice persisted. 'Skarfr, it's me, Hlif. I'm here.'

He only opened his eyes a second, to banish the illusion before flying away, but sea-grey eyes held his and if he dived again, it would be into those eyes and he would be lost in them. *Hlif.*

She was sitting on a stool beside the straw pallet on which he lay, a blanket half over him, half tossed off. Her hand held his, tightening, tethering him to this world.

'Water,' he croaked.

Hlif offered the practical response of holding a leather bottle to his lips, wetting them and helping him sip. Whether that was the water he needed or not, he couldn't say but he felt his wings furl and shrink to finger-size. He flapped them over the blanket and they *were* fingers. He pulled the cover fully over him, embarrassed at his state of undress, waiting to wake up from this strangest of dreams.

'You've been in a fever for weeks,' Hlif told him. 'Rognvald sent you to the healer's house. He and the others are still in Einar's farm and will probably stay there for the summer.'

Skarfr looked about him. A tidy longhouse interior, smelling of cleansing herbs, crushed juniper needles, rue and a sweet hint of dried dog-rose petals. But no healer in sight.

'She was called to a birth, some miles away. I said I'd look after you.' Hlif glanced away. 'I said I'm your sister. The Jarl doesn't know I'm here.'

Skarfr sat up abruptly, which made his head spin. 'My sister! I don't have a sister.'

She shrugged. 'I know but I shouldn't think anybody else does. I'm on Hjaltland to assess the goods salvaged from the shipwreck and organise their transport to Orphir. Rognvald thinks I'm on my way back there and nobody in Orphir will count the weeks I spend here.'

'What about the healer? She'll hear gossip, figure out who you are.'

Another shrug and a mischievous smile. 'If she does, she won't tell. She's one of those women used to keeping secrets.'

Her hand had crept back like a little mouse to nestle against his. He didn't dare ask what this meant so he shut his eyes. His wings did not grow back. The voice remained, low and honeyed.

'Word came from Hjaltland that the Jarl's ships were wrecked. As more news came, I asked about you but could get no sense. Somebody said there'd been one man drowned, a body carried up the beach by Rognvald. Nobody had seen you with the Jarl's men. The stories were all so confused. Ten men had died, nobody had died – all they wanted to tell me about were boxes of furs!'

She whispered, 'I thought you were dead.' Her fingers curled around his, clenching and unclenching. 'And when I found you here, I still didn't know whether you'd live. You were burning up with fever.'

Their eyes met. *Burning. On fire.*

'I've wondered too,' she said, 'whether this is the meaning of my vision for your future. I hope so as the danger has passed now.' She bit her lip, came to some decision. 'I've waited so long for you to grow up and I'm not going to wait any longer.'

He should probably feel insulted but his heart was thumping so loud he could hear it in his ears. 'You're younger than me,' he pointed out.

'I've *never* been as young as you,' she retorted, almost the sparring partner of his childhood. Almost.

'When the fever was high, you called out a woman's name.' She hesitated. 'Never hers. Always mine.'

He heard the scrape of her stool, felt fine wool brush against their joined hands as she leaned over him, one of her gold brooches cold against his chest as her cheek leaned against his, gently rubbed skin against skin. He didn't dare open his eyes but he pictured her every move, her expression. Her lips touched his, curious and soft, as open to him as the sea in his fever-dreams. Were her eyes open or closed?

He had to look.

They were open. Grey pools, flecked with sunlight, welcoming him. He dived in.

When he surfaced again, she held back, sat on her stool, shook her head. 'Not yet but soon. You are still weak.'

He would have protested but his body cried out for sleep and the comfort his spirit had taken made letting go of the world easier than he'd known for years.

Each time he woke, he reached for her, afraid she'd vanish. Once he found her curled up in his arms, too tired to watch him any longer. From then on, that was her place whenever she wished. As he grew stronger, her touch grew bolder and neither could say which day they became lovers – just that they had and with no regrets.

Lingering over her smooth shoulders, which had featured in his dreams for so long, Skarfr discovered where there *were* and, even more exciting, where there *weren't* rosy lace freckles on marbled skin.

Holding his face in both hands, she said, 'There is something you should know.'

He'd been waiting for the catch and he prepared himself. Botolf's lashings all over again. Always punishment after any pleasure.

'You don't see me as I am,' she told him. 'I'm squinty-eyed and snub-nosed, with blotchy skin and ginger hair like a wire scrubbing brush. I'm never going to grow above your chest height and will always need help getting onto a pony or into a boat. I can hardly carry a shield, let alone a sword.

'I can count better than any man and know more about trade than Rognvald does. Men don't like that, except when they're trading of course. The only men who have ever looked at me as if I'm a woman are you and Thorbjorn. And he'd swive a goat when his blood's up.

'Everybody knows this. Everybody sees me this way. I'm plain and shrewish. I don't need the curse to stay unwed. That's the truth and I don't want you thinking I don't know so.'

Skarfr could tell she was serious so he bit back his laughter. He didn't want to make the sort of mistake that had already cost him years of distance from Hlif. Then he told her the truth.

'I didn't think you were pretty when we met,' he confessed. 'And your looks *are* different.'

'Not beautiful like Inge,' she said.

He didn't take his eyes from hers. 'Not like Inge at all,' he said, 'but beautiful. Nobody else sees you from the inside like I do. You light up my life. I don't want you to be other than you are. Perhaps all men see the right woman in this way, beautiful to them, when others see bent noses or coarse hair, blubbery flesh or sharp tongues. I don't *care* a sheep's arse how others see you. You are beautiful to me inside and out.'

His body's confirmation of this was very convincing. All that Skarfr had learned from other women, he gave to Hlif with a tenderness that was for her alone. And what she gave him was worth the danger they faced. Probably. Skarfr was worried about the risks Hlif took.

'Rognvald will exile me if he finds out and he'd never let you come with me.'

'Then we'll make sure he doesn't find out.'

Hlif could be very persuasive.

# CHAPTER THIRTY-SIX

'Why is everybody being so nice to me all of a sudden?' Skarfr asked Hlif when they met by Brogar, the furthest ring of ancient standing stones up above the loch. Far enough from the village for them to be together with only ancestral ghosts for company, who were myriad, according to local tales. Being cursed offered a certain familiarity with the spectral world, however unwanted, and Hlif considered the living as more of a threat to their closeness than the dead. Skarfr would have walked through fire and phantom for her sake so here they were.

'Even the washerwoman smiled at me as she took my dirty clothes this morning.' And she'd be washing them in the loch nearest Orphir at this very moment, scrubbing and gossiping – not about him, he hoped.

Hlif studied his face, traced his mouth with a fingertip, then answered, 'It's a miracle the wind hasn't set your face in the glower you've worn for years now. But I do believe there are smile lines forming ... here—' she pulled lightly at one corner of his mouth, then at the other. 'And here. It's a well-known phenomenon. When you smile, people smile back. And they were terrified of you, with your face like a thunderstorm and a sour word whenever you opened your mouth, making a misery of their lives as well as your own.'

Her words teased and stung like the northerly breeze.

She stood on tiptoe to kiss him but he held her back.

'You know why,' he told her. Botolf. Lost poetry. Sweyn. Lost dreams. Thorbjorn. Lost love. She knew all his hidden self. He flushed. Perhaps not hidden so well if his melancholy humour had been so contagious.

She nodded. This time, he let her kiss him and his arms closed around her slight body, lifted her easily, powerful and protective. Sometimes he was frightened he'd crush her, so fragile she seemed compared with his *glima* wrestling partners. But she revelled in his strength, as if he were a mastiff she'd tamed, her secret weapon.

He growled at her, bared his teeth, and she laughed.

'Why were you never afraid of me?' he asked her.

'I know you,' she replied. 'From boy to man.' She punched his chest, a dragonfly landing on a tree trunk. 'You can be stupid but I'd bet on you winning a fight and you're a good man.'

Skarfr tasted her words, wondering. Was he a good man? He'd never thought of himself in those terms. But he'd often thought of Hlif as a good woman.

She added quietly, 'We know what an evil man is like.'

They didn't name him.

Instead they talked of someone who often spoke of goodness. Rognvald's projected voyage to Jórsalaheim was on everyone's lips and Skarfr couldn't help feeling the buzz of anticipation, even though he would be leaving Hlif behind for years. The saga-story of a lifetime and he would be going.

She seemed resigned to the pilgrimage, more than happy to talk ships, stores, people and planning. Too resigned, he realised later. Too meek.

They would have more than a year together before the parting, which would be temporary, he assured her. With the double standards of a man who wants to eat his bannock *and* save it for later, he considered the time before the voyage as too long to worry about parting and the length of the voyage itself (unpredictable but at least three years) as a short absence.

Hlif never pointed this out but smiled and made their time together sweet in touch and talk. Not that she always agreed with him but her direct opposition in debate was refreshing. He enjoyed being teased and stung. She made him feel he was worthy of such honesty. And they both knew other ways a woman could behave with a man. No, that was not what he wanted.

Their meetings were all the more precious as they were rare, limited by the time and planning necessary to reach their secret places, discreetly. The Jarl was too busy with his own planning to notice occasions when his ward and his saga-maker were missing at the same time. If anyone of lower rank suspected, ascribed a cause to Skarfr's cheerful demeanour, they were unlikely to cause ripples by tattling to their betters.

Winter brought its usual fun and this year Skarfr could enjoy the mummery of the Boy Bishop, a young choirboy chosen to mimic Bishop William for a day, strutting in his prelate's robes, declaring new Holy Days and demanding fanciful forfeits for old sins.

*Now* that *was glowering,* thought Skarfr, watching Bishop William's sour face, mirrored in the boy's. The lad even had the stooping walk, as close to the original as if he were the Bishop's shadow, making all but his model laugh as he blessed all around him.

*A day's humility harms nobody and the sin of pride is such a danger to the gifted.*

The midwinter traditions would not have been complete without a poetry challenge from the Jarl. 'By the time I finish reciting my poem, you should have yours ready, on the theme of that tapestry,' Rognvald pointed to one where an old man wielded a sword, 'and without using any words from my verse.'

> 'The old one standing in the hanging,
> though full of unspent ire,
> rod unsheathed upon his shoulder,
> will not move one woven step.'

Oddi the Little took up the challenge, chanting,

> 'The warrior stoops, preparing
> one fell sweep there
> where the tapestry is cut open.
> Yet he's the one in danger should
> the ships' captains fall to brawling
> once more in this hall.'

The brawling captains showed as much appreciation of Oddi's sly wit as the rest of the audience and Skarfr's heart ached that his own verses were locked in his head. *An aged man in crewel hues, whose sword he cannot use.*

Another time the theme was a man's beard and poetic mead flowed as freely as its bodily form.

And if Hlif avoided the Skottish mistletoe hanging from a beam, she made up for her public modesty with private kisses and Skarfr thought himself the happiest of men. Especially when Rognvald announced an expedition to Norðvegr in the spring and told Skarfr he was to remain in Orkneyjar and report on events there to the Jarl when he returned. Harald was to accompany Rognvald, leaving Thorbjorn in charge.

Skarfr put on a gloomy face, expressed deep disappointment at being left behind and the instant he saw the Jarl's ship disappear over the horizon, he left word that he'd gone sailing to Papey

Meiri. Or fishing off Birgysey. Or visiting friends in Hjaltland. All of which he did, briefly, interspaced with time at the Bu, catching up on events and fulfilling his duty to the Jarl, or in his longhouse, where Hlif would meet him.

They became experts at hiding time. Enough days that they could live together as man and wife, fed and protected by Fergus and Brigid, ignoring the parasite by the hearth, who grew ever more skeletal and no less malignant. He spat impotent threats and vile insults until Skarfr quietly reminded him of what was owed to a host – and the alternative. But he was harmless, a worm indeed. With Hlif beside him, Skarfr even pitied his old master, remembered his verse and his teaching, put the beatings out of mind. Such pity rendered the yellowing eyes more bilious with envy as they watched the young couple's joy, the older couple's benevolent ministrations.

Running along the beach where they had first met, Skarfr and Hlif knew the heady brew of freedom. Breaking bread together, discussing sheep with Fergus and how to smoke fish with Brigid, all the daily practicalities of household management were moments as dear as those when they lay together. No pretence.

Was that when a dark shadow passed over Skarfr's joy? Not fear of the risks they took, for when he was in the Bu, Thorbjorn seemed as self-absorbed as a dragon with its hoard and all was calm in Orphir, sheltered from the storms that gathered in Norðvegr and Skotland.

No, not fear of risks but the knowledge that stolen meetings would never be enough in the future, not now they'd lived together. As Rognvald's return loomed ever nearer, there was desperation in each embrace, even in their plans for the homestead's wool production and cheese-making. Every time they lay together was goodbye as they didn't know on which return to the Bu they would find news of the Jarl's return and they would be stuck there, under surveillance. They would not be able to sneak away so easily, even for a few hours, and winter would make trysts even more difficult.

Besides, they didn't *want* to sneak away.

'I will change his mind,' Hlif said.

But Skarfr knew Rognvald's stance was built on his Christianity and his kindness: unshakable foundations.

'If you bring the subject up, he'll think you have someone in mind and he'll watch you more closely. He has only just dismissed his suspicions of me but if he thought you cared for someone, he might wonder.'

And, although Skarfr had learned enough tact not to say so, what Hlif said about herself was unbelievable but true. Other men did not pay her any attention except as a shrewd businesswoman and trustworthy steward. There were no rivals, for which he was grateful. He needed no other man's confirmation of Hlif's beauty and worth. But that made it impossible for Hlif to misdirect Rognvald as to suitors.

Inevitably, the day came, with shouts and bustle at the Bu. Ships had been sighted. The Jarl had returned with his company of foreigners, all set for a wild Orkneyjar winter before setting off on the voyage that would make a saga of sagas.

Skarfr and Hlif had run out of time. Although he never mentioned it, Skarfr kept remembering the malediction Hlif had cast on him when they were children. Now he was a man, he understood that she'd felt slighted by his foolish declaration that he would marry Inge. But her words could not be unsaid and he was no hero to meet the impossible conditions.

*I will marry you when my curse is lifted and when you are a skald renowned from the Old Country to this.*

# CHAPTER THIRTY-SEVEN

Skarfr passed on to Rognvald the gossip from Ness about trouble brewing in neighbouring Skotland. He did not mention the source of his information and had burned the message signed with the letter I.

'Rumours are abroad that Erlend is pressing his claim to be jarl and he gathers men about him. King David has given public backing to Erlend's right to Orkney.' Skarfr did not press the point that Erlend's right to Orkney was arguably stronger than Rognvald's. Erlend was a jarl's son while Rognvald was a jarl's nephew. But Rognvald was older and he was here.

'Erlend has no support in Orkneyjar and no man here cares what King David of Skotland thinks. He was quick enough to support Harald when it suited him and he enjoys sowing division.' Rognvald dismissed Skarfr's concerns, having already spoken with Thorbjorn, whose analysis always showed his own stewardship as a period of peace and prosperity.

'If Sweyn backed Erlend...'

The Jarl laughed, 'On *that* day, the moon and sun would drink ale together in the banquet hall of the sky. You forget that Sweyn killed Frakork and Erlend is of her family.'

It seemed to Skarfr that everyone was related to Frakork but not everyone regretted her death. He did not say so to her brother-in-law. Rognvald had other reasons for ambiguity in his relationship with the sea-rover who had made him jarl and yet flouted his authority at all turns.

Skarfr was dismissed as lightly as his report and he readily left Rognvald dealing with a thousand and one problems caused by the influx of pilgrims-to-be, from Norðvegr and Ness. Their need of shelter and food would pass the thousand and one problems on to Hlif but she was not responsible for their entertainment. The months until spring, when the ships would finally set sail for Jórsalaheim, would be long and fractious, with more men arriving each month until winter storms confirmed that all those intending to come had arrived.

So many names to remember. The leaders: Magnus, the son of Hávard, Gunni's son; Swein, Hróald's son; Thorgeir Skotakoll, Oddi the little, Thorberg Svarti, Armód the skald, Thorkel Krókauga, Grímkell of Flettuness, and Bjarni his son; Erling, Jón, his brother-in-law, Aslák and Guttorm. And of course, most important of all, Eindridi, the man who'd inspired Rognvald with the idea of sailing for Jórsalaheim.

In addition to catering for his increased entourage and preventing the inevitable violence they'd wreak on each other if bored, the Jarl was calming rumours that he'd been insulted by Eindridi and that he would take revenge.

The Norðvegr shipbuilder had kept his word and when Rognvald reached Biörgvin, he found an exquisite piece of workmanship, with carvings not only on the prow but also on the vanes, ornamented in gilt. A sun vane, showing the ship's orientation by the pointer's shadow, and a weathervane, attached to the mast to show wind direction.

'She goes like the wind,' the shipbuilder told Rognvald and so he named her. The *Wind-cutter*. All considered it a name of good omen and when the wind appeared favourable for the return journey to Orkneyjar, the fleet sailed with the Jarl at its head, as agreed. However, out at sea, the wind dropped, leaving his splendid, heavy ship slower than the others.

From respect, the other captains took down their sails to keep pace with the *Wind-cutter* and there was a good spirit in the company. But when the wind picked up, the Jarl's ship stormed ahead and the smaller boats had to use reefed sails to cope with the conditions. Only two boats rivalled the Jarl's in speed and one surpassed the *Wind-cutter* both in size, speed and splendour.

Eindridi's ship overtook the *Wind-cutter*, proudly flaunting its dragon prow, gilded head and stern, and vibrant paintwork, in flagrant breach of the agreement that only the Jarl of Orkneyjar would have the status of such a dragon-prowed drakkar, as became the leader of the expedition.

Skarfr remembered Thorbjorn's face whenever Sweyn and the *Death-bringer* passed the *Surf-rider;* Rognvald's humiliation was greater as Eindridi had showed disrespect for their agreement, for the Jarl's status and for Orkneyjar itself. This boded ill for the coming voyage.

But while men were placing wagers on a fight and the outcome, Rognvald once more showed himself a bigger man than those who pulled his nose.

He was asked in public what he was going to do about such insolence and he replied, in his usual confident manner, 'Eindridi is a proud man and chafed at keeping pace with those who are clearly his inferiors.' There was no humility in Rognvald's analysis of what had happened. 'Time will tell whether Fortune stays with him or passes him by. We don't need to change our course according to one he follows in the heat of the moment.'

Who would he rather sail with? Skarfr asked himself. Hotheads or a steady head? The answer was obvious and the put-down achieved more than any wrestling bout would have. There was no lingering ill-will between Eindridi and Rognvald as each man had proved his point, in his own manner.

Instead, petty rivalries broke out elsewhere, between different men; a thousand sparks with fewer men to fight the fires than to start them.

Skarfr and Hlif were usually too busy defending their own bed-spaces from those seeking a warm corner in the Bu, or commandeering everything from cabbages to mail coifs, to even try to meet up.

When Hlif whispered, 'The Brogar standing stones, in two hours,' Skarfr immediately suspected the worst. His face must have revealed his feelings because she shook her head, murmured, 'Not here,' and moved away to resolve a dispute over smashed eggs. She had told Skarfr about the unthinkable quantity of eggs needed each week and his admiration for her organisation grew, the more he knew about the number of people involved in getting all the resources required to the ever-increasing population in the Bu, the village and the environs.

Understanding how impossibly busy she was made Skarfr even more surprised that she could find time for a spontaneous assignation. Usually, their rare meetings were planned ahead, to free a few hours when nobody would notice them missing simultaneously.

He leaned against one of the ancient slabs of granite, watching the way she would come, past the Steinnesvatn circle of stones, past the Watcher, a fossilised troll guarding the Bridge of Brogar, which was a narrow causeway between lochs, and up to the elevated knoll where the stones of their meeting-place cast long shadows against a backdrop of water and sky.

She ran the last part, the tools jiggling on her leather belt. He didn't like the new additions of her wand and pouch of rune-stones but he could hardly object to her carrying what she believed to be weapons. And maybe she was right. The witch Frakork had been feared. *Until she was burned in her house.*

'I'm coming too,' she told him as she threw herself into his arms, triumphant.

When Skarfr could speak, without being distracted by the physical charms on offer, he said, 'But I'm not going anywhere.'

She gave him one of those looks which suggested his intellect was lower than an earthworm's and stated the obvious. 'To Jórsalaheim. I've been working on Rognvald, letting him see how difficult it is catering for so many and how I can solve problems for him.'

He looked at her shrewdly. 'You've created those problems, haven't you?'

She tossed her head and some ginger curls escaped her coif. 'I might have.' She rushed on, 'And then this morning, I read the runes for him.'

'Don't tell me – the runes said a red-haired woman would travel on the Jarl's ship or the company would never reach Jórsalaheim.'

'No, silly. Rognvald is much too sharp for such nonsense.' Her voice took on the far-away tone in which she told of her visions and Skarfr shivered, holding onto Hlif as if she might be snatched from him by the gods who spoke to her.

'The runes said that the company would reach Jórsalaheim but Rognvald would be more changed by the journey than by the destination. A woman would change his life. I have seen her, slim and golden.'

Hlif looked at him, her eyes dancing, and her voice was teasing, no longer in another world. 'I know what you're thinking. Inge!'

He did not deny it.

She shook her head. 'No, this is some foreign noblewoman on distant shores but I *saw* her. When I read the runes, my visions are channelled by them and I would never lie about what the gods show.'

Unlike him. Skarfr flushed. Thanks to him, Thorbjorn would always believe *he* saw visions and was hiding them and that Hlif was a deceitful fake. She could call herself a witch, carry a wand, wave it about and cast runes but she would never have any power over Thorbjorn. Skarfr had stolen that from her. He shivered, then reassured himself. She didn't need any power – he would protect her, he vowed, against Thorbjorn, against the gods themselves. And he did not like the idea of her risking this sea voyage.

'All I had to do then was ask to go on the pilgrimage, as cook and steward. Rognvald was already malleable because of the runes, could work out for himself how a wise woman would contribute to a voyage, read minds and read the weather, so I didn't need to point that out.'

'But it will be years voyaging with sea-roving men and staying in barbaric countries.'

Her face darkened. 'I am well used to being among rough men and will be safer on a ship than anywhere here, especially if I am left without Rognvald's protection. And yours,' she added, a little too late for his pride.

He suffered the full weight of her stormy eyes.

'What if Thorbjorn finds out what we did?' she asked.

'That's old news now, buried and forgotten.' Skarfr shook off his forebodings. He was confident that nobody would have any reason to reveal the role they'd played in Inge's escape. 'No, Thorbjorn will relish his own importance advising Harald, with Rognvald out of the way, and will be too busy to look back.'

Hlif looked less convinced but neither of them wanted to waste precious time together on worrying about what might never happen.

'I'll be with you,' she said, her gaze slipping away and he sensed there was something she was holding back.

He took hold of her chin gently, turned her face so her eyes met his again. 'Why is it so important that you go?'

Her voice low, she told him, 'I will go as a pilgrim. In the Holy City, my prayers to the White Christ and to Rognvald will touch him. He cannot help but release me from my doom, let me,' she hesitated over the word, 'be with you.'

*Marry,* he understood but did not say, in case gods more spiteful than the White Christ were listening.

'Oh, *elskan min,* my darling,' he said, voice and heart breaking. Rognvald's mind was flint and grief surely lay ahead for Hlif, even worse than St Magnus' mockery of her prayers. Besides, she herself had laid a bane on their marriage. He would no more be a skald than she would be free of her curse. Married or not, they would continue to defy the Jarl and the fate-bringer Norns, in secret, without drawing attention to themselves.

And although he was full of misgivings — Hlif suffering the hardships and risks of the open sea, the proximity of ship life with Rognvald watching their every move — his heart ached at the thought of leaving her for years.

'We'll manage somehow,' he said, capitulating.

They walked slowly across the Bridge of Brogar, past the Watcher until they could see the other great ancient upright, that stood before the Steinnesvatn circle. The great Óðinn Stone, pierced by a hole: a source of magic, whispered by those who said petitions were granted here that the kirk would never countenance.

'Come,' she bade him, running to the Óðinn Stone, with that quicksilver movement that made him feel like a bear, lumbering after her. Offerings of flowers, bread and cheese lay beside the monument.

She stopped on the other side, hidden by the ancient monolith, except for her hand through the hole in the rock and her voice, which floated eerily towards him with the timbre of her second sight.

He took her hand, small and still, callouses forming at the base of the slim fingers. The granite circle around their joined hands made a ceremonial ring, the serpent around the world.

Time stopped and with the solemnity of oath, she told him, 'I am your Valkyrie and would follow you across the nine realms and into eternity.'

As always, the poetry formed in his head and could not be spoken. 'Jórsalaheim is far enough,' was all he could manage. Was she disappointed? She said nothing. But she did not drop his hand. He plucked up courage.

'Into eternity,' he promised, a lump in his throat, and the inner vows he could not speak were heard by Óðinn. One-handed, he pulled twine from his pouch and bound their two clasped hands. He was pledged to Hlif, handfasted, with the gods as witness. He let Hlif be the one to slip her hand free, taking the twine to her side of the great stone. No more words were needed.

Their stolen hours passed too quickly and life was an endless series of chores for both of them as the days grew shorter and darker, the visitors squabbled more and the spring sailing seemed too far away to keep peace, even as the prospect grew nearer.

In search of entertainment, the Norðmen provoked peaceful villagers into aggression, their buildings vandalised and the farm beasts running amok. Hlif had hidden the large drinking horn and replaced it with a small one in a vain attempt to limit catastrophes after the 'down-in-one' competitions. Rognvald was forever paying compensation and soothing ruffled feathers, devising manly contests with sling and sword, riddles and verse, anything to exercise bodies and minds.

Then came the day that great Thór and the snow *jǫtunn* Skaði waged elemental war against Orkneymen and visitors alike. The day of the Midwinter Solstice.

Feasts and games were ongoing for the midwinter festival and Rognvald had turned a blind eye to the sacrifices planned or practised, in the old manner. The standing stones were no longer a place for lovers as their iron-hard beds showed rusty stains and offerings that were flesh not flower.

The wind had been howling for blood all night, turning men restless and bad-tempered so Skarfr was not surprised to hear of foolish sorties the next day by foreigners who might be used to facing wolves and mountains but had no stomach for Orkneyjar's endless winter gales and grey skies.

However, the level of recklessness was beyond imagination and when two Norðvegr men were unaccounted for, enquiries found that they had intended to fish on the loch of Steinnesvatn.

Cursing, but unwilling to abandon them to a cold fate in the worsening sleet and icy gusts, Rognvald chose a company of Orkneyjar and Ness men to retrieve the idiots. Glowering blacker than the clouds, he asked the Norðmen to stay safe in the Bu as they did not know the terrain. For once, they didn't argue.

Only when the party had set off, wrapped warmly against the hostile weather, did Skarfr realise that a tiny muffled, cloaked figure with them was no intrepid boy but Hlif, with stout boots and stouter determination.

'Madness!' he muttered to her as his lips grew dry and chapped.

'I'll be needed to nurse them,' she said. 'To make sure they're warmed and brought back alive. For the Jarl to kill them as he chooses!'

Soon, the question was not whether the missing men would get back alive but whether Rognvald and his company would.

# CHAPTER THIRTY-EIGHT

F linging icy specks and flurries of snow into their faces by
ever madder gusts of wind, Skaði, the winter goddess,
mocked these puny men who stumbled across a landscape with no
shelter. Not a tree, not a shepherd's hut interrupted the playing
field of the whirlwind, a bleak stretch of grassland with water
beyond. Skarfr hoped the water *was* beyond and not a misstep
away as the world whitened, blinding him so he could barely see
his own hands, freezing even in the wool mittens he'd donned.
Like a land version of the Swelchie, the blizzard turned around the
company in a vortex of stinging snow.

'He's blowing a guster,' the man beside Skarfr yelled in his ear,
as if describing the weather gave them some control over its
impact.

'Ay, and a *moor*.' Skarfr responded in kind, using the local word
for blinding snow.

Stumbling, frozen, each barely able to see the man next to him,
they moved onwards without knowing what Rognvald was
leading them into. His voice sometimes carried above the keening
wind, hoarse but encouraging. Hidden by the whirling snow,

Skarfr reached for Hlif's hand, mitten around mitten, and squeezed. They would come through this.

Such snow was rare and if it came at all, was usually in the months after Yuletide, so the men were ill-equipped for such an onslaught. All the familiar features of their landscape were lost in blinding white. No sun, no ancient stones, no lochs. Heading home would only be an option if they knew which direction to go. Even if they were lucky, they'd walked well over an hour before the snowstorm struck. At their current pace, how long would it take them to retrace their steps? And if they went round in circles? Was that better than mistaking loch for land and drowning in the icy waters?

While such gloomy thoughts vied in his head with verse expressing them, *Skaði's white tears, winter's eagle-food,* Skarfr realised he was walking up a slope. Hlif dropped his hand, pushed past the man in front of her to reach Rognvald, shouted something, but her words were whipped away and Skarfr only knew that she moved in front of Rognvald, walking up some kind of hillock. The Jarl and the men followed, snow now up to their calves and forming drifts that caused more than one to lurch and grab his neighbour.

Then Hlif and Rognvald disappeared. Not just by walking down the other side of the hill and fading from sight: they completely vanished at the crest of the hill. They were yards in front of Skarfr, then they'd gone. When he reached the same place, he saw the hole in the snow, rubble below, a rough descent to ... somewhere. There was no choice but to follow, yelling to those behind him to do likewise.

Scrambling down the steep, tumbled rock, trying not to twist ankles already tired from negotiating hazards hidden by snow, Skarfr could see Hlif and the Jarl taking in their surroundings in silence. As well they might.

This was no cavern but a stone building of ancient and skilled construction, dimly visible in the light entering from the hole in the roof, through which men scrambled, cursing, accompanied by snowflakes which found their way through the opening, dusting the rockfall in white.

'Move slowly till you touch a wall and stand still!' ordered Rognvald, his voice echoing in what must be a confined space.

Skarfr told himself they could climb out the way they'd come, they weren't trapped, they had plenty of air from the hole above. The air was musty, dank, suffocating. And there was something in the quality of darkness, of being underground, as in a barrow, a tomb, but made of stone rather than earth.

No sooner had the thought come to him than he heard whispers, in no language he knew. The hairs stood up on the back of his neck and he knew from the poor attempts at jokes by the other men that they felt uneasy too. But they *weren't* trapped.

'We're all here.' Hlif's voice was calm but then she was used to the dead walking. Skarfr shuddered as invisible beings brushed against him.

'If we light a fire on the rocks here,' she moved to the bottom of the rockfall, a slight figure flickering in the stormlight, 'we'll have warmth and light. There's enough kindling to start it. Someone has been here before us. Vemundr, do you have your touchwood with you?'

'Ay.' The Ness man joined Hlif, brought the precious firelighter out of his metal tin and blew on it. After some perseverance, the smouldering matter flickered into life and breathed fire into the sticks and lump of peat bequeathed to those seeking shelter by whoever had come this way before them.

Nostrils clogged with earthy smoke and ancient fustiness, Skarfr catalogued his surroundings in the flickering firelight. Like penned sheep, even smelling of damp wool, the men were huddled in a large square chamber. The ceiling was a high dome, with the hole in the top where they'd entered. In each of the four walls was a shadow, a recess.

Surely there was an entry? Unless the stone barrow had been walled up after ... whatever ... had been placed here. And where there were barrows, *'haugs'*, as they were known, there were *haug-boys* protecting them, ghostly occupants fighting against the desecration of their last resting-place and against the theft of the goods they would need in the next world.

Skarfr ignored the susurration, the light touch on his face. Spider-webs, he told himself. He saw Hlif's face glow unearthly, as if she walked in two worlds. He dared not reach out to her, this time not only because of Rognvald's ban.

The Jarl ordered four men to each explore a recess, see what was in it and report.

'Nothing,' came three answers. 'An empty alcove one and a half paces deep.'

*Big enough for a body. Someone important.*

Rognvald must have had the same thought. 'Must have been treasures here once.'

'Well, there's nothing now.'

The fourth man reported back. 'It's not a recess – it's a tunnel. You have to double up to walk along, and it's only one man's width, but it's solid, well-constructed. It's blocked at the other end but I think that might have been the way in. I tested it with my axe and it's earth, not stone.'

Rognvald glanced up at the hole in the roof, where snow was still spiralling down from a steely sky.

'We'll shelter here till it stops,' he decided. 'Ottar and Arnfior, take turns using your axes at the end of the tunnel, see if we can free up an entry. If the earth starts blocking the access, leave it. We can always try to find the entry from the outside, now we know the layout.

'Ormr, pace out the chamber's width and length. Note the

point where you're under the hole in the roof. The tunnel's in the middle of that wall so when the blizzard's stopped we can work out the orientation and where to connect with the entry.'

'Why?' asked Ormr. 'It's only some old building with nothing in it.'

'What are we supposed to do while we're waiting?' complained one voice.

Rognvald snapped. 'Are you men or children with your whining and boredom? Don't you sense something in this place?' He glanced at Hlif and once more, Skarfr wondered what she had told the Jarl when she brought him to the hole in the top of the hillock.

'It is gods-touched,' said the Jarl, doing what he did best, taking a hard situation and mastering it. 'See these lines?' He ran his finger along nicks carved in the wall. 'They are smoothed with time, ancient. Maybe they were once sacred pictures.

'And we are pilgrims. So let us mark this place as ours, in God's name, for all those who come to know we were here, when we have gone to heaven. See, I'll begin.'

He took up a shard of stone and wrote the futhark, the runic alphabet, in sixteen careful runes on the ancient wall. Rune-making: one of Rognvald's nine skills. Skarfr thought of the stonemason at the cathedral, marking his building blocks. The men's humour swung from surly to enthusiastic. With an axe or knife-tip, with found stones or with fire-flints, they took turns carving a message to the future, jostling each other for space. This would be their cathedral, one where crude men could leave their mark. A saga etched in stone. They had lived and they had been here.

Checking their runes against the futhark Rognvald had cut into the stone or against each other's work, men put their names on the walls. Vermundr, Ottar, Ogmundr, Hermundr Hard, Anfior son of Stein and Arnfirthr Food *carved these runes*.

The shortest man of the company drew gales of laughter when he perched on another's shoulders to chip into the stone, *Eyolfr Kolbeinssonr carved these runes high.*

The Jarl displayed his skill in another message more fitting for eternity.

*The man who is most skilled in runes west of the ocean carved these runes with the axe which Gaukr Trandlissonr owned in the south of the Old Country.*

With supreme confidence in his own future fame, he didn't even sign it.

'Is that Gaukr Trandlissonr's axe?' asked an innocent, in awe, eyeing Rognvald's weapon, supposedly that of a dead saga hero. His question was met with guffaws and a heavy slap on the back.

'It's a joke! It's like saying he wields Thórr's hammer! It's what poets do,' explained Hermundr, taking pity on the poor soul.

One of the more pious Ness men started a new topic with, *Jórsalaheim men broke this mound* and first Benedikt, then two more men etched crosses, whether from religious fervour or because they didn't trust their runes.

Then Hlif made the men step aside for her to carve her runes on two blocks to the right-hand side of what must be the back wall. She asked Skarfr for his hand-axe and made a tentative mark with the sharp tip but she shook her head at its unwieldy heft. Returning the axe, she pulled the steel-tipped wand from her belt instead and with a steady hand, she scored the stone. When she realised that she might not have enough space, she made the runes narrower so she could squeeze them all in.

*Jórsalaheim-farers broke Orkhaugr.*
*Carved by Hlif, the Jarl's housekeeper*

*Orkhaugr.* In naming the stone barrow, Hlif made them all aware once more of the hostile atmosphere and attempts at jokes fell flat in nervous laughter. The chamber was full of invisible *haugars* and *haug-boys,* revenants and barrow-spirits who hated intruders.

'What do you think happened to the treasure that must have been here?' asked Rognvald, distracting the men from dark thoughts.

'Rats ate it,' suggested one man.

'Big rats with two legs stole it, more like. Whoever broke in before us and left the kindling.'

The Jarl was thoughtful. 'And whoever comes after us will think we took it.'

Hlif said, 'No they won't. Let's make them look elsewhere!' She carved,

*In the north-west great treasure is hidden.*
*It was long ago that great treasure was hidden here.*
*Happy is he who can find the great wealth as*
*Hakon alone carried treasure from this mound.*

Men sucked their beards, slapped their sides and laughed. 'That should send them all off to Byrgisey chasing some Hakon.'

'I wouldn't want to live in Byrgisey and be called Hakon.' Just the thought of some poor man being harassed for his treasure made them laugh all the more.

Then someone had another idea.

'Let's make them think we only just missed getting the treasure so they think the trail's still hot and get their boats to the water faster than a dog to a bone.' He carved,

*What I say is true, that the treasure was carried away three nights before*
*they broke this mound.*

Hlif pursed her lips. 'Shouldn't it be "we" not "they"?'

'I meant "they, the *Jórsalaheim-farers*", same as you wrote,' came the aggrieved reply.

'But—' began Hlif, about to argue.

Skarfr was relieved when she thought better of it and held her tongue. Debate on the finer points of runes and grammar would not have been appreciated.

Luckily, somebody else had an idea to keep the joke running.

'Let's confuse them, make them wonder whether the treasure is hidden here after all!' Oddr set to, marking on the wall,

*Truly it is told to me that the treasure is hidden here well enough. Few know this, says Oddr Orkansor in the runes he carved.*

Imagining the confusion of those reading such contradictory messages briefly lightened the atmosphere again but the shadows still flickered. Skarfr's head felt the pressure of untold years weighing on him, whispering wrongness.

'I want to write something about this place,' said Rognvald, 'something respectful.'

The men watched as their Jarl carved his precise runes.

*This mound was built before Lodbrok's. Her sons were bold; they were real men.*

Everyone knew of Ragnar Lodbrok, 'Shaggy-Breeks', a hero every bit as famous as the Rognvald from whom the Jarl took his name. But 'her' made no sense unless... Skarfr laughed at the wit.

'Why "her"?' asked Hlif, boldly asking what others would not.

'It's making fun of Lodbrok's hairy breeks, suggesting they're unmanly, but of course he was *the* most manly of heroes so it's ironic.'

'Oh.' Hlif's tone suggested she wasn't convinced. Women never did understand the subtleties of skaldic wit.

'Your words are good,' Skarfr told Hlif, trying to take her mind off Rognvald's jokes. She looked at her runes on the wall and he could feel her slipping into the otherworldly trance of her visions.

*Jórsalaheim-farers broke Orkhaugr. Carved by Hlif, the Jarl's housekeeper.*

Stepping back from her work, Hlif turned towards Skarfr, her eyes glowing ever brighter, drawing power from the chamber that was *not* empty but full of ghosts, all hammering in his head as if he were their anvil and they would beat him to fine steel. Urging him to make his mark.

When Hlif spoke to him, her voice was heavy with his doom and he could only obey. 'Make your mark, Skarfr.'

Hardly aware he was holding a shard he'd picked up, Skarfr turned to the wall, found his space on the narrow edge of an upright slab, near the two blocks Hlif had inscribed. Then the dragon breathed fire and Skarfr's world flamed red and gold.

# CHAPTER THIRTY-NINE

Consumed by unearthly fire, Skarfr etched an outline on the wall. Only Hlif remained in this otherworld, protecting him, her arms spread out like wings drying – but even she was mute and static while the gods spoke through his stone. Like Brother Kristian's illuminations, like the stonemason's mark, like Thorbjorn's cormorant, the lines made a shape, like and unlike the creations of those three artists.

Skarfr was conscious only of the shaping itself, not of any influences. Blowing through him, the dragon made an image of itself. Four prancing legs, clawed feet and a proudly arched neck. One huge, slanted eye in the profile of a head looking back over its right shoulder. Tongue lolling as the mouth breathed fire. One scallop at a time, Skarfr added delicate scales on back, neck and head, as if he were scraping the surface with a penknife to find the gold underneath. Tail swinging between its legs, like a penis, like an arrow, swinging up...

And then Skarfr stopped carving, his hand held in a gigantic, scaled grip, the foul stench of rotted meat rolling over him, a voice old and deep as oceans and centuries rumbling through his mind, 'That is enough.'

But it wasn't. Skarfr could see the dragon carved on the wall but he had not finished. There was more he had to say and he struggled, alone against this primeval force unleashed by the tomb, still guarding its lost treasure.

Resonant, scalding laughter ripped through him.

'You wish to wrestle with me, little one?'

'Not wrestle but riddle,' Skarfr told the dragon, drawing on his time with Botolf for all he'd learned of standing his ground and of old stories, dragons and heroes.

More laughter, which surged through Skarfr's guts like a purge.

'Very well then. Three riddles. Guess them and you may spoil my creation in whatever manner you choose. Fail and you join me, guarding this tomb.'

Skarfr swallowed. 'So be it.'

The dragon's words rumbled like an earthquake, reverberating through Skarfr's entire body, not just his eardrums.

*'Who grasps the earth,*
*swallowing wood and water;*
*fears no son of Embla*
*but dreads storms and wind;*
*takes on the sun in*
*a fight to the death*
*that repeats when this great one*
*grows strong again?*

*Small messenger of the worm's lair,*
*guess my riddle.'*

Immediately, Skarfr thought of Jörmungandr, the Midgard Serpent who *grasps the earth* but on second thoughts, this did not fit and he held his tongue until he had the whole picture. *Son of Embla* was obviously *'man'* as all men were descended from the first mother, Embla, made from a tree. The gods didn't fear man, neither did the powers of nature, and they were all *great ones*. But the gods wouldn't fear storms or wind.

'I have it!' Skarfr told the dragon. 'This is a force of nature which *swallows up wood and water* and *fights the sun* by making them invisible. But as soon as the wind gets up, the sun breaks through and he is defeated. *Fog* is the answer!'

The dragon gave a low rumble at defeat and opened its maw, showing two rows of spear-sharp teeth. A blast of yellow smoke preceded the second riddle.

*'What is that wonder*
*I saw outside*
*before Dellingr's Door;*
*two lifeless ones,*
*lacking breath*
*yet blowing briskly*
*they branded the hilt's tongue?*

*Small messenger of the worm's lair,*
*guess my riddle.'*

Skarfr laughed. These were old and easy riddles for a skald trained by Botolf.

The god *Dellingr* had sired *Day*, so this was just a poetic way to say when the imaginary event had taken place, before daylight. And *lifeless ones* were usually objects being described as if animate, for surely the gods could embue life where they chose. *Two* means a pair...

'I have it,' Skarfr told the dragon. 'When there is no air squeezed into this pair, they are flat but when filled with air, they make the fire hot to forge weapons such as a sword, *the hilt's tongue*. The answer is *bellows*.'

But there was one riddle left and he should have hidden his elation. The dragon spat sparks as he roared,

'Who, dressed in black,
travels with swift ease the
eagle path and fish ways, and
carries the wave-rider who is
blind, deaf and dumb,
taking him hearth-wise from the whale road
to where his sword sleeps?

Small messenger of the worm's lair,
guess my riddle.'

Sweat bubbled up from fear or from the dragon-heat, trickled into his eyes, stinging.

The dragon was in Skarfr's blood and bone, crooning to him. *Black, eagle path, blind man* ... the words tumbled round Skarfr's head, making no sense.

'A bargain must be kept,' rumbled the dragon's voice. 'If you don't know the answer, you must say so and join me here, immortal.'

Skarfr played for time, deciphering the easy puzzles. '*Eagle path* is the sky and *fish ways* are the rivers and seas.' Was it a Valkyrie dressed in black? A man blind, deaf and dumb? What sort of man was blind, deaf and dumb? Was it sweat that blinded? He felt as if the answers were behind a locked door and he'd lost the key.

'Parts do not make the whole. What is your answer? Well?'

*Parts do not make the whole.* Skarfr shut his eyes to picture the whole riddle, remembered that skaldic verse so often unravelled from the ending like a skein of wool. The ending. *Home where the sword sleeps.* Death! Then *blind, deaf and dumb* made sense. And it was not Death in black, carrying a sea-rover home. It was a messenger of the gods, it was...

'I know your riddle, great cousin to the serpent who circles the earth.' A little respect might atone for earlier smugness. '*Blind, deaf and dumb* is the corpse of a sea-rover, dead at sea on the *whale road* and the one who carries home his spirit so he may rest in peace, is one in black who flies and dives, one in black *feathers*—' He drew out the suspense, sure of himself.

The dragon's eyes gleamed. He was sure of himself too.

Skarfr knew why, as he'd nearly made the expected error. Any other respondent would jump to Óðinn's bird, the raven, as an answer, despite that bird's landlocked nature.

'A cormorant,' declared Skarfr and knew straight away that he was right, from the flash of fire in the darkened eyes, a wisp of smoke hissing from the forked tongue.

Then the dragon changed tactics, began to croon, hypnotic. 'Well-guessed, small messenger of the worm's lair. You are far too gifted for the life you lead. A bargain must be kept,' sang the voice, irresistible as fishfolk dragging a man down into Finfolkaheem. 'But you can *choose* to join me instead.'

So tempting, to let go of all that hurt, to be magnificent, immortal, have purpose...

A screech of defiance drew Skarfr's eyes to the hole in the roof, where a black bird hurtled down towards him, claws and beak outstretched. His cormorant, coming to take his eyes out. He stood unflinching. As she had given him life, so she could take it. The dragon inside him roared, helpless as the cormorant folded her wings, streamlined her body and dived into the great beast within Skarfr as if she were diving into the sea. He felt their union as she seized the dragon's tail, merged with him.

Containing their spirits in his own, shaking with effort, he finished his carving, etched his brave cormorant, diving into the scaled dragon in eternal conflict and eternal union.

Panting, Skarfr stood, recovering. Hlif lowered her wand and her arms, shrank to her usual proportions, concern writ as clearly on her face as the runes all around them on the walls.

She walked to him slowly, as if they were in some dream-state and held her hand to his head. 'Burning,' she said. 'You're burning up. This is what I saw! I'm sorry but I must do this, focus the fire.'

Skarfr thought she meant the dragon's fire but he was aware now of the chamber they had entered, the rockfall, the fire started by Rognvald's man. She bent down, picked up a piece of hot charcoal and held it in her bare hand without showing any pain. She approached Skarfr and rubbed it onto his right arm, then pressed the seared flesh against the carving he'd made. He heard somebody scream in agony.

He saw Rognvald and the other men, present again, all looking at him. His head was spinning.

'I'm sorry,' said Hlif. 'But all will be well now.'

He dropped to the ground, unable to speak, hearing voices at a distance, as if from another world, but not those from the past.

'By the rood.' Rognvald, swearing. 'He's carved the lion of St Mark. It's wonderful!'

Skarfr could feel the dragon and the cormorant biting some barrier in his head, tearing him open with teeth, claws and beak. He wanted to put Rognvald right but when he opened his mouth, out came a flood of words, undammed, unstoppable.

*'The shroud-pin that broke. An aged man in crewel hues, whose sword he cannot use. No harm to Baldr swore the boulders, bears and all of nature's blades. All but mistletoe made vows to Frigg his mother not to harm a hair on Baldr's head. No harm in mistletoe, thought Frigg so young and green-white innocent, so Frigg his mother thought before her fears shaped tears. One hundred hammer-strokes clinked his heart iron-hard, manly, fit for stormy passage and rough seas, for reddening the raven's claw, an overlap of brothers' wooden shields sealing out the heady drink of women's wiles and words that capsized unwary warriors'.*

'He's moonstruck!' exclaimed Benedikt, horrified.

'No.' Rognvald crossed himself. 'It's poetry. And he will be the best skald among us. If he lives.'

'I'm through to the outside,' yelled the man whose turn it was to hew at the blockage in the tunnel. 'The sun's come out!'

While the drama inside the tomb had been claiming their attention, the blizzard had ceased and the light filtering down through the roof was now gilded.

Within minutes of the first breakthrough in the entrance, a big enough hole had been cleared to allow shafts of sunlight to pierce the chamber, hitting any man who stood awestruck between the tunnel and the back wall.

'Midwinter Solstice,' said the Jarl, crossing himself again, as the alignment of the tunnel and the setting midwinter sun displayed the architectural skills of those whose sacred place they occupied.

'Look,' yelled the man who'd cleared the tunnel entrance.

One by one, they bent to walk along the tunnel, twenty paces long, and each man gasped as he saw the sunlight hit the great standing stone, alone in a far field, before spearing the tunnel and the chamber in its magical light.

Skarfr was motionless in Sól's fire, unable to move. Not moonstruck, sunstruck.

Voided, he closed his mouth and sank into black nothing, leaving behind these little humans and the new tattoo that throbbed on his arm. A cormorant diving into a dragon. His spirit creatures.

# CHAPTER FORTY

Flames danced in the fire-pit and the hall was full of the Jarl's subjects and foreign pilgrims, all celebrating Yuletide. Jórsalaheim-farers saw no dissonance in cheering on the pagan festivities. The two men who'd gone missing on the Winter Solstice cheered the loudest of all, none the worse for their adventure. They'd sheltered under their boat then found a well-stocked farm when the blizzard stopped. Rognvald jovially declared there was no harm done; an adventure added to his saga.

Skarfr sat at the High Table, his stomach in knots, knowing what he must face, remembering a brutal master and a young boy ten years earlier. He was a man now. Ale warmed his belly, instead of souring his guts and turning his mind. *Ale: talk-maker, sense-taker, head-breaker.*

As he raised his cup, the dragon tattoo rippled on his arm. The dragon *and* the cormorant, but only he knew the detail and significance of the coupling. Maybe Hlif guessed but they had not found time alone together since Skarfr had been carried back to the Bu in triumph, a skald touched by divine madness, the dragon carver – or the griffon carver – or the lion carver, depending on men's fancy as the story was retold to those who had not been on the fateful expedition.

One other man had been touched by the gods, lain twitching on the earthen floor of the ancient tomb. But he had merely screamed of *haug-boys* and had taken two days to return to being the dullard he'd been before. In contrast Skarfr wore a blue dragon on his arm and poetry on his tongue. He could taste the words in his mouth, seeking only the occasion to flame forth, no longer imprisoned.

'I told you the time would come,' Rognvald had told his newest skald, with quiet satisfaction. 'That your body would catch up with your mind.'

Was that what had happened? There were many ways to interpret the cause of this change. Only Skarfr knew of the seeds Botolf had sown, denying them light and air. How they'd grown in secret and bloomed in the dragon's fire.

The Jarl stood and issued his familiar challenge. 'Let's make verse.' He looked towards Skarfr and smiled, skald to skald. In private he'd been encouraging, told Skarfr he was ready now, but in public there was no patronage.

Rognvald looked around the Bu, seeking inspiration. When he pronounced 'fire' as the theme, Skarfr knew the Jarl was offering him an easy beginning, a topic with many well-known kennings to string together like beads on a necklace. Like turquoise beads worn by a fiery red-haired woman.

Skarfr felt Hlif's eyes on him, sending support. He risked a quick look, skating past Thorbjorn's dark mockery. He too would remember that night ten years ago. Was he hoping Skarfr would fail again or did he hold some softer emotion for the youth he'd trained in combat? Or both at the same time? Whatever his attitude, Skarfr no longer needed reassurance.

He admired Rognvald's clever lines. Fire as *branch-sorrow* and *tree-foe*, as *house-thief* and *bright wolf of the temple*. The audience showed their approbation, pleased with their Jarl.

Then Skarfr stood, pipe in hand. The shadow of a boy stood beside him, tipsy and scared, not ready for what was asked of him. And no shame in that, except for the adult who'd asked. No, not asked but *demanded* too much, watched him fall and never picked him up.

Rognvald was right. He was ready now. He played a few soft notes, the fire-pit sleeping.

> *'Where flame-food lies flat-dormant,*
> *starved, one touchwood spark will start*
> *the eager flicker-eating force.'*

Then he blew sharp notes like sparks through his pipe, a frenzied crackle that reached a crescendo. The fire caught. Now he echoed the Jarl's fire-song.

> *'Hot-headed son of the giant Forgnjotr, he*
> *leaps and licks, this red howling hound,*
> *life-harm and hall's doom, unleashed.'*

The fire music steadied, a dreamy melody showing what a man saw when he looked into the hearth-flames. Warmth, home, a woman. The wolf tamed.

> *'Holds every hall its Garmr, Hel-hound,*
> *and its Gunnr, Valkyrie who rides this warg,*
> *makes home from Hel, for heroes.'*

A few gentle notes from the pipe lulled the fire asleep again. It was over.

Skarfr waited, never before having felt the silence that followed such a performance. He looked around the Bu, at the listeners seated behind their tables, blinking as they came back from some otherworld of music and poetry. *His listeners: cups brimming with Óðinn's mead.*

Then fists banged on wood, followed by shouting and stamping.

Bemused, Skarfr looked back at Rognvald, seeking guidance. He saw tears streaming down the Jarl's cheeks, unheeded.

The skalds who usually joined in Rognvald's challenges stood up, looked at each other, shook their heads and pointed to the victor.

As if turned into a standing stone, Skarfr could not move, had no idea what he should do, as acclaim for his verse reverberated around the hall. And in the central fire-pit, the flames burned low and steady, repeating the words of his poem to those whose minds were still open.

With the smoothness of an experienced performer, Rognvald joined him, clasped his wrist in homage, called for quiet in the hall.

Skarfr knelt at his Jarl's feet, wondering whether he had erred in judgement yet again, a presumptuous star outshining the sun. What would the punishment be? Rognvald's pathfinder brooch Vegvisir gleamed level with his eyes. The sigil showed many directions for Skarfr, born in this moment.

'When the young man teaches the old, the world is upside down and I must blame the wicked stars for my defeat.' Rognvald mimed a crook-back walk, making it clear he was the old man, making everyone laugh at him and with him. This was his gift, as much as the wit of his rhyming.

He became serious, raised his hands above his head so that his cape fell back and the chain arm-rings jangled and shone.

'Let the world right itself again and know that the court of Jarl Rognvald of Orkney welcomes the peerless skald, Skarfr

Kristinsson, whose name shall be renowned from the Old Country to this.'

Skarfr's heart stopped at the words which lifted half a curse, gave him a flicker of hope – extinguished by Rognvald's next words.

'My man and my skald, Skarfr Kristinsson shall be a credit to me and to Orkneyjar, from here to Jórsalaheim and all places in between, his loyalty as evident as his gods-given talent. I will always reward such loyalty and such talent.'

Accompanied by more banging and shouting, Rognvald broke one of his gold arm-rings and presented Skarfr with four links of the chain. The remaining links went into Rognvald's pouch, saved for some future show of generosity. For the Jarl was the Ring-Breaker, a generous lord.

And Skarfr was a hypocrite, mouthing fealty and yet bedding Rognvald's ward, against his express orders to stay away. He was an oath-breaker if he met with Hlif and an oath-breaker if he didn't. His moment of glory was the moment the gods damned him.

Rising to his feet, clumsy, Skarfr made his way back to his seat amid praise and congratulations. He regained some of the pride he'd felt at performing his best work, the words running beautiful in his mind and slipping easily from his tongue.

'Quite a man now, a *skald* I should say. And one Rognvald values highly. As does his ward...' The insinuation, the sarcastic voice as Skarfr passed him, could only be one person. Thorbjorn.

Such digs were easy to shrug off, with a humble response. 'The gods were with me tonight. I thank them and know that will not always be so.'

But Rognvald's trust was a burden he must carry on his conscience.

Weeks dragged, then flew towards the pilgrims' voyage. Each meeting alone with Hlif tasted of some new delight and some old sorrow. To be so close together on a ship for years would be a shared adventure worth the telling. And Skarfr's would be the voice to tell that saga. And yet, the price of that closeness was the pretence of distance, a daily discipline.

In their old trysting-place by the standing stones, Skarfr lay on the grass musing on the path which had led to this moment, to Hlif warm and contented in his arms. He had followed many false turns but he was sure this was his destiny.

His conscience proved to be a more flexible muscle than he'd thought. Would Sweyn, Thorbjorn or Rognvald himself think twice about loving a woman forbidden to them? Wasn't it a hero's role to attempt the impossible, to be on the horns of a dilemma and ride them with courage, accepting imperfection? He had come to appreciate Rognvald's qualities, as man and leader, and he *would* be loyal – except where Hlif was concerned.

If her hope came true, if the saints heeded her prayers and she gained Rognvald's consent to marry, then all deceit would be ended. Some days he convinced himself that such would be their future. On darker days, he thought of Rognvald's unshakeable Christian conviction that he acted in Hlif's best interest. Skarfr put little faith in prayers to saints but hadn't Saint Magnus given him all he'd asked for in exchange for the precious bird bones? Adventures and dragon ships? A prick of conscience reminded him that he'd vowed silence as a votive offering in hopes Hlif's curse would be lifted. He had broken that vow in spectacular fashion.

But surely that was the gods' decision, not his? After all, he *was* to be a renowned skald, something which made him smile, despite his fears.

Hlif asked him, 'Why are you smiling?'

'The curse you laid on me, that you would marry me when I was a skald "renowned from this land to the Old Country". I might just be that skald. Maybe the cormorant spoke true and I can make sagas. And maybe the first condition of you marrying me is met, so half your curse is lifted.'

Nestled in his arms, she turned to meet his eyes. 'It was not a curse but a prophesy. So it shall be, my love. I swear, by the dragon.'

She stroked the blue-ashed image on his arm, fork-tongue spitting fire and he remembered her watching his possession by the spirits, an ancient priestess with wand raised. She'd channelled the fire into this brand on his arm, saved his life from fever a second time.

His questing hand hit upon her pouch of rune-stones, beside the wand in her belt, alongside who knew what tools she would bring to the pilgrims' aid. Not so helpless.

'I need you at my side,' he confessed. 'I'm glad you're coming too.'

'I know,' she said.

He plaited her loose hair, coiled it back up under the demure coif, pinned it in place as she'd taught him, stroked the back of her neck.

'*O vivid Valkyrie,*' he declaimed, '*your power vaunting,*

*Your helpless hapless hero lays*
*In your lap the deeds and dramas of*
*A myriad marvellous moments.*'

She chewed her lip. 'I like "vivid Valkyrie,"' she decided. 'More.'

Kennings slipped from mind to mouth as easily as fish swam downstream.

*'My vivid Valkyrie*
*Fate-weaver*
*Hearth-maker*

*Rune-reader*
*Heart-breaker*
*Wool-weigher*
*Fare-baker*
*Wand-waver*
*Life-saver*
*Elskan min.'*

'More,' she ordered.

And he knew there *would* be more. Their saga had only just begun.

# EPILOGUE

Orkneyjar was recovering from the influx of foreigners, the frenzy of fitting and supplying ships, the wait for spring weather and tides. Jarl Rognvald had just gone a-viking – or Jórsalaheim-faring as he preferred to call it. There would be honour and saga-stories for the pilgrims, despite the bickering which had marred their departure. Hlif the Housekeeper would be missed in the Bu but nobody was irreplaceable.

Jarl Harald was young but a man for all that, with Thorbjorn's experience to draw upon. Which was just as well. Rumour said that Erlend had declared himself Jarl, reminding Orkneymen of his rights and that *two jarls must heed their people*. Rumour also said the unthinkable had happened, that Sweyn was in intimate talks with Erlend, in a fit of pique against Rognvald, Harald and, most of all, Thorbjorn. It would not be the first time Sweyn put a jarl on the throne – or dispatched one.

But Thorbjorn was a match for Sweyn, and Harald was already their Jarl, so men watched which way the fickle winds blew and waited.

Of little interest in the grand scheme, or to anyone around him, an old man withered and was found dead by the hearth in a longhouse in his home settlement. An Irish thrall buried him in a common mound and burned his meagre possessions, except for a missive on parchment that the old man had told him was to be sent to Skarfr at the Jarl's Bu, after his death.

'Only after my death, mind,' Botolf had insisted, knowing the man could be trusted, however badly he'd been treated. Some men's natures were written so, indelibly honest. *Fools.*

The thrall, Fergus, gave the letter to a tradesman who was heading to Orphir and could deliver it to Skarfr, as per the name on the outside of the parchment. Or so illiterate Fergus assumed. If the ships had already sailed for Jórsalaheim, no doubt the letter would stay with Skarfr's belongings at the Bu, awaiting his return. Perhaps Botolf had repented of his wrongdoings and had some last words for Skarfr, so as to end his life in grace.

When the messenger reached Orphir, he found the ships had indeed sailed. The thrall had asked him to deliver the letter to Skarfr personally or to the kitchen-master but what would a man of such low status know of court ways? The messenger was conscientious so he checked the name on the missive and his low opinion of Fergus was confirmed. The letter was for Thorbjorn. This was good news as he could fulfil his mission and Lord Thorbjorn would no doubt reward the messenger's efficiency, as Skarfr could not.

After reading the missive, twice, Thorbjorn did indeed reward the messenger's efficiency. With a knife in the ribs, in case he'd read the contents, not just the name on the outside.

*Nobody* would know that a gangling youth and his whore had made a fool of him, snatched Sweyn's sister from his grasp and from the satisfaction of vengeance. But now *he* knew. He read the end of the letter once more.

*...installed two thralls – one a woman, even! – as masters, above their status, above* me *in what should be* my *longhouse, bringing shame on*

*all Norðmen. You who are Jarl of Orkneyjar in all but name, my Lord Thorbjorn, you who are a foster-father too – and who understand what is due to one who has raised a child not his own – I know you will not let such unnatural, ungrateful behaviour spread its evil contagion.*

*May the gods reward me as I deserve in the next life for, if you read these words, I have left this one.*

*Botolf Begla, Renowned Skald to the Courts of Snaeland, Norðvegr and Orkneyjar*

Thorbjorn screwed up the parchment and threw it into the fire, his every muscle clenched, his temples pulsing. He sent a message to Harald that he would be absent on personal business for a few days. Then he summoned five men he could trust, had ponies saddled and rode for Skarfr's longhouse.

# AUTHOR'S NOTE

This novel began with a fateful trip to Orkney and an interest in the Viking prince who stopped off at Narbonne on his pilgrimage to Jerusalem. Jarl Rognvald makes a larger-than-life appearance in my novel *Song at Dawn*, Book 1 of *The Troubadours* series, where he is a foreigner amid southern sophistication. I wanted to meet him on his own terms and in Orkney, where Rognvald is a legend.

I knew nothing of Viking Orkney. When I stood as a tourist in the prehistoric burial chamber of Maeshowe and discovered the 12$^{th}$ century graffiti runes made by Rognvald's men on the walls around me, the connections exploded into a story I had to write. Especially when I saw the exquisite dragon carved by one of those men.

Then the work and pleasure of research began. Viking culture is very different from the Occitania of *The Troubadours* series (nowadays southern France and northern Spain), and even though Christianity had gained hold in Orkney, the Norse myths, legends and 'old gods' were part of people's lives.

The pathfinder brooch worn by Rognvald is based on Vegvisir (pronounced VEGG-vee-seer). The only reference to this Viking symbol is in the 'Huld' manuscript: *If this sign is carried, one will never lose one's way in storms or bad weather, even when the way is not known.*

Historians cannot trust the accuracy of the 19$^{th}$ century Huld manuscript and there's no medieval evidence of the Vegvisir but neither is its existence discredited. As a historical novelist, I make my stories from what might have been and in that shadowy borderline between religion and magic, what is more plausible than a wayfinder symbol that looks runic? Also, I find it beautiful, as an artefact and as a metaphor, so Rognvald's pathfinder brooch plays a significant role in *the Troubadours* series.

My research material included shipping charts, videos on Glima wrestling, a forensic anthropologist's report on St Magnus' bones and a historian's reconstruction of Rognvald's shipwreck off the coast of Shetland. The most important primary source, the *Orkneyinga Saga,* was written in the 13th century as a work of literature so it is even less trustworthy than most histories but what great stories it tells!

Given the oral culture before the sagas were written, it seems likely that the poems included were indeed passed down through the generations and I've used several of Rognvald's, in my words. I wrote Skarfr's kennings and verses. The first two dragon riddles are based on the dragon riddles in the *Saga of King Heidrek the Wise* and I wrote the third riddle in the same style, aware that I was following in Tolkien's footsteps and hoping he would approve.

I've taken huge liberties with the poetry because I find literal translations so weighed down with allusions that pages of explanation are needed and the beauty is lost. Apart from the music of the language and use of alliteration, Norse poetry is full of clever puzzles and 'aha' moments – for a Viking audience.

Ploughing through verse-seas is likely to drag the modern reader down into a swelchie. (And yes, 'the Swelchie', a whirlpool, does exist). We don't have the same frames of reference to instantly understand allusions within allusions but the more Norse poetry I read in translation, the more I enjoy it. I did keep some archaic turns of phrase and word order as one characteristic of skaldic verse is to keep the subject and 'aha' moment for the end of the poem. If you want a scholarly translation that still captures the feel of the original poetry, do read Ian Crockatt's superb work.

Where historians disagree or where there is no evidence at all, a novelist can have fun. We can infer that Rognvald was married as his daughter's marriage and husband's name are recorded.

There is also a poignant poem showing grief over his lady's illness, which I'm taking as autobiographical. In one of his poems, he says he proposed marriage to Ermengarda of Narbonne, which suggests he was single at this point, so I deduce that his wife died. But there is no other information about her, not even a name.

If his wife had been an important noble, she might have been named, but for the daughter to make as good a match as she did (from which came powerful descendants) the wife probably wasn't low-born. Given the lack of suitable candidates, I invented Gertrud, a sister of the infamous Frakork. There were indeed unnamed siblings, according to my research, and that family tree offers fruitful possibilities (pun intended).

Hlif's background was inspired by the suggestion that she might be Hlifolf's daughter, in Michael P. Barnes' *The Runic Inscriptions of Maeshowe, Orkney*, an in-depth work analysing each message. Barnes gives alternative readings and draws few conclusions, and the *Orkneyinga Saga* is contradictory and does not match the messages in the runic inscriptions, so I've followed the story as I saw it. All the runic messages I've included in the Maeshowe scene *are* on the walls in the burial chamber, including those anonymous ones that I've ascribed to Rognvald, although he is not named in any of the runes. My feeling is that he could have been there; a man so powerful and confident would not need to sign his work.

Four events are recorded in the runes, which have not been dated exactly beyond 'mid 12th century'. This is the order I've taken them in.

*Hakon/ Hokon alone carried treasure from this mound.*

Some time before the pilgrims broke into the mound, others were there and took treasure away. There would surely have been grave goods but these could have been stolen hundreds of years earlier and the tomb sealed, as it appears to be when the pilgrims 'broke in'. So I take the naming of Hakon/ Hokon in the runes to be a joke.

*The Jerusalem-farers broke Orkhaugr. Hlif, the Earl's housekeeper, carved.*

I take this as a fact, indicating that Rognvald's band broke into and discovered the burial chamber, not Jarl Harald. According to *The Orkneyinga Saga,* Jarl Harald spent Yuletide in Orkhaugr, where two of his men went mad, and there is some confusion about whether it was Rognvald or Harald who broke into Maeshowe and when. Archeologists agree that there *was* a break-in through the roof and I prefer the idea that at least some of the pilgrims' graffiti dates from before their voyage.

*Many a woman has stooped to come here.*

This jibe relies on the pun 'stooped' as the tunnel entrance has no headroom so physical stooping is required. And the more vulgar messages make clear the other way in which women lowered themselves. The burial chamber became a meeting-place for sexual encounters. This must have happened *after* the initial discovery, over time. So it makes sense to me that Harald sheltering in Maeshowe was the fourth event, at a time when the place was entered by the tunnel and known as a shelter.

I've ascribed the dragon-carving to one of Rognvald's men during the first rune-writing break-in but there could well have been further visits by the pilgrims when they came back from Jerusalem and carved some more messages and crosses, and maybe a dragon. Or lion of St Mark. Or griffon with sea eagle. But Skarfr and I know what the carving is, truly.

Another apparent divergence from *The Orkneyinga Saga* is that Botolf, the Icelandic skald, is not dead at this stage of events in the saga version. I've used poetic license and no doubt I'll understand why as further adventures unfold.

The 'real' account of Magnus' murder, as told by Hlif, draws on the forensic report of R.W. Reid, who studied the bones of both St

Magnus and St Rognvald, as preserved in St Magnus Cathedral. His findings do contradict the saga tale of the saint's murder but they also show a high probability that these are indeed the bones of the two saints, so the report was received with mixed feelings. I think it brings history to life to read such an autopsy and find that Magnus had good teeth and Rognvald had rheumatism. You might be surprised to learn that in with St Magnus' remains really were six long bones from birds, as in my story. As with so much of this novel, strange facts made perfect sense to me as I travelled with Skarfr and Hlif.

I hope you enjoyed this journey into the past as much as I did. May we travel dangerous roads together again soon!

# ACKNOWLEDGMENTS

*Many thanks to:*

my editor, Lorna Fergusson, of *Fictionfire Literary Consultancy*;
Babs, Jane and Kristin for your invaluable critiques and support;
The Sanctuary writers' group for providing exactly that and for all
your expertise;
Fran Hollinrake, Custodian/Visitor Services Officer, St Magnus
Cathedral for information on the history of the building and on
masons' marks;
Historic Environment Scotland and Maeshowe Visitor's Centre for
information and support, and for permission to use my photo of
the Grey Mountain Studio pendant showing the Maeshowe
dragon;
Ryerson for being my boats, sailing and rowing specialist;
Lexie Conyngham for a list of starter research books;
Patricia Long, Orkney guide, for sharing her knowledge and love of
Orkney;
Lesley Geekie for being my woman at the scene;
Bo of Glaipnir for Viking knowledge and enthusiasm;
Midwinter Dragon map © Jean Gill, created using Inkarnate.com
and a base map of Orkney from Ordnance Survey Open Data with
inset derived from File Scotland location
map.svg by NordNordWest, created by Wikipedia User Nilfanion;
Richard Baber of GreyMountainStudio on Etsy, Handcrafted
Pictish and Viking designs in bronze, for permission to use my

photo of his pendant of the Maeshowe dragon in my series, including the chapter heading images; Bourbonbourbon, migfoto and kirasolly for the cover images; and Jessica Bell Cover Design for the amazing covers for all my books.

# SELECTED REFERENCE WORKS

*The Orkneyinga Saga* – Project Gutenberg (Public Domain)
*The Saga of King Heidrek the Wise* – Project Gutenberg (Public Domain)
*The King's Mirror* – Project Gutenberg (Public Domain)
*The Saga of Grettir the Strong* (Penguin Classics)

Michael P. Barnes – *The Runic Inscriptions of Maeshowe, Orkney*
Ian Crockatt – *Crimsoning the Eagle's Claw*. The poetry of Rögnvaldr
Ian Crockatt – *The Song Weigher*. The poetry of Egill Skallagrimsson
Jóhanna Katrín Friðriksdóttir – *The Women of the Viking World*
Judith Jesch – *Women in the Viking Age*
Grace Tierney – *Words the Vikings Gave Us*

## Fiction

Erik Linklater – *The Ultimate Viking*
A.D. Howden Smith – *Swain's Saga*

## Historical articles via Academia.edu and Jstor.org websites

Judith Jesch – 'The Nine Skills of Earl Rögnvaldr of Orkney'
Jesch, J. (2013). 'Earl Rögnvaldr of Orkney, a Poet of the Viking Diaspora.' *Journal of the North Atlantic*, 154–160. https://www.jstor.org/stable/26686977
Lucy Collings, R. Farrell and I. Morrison – 'Earl Rögnvald's Shipwreck' (Viking Society for Northern Research)
Collings, L., Farrell, R., & Morrison, I. (1974). I. EARL RÖGNVALD'S

SHIPWRECK. *Saga-Book*, *19*, 293–310. https://www.js-tor.org/stable/48612704

Debbie Potts – 'An Introduction to Skaldic Poetry'

Brenda Prehal - 'Freyja's Cats: Perspectives on Recent Viking Age Finds in North Iceland'

R. W. Reid – 'Remains of Saint Magnus and Saint Rognvald, Entombed in Saint Magnus Cathedral, Kirkwall, Orkney' (Oxford University Press)

Reid, R. W. (1926). Remains of Saint Magnus and Saint Rognvald, Entombed in Saint Magnus Cathedral, Kirkwall, Orkney. *Biometrika*, *18*(1/2), 118–150. https://doi.org/10.2307/2332499

Albert Thomson – 'Masons' Marks in St Magnus Cathedral' (An Orkney Miscellany 1954)

**Online**

www.vikingeskibsmuseet.dk especially the articles, logs, diaries and videos about the voyage of the reproduction longship *Sea Stallion* from Denmark to Dublin, via Orkney.

The Skaldic Project https://skaldic.org/

**Nidavellnir Nalbinding** on Facebook and YouTube, for information and practical demonstrations of this pre-knitting technique, and for the expertise on Viking textiles of Emma 'Bruni' Boast, a Viking-Age Archaeologist and Nalbinding Specialist based in York, UK. Member of the Guild of Mastercraftsmen UK.

# ABOUT THE AUTHOR

I'm a Welsh writer and photographer living in the south of France with two scruffy dogs, a beehive named 'Endeavour', a Nikon D750 and a man. I taught English in Wales for many years and my claim to fame is that I was the first woman to be a secondary headteacher in Carmarthenshire. I'm mother or stepmother to five children so life has been pretty hectic.

I've published all kinds of books, both with traditional publishers and self-published. You'll find everything under my name from prize-winning poetry and novels, military history, translated books on dog training, to a cookery book on goat cheese. My work with top dog-trainer Michel Hasbrouck has taken me deep into the world of dogs with problems, and inspired one of my novels. With Scottish parents, an English birthplace and French residence, I can usually support the winning team on most sporting occasions.

*www.jeangill.com*

facebook.com/writerjeangill

x.com/writerjeangill

instagram.com/writerjeangill

goodreads.com/JeanGill

**Join Jean Gill's Special Readers' Group**

for private news, views and offers, with an exclusive ebook copy of

*How White is My Valley*

as a welcome gift.

**Sign up at *jeangill.com***

The follow-up to her memoir *How Blue is My Valley* about moving to France from rainy Wales, tells the true story of how Jean

- nearly became a certified dog trainer.
- should have been certified and became a beekeeper.
- developed from keen photographer to hold her first exhibition.
- held 12th century Damascene steel.
- looks for adventure in whatever comes her way.

# AMONG SEA WOLVES

## 1150: THE WHALE ROAD

The adventures of Hlif and Skarfr continue in *Among Sea Wolves: Book 2 of The Midwinter Dragon, coming in 2023*

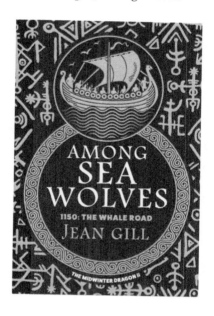

Printed in Great Britain
by Amazon